Words of praise for Michael Reisig's latest!

Having lived in Key West in the la
when Mel Fisher was still hunting
the harbors, and 'square grouper' v .... species,
Michael Reisig's *Back on the Roaᴅ .ᴜ ᴋey West* transports me
back in time. Will Bell and Kansas Stamps face an assortment of
ruthless antagonists and chase adventure with the abandon of the
era, and whether you lived it or not, don't miss the chance to now.
Vivid imagery, strong prose and an exciting plot make this
trip with the boys worth taking. Enjoy the ride!

— John H. Cunningham
Author of the Buck Reilly Adventure Series

Stumbling their way in and out of trouble and fortune, Kansas
Stamps and Will Bell continue to be the idols of what every true
Parrot Head imagines real life in The Keys would be — full
of spontaneous adventure. What a great read!

— Bryan Crews
Former president, Tampa Parrot Head Club

The original thrill-seekers are back in Reisig's latest hair-raising,
quest-filled adventure, *Back On The Road To Key West*. This
laugh-out-loud tale is packed with even more mystery, treasure,
romance, and narrow escapes. A "five-star" experience!

— Tammy Snyder
The Arkansas Book Reviewer

Back on
The Road To Key West

Michael Reisig

BACK ON THE ROAD TO KEY WEST
Copyright © 2013, Clear Creek Press/Michael Reisig
(reisig@ipa.net)
1st Edition, September 2013
Cover design by Powell Graphics
Cover design copyright © 2013 Clear Creek Press

Published by Clear Creek Press
P.O. Box 1081 Mena, AR 71953
1-479-394-4992

ISBN: 978-0-9713694-5-0

DEDICATION

To my lady, Bonnie Lee, who continually strives to make my books, and my life, worth recalling.

CHAPTER ONE

Key West, Summer of 1982

It was late afternoon in the capital of the Conch Republic, last stop in a string of sandy pearls that curl indolently into the Gulf Stream at the Southeastern edge of America — native habitat for the adventure-loving, rum-soaked, and loosely-wrapped. Key West — the southernmost domicile of unabashed hedonism, shameless larceny, and priceless recollections.

We parked our car under the canopy of an old banyan tree on Front Street, a block from Mallory Square, and began a leisurely stroll toward Duval. Our meeting wasn't until 9:00 p.m., and there was time to kill.

On the horizon a gaggle of heavy, gray and white cumulus clouds rose off the sea, swallowing a fading sun as it rimmed them in silver and gold. Above that remarkable display, a blue sky was being washed with streaks of rose and mauve, those colors gradually melding and climbing into the darkening heavens. The waters of Key West Bight reflected the vision, and a collage of sailboats and shrimpers basked in those last rays like contented seabirds drifting quietly into the evening.

The light breeze carried a tart sweetness of key lime and jasmine, buoyed by a crisp aroma of fried fish, conch fritters, and the perennial salty richness of the sea. Music drifted through the air like a fragrance, changing tempo, rhythm, and volume depending on how close you were to the next saloon.

A sense of muddled serenity in the movement of the people on the street suggested that no one was anxious to be anywhere — being right where they were felt…good. There were, of course, some who were well ahead in the unannounced race to inebriety, but hey, this was the islands. Life was a perpetual vacation with an occasional bump regarding love or money.

You either loved The Keys with a born-to-it passion or you didn't care for them at all. You either bonded with the enterprising, excitable Cubans, the slow-moving, easygoing Bahamian people, the misfits, artists, adventurers, alternate lifestylers, and perpetually passionate fishermen, or you didn't. There were those who never wanted to leave and those who couldn't wait to get back to Michigan.

As my buddy, Will Bell, and I strolled onto Duval, decked out in Dockers shorts, tropical shirts, and our best Kino sandals, we were engulfed in the heavy, early evening air. I couldn't help but be reminded of our early days here, and our incredible experiences.

The 1970s were an intoxicating collage of events for us. We had moved to the Florida Keys to become nothing more than commercial divers — tropical fish collectors. But life refused to provide us such simple fare. Upon our arrival to that sun-drenched, palm-covered paradise inhabited by the slightly intrepid and mostly besotted, adventure had come calling, grabbing us by the short hairs and whisking us away. In the process, we discovered a sunken Spanish treasure, became the target of modern-day (if not somewhat dysfunctional) pirates, and found the girl of our dreams (one girl, two dreams, unfortunately — but it worked itself out).

Stumbling along, we had inadvertently become immersed in an international smuggling operation, and had ended up possessing, for a short time, an ancient golden pyramid with very unique properties given to us by a wacky Jamaican soothsayer with a dubious but fascinating heritage. It was all fairly heady stuff for a couple of funky white boys from the mainland.

By the late seventies both Will and I (my name is Kansas — Kansas Stamps) had settled down somewhat, found ladies that satisfied most of our criteria, and had begun to live relatively normal lives. Well, not exactly the shoe salesmen, auto mechanic, stockbroker kind of normal. We were adventurers of sorts, making our living with a diving business and doing a little treasure hunting on the side. Admittedly, we weren't the Harrison Ford *Raiders of the Lost Ark* type of adventurers. More often than not, trouble had a way of finding us rather than the other way around. Neither of us had much of an appreciation for violence or a high pain threshold. We were generally better at talking our way out of situations or out-thinking our opponents. Unfortunately, in the process, we were having such a good time at it all, we lost our wives. Oddly enough, they left us for each other. I remember the scene as if it were yesterday…

"What the hell do you mean 'you've found someone else,' and just how in the hell did it happen to you and Angie at the same time?" I said, my voice coming out a tad shriller than I would have liked.

Celeste shrugged, standing by the counter in the kitchen, dressed in soft white bell-bottoms and a tie-dye T-shirt. "It just happened. It's your own fault," she added firmly, with a mixture of empathy and defiance, one hand on her hip, a wisp of blond hair drifting carelessly across her eyebrows. She brushed it back briskly, as if it were another element of her exasperation. "You and Will are gone half the time on one crazy adventure or another, and that left Angie and me alone here, on a freaking island thirty miles from Key West, and well, damn it, we just got to liking each other's company."

My wife paused, almost contrite, but any attempt at apology was lost to a mischievous smile and the impish glitter in her green eyes. "More than we expected..."

The implication hung in the air like late summer thunderheads, both alluring and ominous, conjuring a brief parade of images in my head, not all of which were unpleasant. I grinned incredulously, pushing my long, dark hair back behind the nape of my neck in nervous reaction. "C'mon, you gotta be kidding me. You and Angie? Like, together? This is a joke, right?"

"If it is, it's on you and Will," she replied. "Your 'joined at the hip' buddy is getting the same news from his wife as we speak."

The phone rang, jarring me from my reverie. I picked it up.

"Are you believing this crap?" Will said without preamble, anger and shock obviously winning out over distress at the moment. "Our wives are leaving us for...our wives!"

It wasn't great grammar but the point was well-taken. The whole thing was like a bomb exploding in the living room of my brain. "How did we not see this coming? Besides that, they're sisters."

"You know Celeste was adopted by their parents when she was thirteen. They're not really related, even though they do look a lot alike, and she goofed us by telling us they were twins when we first met," Will replied with a resigned sigh. "Does that make you feel better?"

It didn't. Not at all...

As heart-wrenching as it was, we discovered over the next couple of weeks that our wives had made up their minds. It was a strange damned thing — to be abandoned in favor of a woman. My head and my ego didn't know quite what to do with it. On the other hand, it didn't seem quite as painful or as hard as being cuckolded by another man. Celeste and Angie weren't really angry with us — hell, they were getting what they wanted. It was Will and me whose lives had just done a major flip-flop.

In the end, the divorces went through without too much rancor or squabbling over things, but that didn't lessen the pain. The girls took Angie and Will's canal home on the west side of Big Pine Key, and Will and I got my place on the southeast side of the island. Will kept his twenty-two-foot Mako workboat, and of course, I kept my Cessna 182 amphibian floatplane that had carried Will and me through so many adventures over the last few years. Angie and Celeste took the little thirty-one-foot sailboat of which my partner had been so fond. They also made us give them half of the ancient coin collection we had — given to us by our strange friend, Rufus, the Jamaican soothsayer, years ago (and therein lies a remarkable story in itself). The coins were so old and so rare that selling only a handful each year and investing intelligently had kept us fairly comfortable. With this new development I realized we might actually have to go back to work — at something.

C'est la vie, amigo. Life stumbles on...

Sometimes you pursue intoxication, like an octopus stalking an old blue crab, rolling out tentacle after tentacle trying to snag it and draw it in. Sometimes it lurks in a darkened corner like a moray, hanging underneath a coral ledge, and just zaps you when you least expect it. That night in Key West, while waiting for our 9:00 appointment, Will and I got zapped.

I think the problems started with Will's sarcasm and twisted wit.

We walked into Captain Tony's on Greene Street just as the last of the sun's rays were gilding the high windows. A four-piece band thumped out a vigorous version of "Brandy" (...*you're a fine girl and what a good wife you would be. But my life, my lover, my lady, is the sea).* The place was already well into happy hour — as if that made a difference in a town whose motto is, "It's five o'clock somewhere." Bartenders and waitresses were scuttling about furiously to the chorus of voices vying for their attention, and over the music bottles clanged, registers sang, and the frenzy of euphoria began to rise as inexorably as the tide two blocks away.

We went in, found a table and ordered drinks, but in the process we couldn't help but notice the alternate entertainment. A rather heavy girl had obviously pulled well ahead in the race for inebriety and had climbed up on one of the tables near the bar. She was wearing a stretched-to-capacity tube top that was losing the battle with gravity as it struggled desperately to contain her voluminous, bouncing breasts. Her way-too-tight miniskirt had risen up past the point of sensuality and was nearing the point of lewd spectacle.

Apparently, underwear had been optional that night and there was stuff peeking out from under her skirt that looked like a Pomeranian might be hiding there.

Will looked at me and muttered with a grin, "How'd you like to see that lumbering at you in a pink nightie?"

In some places, such a spectacle might have driven customers from the bar, but this was Key West, and those who lived there had come to accept its strange amalgam of normal and bizarre in the same fashion we might accept the myriad characters of someone with a multiple personality disorder. It might be weird, but it's never less than entertaining. Truth was, The Keys thrived on the bizarre. As Will used to say, "You want everything the same, every day, live in Montana. In The Keys, the only thing you're certain of is the sun's gonna rise in the east."

Will decided to hit the restroom. He stood up, pushed back his long blond hair with his fingers, brushed down his colorful tropical shirt, then strolled casually toward the head with those long-legged strides of his. He walked by the girl, who was still gyrating like a beached mackerel, throwing her hair from side to side in sensual abandon, the Pomeranian becoming more visible by the moment. He glanced down at the table, then up to her, and their eyes met. "Extraordinary legs," he said with a wry smile, his pale blue eyes sparkling with mischief.

Losing a little of that wild fervor, she returned the smile. "Thanks, big boy." Her eyes danced with a lascivious glimmer. "Extraordinary, huh?"

"Yeah," said my buddy. "Most tables would have collapsed long before now."

Much of life is nothing more than timing. Sometimes your timing is perfect and things go well. Sometimes you just do the wrong thing at the wrong moment.

Maybe her boyfriend had dumped her recently. Maybe she'd heard one too many fat jokes that day. Who knows exactly? But as Will turned to head for the restroom, the girl slowed to a stop as if someone had just pulled her plug. Her eyes widened in shock, which quickly slid into umbrage, then danced right into fury. With a howl somewhere between an attacking Indian and a wild cougar, she hurled herself off the table in a leap that would have done Batman proud (especially remarkable considering she was right around two hundred pounds). Will had just enough time to turn at the sound of the anguished shriek and see the overhead lights eclipsed by the very image of heavy animosity. My partner's eyes suddenly garnered that same look Wile E. Coyote gets when he's just stepped off the cliff. Arms spread and teeth bared, she body-slammed Will like Hulk Hogan with tits. The tube top surrendered its tenuous hold in flight and those giant boobies surged out like airbags in a head-on collision. I'm fairly certain that Will would have been pummeled soundly, and very possibly suffocated by those two gelatinous mountains had I not grabbed a leg and hauled him out from under the enraged behemoth. She was still hurling curses while struggling to get her top back in place as I threw some money on our table, and we made our escape to the outrageously pleased roar of the crowd.

"How in the hell is it that these things always happen to me?" Will moaned, brushing himself off as we paused about a block away.

"I don't know," I said, deadpan. "Couldn't have anything to do with your abrasive wit, could it?"

He grinned. "What makes you think you're so smucking fart? All I did was comment on the legs of the table."

"Whether or not I'm smucking fart has nothing to do with it. She would have beaten you to a puddle of jelly if your loyal sidekick hadn't been there."

Will chewed on the corner of his lip, as he often did when weighing a situation. "Yeah, you're right. Thanks, Tonto." Then he smiled again. "Did you see that freaking chick fly through the air? Did you see that? It was like Fat Albert on crack!"

We decided to work our way down Duval, create a buffer zone from our little escapade. We had actually come into town to pick up some stone crab claws from a friend of ours, Johnny Bolin. He had a boat and a legitimate trap business, but like so many of the folks in The Keys, his occupation had bled almost naturally into the illegitimate. He put his traps out in areas with a lot of the big boys in the business and seemed to pull his at night more often than not, and he somehow brought in more crabs than his few traps could possibly have produced. Everyone expected to find him wacked and drifting in with the tide one day, but until then, he sold crab claws at about half the price of his competitors — mostly at night, and for cash only. We had agreed to meet him at Sloppy Joe's about nine o'clock. We were early. There was almost no alternative but to drink for a while. We walked back to The Hog's Breath Saloon, because it was close to the truck, and settled in for an hour.

We got to laughing about Will and the heavy chick and that led to the retelling of some of our other escapades. We started out with a couple of beers, but somewhere along the line we started adding a shot or two of tequila. If that damned waitress hadn't been so cute and persistent, things that evening might have turned out differently, because by a quarter 'til nine we were pretty well swacked and we still had a stone crab transaction to deal with.

We went back and got our pickup, then drove around to the back of Sloppy Joe's and parked. The yellow streetlamps in the alley cast a pale amber glow, throwing arcane, angled shadows of inky grays and ebonies. The aging bulbs were engulfed by erratic swarms of enraptured insects, drawn to the light in a perpetual summer dance with the same perennial surety and circumstance as the movement of the tides. Ahhh, summer in The Keys.

While surveying the alley I noticed that "Umbrella Man" (one of the many street people so unique that they had been given pet names by the local populace) was asleep in a corner by the loading dock, the perpetual umbrella over his shoulder and his shopping cart next to him, containing all the man's worldly possessions, including his tiny dog. It was campy and melancholic, and charmingly picturesque at the same time. There were others like him — Cigarette Willy, who wandered the streets with a blanket wrapped around his shoulders summer and winter, an unlit cigarette continuously dangling from his lips; and Crazy George, with his strange clothes, wild eyes, and the bizarre tales he told to pry a dollar from tourists and locals alike. It was all part of the colorful kaleidoscope that was Key West.

Sloppy Joe's was unusually sloppy that night. The crowd was extraordinarily boisterous, happy hour having bled into pie-eyed delirious hour. The band was a little too loud, hammering out a shoddy rendition of a Jimmy Buffett song about cheeseburgers and paradise, but no one was complaining. The waitresses and bartenders, as high as they could afford to be and still perform, scampered to and fro, shouting orders to each other like a boarding party in the midst of an assault, while struggling ceiling fans sliced the noise and the stratus clouds of cigarette smoke, sending them swirling back down into the melee. As we entered, we began looking for a fellow with a red ball cap — that was what Johnny told us to watch for. He rarely did his own transactions anymore.

Halfway back, along the wall, there was a guy sitting alone at a small table. He had a purplish ball cap on, which looked close enough. Long, scraggly blond hair spilled out the back and sides of the hat as he hunched over his beer as if protecting it. He was an old guy; as thin as a hungry lizard, with bushy gray eyebrows, deep furrowed squint lines, and the craggy, hardened features of a man who's spent lots of time on the water and in the sun. But his copper eyes held steel in them, and a wisp of wicked humor.

We worked our way through all the seekers of paradise and stopped at his table.

"You got something for sale?" I said, trying to act sober and a little innocuous.

He skewered me with a pugnacious glare. "You got the money?"

I pulled an envelope from my back pocket.

He nodded. "Have a seat."

As we pulled out chairs and ordered a couple beers from the waitress, I couldn't help but notice a couple of guys about three or four tables from us, paying more attention to our exchange than was necessary. They were dressed in tropical shirts stretched by their burly torsos, but they didn't look like tourists — no Hang Ten shorts, more like uptown slacks and hundred-dollar shoes. They looked like they were trying hard to blend in. When they realized I was watching them watch us, they went back to their drinks. About that time the band took a break and things quieted somewhat.

Our new acquaintance glanced around nervously, then reached into his pocket and pulled out a manila envelope. "Okay, let's get this over with." He slid the envelope over to me and I passed him the money, thinking it was strange that Johnny would be giving receipts, and noticing that the transaction hadn't gone unnoticed by the guys in the Hawaiian shirts and Florsheims. *Maybe Johnny is becoming more legitimate,* I thought. I was guessing we'd slip outside and transfer the crab claws from truck to truck. As I stuffed the rather heavy envelope into my jeans pocket, the old fellow looked at me and spoke.

"Tommy Fields told me you was a good man so I'm giving this to you. The money don't matter. My time is just about here." He tapped his heart. "Bad ticker. Doc says less than two months and I'll be on life support." He offered a savage, determined smile. "And that ain't gonna happen. Mostly I'm giving you this to keep it away from Penchant and his bunch."

"Rick Penchant?" I asked, suddenly realizing that we were apparently part of a serious misidentification here. "The treasure hunter Penchant?"

He nodded emphatically. "Yeah, that squirrely bastard."

Will and I exchanged glances. Penchant was fairly well-known in the business. He was also fairly well-known for having the ethics of a spider. If you got in his way he usually had somebody fix the problem. At that point we both knew we should say something like, "We're really sorry, but we're not the people you think we are." But we didn't. What was happening was just too damned intriguing.

The guy continued. "I found that," he nodded toward the envelope he'd given me, "in verily a slit of a limestone cave near Spanish Wells on Crooked Island not two months ago. Stuffed in an old black glass gin bottle and sealed with a cork and rubber tree sap, it was. Been there the better part of three hundred years, I'm guessing."

That brought another glance from Will. Now the boy really had our attention. We had been to Crooked in the Bahamas once or twice.

"But I got a bit of rum in me one night and got a little loose-lipped, and Penchant found out about it," he added.

We didn't know it at the time, but about a mile from us, on Roosevelt Boulevard, there had just been a fender bender. A fellow named Benny Swarez, wearing a red ball cap and carrying a hundred pounds of crab claws in the back of his truck, had just sideswiped a Ford Mustang owned by a Malcolm Bledsow, who was a minor-league treasure hunter and a personal friend of local philanthropist Tommy Fields.

I was reminded of our old Jamaican soothsayer buddy, Rufus, and an expression he used occasionally: "The Gods, they be bored easily, and sometimes they make coincidences. They have a fine sense of humor and irony — these be some of their favorite things."

I exhaled hard, my conscience catching up with me a little. "Listen, we may not be — "

"Don't start with the crap about you don't feel right about takin' this from me, okay?" the guy spat. "Somebody's got to have it. Somebody's got to dig up what's on that map, and unfortunately it ain't gonna be me. Like I told Tommy, just make sure half of what you find gets to my daughter, Vanilla Bean, up on Grassy Key. I'm Jack Bean. That much you better promise me or I swear I'll come back from the dead and — " The sentence was broken by a deep, rasping cough that seemed to exhaust him.

A map! A freaking treasure map! my mind screeched as Will shot me another wide-eyed glance. I turned back to Jack. "Okay, buddy. Okay. I promise. We'll do it."

Without any further ado the old man slugged down the rest of his beer, drew himself up slowly and exhaled hard, then offered a strangely knowing, almost benevolent smile. "Good hunting, *amigos*, and don't forget about my daughter, Vanny." With that he turned and was gone, melting slowly into the miasma of smoke, bodies, and lights.

The two guys behind us let him go. They'd seen the exchange. It was clear what they were after.

"Well, that went remarkably well, didn't it?" Will chimed, easing back in his chair. "We came here to buy a box of crab claws and we're leaving with a freaking treasure map."

"That's the good news," I said. "The bad news is those two fellas over there who have been watching us like vultures waiting for a road kill to quit twitching." Before Will could do it I added tersely, "Don't look at 'em. Just drink your beer."

"Where are they?" Will said without looking.

"Three tables behind you and two to the left."

He nodded and casually pushed his cocktail napkin off the table. As he bent down to pick it up, he took a quick glance. "Big dudes, tropical shirts," he said as he put his napkin back under his glass.

"Yeah, you got it." I looked around at the exits and entrances. There was a hallway by the stage that led to the bathrooms and the back alley. "I think we're gonna need a diversion. You got any ideas?"

Will glanced around, chewing on his lip in concentration. He looked at the stage and smiled. He caught the attention of a waitress, handed her ten dollars and told her he needed to borrow a pair of scissors and a phonebook. When my partner had them in hand, he took a quick jaunt to the restroom. As soon as Will got back, he handed me a thick stack of about two hundred pieces of phonebook paper cut into two-inch by four-inch squares. "Okay, this is what I'm gonna do and this is what you're gonna do…"

A moment or two later Will got up and headed toward the hallway with the restrooms again, but as he got close to the stage he turned and bounced up the three stairs, then walked over to the band's microphones like he owned the place. Waving to the people in the audience, he grabbed a mike and turned it on. "How's everyone doing tonight?" he yelled. "Are we getting right?"

The audience replied with a roar, glasses in the air. When everyone settled down he continued quickly, "Just want everyone to know that Jimmy Buffett will be doing a concert in Miami this Saturday! Yeah!"

That brought another roar. The bouncers slowed their approach to the stage, now figuring that this was a promotion of some sort.

"I got great news for you!" my buddy shouted. "We've got one hundred free tickets to that concert here tonight!"

Another roar.

Will pointed out into the crowd, right at the two dudes who had been paying too much attention to us. "See those two guys with the tropical shirts at the table by the bar?"

I quickly stood, moved over near them and pointed enthusiastically.

"They have the tickets. The first hundred people to reach their table get free Jimmy Buffett concert tickets!"

That was my cue. I threw the pieces of phonebook paper into the air, over the top of the two men, and yelled, "Free tickets!"

A hush filled the room for a moment, as if the air had just been sucked out. Then an old shrimper at the bar stumbled off his stool and staggered toward our antagonists. "I want a damned ticket," he slurred. That was it. In the next second pandemonium ensued, as about two hundred people attacked that table with the frenzy of blood-crazed makos.

At that point, I headed for the hallway and the back door to the alley, where Will joined me. I do remember looking back and seeing those two guys glaring hatefully at us, but that was instantly transformed into the Wile E. Coyote look as the glazed-eyed, slobbering, shrieking congregation charged at them feverishly with outstretched hands like *The Night of the Living Dead on Cocaine.* The last thing I saw was their table going over, asses and elbows in every direction.

I just love it when a plan comes together.

Just slip out the back, Jack, make a new plan, Stan, you don't need to be coy, Roy, just get yourself free. Hop on the bus, Gus, you don't need to discuss much, just drop off the key, Lee, and get yourself free.

— Paul Simon

CHAPTER TWO

"You know, what we did tonight was wrong," Will said from the driver's seat as we came across the bridge to Boca Chica Key, just outside of Key West.

"Yeah, I know," I answered, watching the moon play off the water and turn the mangroves along the road into soft silver wreaths. "But the truth is, what does it matter who finds this treasure, if there is one, as long as Vanilla, the daughter, gets her half?"

"My guess is, it matters to the guy who was supposed to get this map," Will said sarcastically.

"Well, I guess we could get out a phonebook, start with the A's and begin to make phone calls, asking each person if they were supposed to get a treasure map tonight, and if they were, we have it for them. Or we could put an ad in the classifieds tomorrow — 'Have found lost treasure map. Owner can call at 305-872 — '"

That crooked grin slashed Will's face, his large white teeth flashing in the moonlight. "Yeah, yeah. Point taken. Oh well, I guess we'll just have to do the right thing and check this out. That's assuming that there's actually a map in that envelope and there's actually a pot of gold at the end of the rainbow."

There was a map — ancient, brittle, and yellowed, but still remarkably preserved. We sat in the living room of our home on Big Pine Key that evening and studied what some buccaneer had painstakingly drawn and documented almost three centuries before. There had apparently been the taking of a ship. The words, *"A fair Spanish prize taken on the summer seas of 1697"* were written just above the crude image of an island, and a poorly drawn but detailed, exotic-looking cross was shown to the side of the island. *"El Crucifijo de Santa María Magdalena"* was inscribed next to the cross. As I read those words, Will, quite the historian, stopped me.

"I know I've heard of that before, *El Crucifijo de Santa María Magdalena*. Damn!" he said, snapping his fingers fiercely. "Now I remember. That's considered one of the most important treasures lost during the Spanish conquest of the Americas." He paused for a moment, collecting his thoughts. "Yeah, now I remember. It was a monumental gift to Charles II of Spain, cast in the foundries of Cartagena — a physical representation of Spain's Christian dominance over the New World for four hundred years. It was a little

pretentious because Spain had a lot of competition during that time."
He paused. "Seems to me it sailed out of Cartagena in one of the
early 1700 fleets, but it was recorded as lost to piracy. Absolutely one
of the significant lost treasures of that era." He paused again. "You
don't think..."

"There's a damned X on this map," I replied cautiously. "And
two landmarks: 'The great arrow rock,' and 'the mouth in the wall.'
Ya mon, I'm betting you dollars to donuts this boy stashed
something." I looked up at Will slowly, my lips pursed and my eyes
smiling. "Maybe even a particularly valuable cross."

Will got that grin of his, eyebrows dancing. "Ya mon! Ya mon!"

There were two other clues that were significant. The buccaneer
closed at the bottom of the page with the words, *"God bless me,
Captain Catt,"* and the map showed the general shape of the island,
fashioned like an elongated pirate's boot. Will and I had been
through the Bahamas on several occasions and we knew much of its
history. Captain Arthur Catt was a recorded pirate of that area and
era, and legend said he used Cat Island as a place of refuge, and Cat
Island was shaped like a boot...

At about the same time we were examining our ancient map, the
two goons we had ditched in Sloppy Joe's found themselves in a
suite at The La Concha in Key West, standing most uncomfortably
before Mr. Rick Penchant, who was not a happy man. Penchant was
in the process of buying a new home in Key West and had taken
temporary residence at The La Concha until closing. Dressed in an
expensive, emerald-colored, short-sleeved shirt, Levi's and
Topsiders, he shook his head, his big mane of thick, dirty-blond hair
dancing across his shoulders, dark eyes like pools of Arabian crude,
glowering with anger.

"I give you guys a simple job. Snatch a map off of some crusty
old piece of shit and bring it to me. Jesus! The guy's about a hundred
years old! How could you manage to screw this up?"

"He passed it off to two guys before we could take him," the
larger of the two said with just a touch of a whine in his voice. "Then
they tricked us and got away."

Penchant snorted with disgust. "I got fish in my aquarium that
are harder to trick than you two assholes. I knew I should have sent
Stinger. Damn! I can't believe I was this close to that map!" He
waved his hand in dismissal. "All right, all right. Get the hell out of
here before I shoot one of you just to make myself feel better. Put the

word out with the details on these two. Find out who they are. I want what they have. You understand? You either come back with that map, or book yourselves a flight to Ecuador."

The morning sun crept over the horizon, caressing the palms and gilding the still waters of the channel, gradually stealing up the canal and igniting the placid surface in red and gold. As it swept up to the boat dock and the stilt house, splashing the white stucco pilings and walls with its brilliance, a flock of spoonbills in the adjacent mangrove lifted up in unison, their elegant, rose-colored bodies captured in the golden rays and framed in a reef-blue sky — the whole scene simply defying the talent of da Vinci.

I was sitting on the wing of my floatplane, which was moored next to the water, lost to the magic and the moment — feeling really good for the first time in a long time. It had been six months since the finalization of our divorces. For the first month after the separation, Will and I subsisted on a fairly steady diet of melancholy, tequila, and pizza. They had dragged us out of The Gangplank Bar and No Name Pub at closing so many times, taxi drivers had permanently stationed themselves at those locations for our service. Finally, after a couple months of blind abandon and feckless debauchery, we had gradually begun to recover, but it was a painful process, and we realized it was time to get involved in something, start living again. Besides, you can only consume so much tequila and pizza before you begin to feel like you have fire ants living in your asshole.

Will was still asleep in the guest bedroom when I made my way back to the house. I put on some coffee and the aroma brought him around. He came stumbling out, a well-worn pair of Hang Ten shorts clinging to his gangly frame, blond hair tousled and spiked from sleep, blue eyes imbued with enough red in the whites to make him look eerily patriotic. He lurched over with his hand out. "Cof-fee, cof-fee."

Will was such a character. Tall and thin as a mangrove heron, he possessed an easy nature and a clever wit, which often made him the focal point of most any gathering (especially if alcohol or a little herb were added to the equation) — the complete opposite of me. I was of medium height and stocky, with long, almost shoulder-length dark hair, hazel eyes, and more of a type-A demeanor (but similarly entertaining, given the proper assistance). We had met in college and discovered then that we had this weird, cosmic connection — playing off each other as if it were rehearsed, knowing what was coming before the other said it. We shared a passion for the mischievous, constantly looking for something to challenge our wit and whet our slightly twisted humor. We were benign rogues, always searching for a sail on the horizon, an experience to satisfy this intrinsic yearning for adventure. As our two-year intellectual odyssey at Saint Petersburg Junior College neared an end, we came to realize we simply viewed the world differently than those around us. Our friends envisioned dental colleges, accounting offices, and brokerage businesses. We saw sails in the distance — and they carried us south by southwest...

We sat on the deck, coffee in hand, watching the sun scale the last wisps of mottled cirrus streaks on the horizon, climbing up and searing a rose and emerald sky, compelling its transformation into soft summer azure.

Will was holding the map, studying it again. "I wonder why the pirate buried the map and bottle on Crooked Island, with the treasure on Cat?"

I shrugged. "Hard to say. Maybe he had come to a situation he wasn't sure he was going to get out of. Maybe he planned to use it as a bargaining chip at some point. Who knows? The British had major forts on Crooked at that time and they hated pirates."

Will brought the map down and gazed over at the rising sun for a moment, then turned to me and exhaled definitively, his blue eyes alight with roguery. "So, when do we leave?" he said, eyebrows bouncing up and down and that mischievous grin spread across his face.

It took us the better part of the day to purchase the supplies we needed, load them into the 182, and book reservations at a little guest house on Cat, but the following day, as the sun eased its way through the gray, early morning haze on the horizon, we were on our way. I pushed the throttle forward, the stereo speakers in the plane hammered out Three Dog Night's driving lamentation "Mama Told Me Not to Come," and we skipped across the mirrored green surface of Pine Channel, lifting up into adventure once again.

As we roll along this journey called life, each of us experiences an "indelible junction" or two that unequivocally ordains a portion of this voyage. Later, you may look back on it and shake your head with Monday-morning-quarterback clarity and a gratifying smile, or perhaps a wry grimace, but it was nonetheless a defining moment. Looking back on that moment, as we sailed into the blue heavens with visions of gold and adventurous enterprise dancing in our heads, the comforting drone of the engine in our ears and sweet anticipation engulfing us like a mother's embrace, I realize now that was one of my indelible junctions.

So put me on the highway, show me a sign, and take it to the limit, one more time...

— **The Eagles**

CHAPTER THREE

I took us up to five thousand feet and set an easterly course as we soared across the blue-green hues of the Florida Straits, then passed into the shallower, crystalline waters of the Great Bahamas Banks. We drifted over Andros Island and across the deep indigo rift of Northeast Providence Channel, then crossed the long, bony string of islands in the Exuma Cays, surrounded by their distinctive, staggered orange reefs. By this time, the first signs of gray and white cumulus clouds had begun to appear on the horizon, filling with moisture, energy, and the promise of rain. In the last hour of flight we cruised across the dark, nearly fathomless waters of Exuma Sound, finally sighting the distinctive, elongated shape of Cat Island surrounded with the yellow-white aura of its sand beaches.

You can read all you want about Cat, but it doesn't prepare you for reality — that's always the way it is. The whole island is something straight out of an old Hemingway novel. Maybe that's why it's always appealed to me. It's the epitome of the yin and yang of Caribbean life — lazy vistas of aquamarine water and picture book beaches suddenly bleed into jagged iron rock that has no respect for fragile skin and can wear out a pair of tennis shoes in a day. You'll see two hundred-year-old ruins basking like ancient temples, eroding peacefully in the sun and yielding to tenacious vines and sea grapes, right next to brightly colored limestone cottages where descendants of plantation slaves live in a peaceful tropical narcosis. Lazy coconut palms droop over Cat's single main road that lies straight as a desert highway for a mile or two, then suddenly writhes like a snake around the edges of beach and old coral outcroppings. Mysterious blue holes, more than a little daunting and eerie, reside in calm lakes that rise and fall with the tides in the center of the island. One minute the sea can be flat as ice and the sky dotted with nothing more than a few puffy clouds; fifteen minutes later a storm on the edge of the horizon will have swept in and slashed the countryside with warm, heavy pellets, dousing the heat and cleaning the broad-leafed vegetation.

There are several conventional churches on the island, brightly painted and inviting, but the night belongs to *Obeah* and the voodoo rituals that are still the mainstay of religion in the area. Add the legendary creature the people call *nyankoo* — a three-foot, gnome-like minion with a human face that supposedly inhabits the immediate area, and this completes the contradiction that is Cat. If you're looking for Miami-style nightlife, ATMs, exotic resorts and casinos, it's definitely not your stop.

I rolled a wing and banked into a long final toward the small runway at New Bight, backing off the power, dropping some flaps, and lowering the landing gear on the sides of the aluminum pontoons. She laid in as smooth and easy as a pelican in a gentle headwind and I taxied over to the customs building. The warm afternoon wind welcomed us as we deplaned and entered the reception/customs area. Twenty minutes later we were strapped into a little rental car and on our way to Kookie Palms, a small, unpretentious guesthouse in Arthur's Town on the northern end of the island. The first thing we noticed was how absolutely abandoned the whole island felt — very few cars on the road. The simple restaurants and bars were very nearly empty, although the few natives we saw by the road — mostly women carrying their belongings balanced on their heads — waved cheerfully.

Several of those folks waved to solicit a ride, and it wasn't long before we had a carful, the rich, warm accent of the Bahamas flowing through our cab as we traded greetings and questions with them all. Gradually, one by one they emptied out at their destinations. But as the road hit a winding stretch just before Harbour Settlement we saw one last hitchhiker waving pleadingly at us. He was short, maybe five-foot-four, and skinny, even for an islander. His thin arms dangled from the colorful T-shirt he wore and his knobby knees accented legs only a heron could be proud of. He had rich, dark chocolate skin, burnished hazel eyes practically the size of quarters, a huge, disarming smile full of big, square teeth, and long Rastaman ringlets of hair that curled about his face and shoulders like reddish-brown snakes. As we neared him he did this little dance of supplication — arms up in the air, lifted toward us, fingers flittering like he was checking for rain, head bouncing from side to side and feet hopping up and down as if his team just scored a touchdown. It was too much. We had to stop.

He wiggled his way into the back seat, profusely thanking us. "Oh, mons! Oh, mons! Grateful am I much! It gonna rain in fifteen minutes. No wanna get wet unnecessarily."

I looked out the window. There were a few clouds in the distance, but certainly nothing that looked like rain. "You think so, huh?" I said from the passenger's seat.

He nodded emphatically. "Oh, ya mon. Ya mon. Fabio no be wrong about certain tings."

I looked at Will and he shrugged, like, *Yeah, right. Who cares?*

As we drove, Fabio Poitier kept up a running conversation, not the least of which was his contention that he was the illegitimate son of Sidney Poitier. As a street urchin in Nassau, and the son of a hooker who supposedly caught Sidney's eye, he simply took Poitier's last name. He said with that toothy smile, "When you got nothin' in the pot, mon, you got nothin' ta lose."

He pulled himself up, resting his elbows between the two front seats and got a sly smile, his brown-green eyes twinkling with mischievousness. "What you do on dis ol' nothin' island, mons? You ganja boys, huh? Pick up some very many square grouper, ya? Make some crazy mad dash across Gulf Stream, get plenty rich, eat red meat, drink fine rum, screw many white women, ya mons?"

Will and I couldn't help but chuckle.

"Nah," I said, still smiling. "Not our thing. We're here to do a little exploring. Sort of a historical outing, you might say."

Fabio nodded enthusiastically, catching our drift with remarkable astuteness. "Ya mon, ya mon. All kinda tings on dis island. Many old tings buried in de dirt and de sand, mons. Fabio know dis island like de cracks in da ceiling above his bed. Maybe you need a guide, help you explore, help you stay away from limestone sinkholes, banana spiders, and big snakes, not to mention bad juju and little *nyankoo*." He offered a pronounced pause. "Sometimes white people disappear on dis island."

Will glanced at me with a wary squint, eyes displaying a little concern, mouth pinched. It started raining. I looked out the window, then back at my partner.

"Are you bullshitting us?" he said, staring at Fabio in the rear view mirror. "Do you really know this island? Like the interior?"

"Mon, what Fabio don't know about dis flat piece of mangrove, sand, and coral don't need to find your brain. I be right ready, mon, to be your extraordinary and specifically special guide — for a very nominal fee."

We dropped Fabio off at a bar about a mile from our guesthouse, agreeing to meet with him in the morning at the little restaurant across the street from our place.

We had stayed at Kookie Palms before, and the manager — a tall, spry fellow in his late fifties, with a shiny bald head and friendly eyes — welcomed us with two Kalik beers. He showed us to our room of preference by the wooden walkway and adjacent to their old pier, which jutted precariously into the serene Caribbean waters. After settling in, we did a snorkel dive along the sun-bleached sandy shoreline, just for fun, working our way down the beach about a half-mile, staying within a couple hundred yards of the shore. Like most Caribbean islands there were few big fish or lobster close to the beach, but as we moved farther out the scenery wasn't disappointing. The terrain went from flat, sugary sand to rolling, shallow dunes that merged with outcroppings of ancient weathered coral, perforated with crevices and hiding holes. As we moved into slightly deeper water, islands of relatively new growth appeared on the silver-white bottom. Brain coral heads rose from the sands like monstrous mushrooms, vividly decorated with sea fans and other gorgonias, while parrotfish pecked at their coral polyps with serene indifference and small groupers huddled in the shadows, changing colors like chameleons. Nearby, patches of staghorn and elkhorn corals created stunning, intricate labyrinths of orange and gold. Here and there a small school of insanely colorful tropicals hovered in and around the coral like a child's captivating mobile, and the gentle shore surge caressed and swayed it all in a silent symphony of perfect synchronization, engulfing the entire panorama in that hypnotic, mystical, almost magical cadence of the ocean. I was reminded once again of my passion and my undeniable connection to the sea and the islands — a strange thing for a country boy born in the dry, rolling hills of the Midwest.

I was also reminded that most people seem to carry an inherent affinity for a certain region, certainly not always where they're born. Some deny that in themselves, simply locking to a spot like an oyster to a rock, never looking over the horizon, just accepting — refusing to dream. A few of these folks act contented, but most are just fearful of vision and chance. Some of us are searchers, and we need more. We want to find that place that warms the heart — that strikes such a note at the core of our being we simply stand there enthralled, soothed, and a voice inside says, *I'm home.* We want to choose the points for our joys and sorrows before we experience them.

Relaxed and refreshed from our communion with nature, we returned to the guesthouse, and after a couple of quick showers, we pulled out our maps of the island, and our treasure map with its cryptic clues. The X that represented our treasure was near the top of the island, less than a quarter mile inland from a small bay protected by a curving, elongated reef. The clues "the great arrow rock" and "the mouth in the wall" were marked well, but so enigmatic that nothing could be gleaned from them until we investigated the area.

By the time we finished speculating, it was late afternoon and the sun was just beginning its descent into the sulking, cumulus monoliths on the horizon, igniting them in brilliant reds and yellows. The soft, onshore breeze lifted off the tropical green-blue waters, whispering a wistful melody, and the palm fronds outside our window rustled contentedly against a high, silky emerald sky. To be any closer to Heaven you have to have angels on your shoulder.

We put away our papers and decided to go out for dinner and maybe a little nightlife — what there was of it. Malaki, the owner of the guesthouse, had recommended a small restaurant across the street and we remembered it from our last trip, so we threw on some fresh clothes and set out for an evening's entertainment.

The little clapboard and cinderblock restaurant was nothing to write home about, but the "fish of the day" was good and the accompanying fresh vegetables were wonderful. The couple who ran it seemed pleased to get "offshore customers" and took excellent care of us. After dinner we asked about nightclubs in the area, but the question was answered with a shrug and a tad of hesitancy. We were reminded that unless we wanted to drive to the other end of the island to Fernandez Bay or Hawks Nest Resort, we would have to accept the hospitality the few local establishments.

"Dis be da poor end of da island, mon," said our host almost apologetically. "Mos'ly jus' island people." He told us there was a gathering place for music and drinks about three miles down the road. "One you be okay at."

He didn't tell us that there were actually two clubs in that area. We missed our turnoff to the one he mentioned and inadvertently found the second.

Unbeknownst to us, while we were enjoying our dinner in paradise, Rick Penchant's boys were breaking into our house on Big Pine Key. They had coerced a staff member at Sloppy Joe's to show them footage from the bar's security camera in the alley. They got our license plate, figured out who we were, and headed up The Keys to the house. One of the big goons jimmied the lock, and with a quick look around he and his partner slipped inside. Within fifteen minutes they had ransacked the place, ripping out drawers, overturning mattresses, pulling pictures off the walls and checking for safes. They found nothing, of course, but as they were preparing to leave, one of them noticed the checklist I had left on the table. On it I mentioned passports to Cat Island.

The place was a low, concrete block building with a gray, stucco exterior veined with weathered cracks. The covered front porch was shrouded in thick vines of flowering red bougainvillea. There were a few outside tables on the porch — like so many other places in the Bahamas, commonly used for the national pastime of dominoes. The windows were barred, which wasn't that uncommon, and the waning porch light offered a dull glow, casting somber shadows on the vines and the few cars in the parking lot. The muffled sound of reggae music filtered out of the open windows. It didn't carry the gay islands image that we had hoped for. In fact, it didn't look at all like what the fellow at the restaurant described. A worn sign hung over the entrance: The Reggae Cove.

We walked in and looked around, stopping abruptly. Sometimes in life you encounter a situation where you just know you've made a wrong turn. Poor lighting accentuated a thick layer of ganja smoke that hung suspended from the ceiling like the banks of an approaching storm. Two decrepit ceiling fans struggled helplessly to distribute it and combat the heavy summer humidity. The pervading aroma of pot was accompanied by mildew and stale beer. The checkered, black and white linoleum floor was cracked and peeling. From the speakers at the bar, Bob Marley crooned about shooting a sheriff and not being too concerned about it. There were about ten people in the room, all Bahamians, all looking at us with glares somewhere between mild incredulousness and instant contempt. The bartender stood at the bar rail, heavy belly draped in a colorful tie-dye shirt the size of a tent, bulbous Rastaman wool cap on his head restraining so much hair he looked like a black light bulb. The big mirror behind him had been fractured by a bullet. Several patrons sat around the tables, dreadlocks and gold teeth — or missing teeth — being the foremost identifying features. All were playing cards or dominoes. They all stopped and stared — no friendly smiles anywhere. The walls had been painted a gaudy red, completing the image of the original bar from hell. The whole thing looked like a still life by Picasso on acid.

Will whispered to me out of the side of his mouth, "How about we leave now, and come back maybe, the second Tuesday of...never."

Just then a woman emerged from the back room. Quite a remarkable woman, at that, dressed in an inexpensive yellow sarong that hung from one shoulder, draping her shapely, full breasts and caressing her slim frame to just above the knees. She wore simple leather sandals and had a red hibiscus flower tucked into her dark hair above her left ear. Without question she had a rich African heritage, which had given her long, supple limbs and the cocoa in her complexion, but her genetic ancestry had obviously been tempered over generations by liaisons with plantation owners, English traders, and American adventurers, leaving her with the best of both worlds. She was of medium height, but the erect way in which she carried herself made her appear taller. Her skin was flawless — the color of summer honey — and her eyes reflected the yellow-gold of Cuervo tequila with just a hint of hazel flashes as the light caught them. She had long, dark hair that was thick but not coarse; a narrow, slightly upturned nose; and wide, sensuous lips.

Will took one look at her as she stood there staring at us with more curiosity than disdain. "Well, maybe one drink," he muttered, still holding her gaze.

We moved into the room with more confidence than we felt, and took a table near the door in case we had to make a quick escape. The staring continued for a few more uncomfortable moments, then gradually the patrons returned to their drinks and their games. The bartender nodded to the girl and she came over.

"Good evening," she said, her wide mouth caressing the words as they left her lips. She smiled slightly, without a display of teeth, a hint of humor touching those strange eyes. "You boys lost, or just testing the barometer of your manhood?"

"Lost," said Will emphatically. "If you hadn't come out of that back room and stolen our hearts we'd already be a mile down the road."

She chuckled throatily. "Well then, you be on your best behavior, have a drink, and find your way back to that safe resort you came from, mon. The night can be a wicked place on this island."

There was a big guy in the far corner of the room — tall, with the hard, tight muscles of a boxer, heavy black hair ironed straight and pulled back tight against his head like a sixties blues player, dressed in white cotton slacks and a red, open-necked shirt — sitting with two other men, playing cards. He barked something at the girl, and she flinched slightly, but didn't turn. "I will go now and bring you drinks."

As she walked away, Will exhaled heartily. "Lord, I think I'm in love."

"Get in line," I whispered, still watching the sensuous sway of her body as she walked away. But it wasn't just a physical thing. She just seemed familiar, like I wanted to say, "Hi, it's good to see you again after all this time."

A moment later she was back with two Kaliks, the national beer of the Bahamas. After taking money from us she turned to leave. I stopped her with a touch to her arm. "What's your name?"

She shrugged, a slight roll of the shoulders. "What is the name of a night bird that passes by in the moonlight, never to be seen again? And why would it matter?"

Will stared up at her, responding in kind. "Because sometimes in life you find something so striking, so remarkable, that a vision is simply not enough. You have to have a name to complete the space that it holds in your mind and your heart."

She smiled again, exposing her only flaw. One upper front tooth was chipped slightly at an angle. But strangely enough, it added earthiness to her and made her even more appealing. "Carina," she said, but before anyone else could speak, the guy in the corner barked again and the sensual pleasantry fell from her face. "My boss does not like me talking with customers. I will go now."

I was about to say something, but the glower on her boss's face made me think better of it.

A deck of cards lay on the table and I began to shuffle them. Fanning through them, I picked out the ace of hearts. Bob Marley began to relate the importance of "jamming," and Will continued to whine about finding love in all the wrong places.

After about five minutes we had finished our first beer and our lovely waitress returned. "Would you like another, or have you had enough of nighttime in da real islands?"

I couldn't resist the challenge. "Actually, we're beginning to like the place. How about two more?"

Again we got the chip-toothed smile, but before she could get away, Will nodded at her boss. "Is that your boyfriend?"

She shrugged again, leaving it in the air. "I should go."

"What's he going to do, beat you if you spend too much time with the customers?" I asked jokingly, but the look on her face drew the humor from the question.

"He does not beat me too much," she said quietly, but there was a fierce undercurrent in her words. "He know if he does, I kill him in his sleep."

"Whoashit," Will exclaimed, somewhere between comic humor and trepidation.

Carina went to fill our orders. Moments later the big boss man got up and came over, accompanied by two of his card-playing buddies. He pulled out a chair and turned it around, sitting in it and putting his arms up on the back of it. He took one of the unshelled peanuts from the basket on the table, cracked it open, and smiled, but it looked more like disdain fused with poorly suppressed violence.

"When you come in I say to myself, Drako, they just foolish white boys, but now I think you have too much hungry eyes, mon. I think you conch boys need to drink up and go away. You stare too much at my woman."

Normally, Will and I would have been out of our seats and headed for the door, but I saw Carina watching the exchange, and there was something in her eyes — a strange, desperate hope. I just couldn't let her see me simply slink away without a word.

"Man, she's a pretty woman. We weren't being disrespectful, we were just being guys."

The look on Drako's face told me he had already made a decision about us. He wasn't going to be happy without exercising his authority and maybe drawing a little blood. Every once in a while in life you come across someone who just doesn't like you.

Drako's features tightened, his eyes settled into a sly fierceness, and his chin came up defiantly. "Maybe you like my woman. Maybe you fight me for her, huh, conch boy?"

I put up my hands, palms out. "Whoa, dude, now we're way off course. No need for heavy solutions. Hell, man, I wouldn't fight you for her if she was my mother. I have an allergy to violence — makes me bleed, gives me hives." I paused and pursed my mouth in hesitation — I knew I shouldn't do it, yet I couldn't resist. "But I'd cut cards with you for her."

He laughed. Not a pleasant thing. Sounded like a chain saw cutting aluminum. He turned to his friends. "He wants to cut cards for Carina!"

But as he was turning and speaking to his friends, I whispered to Will, "We're gonna need a distraction. You remember that choking act you did at the airport in Key West years ago?"

Will nodded, not at all happy.

"When I look at you."

The big Bahamian turned back to us, eyes still bleeding

animosity. "So, if I cut cards and I win, what do I get?"

"You get to beat the crap out of both of us and keep all the money we have."

Drako thought about it for a second. "No, is not a good enough deal, mon. You 'ave to do better."

"Okay, how about I let you cut off one of my friend's ears?"

"What the fu — " Will shrieked, pushing back his chair.

"I want one of your ears, too," Drako interrupted, the look in his eyes saying he had found a deal he could live with. He sat down across from me, called Carina over, and pulled Will and his chair over closer to him, within reach after he won.

Will took a couple of peanuts out of the basket on the table and cracked them open, eating in a slow, nervous fashion. Carina sat next to me. The other people in the bar, including the bartender, gathered around behind Drako. No one wanted to miss this show.

I pushed the deck over to Drako. He held my eyes while he shuffled the cards, put the deck on the table, picked up about a third of it and turned it over, showing the bottom card — a king of clubs. His countenance cracked into an ugly, triumphant smile. Carina's shoulders fell in disappointment, but her face kept its composure. Will moaned pitifully. I looked up at my partner and our eyes met. I reached over and lifted off another third of the deck, but as I did, Will popped a peanut into his mouth.

There was a collective breath drawn as I held my portion of the deck, but before I could turn it over Will bolted straight up as if he'd just been stabbed with an electric cattle prod. His eyes bulged out in terror and confusion as he reached for his throat and started making muted squawking sounds like a parrot that's being throttled. "Ack! Ack! Ack!" He stumbled away from the table, knocking over his chair, dropping to his knees, and holding his throat with one hand while pointing furiously at his mouth with the other. The sounds coming from him changed to a marvelous wheezing and gasping, completely capturing the attention of the entire audience. Once again I was convinced my buddy had missed his calling. He would have made such an amazing actor. He threw his hands out, waving them as if he were trying to stop a bus, did a full-body shiver, and knee-walked himself over to the feet of the huge bartender, hands outstretched in supplication, the grunting, yelping, hissing noises coming from him sounding something like a goat in the process of birthing a bobcat. The huge Bahamian grabbed Will by his shirt collar and jerked him upright, then wrapped his great, bullish arms around him and squeezed hard enough to make juice. Will's mouth popped open spasmodically and he spit a peanut at the bar hard enough to knock a bottle of Ron Rico off the shelf.

This whole act had diverted the attention of the crowd for a few seconds, but Drako was quick to turn back, his eyes on my hands and the cards. As it quieted down and Will lay wheezing against the side of the bar, Drako said, "Okay, conch boy, no more entertainment. Time to show your card."

There were no eyes anywhere else at that moment. In the background, militant reggae man Peter Tosh chanted through the speakers about poverty and hatred, and getting even.

I looked around at the audience, pausing at Carina for just a moment, then came back to Drako. I slowly turned my portion of the deck over, displaying...an ace of hearts. "Man! I can't believe it!" I cried. "Wow! Talk about luck!"

There was a hugely pregnant pause. Drako's eyes widened in disbelief, then they narrowed to angry slits. "Is not possible!" he whispered vehemently. Throwing his cards at me he surged up, anger spilling out of him as he knocked over his chair. "You cheated, mon! I know you did!" His eyes got killer hard and he drew a thin, terribly sharp-looking stiletto from behind his back. "No one cheats Drako!" he shouted as he moved toward me.

At the same time, Will was being dragged to his feet and thrown against the wall I was backing up to. The others were gathering around their leader, all of them garnering that same bloodlust and outrage as townspeople with pitchforks at the gates of the Frankenstein Castle — all but Carina, who stood in the corner, helpless to change what was taking place.

But at that moment the bar door swung open and three men entered. Two were large Bahamians with shaved heads and heavy, muscular bodies, like WWA wrestlers. But it was the one in the middle who caught our attention. He was a small, wizened man dressed in a traditional African *dashiki* of muted reds and yellows. He possessed the leathery, wrinkled skin of a black rhino, and gray-thatched, thinning dreadlocks fell limply to his shoulders, but it was his eyes that caught our attention. The irises were a deep opaque blue, like the color of the outer reef in winter, and his pupils were extraordinarily large, and black as hatred. At first glance you might have thought he was blind, but a second glance made you wonder if he wasn't peering inside you.

As he entered, everything stopped. There was an immediate and obvious deference as the crowd spread out from the angry knot they had assumed. Drako paused, the knife hand fell to his side, and he nodded, almost in reverence. "Hello, Night Father. We are honored."

The diminutive fellow offered a brief acknowledgment as he moved forward slowly, like an ancient lizard. His face had been a mask to this point, but when he stopped in front of Will and me it became bitter and grave. He studied us in silence, for maybe the longest minute of my life. "I know you," he grated, raising a long skeletal arm with bent, bony fingers that resembled appendages stolen from a coffin. Stretching out his arm, he pointed with a trembling middle finger. "The spirits in de night wind have whispered your names to me." His eyes appeared to swell and the strange aura emanating from him seemed almost tangible. "You come to take something from dis island. Something of metal and stones and greed, taken from de heart of an ancient land." He scoffed. "Proclamations of white man's faith. But Jama, the Night God, will not let you. You will find some of yourself and lose something of yourself on dis island. Maybe you lose your life."

"Damballa, Night Father," said Drako, regaining some of his anger and addressing the older man by name. "Dey cheated me. I want to cut dem."

The old man stared at our nemesis and Drako wilted slightly. "Are you certain dey cheated you?"

Drako paused. His mouth moved but nothing issued. It was obvious he wasn't sure where to go with this. "I want to cut them!" he said again defiantly.

The shaman gazed at him and answered quietly, but his words were full of authority and command. "Dey are not for you to cut tonight. Dey belong to Jama. He will take dem when da time is right." Then his attention returned to us. "Go now, conch boys. Go to your clean, soft beds and thank your Jesus God I come here dis evening. It is not your time tonight." He paused again and a small, wicked smile touched the corners of his lips. "But I think soon come, mon. Soon come."

No one had to ask us twice. We headed for the door like two ferrets released from their cage. But as we did, I glanced at Carina, my head inclined. My eyes asked if she wanted to come. She shook her head almost imperceptibly. This was not the time for her, either.

I can't remember the humid night air and the gentle evening breeze ever feeling better than when we stumbled out of that tavern and into our rental car, bathed in the yellow light of the full moon and gulping in the sweet air of survival.

As he drove, Will muttered, "Well, that was interesting. Nothing like a little after dinner entertainment to get the juices flowing. Except that we almost had our juices all over the floor." He turned to me. "Man, how could you take that kind of chance? How could you possibly know you could pull that off? It isn't like you to be that daring, especially with our ears being the bet."

"You remember when we were sitting at the table and I was shuffling the cards?" I said, staring at the starlight reflecting off the old asphalt on the road.

Will nodded. "Yeah, I remember."

"Well, I slipped out the ace of hearts and put it under my bar napkin, face down."

Will got that goofy grin of his. "Son of a bitch!"

"Yeah. So when you did your choking act — which by the way, was exceptional…you could take that on the road — I pulled the napkin away and slapped the cards I was holding down on the ace, then picked them all up again. Took less than two seconds."

Will shook his head incredulously. "You becoming nastily tricky, mon."

When we returned to Kookie Palms, jasmine and poinciana caressed the night air in waves and the moon was lifting off the almost indefinable horizon, its reflection dancing across the inky, still waters. It was a soothing, comforting sight. We needed soothing and comforting. It had been a long day, and there were promises that this trip was about to become more interesting.

The following morning we met Fabio, our newly hired guide (although the price had not yet been decided on) at the restaurant across the street. He had already procured a table in the back and waved at us.

"Hello mons! Hello mons!" he chattered enthusiastically as we sat down.

The waitress came over, we ordered breakfast, and while waiting, we talked.

"How well do you know the north end of this island?" I asked.

Fabio paused while slurping down coffee. "Plenty well, mon. Plenty well. Like de bite mark from hooker on de head of my extraordinarily large — "

"Okay, okay. I get it. We're going to need to find some

landmarks up there. We'll pay you thirty bucks a day, and if you find what we want, we'll give you five hundred American."

Fabio's face broke into a wide smile. "For dat I not only be your right ready guide, I spit on your enemies and bury dem in a shallow grave!"

As we were paying for our meal, I spotted Carina walking dissolutely along the road, an old suitcase in one hand and a bundle of clothing in the other. I got Will's attention and pointed. A minute later we were outside hailing her. She stopped as we approached, wearily setting down the old suitcase. The sun was already bringing to bear its tropical oppression, and there was the slightest sheen to her golden cocoa skin. It was one of the first times I had envisioned sweat as sexy.

She pulled herself up, gathering her pride. "I leave him," she said without our asking.

"Do you have someplace to stay?" Will immediately asked.

She did that half shrug of hers. "I try to find my sister. Last time I know, she at Orange Creek."

I saw the look on Will's face. I knew what was coming and I didn't try to stop it.

"Wait, you're just gonna hitchhike up to Orange Creek on the chance you might find her?" I said.

She paused, allowing her silence to be her answer.

"Why don't you let us get you a room at Kookie Palms for a few days, just until you can figure this out."

She shook her head adamantly. "No. I cannot do that. For every favor dere is a price, and I do not wish to owe you."

"No price," I said. "We got you into this with that situation last night. At least let us help you out a little. You can pay us back. It's nothing more than a loan."

She hesitated, and Will quickly chimed in, "Just for a few days, until you can find your sister, then you'll be on your own again."

An hour later I had sent Fabio to get a few supplies for us and we had Carina set up in a room next to ours. (We told ourselves it was for her safety, but frankly both of us liked the convenience and possibility it offered, for sadly, we were men well ahead of being good Samaritans.) Just the few minutes with her as she settled into her room left us with sugarplums dancing in our heads, and as usual, we began the typical ritual of competition that always seemed to rise in us when we encountered an attractive woman. And attractive she was. Not as distant and cavalier as she'd been the night before —

more gracious, with an almost simple elegance about the way she moved and spoke. When Will finally succeeded in making her laugh, it was soft and throaty, and as sensual as summer rain on naked skin. But we had to go. We had a golden cross to find. She asked when we would be back and I explained that my buddy and I had some business on the northern end of the island in the jungle. With any luck we'd be back by nightfall. At that point, the owner, Malaki, knocked on the door, wanting to know if there was anything else he could bring the lady. He, too, was obviously smitten.

We changed into blue jeans, heavy khaki shirts, and canvas tennis shoes (to thwart the wickedly thorned vines in the jungles of the Bahamas), organized our packs, set aside our digging gear, and double-checked the operation of the metal detector we'd brought. Then we threw our packs over our shoulders and headed out to the front of the guesthouse to wait for Fabio. We were looking for another chapter in the story of our lives.

It came to mind as we waited in the old wooden chairs on the porch that, actually, most genuine adventures are a combination of diligent preparation and stumbling blind bad luck, usually when you least expect it. But then, it wouldn't be called an adventure if there weren't a dragon or two. That's why exceptional experiences of this sort are generally appreciated more in retrospect. That's why they made alcohol — for the recounting of adventures.

The byproduct of the whole adventure thing is knowledge (and, of course, wonderful barroom stories). Great experiences are borne not from what happens to you, but from how you respond when they're happening. If you're paying attention, encapsulated in the event is learning, which enables you to limit your next battery of mistakes to something new.

While we were waiting, a phone rang in a small, nondescript cinderblock bungalow near the water on the southern side of Arthur's Town. A large Bahamian answered it, listened for a moment, then hung up. He turned and lumbered over to his boss. "Dey leave dis morning for da northeast corner of da island."

Yes, I am a pirate, two hundred years too late. Cannons don't thunder, there's nothing to plunder, I'm an over forty victim of fate.
— Jimmy Buffett

CHAPTER FOUR

The roads on Cat were weathered at best, and the area we needed to get into was at least a mile past the last navigable road, so we had to take the amphibian. It was a half hour back to the airport. As we neared the turnoff to the strip another vehicle was just heading out — a van with a Bahamian at the wheel and three or four white guys accompanying him. When they passed I got a strange feeling in the pit of my stomach. All I had was a glance, but it seemed like I saw a familiar face in there.

Will took a second look as they sped by. "They're in a hurry, aren't they?" he muttered.

An uncomfortable sigh escaped me. "Yeah. Looks that way."

By the time we'd fueled and lifted off, we had lost a good portion of the morning and were anxious to get this excursion underway. It was Fabio's first small plane ride, which left him uncharacteristically quiet. That allowed Will and me to follow the road below uninterrupted, and locate the cove with the curved reef that we needed to find. Twenty minutes later I set the plane down on the placid, gin-clear waters just inside the reef and taxied onto a beach right out of *Caribbean Magazine*. After unloading our packs and the metal detector, Will and I had another look at our map. I stretched it out gently, as much as I could risk with the fragile, ancient parchment, studying the clues. "'The great arrow rock' sounds to me like a more obvious landmark, maybe a large outcropping of some sort."

Will nodded in agreement. "Yeah, and the 'mouth in the wall' might be a limestone cave of some sort. The best thing we can do is sort of mentally overlay this old map over the new one. The X is definitely northeast of where we are, so I think that's our direction."

Fabio interjected that this end of the island had some heavy mangroves near the shore, and that we could circumnavigate them by heading north along the beach for a few minutes, then cut back east/southeast. So, without further ado, we headed down the beach and into the jungle.

Generally, people don't know how harsh and unyielding the interior of most Bahamian Islands can be. There are about a hundred different types of clinging vines and about half of them possess malicious thorns that have eagerly awaited you all of their lives. The other fifty percent will effortlessly embrace and hopelessly tangle you like demented, needy lovers, not to mention the Spanish Spears and wild cactus, both introduced by the Spanish and both of which are abundant, needle sharp, and viciously clever at finding your flesh. It wasn't long before we were reminded about them.

The sea grapes, casuarina trees, and palms on the beach quickly gave way to the heavier interior. Mottled lizards scuttled across the leaf-covered limestone marl beneath our feet, and the last of the morning mosquitoes bombarded us with dogged persistence before absconding with our blood to the leafy darkness of the jungle. An osprey circled high above, watching the invasion of his terrain with a detached curiosity. The air was heavy with moisture and the sweet-sour smell of wild poinciana, salt, and decaying vegetation. Although the animal trail we found made it easier to negotiate, the copses of buttonwood, gumbo limbo, and wild mangoes on both sides were thick enough to daunt much of a view beyond a couple dozen yards.

We continued on into the afternoon, crisscrossing the hillside from the shoreline upward, watching for one of our distinctive clues. There were some granite outcroppings, but nothing that led us to believe they were 'the great arrow rock,' and no one had seen any caves in the granite facings we discovered.

We had been trudging along for about half an hour, moving into the higher interior and cutting our way through the clinging vines, when we saw something ahead of us. Lord, it was just like in the movies. There before us, laced in vines and punished by the growth of trees, lay the aged, gray limestone ruins of one of the old eighteenth century plantation homes rising defiantly out of the jungle.

In the late 1700s and early 1800s, the British Loyalists in the Americas, who refused to offer allegiance to the new United States, immigrated to the Bahamas. Some of them took their goods and their slaves and journeyed to Cat. In a remarkably audacious effort, they carved plantations out of the unrelenting jungle. However, the death knell for their efforts rang in 1834, when Britain abolished slavery. Along with slavery, the plantations faded, and the jungle claimed them. We were standing in the midst of one of those old plantations. It was eerie and intoxicating at the same time.

Slowly the three of us moved into the past, through the grand ruins of the main house and over to the narrow slave quarters — a long building with windows that once contained bars, and only one door in and out. Here and there we could see the remains of an old gin bottle or a fractured crock, or the rusting remnants of an iron pot, and I could almost sense the life they lived — close to the earth, every day a competition, and yet an inherent pride in their ability to challenge nature at its rawest and survive. Huge gumbo limbo trees had pushed their way through foundations of the buildings, parting rock and limestone with the persistence of time. It was absolutely fascinating, but the sun was beginning to move toward the horizon.

Will wiped the sweat from his face with the sleeve of his shirt. "This has been great fun and I wish I could do it another eight or ten hours," he grunted with that quintessential sarcasm. "But I don't think I want to be out here in the dark."

Fabio, who had done a good job of keeping us on track in the dense, easily confusing terrain, nodded heartily. "Oh, ya mon. Dis not da place you want to be when da sun go down. Plenty strange juju wander around here at night."

We had already seen a couple of large snakes (up to six feet in length), along with spiders the size of your palm, and had heard enough talk of *Obeah*, voodoo rituals, and the legendary *nyankoo* — the gnome-like night creature with a human face — to convince us that Fabio might well be right.

I looked at the sun starting to slip into the tops of the foliage. The shadows in the jungle were growing. "Yeah, couldn't agree more. We'll try again tomorrow. It's here. We just have to get the jungle to talk to us a little."

"She talk to us, mon, she talk to us," Fabio agreed. "But de jungle and dis island, dey be like da fickle street mama. You got to tickle her. You got to show her you want dat special honey she give. She like to make you want before she take your hand..."

On the flight back I wasn't disappointed. On the contrary, I was excited. Finding those old ruins, seeing the ancient artifacts, connected me to this island, and suddenly I could feel the people who were there before, as if I had shared that life somehow, centuries ago. It was eerie and exhilarating at the same time. We would try again in the morning. It was out there, waiting for us.

Carina was sitting on the end of the old dock at Kookie Palms, her feet dangling above the water, watching the last bloom of brilliant, flaming pink on the horizon as the earth succumbed to celestial movement and the sun sizzled into a darkening sea. Her hair was pulled back into a ponytail and she had on white shorts and a sleeveless yellow blouse that accented her honeyed skin. Even at a distance we could smell the cinnamon and lime bouquet that was her fragrant signature. We had run the plane back to the airport and driven up the island, dropping off Fabio in the process. Both of us were tired and sweaty, and after a brief greeting a coin was flipped to see who would shower first. Will won, so I sat out on the dock with Carina for a while.

As we watched a V of pelicans glide into the shallow waters near the shore, making that last-minute, ungainly collision with the surface, Carina exhaled softly. "Thank you for allowing me to stay here." She gazed out at the water for a moment. "But Drako will not be happy with any of us."

"We'll worry about him when the time comes," I said with more bravado than I felt, still recalling the light gleaming off that knife blade. I changed the subject. "Have you lived here all your life?"

She shook her head. "No, I was born in Nassau. My mother was a teacher of children, my father was a fisherman, a diver for conch and lobster. He was from France, a *blanc*, like you. But he drown when I was twelve. After that it was hard times." She looked away at the clouds on the horizon and whispered as if the very words were painful. "Hard times."

"But things are looking up," I said with enthusiasm, deliberately breaking her mood. "You're now free of unpleasant encumbrances, and friends with two crazy Americans who are going to take you to dinner tonight. "

"I am also homeless and poor."

"Let's work on one thing at a time. Tonight we eat and drink well, get a good night's sleep, and we'll worry about tomorrow when the sun rises."

"What about you?" Carina said, turning to me. "Who are you?"

I shrugged. "Well, I'm really nothing more than a commercial diver. Divorced. Live in The Keys in a place with my friend. Will and I do a little adventuring on the side. Looking for things people lost a long time ago."

She got a sage look, her eyes registering understanding. "Treasure," she said.

It was a statement, not a question.

"Well, yes, that's the big definition, but I wouldn't say we've been all that successful. It's more of a hobby. Antique bottles, maybe a few coins."

"That's why you are here."

Again, not a question.

"What do you look for?"

"Well, no offense but I'm not sure I want to say too much just yet." I gave in just a little to her inquisitive stare. "Something very old and golden. You might say a relic of some historical value."

Before she could reply, Will came out of our apartment, clean and shiny and in record time, trying not to give me any more one-on-one with Carina than necessary. Having splashed himself with copious amounts of cologne, he reeked like a pimpled, virgin teen on his way to the prom. The game was obviously on.

That evening we drove down to Fernandez Bay for dinner. We sat in the dining room overlooking the perfect circular bay, watching the moonlight dance off the waves as they rolled in perfect symmetry onto the white sand beach, their foamy crests dusted with flickering, luminous splashes of fairy dust phosphorescence. Will, with his offbeat sense of humor, managed to pull Carina from her funk, and she proved to be an absolute treat. Our new friend wasn't overly educated in the formal sense, having attended school through only the tenth grade, but she was a reader, and from that she had a fine vocabulary, a quick, incisive mind, and the wry sense of humor we had witnessed upon our first meeting. It wasn't long before Will and I realized we had discovered a diamond in the sand. The three of us ended up a little drunk, stumbling along the moon-bathed beach, accompanied by a bottle of rum and a thinly disguised desire on the part of Will and me. But it was obvious from Carina's demeanor that there were to be no winners or losers that night. The verdict was still out and it was every man for himself.

When we returned to the pavilion and Carina excused herself to use the restroom, Will turned to me, eyes aglow with liquor and lust. "I'll flip you for her. She's got the hots for me, anyway. Anyone can see that."

"The only thing anyone can see for sure is the drool running down your chin. Man, you're bouncing around like a chimpanzee on crack. I was thinking of doing you a favor and dropping a couple Quaaludes in your rum and Coke."

My buddy got a serious look on his face. "You wouldn't do that to me again, would you, man?"

I chuckled. "I might, for the girl of my dreams. As I've told you before, all is fair in love and war. And I'm not flipping you for her. She's not a freakin' puppy. Besides, it's me she's got the hots for. Your dick is short-circuiting your brain, dude. Not enough blood."

Will grinned. "That's because I got a wanker like a yak. One look at Donkey Boy and the twins and you gonna be officially disqualified."

I opened my mouth to respond, but Carina was coming up the walkway, a look of consternation on her face. The laughter in her eyes had diminished some and she appeared to be uncomfortable. "I am so sorry," she said, one hand holding her stomach and the other extended in apology. "I must have eaten something that disagreed with me — maybe too much rum. I suddenly don't feel so well."

We were immediately attentive. Will went around to get the car and I escorted her to the front of the restaurant. It was a bummer, given all those sugarplums that were dancing in our heads, but we both had a firm rule: never make love to a seriously drunk woman. Projectile vomiting really puts a damper on good sex.

By nine o'clock the next morning we were back in the air. An hour later we were in the jungle again, crisscrossing the hills facing the small bay, but it was about then we realized that, in our haste, we had left the metal detector in the plane. Fabio volunteered to go get it, and because he was the most comfortable with the terrain, we agreed.

It's easy to get separated in thick topography when you're searching for something. We carried hand-held CB radios to keep in touch, and up to that point we had been lucky, but about fifteen minutes after Fabio left, we were pulled apart by a copse of thick buttonwood and large gumbo limbo trees, and before I knew it I could no longer hear Will clomping around. I took the CB out of my breast pocket. "Hey Will, where are you? Lost you about fifty yards ago. Come back."

No answer.

Then the CB squelched. "Hey, Kansas!" There was a pause. "I don't like this…. Whoa! What the hell!" And all went silent.

Fear is a strange thing. There are several kinds, from mild trepidation and sweaty armpits, to shaky hands and stuttering, but the worst is the cold fear of uncertainty, the specter in the darkness — the one you can't exactly see, the one that drives your imagination wild, crawls into your intestines, and digs at you with tiny, mean claws. After about five minutes of calling Will's name in the eerie gloom of the jungle and listening to the empty, forbidding silence, I was starting to feel the tiny, mean claws. A few moments later I came to a small clearing. On the periphery lay Will's hat and machete. I bent down to pick them up, heard a rustle behind me, and that was the last thing I remembered.

"I don't wanna die like this," Will muttered through clenched teeth. "This just isn't how I saw it."

One of the first things you notice when you're hanging by your feet, upside down, is the buzzing in your ears — all that blood draining into your head. This condition is oftentimes accompanied by a rapidly thumping heart, because, let's face it, if you're hanging upside down from the limb of a gumbo limbo tree in the jungle, somebody doesn't like you.

"I don't want to die, period," I mumbled painfully, staring at the two Bahamians in front of us; one huge guy with a machete — a gorilla on steroids with a bald head — and the other, who was slightly smaller (probably only seven feet) with the same sweat-gleaming, dark chocolate skin, holding a heavy cane of bamboo (with which he'd been tenderizing us). "I'd always hoped for lying in bed, naked and pleasurably exhausted when the old ticker lurches to a stop," I added.

As the guy with the bamboo reared back for another round of tenderizing, Will yelled again, "We don't know anything, man! We haven't found any frigging gold!"

Unfortunately, he was right, and we were really screwed because that was not what these folks wanted to hear.

The largest of the two, a jagged scar where his right eye used to be, stopped his partner from whacking me again, then just stared at us for a moment, his single, smoky-colored yellow orb displaying no more compassion than if we were cockroaches. He turned to the man with the cane and barked a few words. Walking away from us, they proceeded to have a brief conversation in a strange language, which sounded like somebody grunting and bleating with a mouthful of marbles. We continued to just hang around.

The sun was past its zenith, approaching the tops of the surrounding trees in the clearing, turning vine and leaf to a soft, elegant gold, reaching out with furtive shadows across the gray-green jungle landscape. As their conversation ended, the faces of our antagonists went grim. The man dropped his bamboo cane, took out a sinister-looking knife and turned toward us.

I shouted, "We have the gold! We'll give it to you!"

Will's body twisted around in the air, his long blond hair falling over his face, eyes filled with incredulousness. "What the hell are you doing?" he hissed. "We don't have squat, dude!"

"Well, you can see how good we're doing with plan A," I hissed back. "I think it's time to try something else."

The men moved over to us. The big guy squatted on his haunches in front of me so he could look me in the face. "Go ahead, *blanc.* I am listening."

"We hid it down by the airplane, in the mangroves," I said. "We had hoped to find more."

The big guy smiled. It wasn't pretty. Whoever had taken his eye had borrowed a couple of teeth, as well. "Just tell us, or maybe you draw a map for us. We find it."

"You couldn't find it with twenty maps and a seeing-eye dog," I sneered. "It's someplace that we'll have to show you."

"He is lying," muttered the other one, a halo of frizzy hair, and hard, black agates for eyes. "Kill them now. They know nothing."

The bald gorilla raised his machete threateningly. "If you lie…"

"Yeah, yeah, if we lie you're gonna kill us," said Will, getting into the plan. "Tell me something I don't already know. All we want is to get the hell off this island! We'll give you the freaking gold! Just let us go."

I couldn't help but smile inwardly. He was such a great performer — a master trickster. We had hopefully bought some time.

Again there was a brief conversation, but more heated — sounded like rocks being thrown against tin siding. Then the guy with the knife turned and moved toward us, menace burning in those black eyes. He squatted next to upside down Will, put the point of the knife at my partner's throat, then drew it slowly up his torso to the crotch of his khaki shorts, stopping there and pressing the point against his more valuable appendages.

"Oh Jesus," Will moaned, "not Donkey Boy and the twins."

The guy grinned maliciously, then suddenly swung the blade in an arch, hard and fast, cutting the rope just above Will's feet. Before my friend had hit the ground, the fellow turned and slashed my rope, as well. With our hands tied behind our backs, we slapped the earth hard, grunting from the shock, our faces almost touching.

"I think he likes you," I said.

"Not funny," Will gritted. "It's not freaking funny."

I was gradually working us back to the area where the plane was, but the boys with the machetes were getting impatient, especially the smaller one. He had just suggested, again, that they kill us and tell "da boss man" to find it himself, when there was a strange sound off to our right, about thirty feet into the heavy brush. It sounded like the soft, plaintive cry of a woman in distress.

"Aaaahh…"

Pause.

Then it came again, more pronounced, almost throaty and sensuous, tinted with heavy anxiety, "Aaaaahhhhhh…"

We all stopped in our tracks and listened. It came again, just a little farther into the brush and more to our right.

"Ooohhh dea' God! I gonna die in dis Godforsaken jungle!"

Everyone's eyes definitely took on a sense of serious curiosity as we glanced back and forth. Then it came again.

"Ooohhh Lawd, I's so thirsty, an' my huge, luscious breasts is all sweaty… and hot…"

There was a pause, several more glances on our part, then another plaintive wail.

"My dress is des' about torn off'a my soft, sweaty body. What I gonna do?" The voice stopped as someone moved off clumsily in the brush, then halted. "Aaaahhh. Aaaahhh…I's so hot…and moist…all dat sweat tricklin' atween my…aaahhh…"

Our captors' eyes now displayed a little more than curiosity.

"I's so slippery my panties is slipping down…slidin' off'a my creamy white…aaahhh…"

The big guy looked at his friend and barked another volley of guttural gibberish, which we were pretty sure amounted to, "You stay here! Watch the white guys!" Without another word he headed off cautiously into the brush. I looked at Will. He raised an eyebrow and shrugged.

The smaller Bahamian herded Will and me over to a big gumbo limbo and roughly shoved us down against the thick trunk, our hands still tied behind our backs. We collapsed and waited, watching the fellow pace up and down the path anxiously. We could still hear our other captor moving into the thick undergrowth, and an occasional seductive supplication from the phantom jungle hottie. Sitting there, I just happened to look up the hill through the trees and noticed an osprey's nest in the canopy above us, the sticks, tufts of fur, scales, and bones from unlucky dinner guests spread out over the sides. As I studied the nest, I realized it wasn't lodged in a tree. It was perched on a huge boulder…shaped like a blunt arrowhead.

"Holy frigging monkey shit!" I whispered to myself.

Will looked at me, concern furrowing his brow. "Don't melt down on me now, dude. There's something happening."

I was about to reply when suddenly there was a hand on my wrists and a sawing motion against my bonds. Seconds later I was free, and I felt someone place a wooden club in my right hand. Will's expression changed to alarm and surprise, then understanding. His hands were free, as well. He glanced over at me. I nodded.

"Yeah, me too," I whispered. But we remained in position, as if we were still bound.

Suddenly, we heard a grunt and a brief rustle in the mangroves. Then it got quiet. We no longer heard the big guy moving around. Our guard was getting nervous. He called for his partner. No answer. He shuffled over toward us, eyes darting quickly from one side of the trail to the other. He called again, standing in front of us — still no answer. His confidence was slipping away, gradually being replaced by growing apprehension, but his sense of brutality was still in high gear.

I whispered out the side of my mouth, "I think we're going to need a distraction here, but the timing is gonna be real important."

"Uh-huh," Will muttered, not quite certain what was coming, but getting ready.

I had never known anyone in my life who could improvise like Will, and I trusted him to come up, once again, with one of his famous "distractions."

The Bahamian stared at Will and me, dark eyes flashing with a final decision. "Where is da gold?" he snarled. "Last chance, *blancs.* Where is it?"

"Told you before, man, we don't know where the gold is," I snapped back. "You might as well just kill us."

"Son of a bitch!" Will hissed, pushing his back up against the tree. "Have you lost your freaking mind?"

"Just get ready," I whispered.

In his stressed-out state, that was all the guy could stand. He barked something in his language and moved into me. The man knelt down so close his rancid breath rolled over me like a beach breaker. (One whiff and I could only assume he must have lunched on the same monkey shit I referenced earlier.) Then he reached for his knife. But at that moment Will stiffened as if he'd just mainlined a quart of brake fluid, eyes wide and bulging like Wile E. Coyote. "Demons! Eviiill spirits!" he screeched in his very best spooky movie voice "Dey come for us! Dey in da jungle all around us!"

The one thing that's pretty well universal in the Caribbean is the belief in, and the absolute fear of, evil spirits. It's an intrinsic part of the culture.

"Aaaiiieee!" shrieked Will, bringing his arm around from his back and pointing over our antagonist's shoulder with a theatrically shaking hand. "Zombies! Zombies! Dey come! Aaaiieeee!"

Well, let's face it, after that performance, even the most committed, card-carrying atheist would want to at least have a quick peek at the approaching zombies, and our boy was certainly no exception. His head snapped around like an anxious squirrel guarding a nut. Just as he did, I yanked my arm out from behind me in a roundhouse swing, the hard, wooden club whistling through the air, and smacked him upside the head hard enough to blind a rhino.

Nothing happened. He still knelt in front of me, although his eyes had lost a little focus, and one hand reached down to the earth to steady himself.

"Whoashit!" hissed Will, starting to edge away like a startled spider.

I hit him again, so hard the club snapped in two, one piece twirling off into the mangroves on the side of the trail.

I couldn't believe it! He was still there in front of me! But his eyes had some odd distance to them now, like the morning after a tequila/peyote party. I waved my hand in front of his face and those glazed orbs didn't move.

Will wiggled back over. "Let me help here," he said confidently, as he pushed the fellow's shoulder with a couple of fingers. Our antagonist tilted limply, then slowly tumbled over, hardly changing position, heavy as a concrete lawn ornament.

Suddenly, Fabio pounced out from behind the tree, holding the baseball bat we kept in the plane (one of the few weapons we could get through customs). He looked down at the Bahamian and got that wide, goofy grin of his. "Not bad for two white boys. Fabio dig da zombie ting. Very funny!"

Will and I just sat there with our mouths open. Finally, Will asked, "What happened to the other guy?"

Fabio slapped the bat in the palm of his other hand. "Dat boy takin' a nap. He out ta lunch — I'm sayin', mon, dere be a sign on da door!"

I had to smile. "How? How did you find us?" I stuttered. "How did you know what happened?"

"When I start back from plane, I see dese two moving into jungle. I go back to plane and get baseball bat. When I get back to where you were, I no find you. So I des follow da path you took. Don' got to be no Hiawatha to follow you. You be plenty clumsy jungle boys."

"And you did the sweaty, hot, creamy breasts thing?" Will asked, his voice carrying a smile and some new respect. "Very clever. Very entertaining."

Our new friend shrugged and grinned again. "Fabio got lotsa talents." Then he straightened up. "But now, I tink we need to be gone, mon. Before zombie dudes wake up from nap."

"No," I said, grabbing the coil of rope at my waist. "Tie them up. I want to know who sent them, and," I said with a triumphant beam, "I've found the first landmark."

While we tied our two antagonists to a large banyan tree, I sent Fabio on an errand. When he returned, I squatted down in front of the largest.

"Who sent you?"

He stared at me, eyes full of fierceness and defiance. "I tell you nothing. You are dead men."

"Okay, have it your way," I said with a shrug. "We're not going to argue with you. Don't have time." I motioned to Fabio. "Bring me the spider."

There was an immediate change in the man's countenance — uncertainty had wiggled its way into his eyes. That drifted right into outright, ugly panic when Fabio brought over a huge black and yellow Banana Spider, which he held pinched between two sticks.

I looked at the arachnid, then back to the man. "I'm not sure how much you know about this spider, but it is the most dangerous in the Caribbean. You're almost better off if it kills you, because wherever it bites you, that section begins to rot like a bad mango. First it swells, stretching the skin to the bursting point, then, finally, the area explodes with pus and poison. Amputation — cutting out all the flesh in and around the wound — is generally the best chance of survival. But by that time most people have lost their minds from the pain." I sighed. "Well, seeing as how there's not going to be any conversation here, I guess we ought to get right to it. Will, hold his legs so I can open his pants and Fabio can drop our little friend into his underwear." I moved close to the man and whispered, "I hope you had some good sex this week, because it was the last you're ever going to have."

As Fabio advanced with the wriggling, deadly creature, the fellow stiffened, eyes the size of dinner plates, and his mouth started moving silently. He caved before I made it to his belt buckle.

"Okay, mon! Okay!" he coughed out in terror. "It was Drako. He send us."

"How did he know where we were going?"

The big Bahamian shook his head harshly. "I don' know, mon. He don' tell us."

Fabio inched the spider closer as I grated menacingly, "Are you sure?"

The guy cringed and pushed himself against the tree. "He get a phone call dis morning. Dat all I know!"

We left our two antagonists bound to the tree while we headed toward the "arrow rock" I had discovered, feeling both excited and uneasy. We were closing in on our target, but apparently there were people closing in on us.

According to the ancient map, the arrow rock and the mouth in the wall formed two parts of a triangle. The third and most important part, the location of the treasure, was shown as what appeared to be a flat rock. We had the arrow, so the mouth in the wall had to be to the south, through some of the thickest jungle yet. We spread out in a line about fifty feet apart, as once again the sun was falling toward the treetops, its rays struggling to penetrate the thick, leafy foliage.

Moving slowly and quietly, I became aware of the life around me — the occasional squawk of a Bahamas parrot, the twitter of monk parakeets, the soft warble of wrens, mocking birds, the rustle of leaves as a startled raccoon or iguana scooted away, and every once in a while a cracking of heavy brush with the movement of something larger, perhaps a hutia (a large, rodent-like animal native to the Caribbean). Like the ocean, the jungle is in constant movement — it's simply more subtle and inconspicuous.

It happened so effortlessly I was amazed. Will was stumbling through the vines and boughs ahead of me when I heard him stop dead.

"Son of a bitch" he whispered emphatically. "The mouth in the wall."

In seconds we were all gathered together, staring at a small limestone anomaly that had drawn itself up from the strata below and formed a narrow cliff that ran for about thirty yards. In the center was a curved horizontal slit shaped like a mouth.

"One more time, now," I said. "We need a flat rock that completes the triangle."

It took an hour of miserable trudging through vines and brush that fought to clutch us with the tenacity of drowning sailors, but finally we heard Fabio shout, "Sweet zombie mama! De flat rock! De flat rock!"

Moments later we all stood staring down at a stone roughly four feet square — very possibly the final resting place of one of the more unique treasures lost on the Spanish Main.

"Let's get this sucker moved," said Will, an anxious gleam lighting his eyes.

The stone was heavy, but no match for the energy of three treasure-hungry men. We had two shovels and we took turns digging for twenty minutes. Finally, there was a distinctive clunk of metal on wood.

Will looked up at me, eyes on fire. "Lord! I'm so excited I feel like a mink in heat!"

Will and I scrambled down into the hole and began working our shovels around the edge of an emerging chest. It was oblong, about two feet by eighteen inches, and as we worked it loose, we found that it was only about six inches deep — very similar to the dimensions recorded in the information about the cross. The wood had deteriorated badly and the bronze bands were seriously corroded, but it had been covered with a skin of some sort — maybe pig, maybe seal — and that had assisted in its preservation.

I don't mind telling you, when we finally pulled it loose, set it on the ground, and snapped off the ancient lock with a shovel, my hands were shaking like a speed junkie. I thought my heart was going to rip itself out of my ribs and do handstands on the jungle floor. I could barely get enough breath to wheeze, "Open...open it!"

Will slowly lifted the lid, and wild, trembling anticipation engulfed us like a tidal surge.

There's nothing quite like gold. It's the embodiment of wealth and greed, the epitome of unabashed prosperity, brazen and gaudy, sweet and seductive, and everlasting. It is the mistress calling from the balcony of your dreams, the seamstress of your imagination, and like a mystical wraith, it can change shape without altering its virtue in the least. It can drive you beyond the limits of endurance, logic, and conscience, and nothing is more capable of bringing out the worst and the best in a man than gold.

The cross lay in what had once been pure velvet. The intricate swirls and etchings carved into the heavy, lustrous gold were absolutely exotic. The emeralds and sapphires mounted into the crucifix were as large as hen's eggs, transfixing in their magnificence. Across the horizontal bar the words *El Crucifijo de Santa María Magdalena* were engraved in elegant script. Slowly, almost reverently, Will reached in and picked it up — the first person to touch it in three hundred years. He held the crucifix with the tender regard of a first-born child, then suddenly his eyes gathered that characteristic feckless impertinence I knew so well.

"Whodang, man. Whodang!" he whispered adamantly with that lusty grin of his. "Welcome to the big time!"

Suddenly, we were dancing around, whooping and trading the cross back and forth for all to see and hold the magnificent weight of wealth. Gradually we calmed down, catching our breath, and Will got out his Polaroid camera. We shot about a dozen pictures with each of us holding it and Fabio shot a couple with Will and me — for posterity. Finally, we realized it was time, once again, to be getting out of the jungle, so we started to pack up. A few minutes later, Will hooked the cross over his shoulder like a happy Jesus and exclaimed to the world, "We be some freaking rich men! I mean filthy, stinkin', skinny hot maids, Porsche cars, sleep until noon and breakfast on the yacht rich!"

"Technically, at the moment, that's true," growled a strange, heavy voice from the edge of the small clearing where we stood. "But wealth, like fame, can be fickle and fleeting."

We all jerked around like that proverbial squirrel guarding a nut, and part-time treasure hunter, fulltime asshole, Rick Penchant stepped out from the jungle. Decked out in the latest treasure hunting attire — beige khaki shirt and pants, matching vest with about fifty pockets, Gucci jungle boots and an imitation U.S. forces jungle hat — he looked like he'd just come from a Tarzan movie set — the epitome of the kind of guy who dressed well but was born with a plastic spoon in his mouth. Penchant moved cautiously forward, pointing a nasty-looking, large bore revolver at us, sizably appropriate for hunting water buffalo. He was flanked by two of his men, who nearly matched his size and girth, but they were definitely not as handsomely attired. They bore the hungry, vicious countenances of poorly fed, badly treated pit bulls.

"Well, it looks like we got here just in time. Took us a while to find you," Penchant said silkily. "Thanks for finding my cross. The map was supposed to be mine, but old Jake Bean had a change of heart at the end."

I saw the heat rising in Will, and so did Penchant. He straightened, shook back his long, dirty-blond hair, and smiled, bringing up his gun with more authority. "Now, we can do this the nice way or we can do this the painful, possibly messy way. Your choice. But the end result, regardless, is going to be me walking away with that cross." He nodded to one of his men and the guy moved over and ripped the ancient artifact from Will's hands.

"I'm gonna find you," I said. "This isn't over."

Penchant shook his head and pursed his lips like a schoolteacher trying to get through to a slow student. "Now you see, that's just the kind of attitude that gets you in trouble." In three quick strides he was in front of me, the barrel of the gun was pressed against my forehead, and his smile had evaporated. His black eyes glistened with malevolence. "Listen, you little piss ant, if I even hear of you mentioning my name again I will weld you into a fifty-five-gallon drum and bury you at sea. Do you hear me? Are you getting this?"

I glared at him silently, realizing I had foolishly let my mouth get the better of my brain. I nodded.

Penchant exhaled heavily and gradually brought down the gun. "That's better," he muttered, some of the fire leaving his eyes.

I exhaled the breath I had been holding for about a minute. But in the next instant he whacked me on the side of the head with the barrel of the pistol. As I stood there stunned, knees almost buckling and blood trickling down the side of my face, he spat, "That's just a little reminder of the serious side of my nature." He turned to his men. "Tie 'em up. It's getting late and I have a dinner date."

Fifteen minutes later Penchant and his men were gone and we were securely bound on the floor of the jungle, a couple of feet from the hole we had dug, all the magnificent elation we had felt dissolving into dark puddles of rage, indignation, and bitter remorse.

"I am going to find that son of a bitch and I'm getting that cross back," I snarled.

Will shifted uncomfortably on the ground next to me, testing his bonds. "Get in line, but first thing's first. Can you reach your knife?"

I carried a small sheath knife which, oddly enough, Penchant's boys hadn't taken. I wiggled over to Will and he was able to pull it from the sheath and cut my bonds. A few moments later we were all free.

As Fabio stood up and rubbed his wrists, he muttered, "You got some stinkin' nasty friends! Son a bitch, seem like everybody in dis damn jungle gettin' tied up. Fabio don' wanna play no more."

Will had turned to face us, sitting on the side of the hole, his feet almost touching the bottom. "Lord! I can't believe this!" he muttered in exasperation, picking up one of the shovels and jabbing it into the pit at his feet. "We go to all this trouble, find the freaking cross, and instantly have it taken away! How much bad luck can two people have?" He started to get up, and with bitter impotence he thrust the shovel into the soft dirt at his feet once more. But as the shovelhead bit into the loam, there was a strangely familiar clunk of metal on wood again. He stopped. I looked over at him and raised an eyebrow. Will exhaled, more in resignation than intrigue, but he picked up the shovel and slammed it into the dirt again. No question, there was that thump again. In a flash I was down in the hole with him and we were digging like two demented armadillos. In moments, a second, much smaller box began to emerge from the earth. It was less than a foot square, but it possessed the same deteriorating wood and decomposing bronze bands. When we finally got it free and lifted it up to Fabio, it had that satisfying heaviness indicating something of value. My heart began a six-minute mile flutter.

We stood around the box with the reverent silence of nuns taking Communion. Will reached down and brushed the dirt off the lid and smiled. "That crafty old pirate buried a treasure under the treasure. Hand me the shovel," he said, tense excitement trembling his voice. Without hesitation he chopped the old lock with the shovel blade, taking off the lock, a piece of hinge, and some of the wood backing with it. Again he opened an ancient box that once held a pirate's dreams. The breath stilled in my chest. Somewhere in the distance a hawk cried out, sharp and plaintive.

The coins, burnished by the late afternoon sun, glittered like lover's dreams — Spanish doubloons, hundreds and hundreds of them, heaped on top of each other in a tumultuous array of fortune. We all knelt by the box, almost afraid to touch them, terrified that when we did, we would awaken from a dream, shaken, trembling, and disappointed to tears.

Finally, Will reached over and tentatively ran his fingers through the heavy cast metal, picking one up, holding it aloft. It gleamed rapturously and my partner beamed nearly as brightly. "We still be plenty rich, dudes!" he proclaimed.

That broke the spell, and suddenly we were grabbing handfuls of coins and holding them up to each other, sprinkling them back into the box and spilling them on the ground while whooping incoherently like drunken pirates.

Having to share the burden of the small but weighty treasure chest, it took us another hour to reach the shoreline. The sun had surrendered to the evening, and a pale, luminescent moon was rising over a mirror-calm inky sea, turning the palms that leaned out lovingly toward the water into soft, onyx silhouettes. A heavy night air carried a fragrance of jasmine and mango, mixed lithely with the brine tang of the sea and the slightest trace of tartness from adjacent mangroves. Night birds called softly to each other, and bats twisted through the darkening sky like acrobatic aircraft, chasing down the evening's brood of insects. The ancient moon's chartreuse reflection captured our little Cessna as it waited for us in the bay — high wings and sleek body perched like a night moth in a tidal pool. I breathed a sigh of relief. Things had not exactly gone as we had planned. A damaged or stolen plane would have capped the adventure for us. Ten minutes later we were lifting off, soaring up into an ebony empyrean punctuated by a million distant fires, all dancing in a perennial cosmic ballet. For a moment I almost forgot that we just had one of the most significant historical artifacts of the Spanish conquest of the Americas stolen from us.

"What the hell are we going to do about the cross?" Will said as I raised the flaps, held in the throttle and gradually eased back the yoke, increasing our altitude. "Not that I'm not pleased as punch with the coins, but we just can't let the son of a bitch get away with this!"

"I've got a plan," I said. "Here's the way I figure it. They didn't come in on a floatplane — they came in on that big Cessna that was sitting on the strip at New Bight yesterday, so they had to rent a boat to get where we were. Fabio, where's the closest marina to the north end of the island?"

"Seabreeze Marina, mon, just south of Arthur's Town."

I nodded, satisfied. "Okay, they've got maybe a twenty-minute lead on us. They have to return the boat then drive to New Bight, a good forty-five minutes." I turned to Will. "You have the pictures we took of the cross, right?"

He nodded.

"Okay, here are my thoughts on this. I suspect Penchant, with his ego, has planned to declare this as a bona fide find. He doesn't have to say where. But we have provenance with these pictures. These show that we found it and had it in our possession. There's a date on the bottom of each photo. This really screws his plans, because it will put a question on his find and possibly throw him into litigation. We can't go to the police because when asked about it he'll just say, 'What cross?' Then he'll get real tricky about selling it underground. Here's what I suggest: I have a reporter friend at *The Key West Citizen*. I say we give him a picture of us with the cross and some of the story on how we found it — not mentioning Cat Island, so we don't get in trouble with the Bahamian authorities. We tell him that it was stolen from us by a well-known treasure hunter, but that we are withholding his name. This eliminates the possibility of Penchant making a legal splash of the find. He'll be forced to sell it in the underground market, and that buys us quite a bit of time to find out where it is and steal it back."

"Oh, that sounds simple enough," Will sputtered sarcastically. "Who do you think we are, Starsky and Hutch? You realize in the meantime he's going to be trying to find us so he can kill us, just because." He took a breath, weighing it all. "And how exactly are we going to let him know about all this tonight, before he flies off with our cross?"

"That's where the photos come in. We're going to fly straight to New Bight Airport. I figure we can beat them there by ten or fifteen minutes. We're going to leave a couple of these photos stuck to the door of his aircraft along with a note saying, *These are for you, the rest are for our attorney.* From there, we hit *The Key West Citizen*, and the game is on."

Will was silent for a moment, then a small smile began to lift the corners of his mouth, his eyes got that reckless gleam, and he chuckled. "What a barroom tale this would make." He looked at me and his face became set, determined, but there was still a sparkle in his eyes as he spoke with a slurred, Mexican bandit accent, "Nobody steals from de *dos amigos*. Push de damned throttle to de wall, *muchacho*, we got a cross to go steal!"

Through all the time we had shared together I had come to realize one thing: there are few things more precious in life than a true friend, and I was reminded of the quote by William Butler Yates — *"I think where man's glory most begins and ends, and say my glory was, I had such friends."* I slammed the throttle to the firewall and we leapt out into the star-speckled darkness.

The airport was closed after sundown, so I just set my radio on 122.2, the standard communications frequency for the U.S. and surrounding areas, and notified any aircraft of my approach, then dropped some flaps and the gear on the amphibian and took her in. There were almost no aircraft at Cat's airport, only a couple small twins owned by locals. I remembered reading that Penchant and his company owned a big Beechcraft B60, and sure enough, there was one sitting on the ramp. We taxied in and stopped next to it. Will got out and stuffed a few pictures in the door, along with a brief note he had written about the photos and our attorney. When he came back, Will and I turned to our little buddy, Fabio.

"I need you to do a couple of things for me, Fabio," I said.

"Here's six hundred dollars and our phone number in the States. Take our car and return it to the rental place, and pay off our bill at Kookie Palms, okay? And let somebody know about Drako's two men we left tied up in the jungle."

"No problem, mon," he said taking the money. "No problem."

"And one last thing. Tell Carina we're sorry we had to leave so suddenly, but we'll be back to see her soon." I looked over at Will, then back to Fabio. "We promise." I took a breath. "And how about giving us a collect call in a day or so, just to let us know everything's okay at your end, all right?"

Fabio nodded.

"Now come here. I've got something else for you." I reached into the aircraft and opened the lid on the treasure chest. I took out a coin. "Each one of these is worth well over one hundred American, just in gold weight. I want you to reach in there and fill your pockets with them."

Fabio's eyes went wide. "You serious, mon? Really?"

"Ya, mon," I said with a smile. "You saved our asses back there. You deserve a cut. Fill your pockets, man. You're an official treasure hunter now."

Our friend's eyes misted and he drew a deep breath. "You damn good white boys. Fabio never forget dis. He remember dis like da scar from da hooker on his uncommonly large — "

"Yeah, yeah, we get it."

He grinned. "You ever need a friend on dis island, mon, you call Fabio. I be right ready." Then he reached over and stuffed his pockets until he had to hold his waistband with one hand to keep his pants up.

Will came over to the plane and reached into the chest, coming out with a handful of coins, maybe a couple dozen. "One more thing, Fabio, and this is important. I want you to find Carina and give her these coins. Tell her to free herself."

With a final handshake from each of us, our faithful friend took the extra coins and the rental keys and disappeared into the darkness toward the parking lot.

I turned to Will. "Time to go home, buddy."

He got that larcenous smile. "Right you are! We got a cross to steal."

If you don't get caught, you deserve everything you steal.
                                        — Daniel Aayeri

CHAPTER FIVE

The flight back was uneventful. A huge summer moon morphed from doubloon gold to pale eggshell and lit our way across the scattered islands of the Bahamas, and by midnight we were clearing Andros, entering the Florida Straits and the final leg of our journey. From there it became a gamble — we couldn't clear customs with seventy or eighty thousand dollars in antique gold coins unless we wanted to go through months of litigation with the Bahamian government and U.S. Treasury authorities, ending up with maybe a third of what we had found, if we were lucky. We would have to come in at sea level and hope that Fat Albert, the government radar blimp on Cudjoe Key, didn't pick us up.

We skimmed along the moonlit waters like a midnight wraith, and the gods of illicit enterprise were kind to us that night. I dropped into Pine Channel about one in the morning and ran the plane onto its mooring at the house. We quickly grabbed the gold (most everything else could wait) and were inside in five minutes. It was then we discovered the place had been ransacked, obviously by Penchant and his people. It was a mess, but nothing was destroyed that couldn't be replaced.

"We'll clean it up later," I said, grabbing a beer from the refrigerator and reaching for the phone on the wall. "I've got to call Kip right away."

"Your newspaper buddy, right?" Will replied. "The guy you saved from the DWI."

I nodded. "Yeah. If you remember, I was coming out of Key West late one night and found his car mated to a telephone pole on South Street, him inside, passed out, drunk as a skunk. We weren't super close friends, but I couldn't leave him like that. I got him out, cut a few wires from under the dash to make it look like it had been hotwired, took him to his house and sobered him up. Then we called the police and reported the car stolen. Saved his job and his reputation." I smiled. "He owes me."

Kip's voice was slurred with sleep but there was an immediate brightening when he realized it was me. "What's going on, man? I gotta bet this isn't a call just to check on my sobriety or my driving abilities."

I briefly explained our somewhat fascinating story (carefully omitting anything about finding any gold coins) and our need for it to appear in tomorrow's paper. The line was quiet for a moment. "Okay," he came back. "Sounds like a hell of a story — ancient artifacts, jungle sorties, nameless villains — but we'll have to move quickly if this is going to happen for this morning's paper. Meet me at *The Citizen* in forty-five minutes."

Long story short, Kip lived up to his promise of repaying my past kindness and somehow managed to squeeze the article in before press time. We went home and slept until noon, then went over to The Big Pine Coffee Shop, got breakfast and a paper, and read the quite fascinating story about ourselves. However, there was another person reading that article about the same time, and he was anything but happy.

"I'm gonna kill 'em," Penchant raved as he crushed the paper into a ball and threw it at the wall. "I'm gonna kill the sons of bitches!"

Penchant's attorney, sitting in the living room of the treasure hunter's suite at The La Concha, kept himself small and quiet. Finally, the attorney took a breath and said, "Whether you like it or not, by doing this, with the pictures they've established provenance. At best, if you went public now, they'd keep you in court for years. Worst-case scenario, you end up losing the cross altogether. My advice is, find a buyer and sell it quietly and quickly. You get the money and none of the hassle."

Penchant swung around, his face a mask of fury. "You don't get it, do you? This was going to be my big find! This would have put me on the front page of every major newspaper in the country! Now you tell me I should just slink off and sell it like a common thief."

The thought occurred to the attorney that Penchant actually was nothing more than a common thief. But there was no percentage in uttering those words. "I'm your lawyer and you pay me to advise you. I don't tell you the truth, I'm not earning my money."

Penchant spat out a fowl expletive regarding the attorney, sex, and his mother, then stomped over to the window, glowering out at the sun-glistened waters below. After a few moments, he sighed angrily. "Okay, okay. We sell it. I want you to start looking for buyers today. In the meantime, you find me those two assholes, and a couple fifty-five-gallon drums."

Fabio called collect that afternoon while we were cleaning up the house to tell us he had taken care of all that was asked of him. "You guys make a pretty big stink around here for tourists, mon. Drako frothing at da mouth. He get a steaming hot, sweaty face and crazy juju eyes, like he having a monkey baby. Not only he lose gold, but I give Carina coins and she leave him like he was zombie wit' leprosy. Just after you take off, de big man wit' yellow hair, who take de cross from you, he go to big plane and see note and pictures on door. He dance aroun' like he possessed by demons, mon. Screamin', shoutin', kickin' airplane — generally having large monkey baby like Drako." He paused and his tone changed. "Carina say she sorry. She never meant to get you hurt, mon."

"What does that mean?"

Again Fabio paused. "She make phone calls to Drako. Tell him where you go."

My stomach knotted. *How could that be possible? How could she do that?*

"I no can explain dat," Fabio said, reading my silence. "A few tings Fabio don' completely understand, mon. Women be one a dem."

Afterwards, I told Will what had happened. "Jesus!" he hissed. "How could she do that?"

"My thoughts exactly."

He exhaled hard. "I can't believe it. She and I had something special. I could see it in her eyes."

"Apparently the only thing you two had in common was the desire to screw each other. But the methods varied."

With the article out in *The Key West Citizen* there was one thing we knew for sure — Penchant would be after us with everything he had. We needed to become scarce — find another place to stay for the time being. We packed everything that was valuable to us, especially the gold coins, then took Will's Camaro and my Jeep Wagoneer and headed up to Marathon. We had taken the coins out of the old chest, and stowed the chest in my closet. I was considering restoring it, if possible, as a memento. We put the doubloons in a safety deposit box at the Marathon Bank and rented a nondescript apartment on the gulf side of town. I moved the airplane up to the Marathon Airport, as well — to have it close and to keep Penchant's goons from sabotaging it.

Marathon was a strange town, never quite recapturing the sleepy Keys essence it had in the sixties. It ended up more like a series of strip malls and restaurants interspaced with resorts trying way too hard to compete with their southern brethren. It could never quite capture the genuine allure or the delightful decadence of the big island at the end of the chain. But for now it was a good place for us to hide out and lay some plans.

"What we need is some way to draw Penchant out, to get that cross out in the open where we can get to it," Will was saying as we sat on our tiny back porch and watched the sun working its way toward the gray, cirrus-banded horizon. "I'm betting dollars to donuts he's putting out feelers to buyers as we speak. He can't hang on to that very long — he's got to be worried we're naming names."

I watched an airplane, a small twin coming up from the south, dropping down for a landing at Marathon Airport. "An article appeared in the paper a while back about his attorney, Jason Wilkes. I would bet that's the man who handles his transactions like this. Penchant's just smart enough to realize he's got to keep his name out of it. I'm thinking we need to have a conversation with Mr. Wilkes. This calls for someone who can appear to be a rich drug smuggler out of Miami, or an independent collector of 'lost' stuff."

"Not a bad idea. I think we can do that part," Will agreed. "One phone call asking about an appointment to see the cross will tell us one way or another if it's for sale."

"Yeah, but if our invented buyer's name isn't on the list, they may get jittery."

Will shrugged. "Maybe, but when the word goes out that *El Crucifijo de Santa María Magdalena* is for sale, even they've got to expect it's going to make some ripples in the underworld." My buddy pulled at his thick mustache for a moment, lost to thought. "So what we need is a convincing representative for us, somebody who's willing to play the game, take a bit of a chance." There was a pause and Will got that larcenous gleam in his eyes. "I'm thinking we need to visit with Crazy Eddie."

I laughed. "Ya mon! Good choice! But we'll have to dress him up a little for the part."

Edward Jackson Moorehouse, nicknamed Crazy Eddie, was one of those "one of a kind" people. They didn't call him crazy for nothing. He had been a pot smuggler in the early seventies, and if half the stories were true, he had taken chances that would have left a normal person with a permanent tic and a Mel Tillis stutter. But Eddie gave up the business a few years back. The scuttlebutt was he'd made a big run and received a serious chunk of money along with a really nice Grumman Goose floatplane. He cut a deal with a friend of his to keep the plane on his buddy's property on the gulf side of Ramrod Key, and rented the back bedroom/bathroom of his friend's house, but he practically lived in his plane. Mildly put, he was eccentric (some would say bald-ass crazy). Nonetheless, he was fearless and clever, and probably one of the best pilots in The Keys.

Eddie wasn't Jamaican and he wasn't black, but he'd spent a lot of time in Jamaica back in the old days — the cowboys and Indians days — leaving him with a vernacular somewhere between black Caribbean and sixties Haight Ashbury. He was in his mid-thirties, tall and lanky, and always dressed in a pair of khaki shorts and a bright, fruit-juicy shirt of some sort. He had a short-trimmed beard, long, sun-bleached blond hair that cascaded down to his shoulders, and a thin, slightly crooked nose that looked as if it might have been the consequence of a disagreement somewhere along the line, but he was still a fairly handsome guy. He had a perpetual tan and an easy smile. Everybody liked Crazy Eddie because he did crazy things, and nobody had better dope than Eddie. An eye patch covered his left eye — the loss a result of too much tequila, a feathered lure, and a careless cast during the frenzy of a mackerel run just inside the reef last summer. As disconcerting as that might have been, the eye patch actually added to his persona rather than detracted.

We were willing to pay Eddie good money for this, but we both knew it would appeal to him so much he'd probably work for Popsicle sticks. The boy just liked "the jazz."

After a quick call and only the briefest of details, our buddy agreed to meet us at Herbie's Restaurant in Marathon within the hour. It was time for the second stage of the plan. I got out a phonebook and found the number for Penchant's attorney. Jason Wilkes' secretary answered on the second ring. "I'd like to speak with Mr. Wilkes," I said politely.

"And whom may I say is calling?"

"You can tell him that names aren't of any import at this moment," I said with a clipped but polite tone. "Tell him that it's only important that we 'cross' paths and talk about Mary Magdalena. I'm sure he'll understand."

"If you'll hold for a moment," she said, confused but cautiously polite.

A few seconds later a man spoke, "Hello, this is Jason Wilkes. How can I help you?"

"Word is you have a unique item for sale, and I'm most

interested," I said, still using my clipped voice and slightly haughty tone.

There was a pause. He was making a decision. "Can I ask your name?"

"You can ask, but my name isn't important. What's important is, I want what you have. If you really have it."

"I don't believe I've spoken to you before," he said cautiously. "How is it that you know anything about my business?"

I sighed as if exasperated. "Mr. Wilkes, if you think you can send out word about something like this and not have it ripple across the backwaters to some degree, then you're not as intelligent as I would have thought. I can assure you when an occurrence such as this takes place, I know about it. If you're interested in selling it at a reasonable price, I'm interested in buying it. Now, if we can dispense with the dancing, I would like to make arrangements for a preliminary foray here. I'm certain you have photos. I'll have my representatives meet with you to see those photos. From there we can arrange a viewing. If all goes well and a price can be agreed upon, we'll all walk away satisfied."

There was silence at the other end as he considered my proposal. "I think perhaps this is possible," he finally said, guardedly. "But —"

I interrupted. "I would want you to know that I'm a very generous man to those who help me. I would like you to know also that my representative will provide a 'gift' for you, personally, to demonstrate our sincerity, and for your cooperation. Mr. Wilkes, do you carry an appreciation for gold, say, gold doubloons?"

Again there was a pause. "Yes, sir, I do," he replied with a little more confidence. (It was "sir" now.)

"Well, I can assure you that at your first meeting with my emissary, you shall have a more personal connection to the Spanish gold escudo. If this transaction should come to pass, your appreciation will be greatly increased."

I could almost feel the greed through the telephone line. "Would tomorrow morning be convenient, say around ten?"

"That'll be fine. My representative will meet with you, and only you, Mr. Wilkes. Do you understand?"

Upon his acceptance of my terms, I hung up and looked at Will, who had kept his ear close enough to the phone to hear the conversation. "An amazing thing, greed is," I said with a smile.

"Ya mon," he replied with that famous grin of his. "Now, let's go meet with Crazy Eddie. We got a cross to steal."

"You're sure it was them, huh?" Penchant said, standing by the bar in his hotel suite.

His man, one of the goons who had been part of the Sloppy Joe's fiasco a week or so before, nodded slowly. "I'm pretty damned sure, but I just got a quick look. They were in separate vehicles, a Camaro and a Jeep, and turning toward the gulf onto one of the side streets in the middle of Marathon. I was coming back from Grassy Key, trying to find that old bastard Jake Bean. His daughter is still at her place but she claims she hasn't seen him in a couple of weeks."

"Okay, okay," Penchant said as he waved his hand indifferently. "I don't care about Bean's daughter. You know the street where they turned off, right?"

"Yeah, just across from the movie theater off of U.S. 1."

"All right, that's all I need from you," Penchant mumbled, waving him away, while drumming the fingers of one hand on the bar pensively. "Get me Stinger," he growled at the fellow as he turned to leave. "Yeah, Stinger."

It took us almost ten minutes to get from our apartment to Herbie's because there was a circus in town and the narrow, two-lane U.S. 1 was backed up for about a half-mile as the traffic wedged into Marathon. About twice a year small circuses came down to The Keys, but this was a big deal, because one of the larger circuses in the country was setting out on a tour of eight South American cities. From there they were headed across the Panama Canal and back up to San Francisco. The entire circus was boarding a freighter in Miami on Monday, so they had decided to do a few shows in Marathon and Key West before shipping out.

We had barely taken a seat in the back of Herbie's when Eddie came gliding through the door with that long-legged, arm-swinging shuffle of his, a combination of unassuming confidence and Caribbean casualness, dressed in his standard attire of a tropical shirt and Hang Ten shorts.

"So, wass happenin' dudes?" he chimed as he took a seat, shaking our hands with genuine enthusiasm. "What's my crazy brothas up to this time?"

I couldn't help but grin. His personality was infectious, but the average person might think he was seven cents short of a dime. You had to know him to understand him. Underneath all the Caribbean, funky sixties personality was a pretty sharp guy. He just didn't like to take life too seriously. It took us fifteen minutes to lay out the history on what was happening and what we planned to do. We knew this could be a little dangerous, so we offered Eddie a thousand dollars for his time if it didn't work, and two thousand if it did. Eddie asked a few salient questions, and at the end of the presentation he got that sly smile.

"This is just radical to the bone, dudes, I mean like, killer cool!" He shook his head slowly. "Eddie never knew two people who could find more ways to get themselves into funky situations." He grinned again. "You dudes are souls of my own heart!" He held up an index finger. "You gotta remember that this whole life gig ain't about makin' it to the grave all clean and shiny and well preserved. It's about slidin' in head first, roughed up, used up, worn out, and shoutin' loud and clear, 'Hot damn! What a trip, dude!'"

Without question Eddie was in, and he agreed to let us buy him a nice shirt, some long pants, and a pair of loafers, accompanied by strange, totally alien things called socks. I explained that he had to appear somewhat sophisticated — to nod thoughtfully a lot and speak as little as possible, and avoid words like "groovy," "funky," and "far out." Really, his role was just to examine the photos, bring one back for us, and set up an appointment for a "viewing" of the real thing.

After breakfast we took him over to our new apartment so he would know how to find us in an emergency. We were standing in the kitchen, chatting about the plan, when Eddie got out his little liquor bottle, the kind they give you on airplanes, unscrewed the lid and took the tiniest of sips.

I grimaced. "You still doing that crap, Eddie?"

He grinned sheepishly. "Just a tiny taste of 'The Tiger' every once in a while."

Our boy liked a little pot and a little alcohol occasionally, so he created a high-test concoction that required only a drop or two, a wetting of the tongue, to keep him where he wanted to be during the day. He took a fifth of Bacardi 151 rum, then added an ounce of "knock your socks off" Jamaican hashish and a single peyote button. He let it distill for three months, shaking it gently every once in a while. When it was ready, Eddie put it into tiny airline sample bottles (only Bacardi Dark bottles so the color looked right). He carried one with him most of the time, and he gave them to friends at Christmastime as presents. But the stuff was so deadly potent that any more than a half-teaspoon in a drink would leave you glassy-eyed and slobbering for about twenty-four hours — I mean bumping into walls while mumbling old girlfriends' names and fascinated with the swirl lines in the stucco on the ceiling. I shook my head and walked over to him, took the bottle and set it on the kitchen counter. "Listen Eddie, this is a really important gig and we need everyone to be straight for it. We'll just leave this here and you can have it back when we're done, okay?"

He offered a sigh of resignation and shrugged. "Okay, okay. Eddie digs. No problem, man."

It was a useless gesture, because he had more at home, but I needed to make a point.

Stinger lounged on the couch while Penchant filled him in. He was dressed in blue jeans, tennis shoes, and a tight-fitting polo shirt. The truth was, Stinger even made Penchant a little uncomfortable. The guy wasn't a big fellow, probably about five-seven, on the slender side, but he possessed the svelte, hard muscles of a martial arts competitor and predatory gray-blue eyes that looked like they weren't quite attached to this world. He was Irish-American, had short-cropped, pale blond hair, and appeared fairly nondescript, but there was just a weird malevolence that exuded from him — an indifference to fear, conscience, or consequence that stared back at you through those strange eyes. Most of us, even the "tough guys," generally have limits to what we'll do, how far we'll go in a given circumstance. But there are some people with whom you realize intrinsically that there are just no limits, no boundaries to restraint or scruples, and these are the really frightening people. Stinger was one of them.

After providing Stinger with physical descriptions, a basic location in Marathon, and an idea of the cars his targets drove, Penchant turned his man loose, as if casting a hunting hawk into the sky after spotting a luckless, lone duck, or maybe two ducks.

Will and I were feeling more confident after our meeting with Eddie. We still had a long way to go, but at least we were developing a plan.

That evening Will and I sat on the small porch of our new apartment, watching the moon come off the shimmering, still waters of the bay and listening to the insects commune as they paid their nightly homage to the streetlamp gods. "I think I've got a plan for this, and I want to run it by you," I said quietly. "It's a little out there, but that's not a field we haven't played in before. It's going to require some disguises, a fire drill, and a monkey."

Will turned in his lawn chair, facing me, big smile. "Okay, now you've really got my attention. Let's hear it."

I took a deep breath. "I don't know exactly where to start, so I'm just going to put the pieces together as I go. Let me begin here. My guess is Penchant is not keeping the cross in his suite at The La Concha. That's too dangerous. Someone, maybe even one of his own people, might try to snatch it. So, I figure he's got it in a safety deposit box at his bank. He'll have to go get it when he does a presentation. Now here's what I suggest. When Eddie goes to the viewing he takes a camera, in the guise of bringing back a final set of authenticated pictures. I know one thing for sure — Penchant isn't going to carry a valuable artifact like that around in a paper bag. He loves show. He's got a nice case of some sort for it. That's a given. Eddie gets us a picture of the case as well as the cross. Then, we set up the buy for that evening, agreeing to return to Penchant's place with the money. He's not going to take the cross back to the bank if it's just a few hours until the sale."

I took a sip of my beer, set it down, and continued. "We find ourselves a duplicate of his case, even if we have to shoot up to Miami in the plane. In the process we pick up a uniform similar to the desk/management personnel at The La Concha. And we need a handful of smoke bombs, which just happen to be easy to get right now because the fourth of July is only a week away." I paused. "And we need a monkey."

Will shifted in his seat anxiously. "Oh boy, that's the part I've been waiting to hear about."

I smiled, certain that I was about to pique my buddy's fancy for diversions. "The monkey's not that hard, actually. Turtle, and his wife Brandi, have a big spider monkey." (Turtle was a longtime friend whom we had saved from imminent disaster several years ago, when he fell in love with the girlfriend of a notoriously dangerous Key West attorney who ran drugs on the side.) "Turtle hates the damned thing," I continued. "Says it's as hyper as a Chihuahua on crack and always crapping on the floor. I know he won't mind if we borrow it. He won't care if we don't bring it back. Hell, he'll probably pay us to keep it. Now here's the more difficult part. We need this monkey to be freaking bonkers at just the right time." I took another sip of my beer and moved on. "I don't know how much you know about Lois Key, a little island on the ocean side, just below

Cudjoe. It's owned by Charles River Laboratories, and there are hundreds and hundreds of monkeys on that island. A friend of mine works for their research station in Key West. They breed the monkeys, or I should say encourage them to breed, then periodically they catch a bunch and sell them to research laboratories across the country. They have developed a pheromone from the secretions of female monkeys in heat that just drives the males wide-eyed, lip-slobbering berserk. I'm talking dick-dragging, monkey sex maniacs that will screw anything that moves. It comes in a spray-mist form. They go into the island twice a year and spray this stuff on the trees and the monkeys, then quickly make a dash for their boat so they don't find themselves screwed to death by sex-crazed simians. I can get a bottle of that tomorrow."

I grinned with reminiscence. "The one thing I know for sure is how distracting a crazy monkey can be. You might remember when we first moved to The Keys and I pulled that trailer we bought in Miami down here with the wacko ex-vet and his spider monkey. I thought I was gonna freaking die when the monkey went nuts going over Bahia Honda Bridge. So, here's what we're going to do..."

The following morning Eddie met with the lawyer, providing him with a dozen gold doubloons and explaining he would receive an additional "gift" of many times that amount if he arranged a swift meeting and held other buyers at bay until the transaction was completed. They set up a noontime appointment for a showing at Penchant's suite. As planned, Eddie arrived on time with the attorney, was frisked, then led into Penchant's living room, all the while clutching his Nikon. It couldn't have happened more perfectly. The crucifix lay on red velvet in one of those new, round-edged, aluminum briefcases. Eddie got nice photos under the guise of needing them for his boss, while dodging questions about who his boss actually was. He did, however, assure Penchant that this had clinched the deal and that he would be ready to return at six p.m. with the agreed-upon price of three hundred thousand in cash.

While Eddie was taking care of his part, we were picking up a spider monkey and a cage from Turtle. In the process, we enlisted him to help us. Turtle (Winfield, actually, but everyone preferred Turtle) had dark hair, large brown eyes capable of displaying a vast spectrum of emotion, and a smile that looked like a toothpaste ad. He was a good man, though not much of a gambler, but his part in this affair was pretty simple. After we obtained a spray-mist bottle of monkey sex madness from my buddy at the Charles River

Laboratory, we met with Eddie at one p.m., got a picture of the case, and learned the deal was set to go down at six p.m.

Will snuck into the employee changing room at The La Concha and "borrowed" a manager's uniform. Then we went over to the local costume shop and bought a long black wig and some makeup, drove out to Stock Island to purchase a handful of smoke bombs at a fireworks stand, and finally headed over to Fast Buck Freddies where we picked up an aluminum case exactly like the one Penchant had, plus a large, touristy-looking Hawaiian muumuu dress.

It was a busy afternoon, but by 5:30 everyone was in place. Turtle had changed into the manager's uniform, and was positioned at the end of the hall on the top floor near Penchant's suite. Will had begrudgingly shaved off his mustache, donned the long black wig and muumuu dress, and rouged and lipsticked himself into a strikingly ugly but acceptable woman. He was waiting near the elevator in the lobby with the monkey in a blanket-covered cage, and the identical aluminum case tucked between his legs, hidden by the overflowing muumuu. I sat in a room on the same floor as Penchant's suite, which I had just taken for the night under an assumed name, having disguised myself by tucking my long hair into a ball cap and donning some large sunglasses beforehand.

At 5:45 Eddie met the lawyer at the bar. At Eddie's request, the lawyer called Penchant's suite from the lobby and asked for his bodyguards to come down and escort them and the money up to the suite. When Penchant's guards reached the lobby there was no sign of Eddie. Then he waved from the bar, not making any move to get up. They cursed in harmony and went over to get him and the attorney. At that point Will, his monkey, and the monkey sex juice stepped into the same elevator in the lobby the guards had just vacated. He keyed a small walkie-talkie hidden in his muumuu and sent the elevator up to the top floor.

While the guards walked over to the bar to get our buddy and the attorney (and waited impatiently while Eddie finished his drink), I received the cryptic message through my walkie-talkie in my room just down the hall from Penchant. I strode over to the cluster of smoke bombs I had duct-taped around the smoke alarm and lit them. Then, leaving my room, I casually walked down the hallway, lighting and tossing a few more around while waving to Turtle to get ready. As soon as the elevator opened with Will, the only flaw in our plan was discovered. A blue-haired, little old lady had gotten on at a lower floor and had accidentally ridden all the way to the top with Will. She had a Pekinese tucked protectively in her arms and a thoroughly aghast expression etched into her countenance, but it was too late to change plans. The hallway was already filled with smoke, fire alarms were going off, and Turtle, dressed as the manager, was already pounding on Penchant's door, yelling that the hotel was on fire.

Well, Penchant did exactly what any sensible person would do with an ultra-valuable artifact in his room and a hotel burning around him. He grabbed the case with the cross and ran. Turtle quickly directed him into the elevator where Will, the ugly woman, stood waiting with a magic bottle of monkey sex and a monkey in a cage. As soon as Penchant was inside, Will pressed the first floor button and backed up behind the thoroughly terrified treasure hunter, who stood a couple feet from the doors, staring at them as if he could will them to open at the lobby, his case gripped tightly in his hand.

My buddy calmly took out the monkey juice and gave the back of Penchant's legs several squirts. The monkey caught a whiff and gibbered excitedly. Penchant was way too focused on the smell of smoke and the slow-moving floor arrow to care. Will hit him with two or three squirts on his ass and the back of his head. Our treasure hunter felt that and glanced around, then down at the covered cage, but it just wasn't high on his list of worries. Through the rouge and the lipstick, Will offered a disarming smile. The monkey got a good sniff of the sex elixir and started chattering wildly, his little hands grasping the bars of the cage door as he screeched beseechingly. The old lady clutched her dog to her breast and stared at Will as if he were mad, but he just gave her a toothy grin and a wiggly-fingered wave. Will hit Penchant again with several good bursts then leaned down, popped the cover off the cage and sprayed the monkey in the face. That was it. The little guy went berserk with slobbering monkey lust, screeching and shaking the barred door with uncontrolled fervor. Will pushed a sandaled toe over to the crate and hit the latch on the door. It was like releasing a demon from hell.

The little simian screamed in passion and hurled himself at Penchant with the sexual energy of a mink mainlining Viagra. The monkey started on his leg, humping with a piston-like madness, working his way up toward our buddy's unprotected groin, sinking those needle-like canines into the man's flesh as he climbed in sexual frenzy. Penchant shrieked with pain and horror, dropping the aluminum case as he stumbled into the wall, knocking over the old lady, who lost her grip on the Pekinese. The monkey, eyes gleaming with carnal madness, continued to scale our antagonist while screeching passionately between love bites, finally reaching Penchant's well-sprayed head. It was there he simply became inflamed, grabbing the man's ears and humping his forehead in passionate madness, ripping out tufts of his reluctant mate's hair in flagrant, exotic ecstasy. Poor Penchant was trying desperately to tear the lusty creature off his face, while screaming scathing expletives about monkeys from hell and hurling himself from one side of the elevator to the other. The monkey was screeching back, probably something like, "Ooohh baby, ooohh baby, you're the one! Don't fight it. You're the one!"

At that point, Penchant and the monkey were pretty much heedless to anything else going on. Will quickly slipped the case from between his legs while snatching up the other one and securing it under the muumuu. Meanwhile, there was no stopping the myopically horny simian. The carnage continued, giving a whole new meaning to the term "monkeying around." When they hit the third floor, the doors opened to a handful of frightened people and Will quickly stepped out. The last thing he saw was our nemesis huddled in the corner with the old lady, his eyes blinking in terror and confusion, saliva running down his chin, great patches of hair missing from his head and dusting the floor around him, clutching his case to his breast and looking like he'd just lost a fight with a cheese grater. The monkey, nowhere near satiated, was rutting the Pekinese in the far corner with the fervor of a sailor after six months at sea.

By this time there was quite a bit of confusion in the hotel, with the fire alarm having gone off, the smoke, and the yelling. All the various members of the Monkey Lust Gang managed to slip out of the building and lose themselves in the crowd gathering on the street.

Eddie, still in the lobby with the bodyguards and the attorney, played his role magnificently, becoming immediately suspicious and indignant. "You shiny-ragged cheese-eaters are trippin', I mean, out of your rabid-ass minds, if you think I'm buyin' into this bogus scene. Me and my man's bread are bookin'. You dig? Gone, like yesterday's lunch. We catch you honkies on the flip side when you got your act together!"

Despite the attorney's adamant declarations of innocence, Eddie puffed up and he and his briefcase walked out into the mass of spectators, never to be seen again.

Penchant spent part of the evening in the emergency room, getting a handful of stitches and a tetanus shot. Then it was over to the barber who sadly had to endure his customer's wrath as he gave the man a burr cut, the last of Penchant's golden locks and the better part of his narcissism cascading to the floor.

When the treasure hunter had recovered enough to be taken to his room, he opened the aluminum case, just to make sure, before putting it away. The people at Sloppy Joe's, several blocks away, could hear his scream over the music.

Sometimes, if you're not careful, you actually get what you deserve.

Adventure doesn't come to you. You have to chase it down. Are you placing enough interesting, freakish bets? Taking enough chances? Playing the long shots?

— **Tom Peters and Kansas Stamps**

CHAPTER SIX

By morning the front page of *The Key West Citizen* featured a photo of Rick Penchant being assisted from the elevator at The La Concha — disheveled, lacerated, violated, and laced with a good deal of blood, sweat, and monkey love. A second photo, taken by a reporter with a roguish sense of humor, showed someone's Persian cat in the lobby, statically fuzzed out in panic, eyes the size of eight balls, firmly gripped by the mad monkey as he gratified himself one last time. The headlines read, "Monkey Business at The La Concha."

I lowered the paper and handed it to Will as we sat in Herbie's. Then I pushed a paper bag toward Eddie — two thousand smackers — worth every penny.

Our partner in crime grinned. "Eddie has made more in one night, brothas, but this was a groovy gig. Harshed that sucka's mellow big time!"

We had pulled it off, the sun was shining, none of us were bleeding, and we had *El Crucifijo de Santa María Magdalena* in our safety deposit box at the Marathon Bank. I just love it when a plan comes together.

After Eddie left, I eased back in my seat. "I think if we were smart, we would be looking for a buyer very quickly. The longer we hold on to that thing, the more chance we have of ending up like Penchant, because you can bet that boy is going to move heaven and earth to find out who took the cross from him."

Will pulled his attention away from the shapely waitress delivering breakfast to the table next to us. "Well, let's face it, he doesn't have much of anything leading back to us. But that doesn't mean I don't agree with you." He gave the waitress another glance as she walked away, then came back to me. "So, how do we find a buyer?"

I took a sip of coffee. "That might be easier than you think. You remember our old buddy, Nick Crow?"

Will's face split into a grin at the mention of the name. "Oh yeah. Not an easy guy to forget."

Nick Crow had been an integral part of one of our "adventures" a few years back — an indelibly imprinted Central American trip that still left me with a tightness in my chest when I thought about it. He was a Tom Selleck kind of guy — tall, tanned, fruit-juicy tropical shirts, bell-bottomed jeans, Kino sandals, and sandy blond hair. But most of all, he was a card-carrying member of The Popsicle Stick Club. He was an ex-Vietnam spotter plane pilot who, like several of his friends, hadn't adjusted well to civilian life without "the jazz" of danger and excitement. So occasionally he and his buddies would fly to Central America, pick up a number of burlap-wrapped, funny-smelling bales, and bring them back to The Keys, a little under the radar. It wasn't really about the money, although that was nice; it was just that every once in a while they needed some excitement in their lives. Nick always said they would have quite as easily done it for Popsicle sticks, but the cash kept him in the lifestyle to which he had become accustomed. If there was anyone who knew people with exotic tastes, and to whom a couple hundred thousand dollars wouldn't seem earth shattering, it was Nick.

While we were having breakfast, Stinger had come up from Key West and toured the neighborhood of his new targets, finding their Jeep Wagoneer. He parked across the street from their apartment. Lighting a cigarette, he exhaled slowly, those feral eyes catching the morning sun and kindling with anticipation. He put the car in gear and drove up the street to its junction with U.S. 1 and parked again.

Hearing Nick's voice on the phone was like biting into a lime after shooting your second shot of tequila. It carried the pleasure of anticipation, but a small part of you tasted the bitter recollection of the last time you had sucked down shot after shot without concern for the consequences.

"Kansas Stamps! The original reluctant adventurer!" Crow said with a chuckle. "So, what's up, man? Haven't heard from you in ages."

"Good to hear your voice again," I said. "Brings back lots of memories. Some I've tried to forget." I looked out the sliding glass doors of our apartment at the gray-blue waters of the Gulf. A front was welling up from the south, pasting the horizon with curdled, gunmetal-gray cumulus. "Well, to tell you the truth, Will and I have a unique situation and we thought you might be able to help. It could be profitable — lots of Popsicle sticks."

"Aaahh, inadvertent adventure has crawled up your leg and bitten you on the ass again, huh?"

I could hear the smile in his voice.

"I suppose we could tie up for a little while. Why don't you come by this afternoon?"

I looked over at Will and gave him a "thumbs up" as Nick set the meeting for one o'clock. We hung around the house for an hour, then headed over to the bank to pick up the cross. There's nothing like up-close solid gold, emeralds, and sapphires to help a person make a decision.

From his vantage point, Stinger watched his prey turn off onto the highway, then he drove back to their apartment, jimmied the sliding doors, and began a leisurely examination of who they were. He always liked to check out people before he killed them.

There's something soothing about driving across the Seven Mile Bridge, Henry Flagler's narrow, concrete masterpiece that arches over that open expanse of clear, emerald-blue water interrupted only briefly by a mottle of sand and palm trees called Pigeon Key. The sea around you is oftentimes as clear as a swimming pool and it's not at all uncommon to see dolphins hurling themselves out of the water in playful loops, watch an occasional shark prowling off the weathered, coral-encrusted pilings below, or to catch sight of schools of winter mackerel breaching the mirrored surface, moving toward the reef in anxious, perpetual motion. Frigate birds swirl effortlessly in the warm thermals above, Vs of pelicans glide by at your shoulder, ever watchful for the careless mullet; seagulls dart about while crying admonitions to each other, or perch indifferently on the graying, guano-splattered railings; and ospreys soar in high circles looking for the next luckless victim that will feed their squawky, demanding broods. It's a carnival of natural wonders in an eight-minute trip.

By the time we'd crossed that expression of man-made ingenuity I was in a better mood. Some of the tension of the last few days was draining from me and the possibility of selling the cross was now becoming a reality. It all felt good.

Nick had a home just down the canal from where my ex-wife and I had lived. It was a modest, two bedroom stilt house — nothing that would portray wealth or station with the exception of a nice little sailboat docked in the canal and a light twin-engine aircraft at Summerland Key airstrip. He shook our hands with genuine warmth and led us out back to some deck chairs by the canal. He was a gambler and a bit of a rogue, but Nick Crow carried a rugged dignity about him that most men envied and women loved. He had an honest, fierce character, and was uncompromising in his integrity — a self-reliant, undisguised man in a world of jokers and fools. Maybe Nick didn't play by society's rules, but he never broke his own code of conduct.

We talked for a while, laughing about our adventures together a few years back, then got down to business. Nick had seen the article that our reporter friend had written for *The Citizen*. He knew exactly what was coming.

"You stole the freaking cross back, didn't you? That's what all the hullabaloo was about with Rick Penchant and The La Concha! He's the one who took it from you. Damn!" he muttered with a wide grin. "You boys are moving into the big time!" Our friend leaned toward us, more serious. "You guys want to sell it, don't you — get out from under it before Penchant figures it out?" He huffed out a breath of disdain between his teeth. "That's if he ever figures it out. The guy's nowhere near as smart as he thinks he is." Nick tabled his opinion of Penchant and looked at us. "Okay, where is it? I gotta see this thing."

Will got the cross from the car and brought it inside, placing the aluminum case on the dining room table and opening it up. Crow whistled softly as the gleaming gold and the brilliant gems leapt out at us. He turned to me, nodding for permission to pick it up, and even he was startled by the weight. "Unfreaking believable," he whispered, studying the design and the workmanship. He set it down reverently and turned to us. "I have a friend who likes shiny old things. I'm betting he's going to have to have this. What do you need to get? Bearing in mind that I'm going to put at least ten percent on that."

Will and I had talked this over. The crucifix was probably worth three hundred thousand or more in a legitimate discovery/sale, but no one was likely to pay that in a back alley deal. We figured we'd be happy with two hundred thousand, half of which would go to Vanilla, old Jake Bean's daughter. Nick seemed comfortable with that, so we gave him a Polaroid picture. He said he'd need a couple of days.

The way home was a jubilant parade of expectation, and wild conjecture — one hundred thousand ways to make our lives better and more interesting, and oddly enough we were looking forward to keeping our promise to old Jake Bean, if he was still alive. Vanilla would be a happy lady. We figured any offspring from that grizzled, coyote-ugly antique could use all the help they could get, and we'd probably have to hand her the money on the end of a stick.

It was just after dark when we got back to our little apartment. A soft fragrance of jasmine and orange blossoms filled the air, blissfully tangled with a hint of sea and mangroves. I opened the door, and as we walked in, Will hit the light switch. There was a man sitting on our couch — short blond hair, svelte build, and weird blue-gray eyes. He was maybe forty-five years old and dressed in gray slacks and a red polo shirt, holding a semi-automatic pistol with a bulky silencer attached to the barrel, aimed at us. He held up a finger. "Now, you're thinking to yourselves, 'Can we get back out that door before he shoots?'" he said with a healthy touch of Irish accent. There was a spit from the weapon and a smack against the wall next to me, creating a clean little hole. "The answer is no, lads," he added calmly. "Now step in and close the door."

We obeyed like well trained, albeit terrified, Cocker Spaniels.

As we moved into the living room, he got up and ushered us to the couch with the muzzle of the gun. "I hate to be the bearer of bad news," he said, "but this is not your lucky day. Appears you've angered somebody, and they've requested you stop breathing — "

"Penchant!" I interrupted angrily. "Right?"

He smiled again, but it didn't reach those cold eyes. "Not supposed to name names. Not professional. Now, before we get to the business of this visit, I have a question or two of me own. This may take a few minutes — may even be painful, depending on how cooperative you are." He paused for a moment, swallowed, and changed course. "You got anything to drink in here? I think I'm getting a cold. Got a sore throat."

Will and I exchanged a glance. "There're some Cokes by the sink, ice in the fridge," Will said. "Who are you, anyway?"

"Doesn't matter." Then he shrugged. "Oh, what the bloody hell, you're not going to be a-tellin' anyone, are you lad? The name's Dunn, Stinger Dunn. Now, you boys just stay right where you are. Relax. We're going to have a conversation before anything bad happens. Unless you don't do what I say, then the bad stuff's going to happen more quickly. You understand?"

We both nodded obediently.

Stinger Dunn got a glass, then helped himself to some ice and splashed some Coke on it all, managing to keep his gun handy and his eyes on us most of the time. He took a sip and leaned against the kitchen counter. "What do you lads know about a gold cross, apparently something me boss lost the other night? You didn't have anything to do with that, did you?"

Just then I remembered the cross was still in the trunk of the car.

I shook my head, looking over at Will. He shook his head and shrugged. Stinger didn't seem convinced. He took another swallow and winced slightly as it went down. That's when he noticed the little sample bottle of Bacardi Dark Rum on the counter — the one that belonged to Eddie, filled with hashish-enhanced 151 rum, and topped off with a dash of peyote. He picked it up.

"Leave that alone," I said. "It was a special gift from my girlfriend before she.... Please, just leave it alone."

Stinger smiled, nastiness just oozing out from between his teeth and dripping down his chin, my supplication hitting just the right button. "I got a feeling you're not going to be a-needin' it anymore, lad, but I'll let you watch me drink it," he said, eyes sparkling with dark humor as he twisted off the top and poured half the bottle into his drink.

Will glanced over at me, a small gleam of hope lighting his eyes. Our new acquaintance had just poured enough of Eddie's magic elixir into his glass to vaporize a water buffalo. The trick was, could we stay alive long enough for the stuff to take effect?

Our antagonist took another solid swallow of his drink and moved around the kitchen counter, back into the living room, and faced us. "Now, I'm going to ask you politely again about the cross." He held up an index finger. "And I'm going to throw in a bonus. The one who tells me where the cross is, gets to live." He took another quick swig of Eddie's Caribbean madness. "That sounds like a pretty good deal, doesn't it?"

We glanced at each other almost involuntarily, then turned back to him, and he grinned.

"Hmmmm, maybe I hit a nerve there."

Without any warning, the gun in his hand spit again and my shirtsleeve twitched sharply. I hardly noticed the pain until I felt blood dribbling down my arm from the clean, superficial slice in my triceps.

"Any volunteers?" Stinger said. "Last chance."

Will sighed, surrendering. "Okay, okay. We know where it is but we'll have to draw you a map. If I draw you a map, will you let us go?"

Stinger Dunn thought about it, head tilting slightly in deliberation. He took another drink. The glass was half empty and his eyes were just starting to slide toward a psychedelic gleam. There was no question Stinger Dunn was buckling into his seat for the ride of a lifetime. "Yeah, sure," he said. "Sure I will." His words carried the same amount of fealty I would have expected from any other sociopath.

"Okay, it's only a little way from here," Will said, reaching for a pencil and a tablet on the coffee table. "Just take me a moment."

Stinger nodded, swaying ever so slightly, like a young palm moved by a morning breeze. My buddy started drawing lines, little squares, connecting them, pictures of trees, asking me questions like, "Was it a big rubber tree, or a mango tree next to the white house? How many feet from the shore to the tree, do you think?"

It wasn't long before our nemesis got bored and shot a hole in the table. "Enough of this shit. Give me the map!"

Will handed it to him submissively. Stinger held it one way, then another, trying to get a grip on my partner's lunacy, while becoming more muddled by the moment. He was losing his grip but he was still very dangerous. Stinger took a final slug of his "rum and dementia" cocktail, then sat it down on the kitchen counter with that slow deliberateness of the nearly besotted.

I knew that one of the byproducts of this kind of high was association, and we needed to distract him as much as possible. I gave Will a quick "follow my lead" eyeball, then turned to Stinger. I started scratching my shoulders and chest. "Man, it's itchy in here. I'm itching everywhere. Are you itchy? Could be from all the cockroaches we have — huge freaking cockroaches, the size of terriers."

Will followed by rubbing his head earnestly. "Itchy. Itchy. Damn, I'm itching all over."

Stinger stood there for a moment, then slurred. "I hate bloody cockroaches," as he scratched his neck and chest, and glanced around cautiously.

"I'm talking big, mean cockroaches — carried off our cat last week," Will chimed in. Then he pointed. "Jesus! There's one in the kitchen!"

Dunn swung around at the imaginary bug, gun first, but quickly came back to us. "We're getting out of here," he muttered, waving the gun erratically. "You're taking me to where you buried the cross! Now!" Then he glanced around once more, scratching his side, and grumbled, "Hate bloody cockroaches."

"It's not far. You'll have the cross in a few minutes," I promised him from over my shoulder as Will and I moved toward the door, hands raised.

"Damned well better," mumbled our captor, taking exaggerated, slightly wobbly steps behind us, eyes becoming slits, looking back once more to avoid being ambushed by a final, cunning cockroach, and scratching his ass.

As we headed out the door, a neighbor's Chihuahua suddenly came charging out of the walkway shadows, yipping and screeching with typical belligerence, scaring the absolute crap out of our snockered hit man. He threw himself against the wall with a shriek and fired three times, his silenced bullets smacking the concrete around the dog, which sent the miserable little twit into an antagonistic retreat, still howling out epithets of umbrage as he bounced back into the darkness.

Eyes glazed, Stinger brought the gun down and groused shakily, "Jesus on skates! Barking bloody cockroaches!"

As Dunn gathered himself together, we continued down a small, overgrown path toward the bay. I glanced back at our captor and could see he was having serious problems with balance. The mosquitoes, which bothered everyone, had become a major issue for him. He was flailing at them and slurring out curses about "bloody miserable bats" as he stumbled forward, but he also stopped twice, inadvertently, to stare at the stars with a glazed appreciation. The gun was beginning to waver. He was still mumbling about having to shoot one of us to show he was serious, but the weapon seemed to have increased in weight, the muzzle dragging downward, and his sense of momentum was fading, like a wind-up toy running out of wind-up. After about five minutes of playing "step and drag it" with Stinger, we came to a large clearing and he paused to stare at the moon as it slid between the branches of a rubber tree, and scratched himself. The gun was forgotten, hanging down at his side now. We had to stop and wait for him again.

"Okay," I whispered to Will, "Let's take him home. I don't want to have to carry him."

We simply walked around in the clearing in a circle and headed back in the direction from which we'd come. Our toasted antagonist bumbled along behind us like a sheep, mumbling the names of old girlfriends, drool running down his chin, stopping occasionally to touch the texture of the dew-glistened leaves around him with the wonder of a demented child.

By the time we got back to the apartment, the cheese had completely slid off of Stinger's cracker. He was reduced to knee-walking, gurgling, and murmuring secrets to himself. His gun was gone, left in the woods. I whispered to Will, "What are we going to do with him?"

My buddy looked at me with that larcenous grin of his. "I know just the place. We're going to send him on a trip — even more distant than the one he's on."

We lifted Stinger off the ground, where he was intently examining a few blades of grass, and escorted our wobbly acquaintance to the car. Will turned north at U.S. 1 and drove for about a half-mile, exiting into the cleared field where the circus was breaking down and packing up for their trip to Miami. The newspaper article had said they would load and board their freighter that night in order to be at sea by dawn. We pulled up in the parking lot and Will got out, looking around at the dismantled circus. Finally, he nodded and smiled. Five minutes later we had managed to escort/drag our obliterated nemesis over to a series of large cages that were being covered with plywood which had been drilled with numerous air holes. There were two fellows, both slim, grimy, and with long hair, who were working on putting the plywood over the animal cages. My buddy handed Stinger over to me.

"Keep him upright for a minute or two. I gotta talk with those guys." He walked over to the men just as they were nailing the last board on a cage containing a big Bengal tiger whose eyes showed the indifference of sedation (a common practice for circuses when they traveled — it kept the animals from hurting themselves, or anyone else). "Hey," he said with a friendly wave. "Boss wants to see you two. Wants to know how you're coming along on closing up the cages. It's gonna be a long night."

The larger of the two issued an expletive and spit some tobacco juice out the side of his mouth. "How are we supposed to finish this if the son of a bitch keeps interrupting us?"

Will held his hands out, palms up, in a deferential fashion. "Hey, I'm just the messenger. You don't want to talk to him, I just go back and tell him you don't have time to — "

"Nah, nah," the fellow grunted, exhaling angrily and dropping his tool belt on the ground. "We'll go. We'll go."

Will gave a quick point in my direction. "We'll pick up for you here. That way you don't lose any time."

The guy liked that; less work for him. He nodded, and he and his partner drifted off into the darkness of early evening. We parked Stinger against a boxed cage. He mumbled something about wanting more Coca Cola. I bent down and patted his cheek. "You've had enough Coca Cola for one night, *amigo*. Now you get to go on a cruise. Lucky you."

In the meantime, Will was walking down the cage line. All of the containers had plywood on three sides. Only the front sides were yet to be done. Suddenly, he stopped, and even through the gloom I could see the gleam of his teeth. He waved and I dragged Stinger over. There, in the corner of the dimly lit enclosure, sat a large, dusty orange orangutan, long, gangly arms folded in his lap, feet tucked up underneath him. A pile of bananas and other fruit had been placed next to him for the journey. From underneath those heavy, brushy brows stared two enormous ebony eyes, softly dulled by the introduction of a strong sedative.

"This is the place," said Will, a grim look of satisfaction on his face combined with a touch of wickedness in those blue eyes He reached back and pulled out the small bottle of monkey lust mist he had evidently taken from the car.

I glanced from the orangutan to Stinger, then back to my buddy. "Whoa! Are you sure? No telling how this is going to work out, you know."

"Yep, I'm sure," he said. "Are you forgetting the SOB was going to kill us? You wanna just let him go with a promise not to bother us again? By noon tomorrow, when he's probably just becoming cognizant, he'll be in the belly of a freighter on its way to South America." He held up the monkey lust juice. "I'm not gonna douse him — just a spritz or two to get his new roommate's attention."

Will looked at the lock on the cage. It was in place but hadn't been clicked down yet — probably the last thing they do, so they can get to the animal if there's a problem. He dragged Stinger to his feet and gave him a couple of quick hits. The orangutan caught the scent and moaned softly, those dark eyes suddenly showing a twinge of interest. I looked at Will and grimaced. Will removed the lock, and slowly, quietly, while watching the big orange fellow in the corner, we slid the man who would have killed us without a hint of remorse into the cage. Quickly closing the door, we waited for a few moments, but nobody had moved, so we closed the lock, grabbed the tools and a sheet of plywood, and began closing it off. By the time we'd made a couple of trips to the stack of plywood and put the last sheet in place, there had been a change in the cage. The big simian was sitting in the corner again, but now he had Stinger on his lap, those long, hairy arms wrapped tightly around his new friend in a more than casual embrace and he was gently licking the back of Stinger's neck with a huge pink and black tongue. The last thing I saw, and I still remember it, was Dunn's eyes, still somewhat lost to the realms of narcotics but widening with a sudden sense of concern, a lingering recognition that all was not right in his world.

In the background, I could hear a portable radio penetrating the darkness with a scratchy version of The Eagles' "Hotel California." *Relax, said the night man, we are programmed to receive. You can check out anytime you like, but you can never leave...*

"Bam, bam," went the final nail into place, and that was that for Stinger Dunn — gone but not forgotten.

All this talk about the best revenge being forgiveness, or outliving your foe, or finding compassion for the person who ripped you a new one, is bullshit. All that really means is you laid in bed, stared at the ceiling and ground your teeth, appalled by your inability to act, covering your hypocritical scat with counterfeit righteousness.

Don't ever confuse virtuousness with fear, or the courage to act with iniquity. One empowers wickedness, the other sends it howling back to hell. The best revenge is seeing fear in your enemy's eyes.

— Travis Christian

CHAPTER SEVEN

Within a week we got a call from Nick. He asked if we could stop by and visit with him, and bring our friend, Mary Cross. He said he had a gift for us from a buddy of his. Two hours later we were driving back over the Seven Mile Bridge, dancing on the edge of euphoria, a paper bag full of Franklins in neat little bundles on the floor at Will's feet.

We went to the bank, put fifty thousand in each of our safety deposit boxes, and took the other hundred thousand home with us. We had a delivery to make.

She picked up on the third ring. The woman's voice wasn't anywhere near as harsh as I had expected, but it was suspicious and all business when I explained that we knew her father and we had recently completed a task he had given us, which required meeting with her and delivering a sum of money. With a good deal of apprehension, she agreed to meet with us, gave us her address and said anytime that afternoon would be fine. She was cleaning fish after being out all morning on the reef. When I mentioned that to Will, he grimaced. "Whooo…like father, like daughter."

The house was located on the ocean side of Grassy Key, set back into a copse of Australian pines about three hundred yards from the water. Surprisingly enough it wasn't quite the ramshackle, dirt dauber structure I had expected. The little A-frame was made of strip-planked cypress with a small, railed deck in front, draped in hibiscus and adorned with a number of potted flowering plants. But the matter-of-fact voice on the phone and the fish-cleaning thing still resonated with both of us. As we pulled up in the driveway, Will said, "I'll flip you to see who has to go up and deliver the money. No need for both of us…"

I sighed and nodded. Will found a quarter, tossed it, deftly caught it, and turned the coin over on his arm, covering it with his hand. "Go ahead."

I called heads. It was tails. Will smiled in satisfaction. His plan had worked nicely.

I knocked on the door and waited. No one answered. I knocked again. Still no answer. I was headed down the steps to go around back when the door opened and a lady stepped out and put her hands on her hips.

"You the guy with the money?" she said, the tone possessing no particular benevolence.

I turned around and stopped, my mouth slightly agape. Her long blond hair was tied in a ponytail. She wore a bright yellow T-shirt and a pair of faded blue jeans, but neither could disguise the nice figure. She had exotic, high cheekbones and pale blue eyes that reminded me of the horizon on the ocean in early morning. Her lips were full, and even without lipstick they carried a soft sensuality. At about five-foot-five, and tanned dusky golden, she was an alluring combination of pixyish appeal and tomboy demeanor.

"Yeah, I'm the guy with the money," I said, trying to recover from my surprise.

"Dad said you'd never show when he found the handful of dollars in the envelope you left him. My money was on him."

As we stood there, appraising each other, Will, who had gotten a look at the girl from the car, quickly scrambled out and made his way up the stairs, coming to a skid next to me. "I'm also the guy with the money," he said, sweeping back his long blond hair with one hand. "Honest, affectionate, and loyal Will, they call me."

The edge of her mouth twisted upward slightly as she resisted a smile. "Vanilla. I'm Vanilla. Vanny. You wanna come in?"

I glanced at Will and his eyes said, "Ooohh, yeah!"

"Well, why not? After all, we've come all this way to bring you a lot of money."

As Vanny escorted us to the living room, which was decorated with more flowers, seashells, and paintings of nondescript artists displaying their affection for life around the ocean, she spoke over her shoulder, "So, you actually found *El Crucifijo de Santa María Magdalena,* huh? Damn, I would've never figured." In the background Don McLean crooned from her stereo about the men that he admired the most, the Father, Son, and Holy Ghost, catching the last train for the coast, the day the music died.

"Yeah, well, it wasn't exactly an easy task, and there are still some repercussions, but the simple answer is, damn right we did!"

Again the mouth twisted slightly and the smile almost escaped.

We sat on the couch and she settled into a chair across from us. I suddenly remembered I was holding the bag of money. I got up and brought it over to her, placing it on the coffee table. "One hundred thousand dollars — your cut. We sold it for two yesterday. By the way, my name's Kansas."

She eased out a surprised breath from between her teeth and picked up the bag, opening it and taking a peek inside, then setting it back down. "Better than I expected. That's for sure. Dad's gonna be pleased."

"So, Dad's still doing okay?" I asked cautiously.

Vanny exhaled, a mist of sadness touching her eyes. "Yeah, today. He's at Fisherman's Hospital. They're trying some new medicine, but even the doctors aren't offering much hope. His heart's just worn out. A lot of hard living and tough times, as well as self-abuse."

"Well, at least you'll have some money, to help out..." I said, trying to brighten the conversation.

Gazing out toward the beach in the distance through the pines, she replied, "Yeah, that'll help. I'm headed in to see him now." She turned toward us and hesitated. "Would you like to come? I think it might do him good...to see it all worked out." Vanny looked at me, straight into my eyes, and I felt something slide loose inside. Then those same remarkable azure orbs pulled themselves to Will. "I would like that."

Will and I glanced at each other. We really didn't have anything high on our agenda, and the truth was, neither of us was exactly anxious for this brief association with Vanny to end. Sometimes you just stumble across someone with whom, in just a few moments, there's an alliance, almost ethereal, without reason or logic. It just appears, inexorably rising like the early morning sun coming off the water, turning everything softly golden. It doesn't happen very often in life and I wasn't really searching for it, but damned if I didn't feel it with this girl. The problem was, looking at Will's eyes, I was pretty well sure he was watching that same sun coming off the water. One of those indelible junctions.

Old Jake Bean was sitting up in bed, clothed in a hospital gown, a couple of pillows tucked behind him, dredging out the vegetables from a Styrofoam cup of soup with a plastic spoon. He looked up as we came in and I watched his eyes take a moment to connect to his memory. "You're the ones who took my map and left me a lousy three hundred dollars." He started to rise. "You got a lot of nerve — "

"It's okay, Dad," Vanny said as she rushed to his side and eased him back down. "They found the cross, *El Crucifijo de Santa María Magdalena,* and they brought us money — a hundred thousand dollars."

Jake sat back, taking that in. He exhaled softly, somewhere

between amazement and disbelief. "Well I'll be picked off a bush and eaten one berry at a time by a pubescent redhead."

"Dad!" Vanny scolded.

"Hey, I'm old enough to wish for anything I want. Doesn't mean I'm gonna get it." Jake surveyed Will and me for a moment. "You found it? You really did, huh?" he said, apparently far more interested in the find than the money.

"Yeah, on a hillside in the jungle on Cat," Will said. "But this whole thing has to stay right here in this room. There were some extenuating circumstances."

Jake chuckled. "Aren't there always? No problem. I ain't got far to go with that secret, and my girl's word is as good as gold." He looked at his daughter. "Well, at least I don't have to worry about you as much now." Then he turned to us with an expression of gratitude, something I was fairly certain was a rare event. "Gentlemen, I owe ya. Thanks for being men of your word. Now, wherever I'm goin', I can relax a little." Those ancient gray eyes sparkled with humor and he leaned toward us conspiratorially. "I'm a little concerned about places called paradise that you can't leave and you can't get a beer. If I go to Heaven — fifty-fifty chance, maybe — I'm sure I'm gonna want to visit some of my friends in hell occasionally."

We talked for a while longer, Will and me telling some of the story about the finding, which lit up the old fellow's face, but Jake was starting to look a little weary and announced it was time for his siesta. Vanny asked for a moment alone with her dad, and we excused ourselves to wait in the hall.

When we got outside the room, Will turned to me intently but I put up a hand, interrupting him. "Yeah, yeah, I know, you want to flip me for her."

He stepped back. "What? You becoming psychic now?"

"This one's not a puppy either, so we're not flipping for her, and besides, I genuinely like this one."

"What? You think I don't? But man, I think she's got the hots for me. This might be the one. I mean, I haven't felt like this since...Carina."

I sighed. "Yeah, and before Carina it was the waitress at The Bull and Whistle, and before that — "

"Okay, okay," he said, waving his hands in placation. "So I got an active libido. It's a curse — comes with having the physical attributes of a yak."

"We're just going to play this one out," I said, holding up my hands, palms out. "Besides, there's no guarantee she doesn't already have a boyfriend, or three children from a previous marriage."

My buddy frowned. "Don't jinx it like that, man. She was giving me those nice eyes. She doesn't have a boyfriend. I'm sure."

At that moment Vanny came out of the room. She took a deep breath, centering herself. "Thanks guys. I appreciate you taking a little time with Dad. You made his day."

"Our pleasure," I replied. "It was great to see him, and it was nice spending some time with you."

"Very nice," Will added with a solicitous smile, not allowing himself to be upstaged.

On the way home, Vanny told us a little about herself and her parents. Her dad had been a shrimper in Louisiana. He met her mother, who was a waitress at a nightclub in Baton Rouge, and they were married six months later. Vanny came along a year after that. Things went okay for a few years, but there were a couple of issues — her father was gone a lot, shrimping in the Gulf, and her mother missed the nightlife. Somewhere along the line her dad found himself with a six-year-old daughter and a wife who had left him for a saxophone player in a road band. Jake had a sister in Marathon, so he and Vanilla moved to The Keys. He got into the lobster business, eventually managing to buy his own boat, and Vanny grew up on Grassy Key, where they built a small home. She was twenty-eight years old, had never been married, but she had "experimented once or twice" with the cohabitation thing. None of it had stuck.

When we returned to the house, we all got out of her car and she shook our hands, thanking us for being so gallant and honest, Will replying that it wasn't anything that we wouldn't normally do. Rescuing damsels in distress was our specialty — we were just those kind of guys. The smile she had hidden finally broke loose. Lord, it was worth the wait.

When Will and I reluctantly got back into the Jeep, Vanny was on the driver's side. When I turned the key, she moved a step closer and leaned down, those blue eyes taking on a sparkling keenness, touching mine, pausing nicely, then moving to Will. "If you're ever in the area, I'd be fine with you stopping by and saying hello."

"We get up this way pretty regularly," I said. "Don't be too surprised if we take you up on that."

As I drove away I could see her in the rear view mirror, standing among those rangy Australian pines, hands on her hips, head tilted slightly, a quizzical little smile touching that wide, inviting mouth. I can still see that smile, late at night, just after I've closed my eyes and just before sleep finds me.

On the way back to our apartment, the conversation danced around our new friend — from her skin and her hair, to a number of other fine attributes she possessed. But at the same time we couldn't help but compare her to Carina, the stunning Bahamian lady who had effortlessly captured our libidos so recently. If it hadn't been for the disappointing news we had received from Fabio about her, it would have been a neck and neck race, the yin and yang of feminine delight, the sultry golden island goddess and the blond Caribbean dream girl.

The full moon is calling, the fever is high, and the wicked wind whispers and moans. You got your demons, you got your desires, well, I got a few of my own...

— **The Eagles**

CHAPTER EIGHT

We picked up a *Key West Citizen* on the drive home. I liked reading the news each morning, and, given the way things were going, I figured it was wise just to keep up with what was happening in our neck of the woods. Sure enough, there was a small article on Penchant, saying that he was taking some time away from The Keys, traveling to South America to research some of the possible Spanish treasures lost near the coast of Colombia and Panama. I was certain he was looking to be gone from the area when our bodies showed up in some shrimper's net. With his ego, he probably wanted to give his hair time to grow out as well, and let all the monkey bite wounds on his legs and face heal up. All this was excellent news. It meant we could return to our home for a while. Penchant had no idea that his assassin was locked in a box with a giant monkey, also on his way to South America.

Once we got home, we cleaned up the plane, stowed all our gear from the Cat Island trip and settled back, relaxing for the rest of the day. The following morning, over coffee on the deck, Will looked at me and said, "I think we should call Vanny, just to say hi, you know. Maybe ask her out to dinner — the three of us."

I set down my coffee cup. "We just left her place yesterday afternoon. Sure you're not rushing things?"

Will shook his head. "No, not at all. It's not fair to let the girl suffer. I know she wants to see me again, and she might even like to see you, you know, like a friend."

I could just barely hear the stereo in the living room — Paul Simon softly cleaving the warm, morning air with "The Boxer."

"All lies and jest. A man hears what he wants to hear and disregards the rest..."

I smiled. "Yeah, you're probably right. I'd make a great friend."

My buddy nodded adamantly. "Yeah, yeah, you would. We might even name our first-born after you."

"I have squandered my resistance for a pocket full of mumbles, such are promises..."

Will called Vanny, and I picked up the phone in my bedroom. He explained that we were thinking of having dinner at The Key Colony Beach Restaurant in Marathon and we wondered if she would like to join us. There was little hesitation before she agreed. Just hearing her voice again lit small brushfires in nebulous regions of my senses. Will was going to be so disappointed when the best he got was a child named after him.

It was a Wednesday night in late summer, so the dining room was relatively quiet. We picked a table by the window, looking out at the ocean. The sun was four fingers above the horizon, playing hide and seek with puffy, evening cumulonimbus clusters, piercing the clouds with dazzling spears of golden rays and rivaling Rembrandt's best works. A few minutes later, Vanilla Bean came through the entrance to the dining room wearing white cotton bell-bottoms sheer to the point of silhouetting her legs in the afternoon light, an emerald blouse just soft enough to define the contours of her full, buoyant breasts, sandy blond hair flowing down over her shoulders, and blue eyes sparkling.

"She cleans up really good," Will whispered almost reverently.

"I'm just gonna ask her to marry me now and get it over with," I mumbled.

When she reached the table, both Will and I sat there like two religious pilgrims who had finally reached the shrine, still trying to get our mouths to work.

"Are you going to offer me a seat, or just gape at me?" she asked with an impish smile, hand on hip.

"I don't know about Will, but I'd like to gape for a few more moments," I said.

She chuckled as Will quickly got up and pulled out a seat for her. Looking at that woman, I realized I didn't want just feckless mingling here. I wanted meaning and passion. I wanted something that held reminiscence and longevity — but I'd certainly settle for feckless mingling if I had to. This one wasn't getting away without selling me some memories.

Our waiter came over and we ordered drinks. In the background Bertie Higgins sang about old, late-late shows, about sailing away to Key Largo, and finding love once again, just like Bogie and Bacall.

It was a marvelous evening — a glorious setting sun, rum drinks, great dinners, and an absolutely stellar companion, the whole thing marred only by the constant competition between Will and me. I caught Will trying to stuff a Dramamine patch in my rum and Coke, and he kicked me in the leg from under the table as I attempted to toss a Quaalude into his mashed potatoes. Both of us were afraid to leave the table for fear of skullduggery.

When Vanny excused herself to use the ladies' room, Will turned to me. "Can we call a truce? I gotta pee so bad my teeth hurt, and I can't relax wondering if you haven't borrowed a tab of acid from Eddie."

I grinned. "You never know…" He grimaced and I held my hand up. "Okay, okay, a truce."

Vanilla Bean proved to be an excellent conversationalist. She loved music and books and she could match us comfortably in her knowledge of fishing and her understanding of the sea. She had a throaty, sensual laugh and a clever wit, and when it all wound down, dinner finished, stars having replaced the sun and the waiter presenting the check, I would have gladly paid another hundred dollars just to do it all again.

As we stood outside by our cars, there was that awkward moment between leaving and not wanting to, and in this case not knowing exactly what to do, but Vanny eased it by coming over to me and giving me a hug. As she pulled away, her eyes stayed with mine for a few seconds, and I was certain I saw flecks of fire in those blue pools. Then she quickly went over to Will and hugged him with equal passion, and as much as I hated it, I was pretty sure they experienced that same connection for a moment, as well. Finally, she backed up and sighed. "It was a wonderful evening, gentlemen. We have to do this again some time. But I should go now, before I throw sensibility to the wind and take you both home."

I heard Will's intake of breath over my own. We involuntarily glanced at each other, eyes like lemurs on acid.

She laughed, breaking the spell. "Take it easy, cowboys. Breathe. Breathe. Just joking." Then she got this weird sparkle in those summer-reef orbs. "At least tonight."

The first few minutes of the journey home were very quiet. Will finally glanced at me, then back to the highway. "You don't think she's serious, do you? About…"

"Hell, how do I know?" I said, still staring at the road, just a little uncomfortable. I was all for reckless revelry, but first off, the only threesomes I'd ever had were women and me. Secondly, I liked Will real well, but not enough to have his junk dangling around that close to mine. Sex was a little more personal to me.

"I think she was just teasing," he said. "Besides, I'm not that hot on sharing certain things, like my toothbrush, my popcorn, or my women."

I exhaled softly. "Glad to hear it, buddy. I feel the same way.

This whole damned thing is way too reminiscent of Banyan McDaniel." (Banyan was a hot, delicious, absolutely crazy chick we had both fallen in love with years before. She made us wide-eyed, moonstruck mental before dumping us for a conga player in a Caribbean steel drum band.) "We're just gonna have to play this one out, maybe cut cards for her."

Will guffawed lightly. "Like hell! I'm never cutting cards with you for anything after that Cat Island affair."

The following day we took our twenty-two-foot Mako out to do some diving, but on the way back one of the twin 125 Mercury engines started missing badly. Will, who was a passable mechanic, popped the cowling and looked it over, but couldn't find the problem. We were only about a half-mile from Sea Center Marina on Big Pine, so we limped in and had one of their mechanics look at it. While Will was speaking with him I wandered down the dock, enjoying a pleasant breeze and a warm sun. I finally sat down on the old weathered boards, leaning against a piling, watching a variety of sea life moving endlessly around the pilings below. Small snapper, parrotfish, sergeant majors, and The Keys' ever-present grunts, worked their way in and out of the shaded water beneath me in a perpetual panorama of competition for the Gulf's bounties. My back against the sun-warmed wood, I closed my eyes, dozing pleasantly.

"Aahhh, sleeping in the sun like a lazy lizard, mon. A benevolence of the Great Tortoise still caresses you, and the wind smiles at your blessing." That voice, the timbre, and accent brought me around instantly. I knew it all too well. *Rufus! God! Rufus!* I opened my eyes and squinted through the late afternoon sun. There he was, sitting on the dock across from me, leaning against an adjacent piling. He hadn't changed at all — tall and gangly, shoulder-length dreadlocks, same weird gray-blue eyes and gap-toothed smile, the sun reflecting off his soft mahogany skin, and the same sweet tang of ganja emanating from him, as always. He wore an old pair of khaki shorts and a Bob Marley T-shirt that looked like it hadn't been washed in weeks.

It had been a couple of years since we had seen our old buddy, the crazy Rastafarian soothsayer. Maybe crazy wasn't fair. He was an incredible character who not only seemed to march to a different drum, but apparently knew the guy who made the drums. Rufus claimed to be the progeny of an ancient race, and was gifted with the eerie disposition of oftentimes knowing what was going to happen well before it happened, as well as possessing odd potions and "magic gumballs." Truth was, it was he who got us involved in the golden pyramid caper several years ago, which probably took years off my life. But it was also Rufus who had given us a "very special present" for our efforts — an old Mason jar filled with hundreds of ancient, extremely valuable coins, and a strange list of upcoming companies to invest in as we sold the coins.

"Aaahh, my olden friend, Texas."

"Kansas," I said. "Kansas."

"Ya, mon. Ya, mon. It is good to envision your countenance again. I think you are well, yes? And your lengthy accomplice, Willmon?"

"Will. Yeah, we're okay." I sighed. "But as usual, it's been complicated."

Rufus nodded sagely. "Life without complications is like good fish without lime — you can eat it, but it not so interesting." He cocked his head. "Interesting fish lately, hmmm?"

"Yeah. A little too much adventure, even for us."

Rufus nodded. "You know, mon, life a lot like Chinese puzzle box — you pull off top and dere is something else inside, den something else." He paused. "I think maybe soon you find another puzzle box."

"Oh Lord, Rufus, don't tell me you're setting us up to be a part of another one of your convoluted, freaking schemes."

My old acquaintance sighed benignly and held his hands up. "We all part of universal pinball machine, some of us levers —"

"Yeah, and some of us are little balls. I know. I know. I've heard this before and you're freakin' me out. The last time we got involved with you, on that damned pyramid thing, we nearly got our asses killed."

Rufus held up a finger. "But you also get plenty nice gift, huh?"

I knew he was referring to the coins he had given us, and he was right.

Evening was closing in and he looked out at the sunset for a moment, admiring Mother Nature's sweeping ostrich feathers of gray, windswept clouds stretched above an orange bloom on the horizon, the fiery colors of a summer sky brushed into the plumes, igniting them. He sighed at the magnificence. "Dis whole thing, life, a lot like da tides, mon." He swept his hand outward. "Water go out." Then brought his hand back. "Water come in. We all like tiny fishes — better to move with tide dan against it."

"Rufus, c'mon, man. Not again…"

The big Jamaican got up, came over, and sat down next to me, our feet dangling off the edge of the dock. "Sometimes dere be treasures inside of treasures, mon," he continued as if he hadn't heard me. "Things dat bring good make life better for other little fishes. Maybe dere be gift here, from my people's people to your people's people. You know, mon, my people be here long before first pharaoh built stone triangle to his ego. You not be da first person we talk to — da Vinci, Franklin, Tesla — names I remember from my parents, and dey remember from deres. Knowledge come in two ways, mon. You divine it yourself or pay attention to clever friends. My people have been clever friends for a long time. In between, da wisdom of the Grand Messenger assists." He paused, half-tilted his head in that distinctive fashion of his, and smiled. "You can always walk away. But maybe I think you like a little complication. You be like da tiny wrasse dat cleans da moray's teeth. You like taste of life better when you swimming close to fangs." He patted me on the shoulder. "You and Willmon a couple of da more interesting pinballs I know. I think you have some interesting journeys coming up, but maybe not totally pleasant, so, like before, many years ago, I give you little gift — a special magic gumball."

Rufus reached into his pocket and pulled out a small, blue ball, exactly like one of the gumballs you would buy in the round bubble machines. He held it up. "Dis be a *blind ball*," he said, then he closed the fingers on both hands into fists. "Throw it hard, on ground or against wall, and close your eyes. When dey gumball cracks, however it cracks," his fingers flew open. "Poof!" he whispered harshly. "Everybody go blind around you for five minutes." My Rastaman friend shook his finger sternly. "Do not open eyes for ten seconds after throwing ball, or you, too, be blind as dead mud duck!"

"Oh, crap," I grunted, realizing we were definitely stepping into deep caca again. "No, I don't want this, Rufus. Why me? Why Will and me? Surely there must be lots of other people who could take care of this for you."

The mystical Rastaman shrugged. "You both be very clever — like cagey seagull who steals from other birds. You perfect combination between talented and expendable."

"Yeah, great, that makes me feel really good."

He paused. "Dere is, of course, special present, like before."

That did stop me, because the last present had been very good. Those antique coins had kept us in modern dollars for a long time.

The seriousness passed from his face and he smiled. "Do not

worry. You be clever seagulls, get new experience to tell in rooms of drinking and merriment. The Grand Messenger of Da Wisdom of Ganja say, 'He who does not taste da mango, does not know what da mango tastes like.'" Rufus exhaled and stood up. "I must go now — catch the tide. Cool driftings, mon. May your life egg break cleanly and Da Great Tortoise grant you a moonlit path to da sea."

I couldn't think of anything to say but, "Oh crap. Not again..."

With the boat engine fixed, we took the next day to dive for lobsters on the patch reefs in Hawk Channel. Will had recommended we have Vanny over for dinner one night during the week. After the first dive, we were sitting topside, having unzipped our wetsuits and turned off our hooka rig (a gas engine which ran a compressor, feeding air into a volume tank and a couple of one hundred fifty-foot reinforced rubber hoses that ran off the tank. They attached to the second stages of regulators, built into our backpack harnesses).

I turned to Will and said, "You'll never guess who I ran into yesterday."

He looked up. "Who?"

"Rufus."

Even through the redness and pinched lines on his face from the mask, I could see his color drain. "Rufus, huh?"

"He's got another 'quest' for us and supposedly another very special gift for our trouble."

"No."

"No what?"

"No," Will said, shaking his head emphatically. "The last one almost got us killed."

"That's what I told him."

"We don't have to do it. He can't make us."

"That's what I told him."

Will scrunched his lips together and wiped the seawater from his face in a reflective, nervous action. "Man, just hearing about this makes me feel like a Hobbit on my way to Mordor." He paused. "What's the very special gift? The last one was pretty good."

I looked out across the sea. The surface was throwing up a light chop, not quite enough to create whitecaps, but still okay for diving. "Don't know. He didn't say."

With a sharp exhale, Will asked, "When is this thing supposed to happen?"

"Don't know. You know how Rufus is. There aren't a lot of

dates and times. Most of it depends on the mood of The Great Turtle, the Grand Messenger, and clever seagulls."

My buddy ran a hand over his face again, massaging his cheeks where the mask fit too tight. "Doesn't matter. He can't make me."

I shrugged. "He seems to think he won't have to — something about finding treasures in treasures and Chinese puzzle boxes."

"Now I understand completely," Will huffed as he picked up his mask. "I feel much better. Did he mention anything about mangoes or pinball machines?" he added sarcastically.

"Yeah, as a matter of fact, he did."

Will blinked in amazement. "Sounds just like freaking Rufus. C'mon, let's do one more dive."

That afternoon when we got home, I called Vanilla and asked her if she'd like to have dinner with us the following night at our place.

"Will it be safe for a girl, you know, alone and helpless at the home of two men?"

I quickly explained that it was just dinner. We weren't those kind of guys.

"Too bad," she replied with a wry smile in her voice. "But dinner would be nice."

The dinner date was simply wonderful — another adventure in conversation, competition, and innuendo — the competition between Will and me, and the innuendos in all directions. Vanny was charming and intriguing, but at the end of the night neither one of us was any closer to eliminating the competition. We did, however, advance to a serious hug and a brief kiss for each of us. In the end, standing on the marl rock by her car, moonlight dancing over her golden hair like a consecration from Heaven, she gazed at us, shook her head, and sighed.

"What's a girl to do? What's a girl to do?"

Before the lights of her car had disappeared, I turned to Will. "Okay, I'll flip you for her."

Will took a step back. "Whoa, cowboy. I'm not giving her up that easily now. The best I'll do is flip you for the first date. Winner gets to ask her out, by himself, just two people. No more of this 'step and drag it' *ménage à trois* crap."

I thought about it for a moment. "Done. Pull out a coin and flip the sucker."

I slept like a baby that night, even over the cursing and whining of Will in the other room. But in the next few days a couple of things happened that made life far more "interesting" for this pair of clever seagulls.

It's all right now. I learned my lesson well. You see, you can't please everyone, so you got to please yourself.

— **Ricky Nelson**

CHAPTER NINE

The next day Eddie and Will went into Key West to get a part for the Goose, and probably have a couple of drinks downtown.

I had a number of plans myself, not the least of which was calling Vanny. She answered on the third ring, and after a few pleasantries I simply blurted it out. "I'd like to know if you'd consider going to dinner with me tomorrow night — just you and me."

There was a silence on the other end and I quickly began to think this was a colossal mistake. Then she said, "How does Will feel about this?"

I exhaled the breath I'd been holding. "Well, I can't say he's overjoyed, but he has agreed to it."

"You flipped a coin, didn't you?"

God, she was a savvy chick. "Yeah, yeah we did."

The tension was gone when she replied, and I could hear that smile in her voice. "Well, congratulations, lucky winner."

After the phone call, I decided to check my closet for some clean duds, something extra cool. In the process, I noticed the old chest that had contained the coins we found on Cat Island. I had wanted to restore that, so after having a quick look at clothes, I picked up the chest with the intent of taking it downstairs to our workshop beneath the house — maybe start the restoration process by cleaning the brass on it. I got outside and started down the stairs, but missed a step. Grabbing for the rail, I lost my grip on the box and it slipped from my hand. As it hit the steps, the fragile container bounced hard and tumbled down the stairs. One of its hinges on the lid broke loose, and the bottom cracked open like an eggshell. With a harsh expletive I stumbled after it and picked up the remains, but I immediately noticed that there had apparently been a false bottom built into the chest. In the small, now obvious compartment, was an envelope of some sort — brittle and aged, but nonetheless an envelope, sealed with cracked red wax. I pulled it out and sat down on the stairs in amazement as I held something that had been written by someone well over three hundred years ago. With my pocketknife, I gently pried loose the flap and took out the yellowed, brittle pages. Fortunately, I spoke Spanish well, and although it was Castilian and somewhat more difficult, it was manageable. I took a deep breath and began to read.

Just as I was finishing, Will and Eddie pulled up. Coming over, they stopped in front of me.

Will stared at the shattered box. "Wow, man, what happened to the chest?"

I looked up, still a little in awe by what I had just read. "Dropped it on the way down the stairs."

"Bummer," Eddie said. "Stone cold bummer, dude. Too bad."

"No, too good. You have no idea."

Will cocked his head at my strange answer. "What are you reading?"

In just the few minutes it had taken me to read the letter, I had already realized we'd been cast into another quest, and I understood with some degree of reverence the remarkable clairvoyance of our Rastaman buddy, Rufus. I also realized that this was going to require the services of Eddie and his big Grumman Goose amphibian. "Treasures inside of treasures," I muttered to myself. "Chinese boxes — you lift off the lid and there's another box inside…"

My friends looked at me as if perhaps I'd been in the sun too long.

"C'mon my little Hobbits, I have something to read to you," I said, rising and heading up the stairs without another word.

Once we were all seated in the living room, I carefully adjusted the ancient pages and began to read a letter written by a Spanish conquistador over four hundred years ago.

My dear Juan,

I have sent this message to you in our family's surreptitious fashion because it is paramount I make you, and only you, aware of a profound discovery. I have come upon something that is beyond the boundaries of man's imagination, and as prehensile as it may sound, I care not to share it with others. But I am a soldier and there is still a conquest at hand, and I fear that if I should suffer harm before I return, this knowledge could be lost forever. Therefore, I am providing you with this letter.

I looked up at my friends. I definitely had their attention.

This that I have unearthed, I cannot entrust to anyone else. It must return with me, to Spain, and to our family. My brother, I have truly discovered a tool of the Gods, or the devil's own scepter, I know not which. Bear with me as I try to explain:

A few months ago as we closed on the Incan city of Cajamarca, I led a portion of the final assault, along with my commander, Francisco Pizarro. In the fracas I spotted one of the chieftains retreating with his royal guard. My men and I fought a running battle with him and his contingent as he retreated into the city. In short, his soldiers died protecting him and he slipped away into the heart of his own palace. We followed, through the quarters, to his personal chambers. But when we finally burst down the doors he was nowhere to be found. It took several minutes of searching, and had I not been of nobility and understood the value of secret chambers, I would never have noticed the finest of clefts in the stone of the west wall, which had been covered by a tapestry. It took many minutes of prying with our swords, but finally the hidden latch gave and the stone door slid outward. Once inside the small room, two of my men and I found the man huddled in the corner, dying of a severe wound to the chest. But the contents of the chamber startled me. There were diminutive golden idols, chests of decorative gold and silver items, and numerous small boxes of rare stones.

"Really got my attention now," muttered Will.

I started again.

Not to belabor this in the telling, it was later that day as we inventoried the room that I found an item wrapped in soft dyed wool — a scepter of some sort — a rod perhaps a vara in length, with the girth of a sword hilt, made of what seemed to be a thin covering of gold but light enough to wield comfortably.

I stopped. "If I remember correctly, a *vara* was a Spanish yard, somewhere around thirty-two inches."

"Thanks, Mr. Wizard," said Eddie, obviously captured by the story. "Back to the program, dude."

At one end of the rod was a small, sparkling clear globe, and at the other a many-faceted crystal that came to a point. There appeared to be indentations in the center of the rod, where one's fingers might hold it — to point it. As my fingers clutched the ancient grip, a notch gave when I squeezed it, but nothing transpired. I know not why to this day, but there was something about the weathered antiquity of it — the design and the strange emblems on the shaft that seemed to be inconsistent with all we had seen of this civilization — that made me place it aside.

By the time we left the palace with the spoils of conquest, the sun had set and the moon had risen. Still not exactly understanding why, I had taken with me the strange scepter wrapped in the blanket and stuffed in the saddlebag of my mount. The next morning, as was my habit, I had the groom saddle my horse and I rode out into the surrounding hillside to survey our position. After dismounting, I was sitting on a rise looking out over the valley, my horse tethered near me, when I remembered the scepter. I walked over and removed the strange device from my saddlebag. As soon as it was clear of the bag and the morning sun struck it, the globe on the one end began to sparkle, then glow. I was so shocked I dropped it and leapt back, muttering something about the work of the devil. But it just lay there, the globe continuing to glare. I must admit I waited several minutes. Finally, I gathered my courage, stepped over and picked it up. But as I gripped the indentations, the notch beneath my fingers clicked and the scepter began to vibrate softly. Suddenly, the crystal on the front of the wand began to glow, and a translucent, shimmering beam, flickering and wavering like a desert mirage, flowed out from it.

There was a huge felled tree not fifty varas from me, taken down by recent winds, for the ball of tangled roots at the base was plain to see. The beam struck it inadvertently, and reacting from the shock of what I was experiencing, I turned my body slightly (the wand turning with me). There before my eyes I witnessed a miracle, or the devil's wiles, for the tree simply lifted up, ten varas off the ground, and sailed upward with the direction the scepter's crystal point, magically reposed in midair. So unnerved was I that again I dropped the scepter and jumped away from it. In that same instant, the colossal tree fell to the ground with a thunderous crash.

I have never been considered a cowardly soul, but I will admit it took me several moments to quell my shaking hands. Finally, I returned to the scepter, as curious as I was fearful. I offered a small supplication to our Lord, crossed myself, then slowly, carefully, picked it up and turned toward the fallen tree. I gripped the handle and felt the notch depress beneath my finger. Instantly the device trembled and the flickering mirage leapt from the stone in front, striking, then fixing on the tree. This time I held my fear and carefully lifted the front of the wand. To my never-ending surprise the tree simply lifted off the ground as if held by the hand of God. At that moment, I knew I held the power to change the world.

I know you will think I'm mad when you read this, brother, but several times afterward I slipped from my encampment and practiced using this device, moving immense boulders and felled trees like children's toys. With this scepter one person could move the stones of the great walls of our own Maracan Castle as if they were made of the lightest cork, and place them wherever they wished. Believe me not if you choose to, but hold close this letter, and secure it in the safest of places.

While Pizarro consolidated his power in the region I was ordered farther south, moving into the last regions of the Inca Empire east of the great lake the Incans called Huinaymarca...

Will interrupted, "That's one of the names for Lake Titicaca in Bolivia."

"Right you are," I said, continuing on.

But as we traveled and fought, I felt less safe in the possession of this magical device I had discovered. I began to feel an eerie premonition that my time might be at hand. When we reached the area the natives called Tiahuanaco, we came to the ruins of a truly ancient city — enormous slabs of stone, with sizes and weights that staggered the imagination. There were interconnecting walls of dimensions beyond belief, cut and assembled with such a precision that the honed point of my dagger could not slip between the slabs.

"Damn!" exclaimed Will, waving his hands in the air like he was fending off gnats. "I know exactly where he's talking about! The place is called Tiwanaku and Puma Punku! I remember reading about it while researching the Spanish conquest of South America. Puma Punku is an absolutely amazing engineering feat. No one's got any idea how they cut and moved those stones."

Eddie and I looked at him.

"Okay. Okay, go on," he muttered. "Just supplying a few details."

I continued.

The concept of moving behemoths like these a single vara seemed no more possible than touching the sun. Yet here they were, although many had been scattered as if a great catastrophe had befallen the city in some distant time. Suddenly, intrinsically, I knew beyond a doubt that this was the home of this scepter of the gods I had discovered.

With my haunting premonition and the nagging fear of discovery, I hid my strange device in the hills, less than half a legua from this curious, aged city.

I paused again.

Eddie anticipated me. "Okay, Mr. Wizard, how far is a *legua?*"

"Getting into this, aren't ya? I may charge you fifty bucks for the complete translation."

Eddie got that goofy grin, edged with a little roguery. "And Eddie maybe drop a tab of acid in your hot cocoa — harsh your mellow when you're least expecting it."

"Hmmm. Okay, you win. A *legua* is a little less than three miles, so we're talking about a mile and a half." I went back to the letter.

Just north of those ancient ruins stands a huge granite cliff, the face of which is easily 1,000 varas across. Near the center of the cliff is a huge, V-shaped rift extending to the ground. Close to the base of the V, there is a cleft in the rock, just wide enough for a body to enter the interior of a cave, approximately ten varas deep by five wide. The scepter is buried in the soil at the very back. If I fail to return, seek this out. It is yours, and all the wealth and fame it brings will raise our family to the status of our grandfathers once again.

Finally, brother, my impression is that the Incan leader who died trying to escape me had never discovered the scepter's power. I am of this mind because apparently the only drawback of this device is that it must enjoy the companionship of sunlight at least two hours a day to function at its most remarkable capability. Without that, it becomes inert.

I have prepared the chest that hides this letter to be shipped to the coast by special envoy, along with some minor spoils of the latest campaign. From there the envoy will sail to Cartagena and join a fleet to Spain. It is my fervent hope that you receive this message intact, and that I shall see you again. I wish you and our family good fortune.

Until then, your grateful brother,
Hernando de Amargo

The room was quiet for a few moments after I had finished. Will slowly shook his head, eyes gleaming like two golden sovereigns. "Whoodang! Now that's a treasure tale if I ever heard one."

I nodded, then softly muttered, "Wonder what a device like that would be worth on the open market? Imagine the engineering potential — the military prospective. What if it could be duplicated and you held the patent?"

"Ya, mon!" Eddie said enthusiastically. "Ya, mon! Eddie could live in the fashion to which he wants to become accustomed."

"Avarice aside, think what a gift this scepter would be for mankind if it could be reproduced," Will said.

I sat looking at the yellowed letter. "Here's the odd part. There's well over a hundred years between the writing of this letter and the buccaneer era of Captain Arthur Catt in The Bahamas. How is it that the chest ended up with him?"

Will chewed the bottom of his lip for a moment, thinking. "I remember reading that storage containers — chests, for instance — were commonly used over and over again in those days. Stripped of their original possessions, they were loaded with cinnamon, or liquor, or gold coins and sent on — or buried, in this case. It's my guess that the box may have been waylaid somewhere along the journey and probably made several stops before it ended up in a pirate's lair on Cat Island."

"But nobody ever found that letter," Eddie replied.

"Not nobody," I said with a smile.

The three of us talked for the next hour, laying out plans on how we could tackle this project. It was obvious that we needed a way into and out of Bolivia that didn't require conventional airlines, something that would allow us to get out in a hurry if we had to. That's where Eddie and his Goose would come in. It had more range and could deal with adverse weather better than my little Cessna. The project would take at least several weeks in preparation — passports, visas, research, and equipment, just to begin with. We had laid some preliminary plans and divided up some of the responsibilities, most of what we could accomplish for the day, when there was a knock at the door. Will got up and went over. He opened it and just stood there, a look of surprise and cautious emotion on his face. Just beyond him I could see her, the sun cascading down on her long, raven hair and perfect golden skin, those Cuervo eyes staring at him with uncertainty and trepidation, but also burnished with an unabashed gladness. Carina!

She stood there with a suitcase in hand, dressed in a soft, white cotton shift that outlined the contours of her body — hesitant, insecure. "Hello, Will," she said.

His mouth moved but nothing came out, and like a robot, stiff and confused, he backed up and let her in. I had forgotten how beautiful she was. Not so tall, but elegant, smooth, and perfect, every part of her a work of Michelangelo. Even captured in this moment of uncertainty she didn't walk, she flowed with a movement akin to an osprey in flight, every motion a nuance of delicately controlled energy, and those eyes — cool and entrancing, yellow-golden like a hawk, but capable of a vast spectrum of expressions.

I found myself rising from my seat, hardly recognizing my feet were carrying me over to her. When we stood in front of Carina she said, "I had to come and find you. I had to explain. I left Drako the day you left the island." She paused, gathering her words carefully.

"This is something I should have done long before. Sometimes we value the security of today beyond the possibility of tomorrow. You give me means to take the chance. I am grateful."

Words didn't just tumble out of her mouth as they did with most people. She tasted them with her tongue and caressed them with her wide lips before letting them go, and they left with regret. She made vowels an erotic delight. Watching her speak was more sensual than watching most women take off their clothes.

"I thought you left Drako before that. Before you came to stay with us," I said, entranced, but not ready to release the animosity I had built up for her betrayal.

Carina took a deep breath and expelled it slowly, her face filled with anguish, then she spoke quietly. "You are right, that's what I told you. The night you left the bar, the night you cut cards with Drako, he was so crazy he was going to kill you. But the words that the old shaman spoke made me think that you were there for treasure. I told Drako this. I told him I would go to you, find out what you do — if he promised not kill you. Yes, I deceived you, but I trade your lives for your treasure. I make Obeah sacrifice, and pray to Jesus. In the end, you trick Drako and keep the treasure, and I am pleased."

"Why?" Will said. "Why'd you do all this?"

She exhaled hard again and looked up at the ceiling, then brought those golden eyes back to us, shaking her head slightly. "I do not know. You were nothing to me, and yet you were something. Sometimes you meet some people and your spirits touch, like old friends. The taste in your mouth is sweet and it carries a memory that your mind cannot see, it can only feel — like the early morning shadows on the water, before the sun has blessed them and they slide away into the breeze." She paused and smiled, almost embarrassed by her description. "I don't expect you to understand."

But I did understand. I felt it also that night — an instant rapport, very similar to what I experienced with Vanny. It seemed bizarre that I should encounter this twice in only a few weeks when I could only remember it happening perhaps once before in my life.

"Come on in, Carina," I said, extending my hand. "I'm sure it's been a long trip for you."

Will, whom I realized was feeling much the same, quickly took her suitcase and brought her inside, thus ushering in a whole new dimension of complication for our already "interesting" lives.

For the time being, the new adventure was forgotten. Well, not forgotten, but temporarily shelved. After introducing Carina to Eddie, we all sat in the living room and talked like old friends, Carina telling us about the antics of Fabio, our Bahamian buddy with his newfound money, and how she managed to find us.

I sat there watching her talk, her wonderful facial expressions, and the sound of her voice, like the rustle of a fast-moving tide over sand — soft, yet momentous in its width and depth. I found myself comparing her with Vanny. Truly, they were two vastly different women, but each carried her own set of charms, her own powers. They were like the moon and the sun, like Cleopatra and Nefertiti, or Marilyn Monroe and Katherine Ross — at some point, perspective blurs and it all becomes subjective. Looking over at Will and his glazed eyes, I could tell that he, too, was struggling with subjectivity.

In the background, Jim Croce whispered from our stereo about time in a bottle.

If I had a box just for wishes
And dreams that had never come true
The box would be empty
Except for the memory
Of how they were answered by you.

CHAPTER TEN

We asked Carina if she had a place to stay and she shook her head. It was plain that our lady friend was not going back to Cat anytime in the near future, so we offered to have her stay with us for the night. Carina thanked us, but declined, saying she would get a motel room on Big Pine Key, then make some decisions in the morning. We took her over to The Big Pine Motel and got her signed in. That night we had dinner at The Baltimore Oyster House, where we drank and ate, and drank some more, immersed in conversation, laughter, and, of course the perennial competition between Will and me. Carina possessed a remarkably intuitive intelligence and little got by her, even though she was somewhat out of her element. The fact that her father had been French, and her mother's father English, had given her more of a European than true Jamaican dialect and a broader understanding of the world. Regardless, with her exotic looks she was the center of attention. Will and I got about as much consideration as the lobster and crab mounts hanging on the walls. One of the waiters walked into a wall with a full tray of food, paying too much attention to her and not enough to his feet. It was a wonderful night.

We dropped Carina off at her motel and drove home. Moonlight splayed across the hood of my partner's Camaro and stars raced overhead like glistening silver kestrels.

"Is it always going to be like this?" Will asked, to no one in particular. "This complicated? Just when our lives seemed to have settled down, after being mutually dumped and emotionally scalded by our wives, we find not one, but two women whom we both want — probably because we're both about as crazy greedy as a monkey chasing a mango truck. Then, if that weren't enough, the mad Rastaman shows up again and drops another wild Hobbit quest in our laps. If we were smart people we'd say 'no, thank you, we don't need to be chased, shot at, and generally sought for punishment in one sort or another, again.' But you know what? We won't. And you want to know why? Because we're both about as crazy greedy as a monkey chasing a mango truck."

"There is the adventure part," I said. "The excitement, the barroom tales."

"Yeah, there is that." My friend shrugged. "And I guess the truth is, I'd really like to see that cool wand — a device can move anything you point it at."

"Yeah, that would definitely be far out."

A tiny smile edged the corners of Will's mouth. "I guess we just be two crazy freaking monkeys, mon."

The next morning we picked up Carina and took her to breakfast at Island Jim's. During the meal she laid a bombshell on us — she had decided to stay in The Keys. She would stay the six months that her visa allowed and begin the process of dual citizenship. Will and I offered to help her look for an apartment, saying that we would cover her rent for a few months until she got settled in. It was the least we could do for her attempt to keep us alive on Cat Island.

She argued at first, but finally agreed. "As a small expression of my gratitude I would like to take both of you to dinner tonight," she said.

We both agreed eagerly, then I suddenly remembered my date with Vanny. "Aaahhh, I can't do that tonight," I said hesitantly.

Will knew exactly why and pounced on it with both feet. "Oohh, that's right, you can't come tonight, can you?" he said with a triumphal, glittering smile. He turned to Carina. "Kansas has a date — pretty little thing who lives on Grassy Key — just crazy about him."

I shot a scalding glance at Will, then, turning to Carina with the innocence of a saint, I sighed and said, "Actually, it's Will's girlfriend I'm visiting. She wanted to see me — needed someone to talk to. He's been cheating on her again, faithless, profligate bastard that he is. There's probably half a dozen little rapscallions running around in The Keys with that distinctively hooked nose."

Will looked like he'd been stabbed with an ice pick, but recovered quickly. "Well, she used to be my girlfriend, but Kansas snaked her away while pretending to be helping us with our relationship. She likes him really well now. If it weren't for his virulent outbreaks of herpes, they'd probably be living together. Then, of course, there's the bipolar problem. He's got the mood swings of a pregnant squirrel monkey."

Carina was a very quick study. She could tell when she was being played. She smiled. "Gentlemen, you're working too hard at this. Let the moon change the tides. It is not my plan to interrupt your lives. Let us float with the current for a while and enjoy."

That night I had a wonderful dinner with Vanny, while Will took Carina into Key West for drinks and to watch the nightly "sunset celebration" at Malory Square. I didn't know what happened with Will, but I knew what happened with me, and I enjoyed every minute of it.

I got home in the early morning hours, a bit disheveled with a permanently embedded smile on my face. I hit the head, went to bed, and was asleep before you could say, "Whoodang!"

When I finally got up, Will was reading the paper in the living room. He turned to me, and almost simultaneously we both said, "Did you have a good time last night?"

"Yeah, I did," I replied, barely able to conceal my pleasure.

"So did I," Will added. "That Carina is an amazing chick. I mean, just amazing."

The implication settled into the room like an elephant.

"I would have to say the same for Vanny."

Will closed the paper. "But that doesn't mean that I'm not still interested in Vanny. This is a complicated situation. Not a time to be hasty. You have to see a couple sunrises and sunsets before you know what you like best."

As much as I enjoyed the evening with Vanny, my pal was right. The girls we were talking about so cavalierly had their own choices to make. Just as Rufus told me the other day, "He who does not taste the mango does not know what the mango tastes like."

We managed to find Carina a furnished apartment on Big Pine, and she settled into life in The Keys quite well. That was the easy part. The next month or so became a strange but fascinating game of musical chairs, and an emotional collage of competition in numerous directions. The women we'd become so taken with were not fools. They knew what was happening, but apparently they were equally as concerned with making sure which mango tasted the best, so to speak.

Personally, I was still struggling with the whole thing. I loved the frankness and earthy beauty of Vanny, and we shared a love of the ocean and the outdoors, which had created an undeniable bond between us. Lovemaking was passionate, verbal, and exhausting, with few holds barred, but afterwards she softened like a kitten, curling up into me as the moon from the bedroom window bathed us with its blessing. There was a sense of contentment and belonging with her that I had rarely found.

Carina possessed a remarkable, unfeigned sense of finesse and grace, like a lioness. She was clever and naturally intelligent, and never boring. Conversation flowed without effort. Lovemaking was a slow, sensual, erotic process, which carried us through numerous stages of passion and into extraordinary crescendos. But at the same time, there was a part of her — an innocence hidden just beneath the folds of composure — like a young girl so willing to please and so easily satisfied. It was a strange and wonderful combination.

However, the major fly in all this exotic ointment was that everywhere I went, I knew my buddy had been there, too. At first it wasn't so disturbing. No commitments had been made, and it was somewhat of a game, but as we moved along it was obvious, at least to me, that this "tasting the mango" thing had a shelf life. It had to be resolved before it simply dissolved into banal hedonism. We had to decide if banal hedonism was okay, or if there was more here that we wanted. As for me, I had begun to realize perhaps I wanted more, and I was beginning to see with whom I wanted it.

During this time we were also involved in a full-scale preparation for the new journey Rufus had cast us into. We began to work on visas, and Eddie had to update his passport. (Most of his overseas flying, when entering foreign countries, had been done at sea level and hadn't required any identification.) Eddie's Grumman Goose needed a little work on one of its engines and a mechanic's look at all the landing gear hydraulics. There was also a goodly amount of equipment and supplies to be purchased. Most importantly, Will and I needed to do some research on where we were going — everything from local towns and available landing strips in the area, to a history of the ancient ruins of Puma Punku and the terrain challenges we could expect. The language wouldn't be too much of a problem. All of us spoke Spanish fairly well and we could struggle through the dialects.

The following day my partner and I decided to head down to Key West and visit the library to do a little research on the Spanish conquest of Peru and Bolivia, and a commander named Hernando de Amargo.

We arrived at the library a little before noon. As we walked toward the entrance I saw Umbrella Man sitting on the bench out front, his tiny Chihuahua curled up on top of all his worldly belongings in the fellow's perennial shopping basket. He was reading the comics in *The Citizen*, and chuckling quietly to himself, his enduring umbrella resting over his shoulder. Once an important man in Key West, he was now reduced to handouts, and reading yesterday's wrinkled news.

"Fate is a fickle mistress," muttered Will, shaking his head.

The lady librarian, mid-fifties, thin as a street waif with mournful brown eyes and short, heron-gray hair listened patiently as we explained what we were looking for. "It's not a category in which I'm well-versed," she said quietly. "But you're in luck. There's a gentleman here today who is fond of Spanish Main history."

He was sitting in the back of the library at a small table — an aging gentleman dressed in faded blue jeans and an equally weary tropical shirt. He possessed a balding crown with strands of gray hair sparsely embedded around it, stubbornly defending their tenuous hold, and he had a slightly disappointed mouth, but his sparkling blue eyes belied his age and offered intelligence and humor. Will and I introduced ourselves, and he, in turn — John Potter, formally of the Institute of Historical Studies at the University of West Florida, now entrepreneur of beachcombing and connoisseur of Red Stripe beer introduced himself. He had lots of time, and spent much of it at the above endeavors, as well as researching Spanish and Incan history at various libraries. We had indeed been lucky. We had found a proverbial needle of knowledge in a haystack of historical indifference.

Will broached the subject of the Spanish conquest of the Incas, and in particular an officer named Hernando de Amargo. Our new acquaintance mulled the name for a moment, rolling it over in his mind, then excused himself. He returned with a large, ancient-looking book and began to comb through it while emitting a series of inquisitive sounds, from "hmmms" and soft teeth clicking to pronounced "aahhs." After a few minutes, he issued a definitive "aahh-ha!" He looked up at us, decidedly pleased with himself.

"Your Captain Hernando de Amargo did most definitely exist, and as you mentioned, was indeed a part of the conquest of the Incan city of Cajamarca. He continued serving with Pizarro's army through to the early part of 1533, where records show he was killed in a skirmish near the province of Tiahuanaco."

Will and I looked at each other. Will's eyebrows bounced like Groucho Marx's. Far be it from us to wish someone an early death for our gain, but this was huge news. It meant that Amargo never made it back to Spain, and his brother never got the information about the ancient scepter.

I decided to push our luck. "How much do you know about early Bolivia and Peru — like, say, pre-Spanish Bolivia?"

He paused for a moment, appraising us, eyes twinkling with curiosity and a strange sense of insight. "How far back do you want to go?"

Will picked up the conversation. "Well, ironically enough, we're interested in the settlement you mentioned earlier, called Tiahuanaco — the pre-Incan part of it. There's supposed to be some really old ruins in that area. Lots of massive stone blocks that lock together tightly. A very old, amazing site."

The twinkle in his eyes gave way to incredulity. "You're the ones," he whispered quietly, obviously amazed.

My buddy pulled back a little, a questioning look furrowing his brow. "What do you mean, 'the ones'?"

The guy shook his head as if still trying to get a grip on this whole thing. "A few days ago I'm in the restroom, here in the library, at a urinal. This guy comes up, large Jamaican fellow, dreadlocks to his shoulders, chocolate eyes, big toothy smile, and starts using the one next to me. Out of the blue he says, 'You know, mon, life is like great cosmic pinball machine. Some of us levers, some of us little balls, bouncing around, being pushed in different directions. But sometimes da gods, who play da game, dey get bored and make a coincidence. Da gods have a fine sense of humor and irony — deese be some of dere favorite things.'

"Now, I'm trying to mind my own business, get the lizard put away and get the hell out of there, but as I turn to leave the guy says, 'You have two tiny pinballs headed your way — little Hobbits on quest. Be da lever, mon. Become da virtuous mango and feed dem with knowledge.'"

"Son of a bitch!" I whispered. "Rufus! That was Rufus!"

Will nodded adamantly. "Sure as hot fire and wet rain."

John, our historian, stared at us for a moment, still having a tough time grasping what was taking place. (Rufus had that effect on just about everyone.) "I don't know what his name was, but I'm bettin' sure as hell you're the two 'tiny balls' I'm supposed to help." He sighed, not in an unpleasant fashion. "Okay, I've always liked scavenger hunts, so what do you want to know?"

I exhaled softly. "We need to know about the old ruins there. They're called — "

"Puma Punku," he said before I could finish. "You know how many people in this town could actually tell you about Puma Punku? Or even pronounce it correctly?"

I shrugged.

"One," he said. "Me." He grinned broadly, slightly yellowing teeth exposed almost skeletally in his wide mouth. "Now how's that for a bloody coincidence?"

Our new friend scooted his seat in closer to the table, almost confidentially, and instinctively we did the same.

Then he began. "It just so happens that Puma Punku has been one of my hobbies for a long time. Years ago, as a young man, I had the occasion to visit it and the place left an indelible mark on me. There's a feeling — like other-worldly, man. It's like seeing the Great Pyramid for the first time. You just know there's something there — more than meets the eye. We like to think we're the best thing since cream cheese, that there's never been anything before us with the intelligence, or the technology, or the sheer drive to accomplish. But when you stand before the Great Pyramid and contemplate that engineering triumph, let alone all the undiscovered possibilities it holds, well, you just damned well know it wasn't made by a bunch of witless slaves gleefully rolling two-hundred-ton blocks along on friggin' palm tree trunks."

It was way more information than we wanted, but the guy was on a roll.

"You want to know something? The Egyptians were just huge on recording things. They recorded every ruler they had, every wife and every child he had, all their pets, and every time each one of 'em took a crap. They recorded all their harvests, plagues, victories, conquests, defeats, and celestial movements, and described every tool and every weapon they ever made. But you know what? There are no recordings anywhere of how the Great Pyramid was built. Oh yeah, later on they recorded information on smaller imitations, but the big one was the real thing, and it was made by people whose expertise and technology would make most of what we do today look like dirt daubers building mud nests under the eaves of your house. That's exactly the same way Puma Punku makes you feel. You just know that there are all kinds of things we haven't begun to figure out."

He took a breath and exhaled slowly, cooling himself.

"Okay, you wanna know about it, so here goes. It lies in Bolivia, midway down the western border, about fifteen miles from Lake Titicaca. It's off the beaten path, but there are some roads to the area. There's a great deal of speculation as to its date of origination, but the argument runs back as far as 12,000 BC. Evidence suggests that there may have been two cultures at Puma Punku — one, an antediluvian civilization that actually built and occupied the city, perhaps like an outpost of some sort, then abandoned it; or maybe it was destroyed in a cataclysm, like the Great Flood, then possibly the

area was occupied by an indigenous, slowly recovering civilization."
He paused for a moment, his eyes scanning the area to see if anyone
was listening to our conversation, then resumed. "There is also
serious argument regarding the stone blocks that the city was built
from, and the indigenous population's ability to cut and transport
them. The terrace of Puma Punku is comprised of perfectly cut
sandstone blocks, some of the largest weighing over one hundred and
fifty tons. Based on chemical analyses of samples from the individual
stones and area quarry sites, archeologists have determined that these
blocks were cut and carried up a steep incline from a quarry almost
ten miles away." Again he paused and stared at us. "One hundred and
fifty-ton blocks moved ten miles, uphill. Good trick."

Fifteen minutes later we thanked John Potter for his time and
headed home, far more educated and certainly more convinced that
this wild goose chase may well have a goose in it. On the way home
we discussed our latest revelations. There was no question that Rufus
was right. We were locked into something extraordinary.

Will turned to me as I drove. "This whole thing is a lot like that
Coral Castle in South Miami."

I looked over questioningly.

"You know, the guy who built an entire castle out of megalithic
limestone blocks — Ed something, a Lithuanian dude. He quarried
the blocks, each between fifteen and thirty tons, and put them in
place by himself, mostly at night. There's a lot of speculation that he
had developed a form of electromagnetism. He claimed to have
figured out what the ancient Egyptians understood."

I scrunched my mouth in thought. "The way I figure it, that
makes a lot more sense than palm tree trunks and zillions of sweaty
slaves. I'm thinking some of the folks who came before us were a lot
smarter than we want to give them credit for being."

"Yeah, there are dozens of sites around this planet with
megalithic structures supposedly built by primitive peoples, all using
those same logs, many of them in places where there weren't any
trees. The problem is, we don't like the idea of not being unique —
too hard on our egos."

Regardless of our fascinating love lives, we realized that there
was another adventure calling us, and it was time to be underway, to
set out on the road to Mordor once again. We figured with Eddie's
extended-range tanks on the Goose, we could hopscotch from Key
West to Cancun, then down to San Jose, Costa Rica. From there it

was into Quito, Ecuador, for more fuel, then down into Lima, Peru, and finally, one last hop into La Paz, Bolivia, where we would either rent a vehicle to take us the final leg into the Tiwanaku/Puma Punku region or find a strip in the area for the plane. It was a three-day trip with an overnight in San Jose and La Paz.

We met with our two lovely ladies individually, and explained as much as we could, saying that we hoped to be back within a couple of weeks, and not to forget us. Neither was overjoyed with the revelation, but both of them found the concept of a device such as we described absolutely fascinating. In addition, they both understood that adventure was a part of our nature, and beyond their concern for us, they dealt with it relatively well.

So, early one misty, gray morning we piled aboard the Goose and buckled up. Captain Eddie slid the big, beautiful bird into the water and out into the center of Niles Channel. He snapped on the oversized speakers in the cockpit and instantly we were engulfed in the sonorous power of Styx and "Come Sail Away." Eddie got that trademark psychedelic gleam in his eye, lit a joint, and whispered, "Let's boogie, dudes. Adventure calls!" He pushed the throttles forward and the belly of his airplane slapped across the calm waters, the huge, air-cooled, nine-cylinder Pratt & Whitney engines from atop each wing whining like hunting dogs begging for release. A new sun eased through a stratum of soft, pink-laced clouds on the horizon, igniting them with purple and gold, and kindling the somber, early morning heavens as our plump, magnificent bird broke its bonds with Earth and soared into the sky.

A gathering of angels
appeared above my head.
They sang to me this song of hope,
and this is what they said,
They said come sail away, come sail away, come sail away with
me lads,
Come sail away, come sail away, come sail away with me ...

Remember what Bilbo Baggins used to say: It's a dangerous business, Frodo. You step out onto the road, and if you don't keep your feet, there's no knowing where you might be swept off to.
— J.R.R. Tolkien

CHAPTER ELEVEN

Leo Lickker was having a bad day. Actually, he'd been having several bad days, and the forecast was partly cloudy with more of the same. He and his lady, Lucinda Aquiar, had found themselves afoul of the law, and it looked like a change of residence was in order. It wasn't anything new to Leo; seemed most of his life he'd been afoul of something.

Leo Lickker, aka Richard Lickker, wasn't a bad-looking guy, with curly black hair; dark, slightly mischievous eyes; and an acceptable smile. But at five feet one inch, he had always struggled for respect. On top of that, he had simply started out in life on the wrong foot. His parents were either abysmally naïve or possessed of a wicked-evil sense of humor. By junior high school his first name had been abridged to Dick. You know you surely have one foot firmly embedded in social hell when your name is Dick Lickker. By the time he reached high school, his stutter had commenced. By graduation, poor old Dick could barely get out a sentence without a significant stu-stu-stutter. So, what had started out as a normal, albeit somewhat reserved child, became an angry young man with a chip on his shoulder and a disregard for the conventions of society. If he'd been a little brighter he would have made a good politician.

His father was Cuban and his mother was the daughter of low-level Italian mafia, which left him with a unique Havana/Bronx vernacular and a penchant toward crime. As soon as he got past high school he became a runner for a bookie — it didn't require much conversation. Gradually, he advanced to a "collections agent," but he wasn't always successful at that because Dick just wasn't very fearsome-looking, and it did require some conversation. It's hard to take someone serious when they're verbally lurching through what's supposed to be threatening dialogue. The moment Dick turned eighteen he had his name legally changed to Leonard Lickker. He liked the name Leo. It sounded tough. Leo did manage to get his own apartment, which should have made life more interesting, but he wasn't doing well with the women, so he decided to attend a seminar for "Individuals With Social Challenges" — guaranteed to boost your confidence. It was there that Leo met Lucinda.

Lucinda Aquiar was tall and thin as a stork, with long dark hair, and sloping, but definitively upturned breasts. Her skin was a soft, reddish cocoa, the result of a Mariel Cuban father and a Brazilian mother. Her eyes were cold turquoise, stunning without question, but they never seemed to light, regardless of the situation. She had a wide nose and a full mouth. She was one part startling, one part intriguing, and two parts purely dangerous. Like a lioness with a wound, she was never quite comfortable or totally reachable, and although Leo was immensely attracted to her, he was hardly ever certain how she would react to a given situation.

The one aspect of Lucinda Aquiar that thoroughly cemented her relationship with Leo was that she was a mute. She couldn't speak a single word, but was adept at sign language, and could read and write. When they made love, however, the smallest of sounds escaped her throat, like the mewing of a tiny kitten, and she signed furiously, thrashing the air above his back, screaming sultry, passionate, profane words with her hands.

There was one other aspect of Lucinda that left Leo more than a little uncomfortable. She had a pet — a Brazilian Wandering Spider, considered to be the most venomous spider in the world — which she kept in a small wicker basket. She called it Bobo. The spider was capable of killing with one bite, but Wandering Spiders were often known for a quick strike that would release a lesser amount of venom, often causing a death-like coma lasting as long as a week if the victim survived. Leo understood intrinsically it was a weapon she had used before to protect herself, maybe out of vindictiveness or anger, or both. Although this part of her frightened the crap out of him, their strange bond and passionate lovemaking drew him like the sun to the horizon. They were an odd couple, the small, pale Cuban and the tall Brazilian temptress, but they were a couple nonetheless. Leo, of course, spoke Spanish and English, and Lucinda understood both. Lucinda taught Leo sign language so she could communicate with him.

The only real problem (beyond a freaking spider whose bite could kill you in less than two minutes) was they just weren't making enough money. They fell in with a crowd that had taken up the enterprise of stealing yachts — boarding them at sea, throwing the occupants into the water (generally with life rafts), then hooking up with some of their compatriots from Cuba in the straits just off Key West. Their friends would take the yachts into select harbors along the Cuban coast, make some superficial changes, create acceptable registrations, and sell them along the eastern coast of Central

America.

Leo and Lucinda participated in a couple of heists at sea, but once again Leo's stuttering became an issue, which was exacerbated when he got nervous. The scene might go something like this...

"Pu...pu...pu...chu...chur hands up! Dis es una hi...hijakin'!" Boat owner, with a smile, hands on his hips: "Wilson put you up to this, didn't he? That guy, he's too much! 'Pu...pu...pu...chur hands up!' I love it! I love it!"

Leo, shaking his pistol at the guy: "Don' you mess wi...wi...with me, assahole! I ch-choot chur nuts off an' dance on 'em!"

Boat owner: "Fabulous! Fabulous! You're an actor, aren't you? Damn, you're great! I bet you work at Wilson's dinner theater, right?"

Leo's eyes blink a couple of times in disbelief and the gun lowers a little. "Unabefreakin'alievible," he mutters incredulously, not exactly sure what's going on.

"Okay, tough guy, give me the best you got!" snarls the boat owner, getting into this, enjoying himself. "You don't scare me."

That was it for Leo. Anger was cleanly edging out incredulousness. No freakin' body talked to Leo Lickker like that. His hands and gun come up, waving around in flagrant disregard for the direction of the muzzle. Leo's feet begin a frustrated little dance. The people with him are backing up as he focuses on the boat owner, puffing up like a little Cuban toad, eyes wide with indignation. "Chu wan' sona' me, assa...assahole? 'Cause you gwenna get son', and ch...chu not gwenna like it!"

The boat owner, undaunted by Leo's display, is shaking his head in admiration and smiling again. "Absolutely amazing! I love the accent!" He takes a couple steps closer and gestures with his hands. "Can you do it with like, an Al Pacino voice — you know, in *Scarface* where he's snorting all that cocaine and shooting people with the machine guns? Go ahead, do it again, from the top, but try it without the stutter. It takes away from the realism."

Bam! Bam! The pistol's report gets everyone's attention, particularly the boat owner, who now has a hole in the top of one of his fifty-dollar boat shoes.

"Es dat real enough, assa...assahole? Unabefreakin'alievable! Al fr...freakin' Pacino! Sonabitchin' gringo *tourista!*"

Unfortunately, Leo had just started getting a little better at his job

— less stuttering, less shooting — when the FBI busted one of the runs being made by another part of the organization. Word was, the boys were naming names. The Feds had already hit two houses and arrested several gang members. Leo figured it was time to get out of town — *mierda*, out of the country! Maybe Central or South America for a while, until it cooled down — just like those crazy gringos, Butcha Cassidy and Sunadanca Kid.

You got to know when to hold them, know when to fold them, know when to walk away, and know when to run...

— Kenny Rogers

CHAPTER TWELVE

The first half of our trip went smoothly, from Key West across to the coast of Mexico then down into Central America. We reached the eastern shores of Costa Rica well before dark. The sun was still two fingers above the horizon as the lush tropical mountains rolled up at us. Then the cloud cover peeled away, revealing the capital city of San Jose, nestled on a high plateau in the Cordillera Mountain Range. After clearing customs, we got a motel near the airport, grabbed some dinner, a few hours' sleep, and were back in the air just after sunrise.

By the end of that day we had sailed over Panama, Colombia, Peru, and climbed into the high altitudes of Bolivia. Finally, by late afternoon Eddie was making a final approach into the airport near La Paz, the sprawling shantytowns of El Alto spreading out around the steep terrain below. Eddie handled the approach and landing in a remarkably professional fashion and we were directed to the area for noncommercial flights. With visas and passports in order, customs was relatively simple, and an hour later we were in a motel a couple of miles from the airport. Will and I got a room with two double beds, and Eddie got a single room next to us with a connecting door. The first thing we all noticed was the altitude change. At over ten thousand feet above sea level, breathing becomes a matter of acclimation. Nonetheless, we were in high spirits. We were on our way into a new adventure — another pot of gold at the end of another rainbow.

Throughout the night and the next morning we all found that breathing was still a problem, so we decided to stay outside La Paz for another day to give us a chance to acclimate. We had chosen a nice, two-level motel just on the outskirts of town — nothing fancy, but it had its own restaurant and it catered to Europeans and Americans. At breakfast I asked the concierge if there was someone in the area who could serve as a driver for us and provide some firsthand information on Tiwanaku and Puma Punku.

The fellow looked over at the lounge, then the lobby. Finally, he glanced back at the lounge and returned to us. He sighed with what seemed like a touch of disdain. *"Si, señor,"* he said. "There is one." He tilted his head toward a fellow sitting at the bar, sipping a cocktail at 9:00 a.m. "Caesar can help you, if you can catch him between drinks and chasing women."

"Sounds like my kind of guy," Will whispered behind me.

Caesar was a little overweight, but he wasn't a bad-looking guy. He had dark hair, a little long, falling over his ears, clever brown eyes, and wide lips that looked almost feminine. He was dressed in a Latin guayabera shirt and a pair of blue jeans. As we approached him, those brown eyes and the wide smile told me he was a bit of a hustler, as well.

We introduced ourselves and I told him we were looking for a little information on some places and things, and maybe a driver who knew his way around. His eyes gleamed with a sly understanding. "No problen' *amigo*, no problen'. Caesar know everything in this blinkin' town. He know the clubs, the women, the best deals on anything." He looked us over a little, gauging us. "Maybe you wan' son' of de ..." and he touched his forefinger to his nose, "de Bolivian special, huh? Or maybe son' special smoke?"

I shook my head, although I did see Eddie perk up when he mentioned the special smoke. "No, man, not our thing," I said. "We need some information, maybe a driver for a couple of days. How much do you know about Tiwanaku and Puma Punku?" I could see his countenance glaze over with that "just another *tourista*" look. But he quickly perked up. A gig was a gig.

"Sure, man, I thinks I know every damn hill in that place, know all the histories better than *los profesores.* Caesar know every rock, every lizard and every hawk for a hundred miles." He got that sly look again and edged a little closer, nodding his head as he spoke. "Caesar know de back roads, secret places — de places *touristas* no go. You want to see de secret *brujas* ceremonies? Wild naked dancers? Drink magic elixirs — make your *jumbas* like baseball bats, have many fun, good times? Huh? Huh?"

Will and Eddie were chuckling behind me. Will was muttering that this guy could be Cat Island Fabio's older brother. "We're interested in the ruins. In particular, Puma Punku," I emphasized.

Caesar cooled his jets a little and got into the theme, realizing this wasn't going to be an *Americano* "Girls Gone Wild, toot your brains out" gig. "Sure, man. Okey-dokey, man. I be cool with it. I thinks Caesar know all about Puma Punku. Caesar's great-great-great-grandpapa live in Puma Punku. Help make stones." (Which, of course, was absolutely preposterous, considering we were talking maybe ten thousand years ago, but our boy was on a roll.) Caesar threw his hands up theatrically, eyes growing dramatically large. "I thinks he was sacrificed to Sun God! Not making stones fast enough! Doin' de *nuka nuka* with celestial virgins!"

I don't know why, but we decided to hire him — maybe just for the entertainment value. I told Caesar to meet us out front in half an hour. The plan was simple: we would take a trip to Puma Punku by car, which we understood to be about an hour and a half ride. We would spend the day there and get a firsthand look, determine if there was a landing strip close by, what the roads were like, and see if we could find the "huge granite cliff" about a mile and a half from the ruins, where an incredible anti-gravity device was supposed to be buried.

Caesar was waiting patiently for us, his 1969 Chevy Bel Air parked off to the side of the entrance. Once we got our gear into the car, I realized that I had to pee. I told Caesar and Eddie to wait a moment. Will, who had a nervous bladder by nature, said he'd better second that emotion. We hit the restroom in the lobby. There was no one but us — I glanced under all the stalls quickly just to be sure.

"Damn, it's starting to get exciting again, buddy," I said, up against the urinal. "We're on our way after another treasure, one that's been buried over four hundred years, and dates back God knows how far."

Will nodded. "I'm so excited I can barely pee. Gold always does that to me. Imagine finding this damned artifact. It's not just the gold, really, it's the intrinsic value of what this thing is capable of doing. It's damned near priceless."

I couldn't help but grin eagerly while I zipped up. "Let's go, partner. Destiny awaits!"

As we closed the door and headed out to our destiny, the bathroom was quiet for a moment, then a stall door at the far corner opened slowly, and out stepped little Leo Lickker, fresh in from Miami. He had been perched on top of the commode like a chubby toad, doing a couple quick hits of cocaine — just to get his day rolling. He was smiling.

We had barely cleared the parking lot when a second car pulled away from the motel. There were two passengers — Leo at the wheel and tall, bronze Lucinda next to him, smoking one of her unfiltered cigarettes.

Caesar proved to be a pretty reliable guide. He knew the roads and was able to show us a rough but passable airstrip only a couple of miles from the ruins of Puma Punku. The strip had evidently been used by a silver-mining operation a decade earlier.

Finally, we came into the ruins of Tiwanaku, near the southeastern shore of Lake Titicaca. Tiwanaku, precursor to the Incan culture, once capital of the major power in the region for over five hundred years, was filled with temples and small pyramids somehow built with massive, solid blocks of stone not indigenous to the stark, flat plateau. Wispy gray clouds cached the sun, a somber wind whistled through huge, square portals, and dust devils swirled anxiously in the timeworn alleyways, calling their ancient brethren in brittle whispers. It was a startling experience, but the next stop, Puma Punku, was simply beyond belief.

Called "Door of the Panther" by the Andean peoples, it was thought to be, in Incan traditions, the site where the world was created — intricate, magnificent architectural designs of monolithic stones in unimaginable weights — a monument to man's ingenuity that left the senses stunned and the ego humbled, and unequivocally reminded us we were but a small epoch in the history of this planet. It was just as John, our historian buddy in Key West, had said. "…you just damned well know that it wasn't made by a bunch of witless slaves gleefully rolling two-hundred-ton blocks along on friggin' palm tree trunks."

It was mid-afternoon by the time we headed north out of Puma Punku on an old dirt road, aiming for the granite cliffs that conquistador Hernando de Amargo had mentioned in his letter. True to his writings, there were cliffs rising up in the distance. Traveling toward them over the dry, hard terrain littered with rocks and scrub brush, we knew without a doubt this was the right place. We were still a quarter of a mile away when I spotted the v-shaped rift cutting through the granite face from top to bottom.

Leo and Lucinda watched from their vehicle on the high ground at Puma Punku as the car they were following moved toward the cliffs in the distance. Leo followed the dust trail with his binoculars, seeing it stop at the base of the steep mountain. He nodded to Lucinda and they drove onward slowly. Stopping behind a small bluff perhaps three hundred yards from the other vehicle, they both got out, taking a position where they could watch without being seen.

At the base of the rift I turned to our driver. "Okay, Caesar, this is what I want you to do. Go back to the Puma Punku ruins and wait there for an hour. Then come back and pick us up. Can you do that?"

Caesar sensed something was up. "Chur, no problen', man." He got that sly smile and his eyebrows danced up and down. "Chu got special meeting, huh? Way out here in no place land? Chur, man,

Caesar don' hear nothin', don' see nothin'. Ees totally blinkin' okey-dokey with me."

We got out with our canvas duffel bag, which contained a couple of folding shovels and a metal detector.

Caesar glanced at the bag. "See chu in a hour, you tricky *Americanos*," he said with a grin. "No, man, we don' want no smoke, no blinkin' blow," he added sarcastically. "We just *touristas* who want to see ruins. Right, *muchachos?*"

As soon as he was out of sight we began to search the walls on both sides of the rift for the small cleft that held a cave. A good deal of shrubbery and small trees grew against the walls where there was shade, but it wasn't long before Will called out, waving to Eddie and me.

There it was, a small fissure in the granite, barely wide enough for a person to get through sideways, well hidden by heavy growth. In seconds we were inside, our flashlights glowing on the rough rock walls of a small cave. There was a fetid smell of animal feces, and the air was dry and cold. Small animal bones littered the floor. I pulled out the metal detector and, after a quick ground balance and squelch adjustment, began sweeping the floor. The first minute or two yielded nothing, not a single ping. I paused to make a slight depth adjustment, mumbling something about this being a long way to come on a wild goose chase, but as I brought the head of the detector around, the machine pinged softly. We all held our breath. I brought the head back in a wider arc and the machine chimed loudly. Another couple of sweeps and I had a target pinpointed. Initial indications on the readout showed the possibility of non-ferrous metal at approximately a foot deep.

Eddie, shovel in hand, looked at Will. "Well, don't just stand there like a stoner at Woodstock, man. Let's dig that sucker up!"

In moments we were on our knees, digging furiously, widening out the hole as we went. At about fourteen inches, Will's shovel hit something with a muted clang. He looked up at me.

"Could that be fortune calling?"

I grinned. "Slowly now, easy. Let's not break anything."

Gradually, under the glow of my flashlight and the careful work of my friends, a narrow outline appeared. It was once a heavy, furred skin of some sort, but it had deteriorated into a papery thin, practically translucent membrane that shredded as we touched it. Underneath, something shone at us through the dirt — that obdurate, persevering, unshakeable gleam of gold.

Slowly, with their hands, Will and Eddie pushed the dirt away and gradually a form took shape — the lustrous gold shaft; a cold, glistening crystal at one end, and a polished clear globe at the other. Gently, as if it were his own child directly from its mother's womb, Will brought the scepter up from the soil where it had lain, last touched by a conquistador four hundred years ago. He pulled away the last shreds of hide that covered the device and held it up. A trellis of sunlight breached the crack in the wall, brushing our scepter, and the clear globe suddenly flickered, then glistened. A second later there was the softest hum, like a refrigerator cycling on, and the wand began to vibrate ever so slightly.

We stood there, awestruck.

"It's true," whispered Eddie reverently. "It's true. Wicked to the bone, dudes. To the bone!"

"Mucking fagnificent," muttered Will, still staring at it, eyes misted with incredulity.

I gently took the scepter from my friend's hands, surprised at how light it was, and turned toward the cleft in the wall. "C'mon, my little Hobbits. Let's take it for a test ride."

"Ya, mon," they said in harmony. "Ya, mon!"

When we got outside, the sun hit our wand. The globe at the rear began to glow and the vibration increased. My finger found a small protuberance in the grip. A boulder lay about fifty yards from us — maybe four feet tall and the same in width. I pointed the wand at it and pressed the button. There was a sudden, audible moan and a translucent, shimmering beam, wavering like a desert mirage, streamed out from the scepter and held the boulder. I looked over at Will and Eddie, whose lemur-like eyes filled with apprehension and excitement.

"Do it, dude," whispered Eddie. "Do it!"

"Oh, yeah," Will chimed. "Go for it!"

I raised my hand a few inches, but nothing happened. The beam rose where it was aimed, but the boulder didn't. "Hmmm," I muttered with a frown. I brought the beam down onto the boulder again and pressed the "trigger" again. This time when I raised the beam, the boulder simply broke loose from the ground with a shudder and rose effortlessly ten feet into the air. We all shuffled backwards in astonishment.

"Whoashit!" exclaimed Will as he sucked in a breath and uttered a second, bawdy expletive about sex and ducks.

I moved the wand to the right a few inches and the boulder sailed across the field fifty feet and stopped in midair. "You gotta press the button a second time for the beam to lock in on the target," I said with new understanding. I pressed the trigger again. The beam drew back into the device with a "whoosh" and the boulder thudded heavily to the ground.

"Righteously psychedelic! I mean, slammin' dude!" Eddie muttered. "Man, I'm telling you, this is like inventing the freakin' light bulb!"

Leo turned to Lucinda and she signed furiously, eyes wide with wonder.

"Yeah, chu ri…right, baby. We jus' won de lottery. We need to take dis li…li…little toy from dem, quick."

She signed again for a few moments.

Leo thought about it briefly and smiled. "Okay, okay, chu right. I like dat. Let Bobo help us out tonight."

Years ago Lucinda had explained to Leo that Bobo, her Brazilian Wandering Spider, was given to her by a shaman in Sao Paulo during a special ceremony that made Bobo her "spirit friend." She was given a reed whistle that emitted a sound almost out of the range of human hearing. She could turn Bobo loose to wreak his havoc in a confined area, and afterwards blow the whistle. The spider would return to her and/or the reed basket it stayed in.

Leo ran his hand over his stubbly goatee. "There's two of dem in that room."

Lucinda signed again, explaining that Bobo had killed twice for her before. He was drawn to body heat. They could slip Bobo into the room that night, let him do his thing, then leisurely search the room in the morning without having to fuss with live people.

There was no point in further tests. We had the real thing, and we could see the trail of dust coming our way from Caesar's car, so we put everything into the canvas bag and were waiting as our driver pulled up.

Caesar offered a knowing smile. "Did chu have a nice little walk in the desert, *amigos?"*

I nodded. "Yeah, yeah we did. Time to go now. But we need you to take Eddie to the airport tonight, okay?"

Our plan was to get Eddie's Goose to the little airstrip by Puma Punku the next morning. We'd meet him there and make a dash out of the country. Bolivia didn't have radar/flight observation facilities like the States, so it wasn't a big deal getting out. However, getting back home could be a little tricky.

Two hours later Eddie was on his way to the airport at La Paz and the sun was edging the horizon. The motel was unusually crowded with clusters of noisy, excited people. I asked the concierge what was happening and he explained that tomorrow was the Bolivian Independence Day Festival, a major celebration involving dances, bullfights, parades, fireworks, and many drunk people. We headed to our room, got cleaned up, and went to dinner. Eddie had promised to call us later that evening to confirm all was on target.

Leo and Lucinda strolled down the hallway to the room. Cradling her basket under an arm, Lucinda leaned against the wall and lit a cigarette, casually exhaling at the ceiling while Leo picked the lock. Once inside, Lucinda knelt and released Bobo from his basket, stroking his furry brown back briefly and whispering an incantation. In seconds the spider was gone, scuttling underneath one of the beds. They closed the door and smiled at each other. Lucinda bent and kissed Leo on his forehead. The couple walked away holding hands — the tall, bronze Brazilian and the crazy little Cuban.

After dinner we returned to our room. I had barely closed the door when I knew something just wasn't right. My first hint was the man with the pistol sitting on the bed by the sliding doors. "Son of a bitch," I whispered incredulously. "Stinger!"

Sure enough, it was our old nemesis, dressed in nice gray slacks, a pale blue Lacoste pullover and a light jacket, but a little worse for the wear since we'd seen him last. He had lost an ear — gone, looked like it might have been ripped off, leaving a trimmed stump. He also had a ragged scar over his left eyebrow. That eyelid was partly closed, the pale gray-blue eye drifting downward and to the side, as if it had found something curious in the corner of the room. It appeared he was missing a finger or two, as well. Although he was wearing his blond hair longer now to cover the missing ear, it looked like there were thin patches where it was just beginning to grow back.

"Well, well," he said, his Irish brogue a little thicker than I remembered. "What do we have here but the lads that left me in a cage with a horny bloody gorilla." He sighed — not necessarily angry, but not fondly reminiscent either. "There's parts of me that'll never be the same, but one of the things that kept me going, finding me way back from South America, was the thought of you two lads." He brought the silenced pistol up and the menace in his voice thickened. "What kept me going were the pleasant thoughts of our reunion, and here we are, lads. Together again." To emphasize the statement, his pistol spat and the lamp on the nightstand next to me exploded. "Come in and pull up a seat," he said, pointing to the chairs at the small table. "Now!"

We quickly obeyed. Stinger pushed himself up against the headboard of the bed, gun resting on his bent knees, still pointed at us.

"How'd you find us?" I asked. "How in God's name did you track us here?"

Stinger scrunched his mouth and smiled a little — not a happy smile.

"Coincidence. Luck, as much as anything. I don't know if you know it, but your pilot buddy, Edward, has a minor character flaw. A lack of discretion, you might say, when he gets one on. Mr. Edward Morehouse had gone into Key West a few days before your departure and gotten himself glazed. He got to telling a waitress he'd picked up about this 'far out gig' he was headed into, how he was going to Bolivia to find an ancient golden device — and probably a freaking treasure, as well — probably make the Tutankhamen find look like a box of bloody baseball cards."

He saw the look of dawning comprehension on our faces and grinned with satisfaction. "As fate would have it, I just happened to know that little lass meself. She picked up a little money visiting with me on a 'professional' basis occasionally. The lady offhandedly told me the story. She was a clever girl, she was. Even remembered the names of Edward's partners, and the name of the place — Puma Punku. It was easy from there. I just kept an eye on you two, and when you flew out, I figured you'd need a couple days to make the trip. I got a commercial flight and headed south. At about the appropriate time I just started watching the arrivals gate for noncommercial aircraft at La Paz Airport." He grinned again. "And there you were in all your eager glory."

"Son of a bitch!" Will hissed.

"Pretty amazing coincidence, I have to admit," Stinger said, taking a moment to look at his left hand, which was definitely missing a finger. "Maybe it's just something I deserved, or you deserved. But you know, you're lucky lads, because I'm going to give you an opportunity to redeem yourselves. I'm going to give you a chance to give me what you've found."

It was about then that I noticed a huge, furry spider working its way slowly up the bed cover. In a moment or two it had crawled onto the headboard and was creeping its way across the top of the board, edging toward Stinger. A brief glance at Will assured me that he saw it too. It was a small chance, but it was still a chance. We needed to keep Stinger occupied.

"Listen, sure, we'll make a deal with you," I began anxiously. "We'll give you what we've found. You're just not going to believe it. I'm talking gold, lots of it, and a device that's absolutely unbelievable."

Stinger straightened up at those words. "So, where is all this finery, lads? Like me mum always said, 'the proof is in the pudding.'"

By this time the spider had reached his shoulder and those long hairy legs lithely stepped across onto Stinger's jacket. We needed to keep him busy, so I picked up the pace.

"Stinger, you just can't imagine what we've found. It's something that's going to change the world — a device from an antediluvian civilization that has powers never seen before. We could share it. We could all be rich men!"

"Sure we could, lad, just you boys and me, as rich as Croesus," he said, but his eyes didn't agree with his mouth.

The spider was on his collar now, those clicking, venom-dripping mandibles only inches from Stinger's throat, the warmth of the man's skin piquing the arachnid's senses of aggression and hunger, just like a staked lamb to a tiger.

"Listen, man, all you have to do is let us go," I pleaded. "We don't want the gold — "

At that moment Bobo reared up on his hairy haunches and leapt, burying those hooked fangs in the side of Stinger's neck. The Irishman lurched at the pain and instinctively struck the spider away, but it was too late. "Holy bloody Jesus on skates!" he shrieked, jumping up on the bed and firing the pistol, its muted bullets chasing the spider across the bedcover as it scuttled to the floor and under a bed.

"Lord Almighty! The bloody bitch bit me!" our nemesis screamed, ripping open the collar of his shirt and placing his hand on the bite.

Will and I were frozen in our chairs, gripping the table with terror and fascination. There was no running. I had no idea what to do next.

"That's a Mongolian Red-eyed Tarantula!" Will yelled, blurting out the first thing that came to mind.

"A bloody what?" cried Stinger in terror.

"Get your head down, so the poison doesn't rush to your heart!" Will shouted. When our bitten buddy hesitated, Will cried out again. "Get your head down between your legs! It's your only chance!"

Now, neither Will nor I had any idea what had bitten him or how deadly it was. We were just trying to get out of this alive. I quickly followed my buddy's lead. Turning to Will, I cried, "You have the spider bite antidote in your flight bag, don't you?"...my eyes stressing that he follow my lead.

"Yes! Yes! It's in my bag!"

Stinger started to raise his head.

"Keep your head down!" I yelled. "It's your only chance! Only one in three survive the bite of a Red-eye!"

"Get the bloody antidote!" the Irishman bellowed, head between his legs. "Get the bloody antidote!"

I rose cautiously and moved toward the door, nodding at Will, motioning him to follow. "Quick, Will, show me where the bag is!" I rasped. "It's our only chance to save him! God! A Mongolian Red-eye, of all things!"

Stinger started to lift his head again.

"Keep your head down!" we both screamed, and he responded like a scolded puppy. We slid over to the closet, which was next to the room entrance, pulled it open so our wounded antagonist couldn't see us, then opened the door to the room and booked down the hallway like a couple of scalded ferrets. We hit the stairs at a run and didn't stop until we were in the lobby, which was unbelievably crowded because of the independence festival. There were people everywhere in costumes, drinking, laughing and generally having a good time. I looked over at my friend, catching my breath.

"That was pretty smucking fart, the Mongolian Red-eyed Tarantula thing."

He got that famous grin, "Yeah, it was, wasn't it? Just popped right out of my mouth."

We stayed outside in the shadows of the motel for about a half hour, watching for Stinger. When he didn't show, we finally worked up enough courage to go back to the room.

I slowly opened the door, an inch at a time, both of us listening intently, hearts hammering out an AC/DC bass drum beat. I had only managed a few inches when the "Mongolian Tarantula" came scurrying out the door and over the tops of our feet. With shrieks that would have shamed pubescent girls, we apparently grew wings, because the next thing I knew I was halfway down the hall and Will was right behind me. The spider had disappeared down the stairwell. Finally, we bucked up what was left of our courage and returned to the room. Once again I gradually opened the door. No sound from within. We edged around the opening, gently closed the closet, and stared, somewhere between horror and relief. Stinger lay on the bed, arms splayed out, eyes staring at the ceiling, not moving. I sidled over cautiously and stood by him for a moment. No change. I touched his cheek. Nothing, a little cool. Finally, I touched his eyeball with my finger, the sure test. No response.

"Good God, he's dead!" Will whispered. "We killed him!"

"We didn't kill him, a freaking, hairy-assed spider killed him."

"But —"

"Let me remind you, he was going to shoot us."

Will exhaled. "Yeah, you're right." My friend looked over at Stinger. "Man, that giant monkey did a job on him." Then he glanced around nervously. "Whatta we do now? We got a dead guy in our motel room. Do we just call the front desk and ask if there's an extra room service charge for taking out dead people?"

"Yeah, that does pose a problem," I said with a frown. "But we are blessed with a natural distraction — the festival. First off, we've got to get him out of our room. Here's what we need: a couple pieces of rope, your wide-brimmed baseball cap, my dark sunglasses, and a little luck."

A few minutes later we sat on the bed with Stinger between us. His right ankle had been tied to my left ankle, and his left to Will's right, enabling us to make him "walk" as we walked. The broad-billed hat was pulled down over his face and he had on my sunglasses. We stood up and pulled his arms over our shoulders in apparent camaraderie, and headed out the door — just three guys a little tipsy, celebrating Bolivian Independence. When the elevator door opened on the first floor, the lobby was packed with locals and tourists.

"Lord!" whispered Will. "What now?"

I glanced around. I hadn't expected it to be this crowded. "We need to rent a car for a few hours, take Stinger out for one last ride into the desert." I looked over at the lobby and saw an empty couch. "C'mon. I need to untie myself and see about a car."

We stepped and dragged Stinger over to the couch and sat down in unison. I discreetly untied my ankle and put Stinger's arm up on the back of the couch in casual repose. He slid down just enough to look quite comfortable. "You hang out with spider man. I'll be right back."

Will nodded. "Don't be long. My friend's just dead on his feet."

"Yeah, yeah, dead to the world, I'm sure."

Looking for a rental car took longer than I expected. Meanwhile, Will got an attack of nervous bladder, and decided to make a quick run to the restroom. He untied his ankle, reached over to the coffee table, pulled a half-smoked cigarette from the ashtray and stuck it between Stinger's lips. He patted our buddy's cheek. "Yeah, yeah, I know. You said you were going to quit. But one more won't kill you."

Stinger looked good — one arm casually thrown over the couch, apparently staring straight ahead, very cool. It looked like Lady Luck was shining on us.

Will got back just as I returned with bad news. There were no more cars for rent and there was no answer at the number Caesar had given us. Just then I saw a bus pull up out front — one of those big commuters that runs regularly into the city. I glanced over at my friend.

"C'mon. We're going to take a bus ride." We retied our ankle strings, pulled Stinger's arms over our shoulders and headed out to the bus.

"The *tres amigos* again," Will said with a smile.

I looked out at the people getting into the bus. "Not for long."

We were quickly surrounded by a babbling gaggle of excited, costumed, well-lit locals headed to the festival in the city. Getting Stinger up the steps of the bus was a bit of a trick, but everyone thought he was sloshed, just like them. They patted him on the back and laughed as we found three seats on one side of the aisle. Quickly untying our legs, we moved our recently departed nemesis over to a window seat and got him comfortable. Will bummed a cigarette from a guy across the aisle, took a puff, coughed, then put it between Stinger's lips, pulling his hat down and adjusting his glasses. He patted Stinger on the shoulder affectionately.

"Well, ol' buddy, it's been real and it's been fun, but it hasn't been real fun."

As the bus driver started the engine, we got up, walked down the aisle and stepped off the vehicle. A minute or so later I got a last look at Stinger, enjoying his cigarette with a woman sitting next to him, talking his ears off — or at least one of them. And that was that for our Irish adversary, riding off into the sunset in a blue and yellow Bolivian bus.

Clowns to the left of me, jokers to the right. Here I am, stuck in the middle with you.

— **Steelers Wheel**

CHAPTER THIRTEEN

We had just ordered our third round of drinks, celebrating survival, when I saw Caesar walk by the entrance, headed toward the lobby. I flagged him down and when he came over to the bar I told him we needed his services again tomorrow to get us back to the airstrip by Puma Punku.

"No problen', *amigo*," he said with an understanding grin. "I see chur two friends leave a while ago with chur bag, so I guess business is done, huh?"

My gut froze. I grabbed his arm. "What do you mean, you saw our friends with our bag?"

He pulled back. "Hey, chu know, de tall Brazil woman and de *pequeno* Latino. Dey have de canvas bag, man. I just think dey were friends — "

"Stay right here," I said. "Don't move. We'll be right back."

Before I could say another word Will was halfway out of the bar, headed for the elevator.

It was gone. Our room was trashed and the bag was gone.

"Who in the hell?" Will hissed angrily. "How in the hell? No one knew about this but us!"

"Forget that line of thought," I said. "Someone was onto us. We've got to get back downstairs. Find out what Caesar knows."

"Me *amigo*, Rodolfo, he say he take de man and de woman to Hotel Triaca, near de airport," Caesar explained. "It was about an hour ago. He say de man talk about leaving tomorrow morning for Costa Rica."

I looked at Will and he nodded, blue eyes glittering intently. "You bet, man. Let's go."

When we got to Hotel Triaca, Caesar spoke with the manager at the front desk and got their names — Leo and Lucinda, from Miami, Florida. That, and a twenty-dollar bill, told us the couple had booked a cab for the airport at nine o'clock the following morning.

I glanced around the lobby, then back at Will. "We're going to need a diversion here. You have any suggestions?"

Will thought about it for a moment, smoothing down his mustache in concentration. Then he smiled. I knew that smile.

"Okay. Nine chances out of ten the taxi's going to pick them up under the covered entranceway." He pinched his lips together with thumb and index finger, then pointed that forefinger at me. "I'm going to need some ketchup, some of those fizzy candies — Pop Rocks, yeah, I saw some in the lobby — and about two hundred Bolivian dollar bills in two unbound stacks. You're going to need your coat." He smiled again. "Like Rufus would say, we're going to become clever seagulls."

The next morning our two thieves walked out the front doors of the Triaca right on time. Leo, in a fruit-juicy shirt, white slacks, and tennis shoes, was carrying our bag; and Lucinda, in a slinky, red cotton tube dress, had a small wicker basket tucked under her arm. Just before they got into the back of the taxi, Will popped three of the fizzy Pop Rocks into his mouth. Once Leo and Lucinda were seated and the driver settled in behind the wheel, my partner squeezed three packets of ketchup into his mouth, as well. When the driver put his car in gear and it rolled forward, Will came stumbling out from the side of the building and careened into the front side of the moving vehicle. He bounced off the fender, hands flying up, and spilled to the ground with a blood-curdling shriek. As the driver slammed on his brakes, Will let the fizzy red ketchup mixture spill out of his mouth.

"Oh, sweet Jesus! My neck is broken! Snapped like a freakin' chicken!" he screamed, struggling to his knees and letting his head sag dramatically to one side of his chest, Pop Rocks and ketchup spewing everywhere, providing a convincing spectacle. Will knee-walked his way over to the front of the car and slammed the hood with his fists. "You done killed me! Took me in my prime!" Throwing up his arms dramatically and raising his face to the sky, he cried, "Oohhh, Mama, I'm-a-comin'! I'm-a-comin' to see you and Elvis!" He threw back his head (despite the broken neck) and howled, "I'm a-dying! Goin'… goin'…" And with a dramatic cry my buddy crumpled backwards, sprawling out on the pavement, staring up at the sky, arms spread out.

The terrified driver was out of the car immediately and coming around. Will peeked over at me and winked ever so slightly as I stood quietly to the side of the hotel entrance, then he went back to the performance. The fellow knelt and tentatively touched him. Nothing happened. The man touched him again, and suddenly my partner snapped up and bellowed, "I see the light!" The driver burbled a healthy shriek and tumbled backwards. "I see the light, a tunnel of light," Will re-emphasized loudly, looking upward with glazed eyes. "It's Jesus a-comin' for me! Jesus and a band of angels in a sixty-seven Mustang!" Then my wounded buddy collapsed again, performing a wonderful full-body death tremble — arms fluttering, legs shaking, heels banging on the pavement. This was just too much for Leo and Lucinda. They got out and rushed around the car, kneeling next to Will and the driver, hoping to quell all the attention that they didn't need.

I casually walked up to the car from the rear, opened the back door on the opposite side of the crowd that was gathering, unzipped the bag, and grabbed our golden scepter. As I was backing out of the cab, I noticed the wicker basket the woman had been carrying, and my curiosity got the better of me. I lifted the lid slightly. Two hairy spider legs clawed at the opening. Squealing like a pig, I slammed down the lid, and scrambled out the door backwards. But about then, Leo got uncomfortable about leaving his prize, and started to turn around. Will came to the rescue, reaching up, fiercely grabbing the Cuban by the lapels of his shirt and pulling him down. "Tell me your name, please. I don't wanna die without knowing who tried to save me!"

Leo, thoroughly shaken up by all this, stuttered, "Le...Leo Li... Li... Lickker."

Will fell out of character for a moment and grinned. "Leo Licker! Thank God your first name isn't Dick!"

Leo looked like he'd been slapped, then his eyes narrowed. "Ees a go...good thing chur dying, *amigo*," he hissed, pointing a finger at Will. "Ees a good thing."

By that time, I had stuffed the scepter inside my coat, strolled around the back of the car and melted into the crowd. I walked over to where my partner could see me and nodded imperceptibly.

At that moment Will stiffened like a stroke victim and shouted, pointing at the sky. "Wait! Wait! Holy freaking cupcakes! It's Jesus, with jumper cables and a twelve-volt battery! Ooohh, bring 'em on, Jesus. Slap me with them puppies! Jolt me with the holy juice!" Will rose to his knees, reached out and snapped the antenna off the car's hood, then held it over his head with both hands. "Throw the switch, Elvis! Gimme the juice!" He did another remarkable body tremble, shaking like a cocained epileptic, then collapsed, dead still. There was a shocked intake of breath from the people around him, then silence. One moment, then two, and finally the crowd released the breath it had held. He was gone.

Everyone had just started to relax when Will's eyes popped open and he snapped to a sitting position. Several people shrieked in fright.

He leapt to his feet with a flourish, wiped his mouth with the back of his hand and raised his eyes to the sky. "Lord Almighty, I'm healed!" he cried. "I'm saved like Moses from the stomach of the whale! It's a miracle! Like David of Nazareth parting the Red Sea! A freaking miracle!" He straightened up, reached into his pockets, and pulled out two huge wads of hundred-dollar bills. "Praise Jesus!" he screamed and threw the money into the air. "Praise Jesus!"

A collective gasp rose from the crowd. But as the bills floated down around the car, all reverence for the miracle they had just witnessed evaporated, and pandemonium ensued. While Leo and Lucinda struggled toward the car through the brawling congregation, Will eased himself out of the fracas and met me on the far side of the entrance. He swished the car antenna through the air a couple of times, like Zorro, then nonchalantly tossed it off to the side. "Nothing like a good miracle to get the juices flowing," he whispered as we walked away.

I nodded. "Praise Jesus!"

It wasn't until Leo got to the airport that he would have a chance to check the bag. But by that time Caesar had us halfway to the airstrip at Puma Punku.

A crisp, cool wind whisked across the flat plain of scrub brush, rocks, and reddish-brown dirt. The cloudless, blue-green sky stretched off into the horizon as far as you could see. Eddie and the Goose were waiting for us — Eddie sitting under a wing in one of his folding chairs, smoking a joint.

Our friend got up and walked over anxiously, getting the car door for us. "Wass up bros? Give Eddie the skinny. Do we still have the magic stick?"

I got out and combed back my long hair with my fingers. "Yeah, man. We're good, but it is time to go." I turned to Caesar and handed him four hundred dollars. "Thanks, buddy, appreciate all your help. We'll catch up with you next time we're in these parts."

Caesar counted the bills and grinned. "You betcha, *muchachos*. You be lot more blinkin' interesting gringos than the mostly ones I get."

Five minutes later we were buckled into our seats and on the threshold of the old gravel airstrip, Caesar just a curling line of dust in the distance. I was in the copilot's seat and Will in the first cabin seat behind us. Eddie was doing his cockpit preflight, checking magnetos, oil pressures, and sucking down the last of his joint.

Finally, our pilot nodded, satisfied, and slapped the switch to the cockpit speakers. He got that psychedelic gleam in his single eye, exhaled a last lungful of reefer, and pushed the throttles forward. Van Halen suddenly pounded the cockpit with "Runnin' With the Devil," loud enough to made us wince. As we lurched down the runway and lumbered into the thin air of the Bolivian mountains, Eddie yelled, "Get down, get right, and get tight brothas! We be on our way to another adventure!"

We had no idea...

Rather than "run the big pond" (the wide stretch of water from the South American coast to Jamaica and Cuba, and nothing to touch down upon if something goes wrong), we decided to go back the way we came, up through Central America. Going back from south to north on the big pond you saved some time, but you had to get clearance from the Cuban government to pass through their "corridor," which alerted all authorities of your presence. With our new "magic stick," we weren't ready to risk the plane being searched any more than necessary.

Our first day went fine, with the exception of a headwind. We refueled in Ecuador and made Panama City by nightfall. Again we spent the night at a motel by the airport and were back in the air just after sunrise. Our flight plan for the way back would take us across the western ends of Nicaragua and Honduras, then into Belize to refuel.

After we were in the air, I took the controls for Eddie and let him nap — he wasn't much of an early person. By eleven o'clock we were back on the road to Key West and he was feeling chipper. He took over and I settled into a seat in the cabin with Will. We talked a little about what we would do once we got home, then fell into an easy repose, listening to the steady, almost hypnotic drone of the big radials on either side of us.

After a few moments, Will spoke without looking at me. "So, what do you think about this situation with Carina and Vanny?"

I knew exactly what he meant and was grateful that he had broken the ice. "Well, I assume you're talking about this crazy merry-go-round we're into." I sighed, confused and a little uncomfortable. "I've gotta tell you, it's the strangest damned thing that's ever happened to me. I feel like a dog with a bone — don't know whether to eat it or bury it, but I sure as hell don't want to give it away." I looked at my friend. "You know what I mean?"

Will chuckled. "Yeah, Fido, I sure do. You know, it's like

they're both incredible girls. Each has her own unique qualities." He grinned lasciviously. "I gotta say it, I think Carina is part minx. I mean that girl can do things with her — "

"No, no, no, no!" I cried, holding up my hands. "I don't want to hear about it. I'm happy with what I know firsthand."

"And Vanny. God! Did you know that girl can — "

"Ya, ya, ya, ya, ya!" I yelled with my hands over my ears.

Will smiled again and sighed. "If I could roll them up into one girl I'd marry her tomorrow." Then he became more serious. "But you know, I've got to admit I'm getting a little edgy with this sharing thing. I wish I was just absolutely sure..."

"I think I'm getting closer on the decision thing," I said quietly.

Will turned toward me. "Really? You want to tell me? 'Cause I think maybe I am, too."

I shook my head. "Nah, not at this point. I've got to wait it out a little longer. Maybe just being away from them will help me with my decision."

Out of the blue, Eddie called to us from the cockpit. There was a look of concern on the face of our normally jovial friend.

I sat down in the copilot's seat. "What's up?"

Eddie was staring at the fuel gauges, tapping one every once in a while with his finger. "The starboard engine's been harshin' my mellow for the last half hour. I was gonna get that carburetor rebuilt. It was getting a little bogus every once in a while, but then the problem would go away. Started missing when we entered Nicaragua." He took a breath and adjusted the mixture controls. "Now the port's missing, as well. We may have picked up some bad fuel in Panama, maybe off just enough to bum out that carburetor." He looked out below the aircraft. "Hell of a place for a bum-up. Nothing but a hundred miles of freakin' jungle in any direction."

Will had already squatted next to us, and had heard what Eddie was saying. He'd gone pale at the thought. "Man, you don't really think the engine's gonna quit, do you?"

Eddie adjusted the pitch of the aircraft, then tapped the mixture controls again. "No way, man. That ain't gonna happen. Nobody has luck that bad."

Just then the exhaust on the starboard engine coughed out a rich burst of gray smoke and sputtered. Our pilot bounced the mixture forward and brought the nose down a little.

"But Eddie been known to be wrong."

Five seconds later the engine coughed again, spit out another belch of smoke, sputtered, and died.

"Ooohh, harsh bong, man. This is seriously bumming me out," Eddie whispered tensely as he drew back the power on the wounded engine and feathered the prop, then added power to his port engine while stomping on the rudder and working his trim to keep us as straight and level as possible. He glanced at me. "Get on the radio and try to get Managua, let them know we've got problems, while I try to keep us in the air. We're gonna have to head east for the coast so we can set her down, but that's the better part of seventy-five miles, at least."

Suddenly the port engine missed distinctly for a moment or two.

"Downer, man, serious downer," Eddie groaned. "Bad freakin' fuel for sure."

I tried to reach Managua radio without success (probably too far out with a mountain range between us). Eddie trimmed the Goose while working the mixture control and the rudder, trying to keep the old girl flying. But the good engine was getting less good all the time, missing and spitting and generally informing us that it probably wasn't going to take us where we wanted to go.

I could see a couple of large rivers below, flowing eastward toward the Caribbean. I tapped Eddie and pointed. "Worse comes to worst, we should be able to set down in one of those."

Eddie nodded. "Yeah, man. Good plan. But right now I'm gonna suck every bit of life out of this jive turkey I can. I swear on the virginity of my kid sister!"

"I've met your sister," Will yelled over the whine of the engine. "That ship has sailed!"

In the end, the old Goose gave us all she could, but with one engine gone and the other missing badly, we were steadily losing altitude. As we watched the terrain below grow thick and green with jungle, Eddie picked a straight stretch of muddy-brown river that looked just wide enough for the Goose's long wings. We were still three hundred feet above the water when the port engine gasped one last time and stopped dead. Eddie quickly feathered the prop, dropped twenty degrees of flaps and pulled back the stick as we swept down in a barely controlled crash. Wind whistled around the cockpit and an eerie silence engulfed the plane as the river rushed up at us.

In the back, Will muttered bitterly, "I'm never flying over any terrain ever again that doesn't clearly have a 7-Eleven in sight."

We smacked the surface hard, nose practically tunneling into the

turbid waters and snapping us against our seatbelts with the force of a
head-on. As soon as the forward motion stopped and we bobbed to
the surface, I checked on everyone. Eddie had a cut on his forehead
from the instrument panel and was a little dazed, but okay. I could
hear Will cussing about having changed his mind — he was never
flying anywhere ever again. When he got home, he was locking the
doors and having pizza and beer delivered for the rest of his freakin'
life. But he was already opening the hatch. The current started
carrying us lazily downriver, angling our aircraft toward shore. A
bend ahead would have us touching the dense shoreline.

We moved into the cabin and found the mooring line. I coiled it
up and threw it over my shoulder, then slipped out the hatch and
climbed up onto the wing. Within a few minutes our plane nudged
against the shore. I shuffled out on a wing and dropped down into
fairly shallow water, walking my line out and tying it to a large ficus
tree. The Goose swung around with the current and edged against the
bank. My friends jumped out of the hatch and onto the marshy soil at
the edge of the jungle.

An hour later we sat on a piece of high ground, pleased to be
alive, but pissed beyond belief that we were in a nearly uncharted,
mosquito-infested, snake and alligator-ridden, probably headhunter-
populated piece of absolute nowhere. Not a 7-Eleven in sight. To
make matters worse, our radio had taken a solid hit during the crash
landing and was performing somewhere on the level of a rock. We
were about two hours from sundown and already the jungle was
coming alive. Shadows were growing longer and the animal trails
darker. Broad leaves and twisted vines were beginning to blend into
each other. We could hear harsh squawks from parrots and the
screeches and hoots of monkeys in the treetops. Large gray and blue
herons stalked their prey along mangroves at the river's shoreline,
and above us, harpy eagles rose and dipped in lazy swirls. But it got
worse from there. Alligators grunted from thick reeds near the banks,
and occasionally we heard a distinct lumber and splash as one slid
into the water. Deeper into the jungle, a big cat, probably a jaguar or
a panther, coughed out a husky roar, and another answered in the
distance. Will leaned against a tree and reached for a vine to steady
himself, but the head of the vine opened its creamy white mouth and
hissed at him. Fantasy Island this was not.

Adventure... Yeah. I guess that's what they call it when somebody comes back alive.

— **Mercedes Lackey**

CHAPTER FOURTEEN

As the sun touched the river, burnishing it with a copper brilliance, we retreated into the plane. By the very grace of God, Will and Eddie had stocked up on supplies for the trip — lots of bottled water and a dozen sandwiches along with bags of chips, crackers, and candy. But even all their largesse wouldn't last the three of us very long in a steaming equatorial jungle.

That evening we were sitting in the cabin by the open hatch, gratefully accepting what little breeze there was and fending off the hoards of ravenous mosquitoes, when we heard the drums — a menacing, monotonous rhythm that floated on the air like the dark wings of a bat.

"Probably announcing our arrival," Will said. "Your order is ready — all white meat." As we chuckled darkly, he shouted into the night, "Don't bother with the tall one. Poorly shaped head, not suitable for mounting!"

"Nicaragua, of all places," I moaned to myself. "What a rotten choice for a crash landing."

Will looked over at me. "Yeah? How's that? Is there ever a good choice?"

I shook my head dejectedly. "The country's in a constant state of siege. The old President Somoza supporters are fighting the old Sandinistas, who are fighting the new, non-Sandinistas, who are dealing with Daniel Ortega and his communist buddies who want to turn Nicaragua into another Cuba, and all of these folks are fighting the Contras, and they are fed by the U.S. and the CIA. Their rule of thumb is to shoot strangers first and ask questions later. On top of that, there are smugglers and pirates all along the coastline, and an indigenous population of natives who have been beat to shit by everyone and have learned it's better to pop someone with a poisoned arrow and disappear into the jungle than deal with any of it."

Will blinked a couple of times in disbelief. "Thanks very much, Mister Wizard. My confidence has soared. Next time, save the guided tour. I felt much better in simple, frightened ignorance."

Between dreams of being a chicken chased by natives, and the splashes, shrieks, and hoots of the jungle river, I don't remember sleeping much that night. When the sun finally broke over the horizon, catching the river and turning its surface into rippling, iridescent scales, I was ready to get up. I wanted out of that place.

With the sun came the humidity — thick and hot as chicken broth. The air was filled with the musky scents of river mud and deteriorating flora, combined with the subtle aroma of wild orchids, alamanda, and passion flowers from the nearby jungle. It reminded me of the out islands in The Keys during early summer, and for a moment, like so many travelers who seek adventure in foreign places, a touch of nostalgia and longing washed over me like a warm, onshore swell, and I found myself just a little desirous of the safe haven I had left.

We ate a sandwich apiece and drank some water. Will and Eddie popped the cowling on the port engine to have a look at the carburetor. I did what I could with the radio, but the landing appeared to have damaged the housing and crushed a couple of transistors. Toward afternoon we had eaten another sandwich each and sucked down more of our precious water, but were no closer to getting out. I found a pole spear in the back of the plane with some of Eddie's personal belongings, and walked the shoreline for a half hour, managing to spear a couple of small fish. There were flippers and a mask in the plane, as well, but I wasn't hungry enough to brave those waters yet.

By the end of the day, the sun and its relentless heat had sucked away our energy and left us burned, beaten, and forlorn — and more than a little frightened. We talked about untying the plane and trying to drift toward the ocean, but it was doubtful that the river was wide enough to carry us very far. We had just eaten a meager meal of baked fish and another sandwich, and were settling in for the evening when we heard the drums again, but they were closer now.

I was sitting in the hatch when I noticed movement near the mouth of an animal trail less than fifty yards from the plane. As I stared, a face appeared in the shadows — small and brown with black and ochre slashes on the cheeks, and long, dark hair. Moments later, just a few yards away, another appeared, but this one stepped out from the foliage — a bantam, reddish-brown man in a loincloth, carrying a small bow and a sheath of arrows. His eyes carried no affection, no particular fear. He was in his environment; I was the interloper. He studied me for a moment, then disappeared, simply faded away as if a magician had waved a cape in front of him. A small chill ran down my spine as I thought about those indifferent eyes.

Just then Eddie yelled out, "Dudes, we got company! Restless natives."

A blood-red sun was slipping over the rim of the jungle, and as it did, our visitors were becoming bolder, showing themselves here and there, moving continuously closer. We retreated into the interior of the plane. Will stepped up to the hatch, holding his hands out wide like the Great White Father. "We come in peace," he cried. "We wish you no harm. Our great bird fall from sky with crippled wing." Locking his thumbs together and wiggling his fingers, he provided an imitation of a bird falling.

"Oh, Lord," Eddie muttered, rolling his eyes.

The natives continued to move closer. Will was running out of ideas. "We bring greetings from great Jesus God. Jesus loves you."

An arrow suddenly slapped the fuselage next to his head and he zipped back inside the plane quicker than a rabbit can blink.

"Tough crowd out there," he muttered, but the humor was dampened by the fear in his eyes.

Another arrow slapped the plane and a third found its way through the hatch, bouncing off an interior wall.

Eddie got the flare gun out of the emergency pack and loaded it, a fierce sense of desperation in his one, bright eye. I grabbed the pole spear. Another arrow slapped the plane.

"Now I know how they felt at the Alamo," Will gritted as he rummaged through a pile of junk in the back of the plane, coming up with a baseball bat. But as he stood up, we heard it — faint, well in the distance, but distinctly American. Somebody singing a Beatles song.

"He's a real nowhere man, sitting in his nowhere land, making all his nowhere plans for nobody..."

The voice was raspy, like someone dragging a file across glass, but it carried a deep timbre, as well — an old voice, one that had sung many a song, sad and light. Tonight it carried just a wisp of liquor in the notes, giving it a touch of melancholy.

"Doesn't have a point of view, knows not where he's going to, isn't he a bit like you and me..."

The natives, whom I could clearly see gathered in the shadows at the jungle's edge, suddenly began to fade like graveyard wraiths.

"I don't know who that is out there, but I'm gonna kiss him on the mouth when we meet," Will declared with great relief.

"Let's not go creating any bad impressions right off the bat," I said. "How about we just shake his hand to start with? If he winks at you, then you can kiss him."

I grabbed our only flashlight, then crawled out of the hatch and onto the wing. Swinging a beam of light across the darkening water, I shouted. "Hello out there! Hello!"

Out of the gathering mists came an old, badly weathered, low-draft steamer, maybe thirty feet in length, with a small cabin forward, and the boiler, stack, and engine aft. The paint was chipping and peeling. Wood rot had eaten away at her rails, and the anchor at her bow was rusted with age. My first thought was Humphrey Bogart's famous *African Queen*. From the helm in the wheelhouse, a figure leaned out a window and called back, echoing surprise, and caution. "Allo to you, stranger. *Que pasa?*" As the sound of the engine curled away to neutral, the figure stepped onto the deck and called again, a degree of disbelief in his raspy, deep voice. "Now what do you be doing here with a pretty floatin' plane like that?"

"Engine trouble brought us down," I yelled. "Sure could use some help."

The fellow nodded without a word, returned to his cabin, and moments later the boat edged toward shore.

"Wait! There are natives out there, and they're not friendly," yelled Will.

The guy leaned out the cabin window again. "Not to worry, *mon ami*. Not to worry. I have sort of an agreement with them."

His accent was a strange combination of French and Spanish with American colloquialisms thrown in, and I noticed, now that we were closer, that he carried a large iguana on his shoulder with an ease that represented a longtime relationship, and there was a bottle of tequila in his right hand.

"What the hell is this all about?" I muttered to myself.

As our new acquaintance moved toward the shore, he took up his singing again, another *Rubber Soul* Beatles tune — *"Michelle, ma belle, sont les mots qui vont très bien ensemble..."*

A few moments later he had nudged the bow of his boat onto the bank and a second, smaller man appeared, obviously a native indigenous to the region — thin and quiet, taking orders from the man without question. The native hopped ashore and tied off the boat while the owner crawled over the stern and into a twelve-foot skiff with a small outboard engine that they towed behind, firing it up and motoring over to us. We met him at the hatch, secured his skiff and pulled him and his bottle of tequila aboard. He was tall and fairly husky, with a full, sun-bleached beard, bright hazel eyes that were intense yet strangely unreadable, and he had a mouthful of big, slightly gapped teeth. His dark hair was long and thin and he covered it with a ragged old seaman's cap. He wore a weathered khaki shirt and a pair of beige denim pants, which had seen much better days. We introduced ourselves, settled into the four seats at the front of our aircraft, and soon fell into a conversation. In the process, our new acquaintance gave us a little history on himself.

His name was Jean-Paul Lavette. Originally from France, he had settled in Louisiana and had become a shrimper. He genuinely liked his captain and was greatly saddened when the man died suddenly, leaving him his boat. *"C'est la vie."* Jean-Paul sold the boat and decided to try gold nugget dredging in the Central American rivers, which his old boss had often told him about. That led him to Nicaragua and the purchase of his present craft about two years ago.

He smiled willingly and laughed in a jolly fashion, and our hopes of surviving this situation rose considerably. But, without question, he was an odd fellow — he pronounced each word too cleanly, his mouth molding each syllable and his eyebrows bouncing with each important part of the sentence, like Long John Silver in *Treasure Island*. The lizard on his shoulder enhanced the image. Every once in a while he would pull a piece of leafy vegetable from his breast pocket and hand it to the iguana. "There you are, my little lovely, there you are," he would whisper in an endearing fashion. When he caught me staring, he spoke offhandedly, "Isabelle and me, we been together for a long while. She's done better with me than me wife, she has."

"Are you still married?" I asked innocently, making conversation.

He frowned at the thought. "Sadly, no, *mon ami*, I am not. I really cared for that woman. Cherie was her name." He paused, looking out at the river from the copilot's seat. "But, in truth, she was a little too assertive. Did not listen well. She fell off the boat one night and an alligator got her." He offered a small shrug, eyebrows bouncing up and down. *"C'est la vie*, I guess." He took a swig from his bottle, then held it out to us. We politely refused.

Will changed the subject. "You showed up just in time. The natives were closing in, but they disappeared when you showed up. You must be the bad guy on this river."

"No, *mi amigo,* but there is a situation with the natives and me," Jean-Paul said with a chuckle. "They think I have magical powers — that I am crazy, and their shaman has granted me protection."

"Why, dude?" said Eddie "You got some heavy mojo or

something?"

Our new friend looked out at the jungle for a moment, then came back to us. "No, I do not, but there are two things that protect me. All crazy people in the *Miskitos* clan are sacred, and only the mentally touched sing. It so happens I sing all the time. But most importantly, when I first get here they attack me, and one of their very poisonous arrows struck me in the chest." He paused to let that sink in, then continued. "Fortunately, a miracle in itself, I had been reading a James A. Michener novel — very big book, five hundred pages." He held his hands out, palms upturned. "Three hundred of them descriptions of mountains and oceans being made." His eyebrows bounced again. "I had tucked it in my breast pocket. The little arrow struck the novel, but did not go through it. *Sacré bleu!* It was a miracle, in many ways. I stood there with the little poisoned arrow sticking out of my chest, and the *Miskitos* standing around me, waiting for me to crumple and die. But no," he said, finger wagging at us. "Jean-Paul does not die. He rips the arrow from his breast and throws it to the ground." He produced a reminiscent smile. "Now I think I am dead for sure — that they will shoot again a dozen times and I will be food for the alligators in minutes. So, in a last moment of defiance, I close my eyes and sing a Beatles song — 'Yellow Submarine'! We all live in a yellow submarine, a yellow submarine, a yellow submarine!" He paused again and slowly shook his big, shaggy head. "When I open my eyes, natives all gone. I am alone. Since that day they never bother me."

"Hell of a story," said Will. "And I thought I had a few interesting tales."

"And you've been living out here in the jungle, with just your little native buddy, all this time?" I asked.

The big man exhaled hard, as if I had struck a nerve. "No, *mi amigo*, I came here with a partner. I really liked that man, but he eventually contracted an incurable affliction, and he was suffering terribly with it, so I had to put him out of his misery."

Eddie pushed back in his chair, shocked. "Ooohh, man, that's a harsh bong. What did he have?"

I was thinking probably leprosy, or maybe malaria.

The Frenchman drew a breath and held it for a moment, then hissed it out through his teeth. "Greed."

"Greed?" we echoed.

"*Oui, mes amis*, greed. It's a terrible disease. We were dredging gold nuggets from the streams that feed the river. He was stealing my gold at night while I slept. He had found my cache, and was stealing from me, a few nuggets at a time. I hated to do it. I liked the man. But he insisted I punish him in some fashion, so I made him walk the plank. I forgot it was mating season for alligators. S*acré bleu,* they get so testy during that time. Besides, I caught him with my Isabelle twice, stroking and feeding her."

A graveyard silence filled the plane for a moment. There was no good way to respond to that.

Suddenly, Jean-Paul brightened. "*C'est la vie*" he said, stretching out his arms, palms up. "Sometimes that is life. The good and the bad, eh?" He looked around at us, smiling, as if the conversation had never happened. He took another belt of tequila. "So tell me, how do you come to this place, *amigos?*"

We all glanced at each other.

I responded. "We were coming back from Bolivia," I said. "Had some business down that way."

Jean-Paul's eyes narrowed in a cagey fashion and his mouth molded the syllables in an exaggerated manner, eyebrows dancing. "Aaaahh, perhaps moving duct-taped bundles from one place to another, *oui?*"

"No, no," Will replied hastily, not wanting to present the wrong image. "We're treasure hunters." As soon as the words were out of his mouth, he realized the mistake he'd made. "Well, I mean, we sometimes look for old things, not really treasure hunters exactly —"

"*Amigo*, it is not my business," Jean-Paul interrupted, holding up a hand. "What do I care what you do?" But there was a gleam in his eyes — faint, and flickering only for a second, like the fleeting green flash that appears on the horizon the very moment the sun is swallowed by the sea at the end of the day.

Changing the subject, I asked the question that was on all of our lips. "Jean-Paul, can you help us get out of here? Take us downriver to a settlement on the coast so we can hitch a ride home or find a mechanic and some good fuel? We'll make it well worth your while."

The big fellow mulled it over for a moment, then shrugged. "*Oui, oui,* I suppose I can, but it is a two-day trip to the coast, and even then it is a very small town, mostly run by smugglers who get shipments from Colombia and carry them into the southern U.S."

"I'll deal with the freakin' devil if he'll fix my plane," Eddie said adamantly.

"I would be careful about that, *amigo*," our new friend said. "If they know you have a seaplane back here, they will kill you and take your plane. If I was you, *ami*, I would be making other plans." I could see him weighing his thoughts for a moment. He took a piece of leafy vegetable from his pocket — looked like raw spinach — and fed it to the lizard, which slurped it down with a slow indifference. "Aaahh, there my lovely," he whispered, stroking the iguana's back, completely detached from us. Then he returned, and continued cautiously. "In Camerone, the small town on the coast, there is a petite runway where the smugglers keep their planes. Usually only one or two guards, high or drunk most of the time. You could maybe steal a plane." He cracked his neck by turning his head from side to side in a pensive manner. "I could take you there and watch your plane while you're gone," he said, smiling cleverly, and more certain of himself. "For a most insignificant price."

He had us, and he knew it.

"How insignificant?" I said.

He shrugged nonchalantly. "Perhaps twenty thousand American."

The air hissed out of us simultaneously, and Eddie answered for all. "You gotta be trippin', man. You're a few clowns short of a circus if you think we're paying that kind of bread! Even if we could!"

Jean-Paul did that half-shrug of his again and took another hit from his bottle. "Most of the details in the negotiations of life are not based on reason, but need, *amigo*. However, I am willing to entertain a counter offer."

At that, Eddie was halfway out of his chair. "How about you entertain this. How about you take that freakin' lizard and stick it —"

I leaned over and grabbed his arm, pulling him back down. "How about three thousand?"

"Ten," Jean-Paul replied.

"Five, and that's a lot of money for a two-day jaunt."

The big Frenchman thought about it for a moment and suddenly smiled broadly. "Very well, *mis amigos*. For five thousand American, and because I like you, I will gladly take you to Camerone and watch your plane while you are gone, but I would like a down payment of some sort, to secure our agreement."

We glanced at each other and I spoke for us. "We don't have much money with us. We could probably come up with a thousand."

Jean-Paul rubbed his beard in consideration. "That is not much. Maybe you have something you found recently, something old maybe, you could share with me?"

"We didn't find anything old this time." I said. "Maybe we could manage two thousand."

The Frenchman's eyes told me he wasn't convinced I was telling the truth, but he finally nodded. "Very well. Two thousand it is, with three more when you return." Once again the guileful countenance dropped away and he laughed heartily, holding his bottle high. "Besides, I need to go into Camerone for supplies. In the end we all win. That is good, no, *mes amis?*"

We agreed to shove off first thing in the morning. Jean-Paul would leave his native companion with the plane. We would need a little time to gather together our important equipment (including the bag with our ancient anti-gravity device), and to pull a few of the more expensive electronics from the Goose, just in case his little caretaker ran into trouble, or became trouble. Jean-Paul finally excused himself, saying he would dock at the shoreline, and that he looked forward to a safe and prosperous journey for us all. Then he laughed again and stumbled into his skiff, slipping off into the darkness, whispering drunkenly to the lizard and singing, *"She's got a ticket to ri-hide, she's got a ticket to ri-hi-hide. She's got a ticket to ride, and she don't care... My baby don't care, my baby don't ca-re..."*

As the last of the light faded in the interior of the aircraft, we sat down in our seats again and looked at each other.

"I gotta tell you, I don't know whether to feel good or thoroughly concerned about all this," I said with a sigh.

"After spending the last half hour with that guy, I couldn't agree more," said Will. "But it's not like we've got a lot of options."

Eddie rubbed his good eye with the back of his hand and leaned into us. "I'm gonna tell you right now, that dude is a funky bummer. You dig? He seriously harshes my mellow. I don't know if you dudes were paying close attention, but every person he's had any sort of relationship with has ended up dead one way or another. The owner of the boat he worked on suddenly died, leaving him the boat. Hmmm. His lady, who obviously got to annoying him, 'fell off the boat' and got ate by an alligator; and his partner, who may or may not have been stealing from him, got plugged and dumped in the river. The way I see it, the only things that are benefiting from his relationships are alligators. And that freaking, 'lovely' lizard licking his ear! Jeez! It gives me the willies!"

An hour after sunrise we were loading our gear onto the tramp steamer. The little cabin, not much more than a closet, was our captain's. We were left with the open deck on the forecastle, which was partially covered with a canvas sheet. Jean-Paul watched like a hawk as we loaded our few belongings and our electronics gear. His attention was particularly piqued when I started aboard with the canvas bag that held our ancient device. He came forward casually, reaching out. "Can I help you with that, Mr. Kansas?"

I pulled back in reflex, more than I meant to. "No, I'm fine, thank you. Just a few last incidentals from the plane."

He smiled, lowering his outstretched hand. "When you have stowed your 'incidentals' we will be ready to weigh anchor. The sun, she already longs for the pleasure of our bare skin."

We were used to the heat and glare of the sun off the water, but the equatorial humidity was something else — thick enough to ladle with a spoon. It was a continuous sauna that broke only slightly in the early morning hours. We'd been chugging along for about eight hours, and it was late afternoon when Jean-Paul called for a fuel stop, saying we needed more wood for the firebox, which heated the water in the boiler, producing steam that ran the engine. I was hesitant to leave the boat, but the Frenchman insisted we all pitch in so it could be done as quickly as possible.

"My reputation as a crazy person does not extend across the entire jungle of Nicaragua," he said with a grin as he leaned into the wheelhouse and pulled out an old, bolt action Remington 308 rifle. "And you are not known at all. There are *Miskitos* who would trade their favorite wife for your head!"

We entered the dense jungle, trying to stay within calling distance of each other, piling what dry wood we could carry into our arms and carrying loads back, but it took time. On the second trip we were well into the jungle, Will and I to one side of the trail, Eddie and Jean-Paul to the other. After about five minutes I found I could no longer hear the Frenchman. I yelled to Will. He responded and we met up. Together we tried to hail our captain for another couple of minutes, without luck.

Eddie showed up moments later. "I think we need to book it back to the boat, bros. I don't trust that dude."

"Maybe something's happened to him," Will said, looking about cautiously. "Maybe natives…"

That certainly encouraged the vote for heading back to the shoreline. We were about halfway there when off to our left, Jean-Paul came stumbling out of the woods, belting up his pants. "Aaahh, *mes amis.* You miss me, no? The call of nature struck. I think too much tequila last night give me the lusty squirters." He hitched up his pants with both hands. "Come, a little more wood and we escape this place, before our heads become conversation pieces!"

Four hours later, as the sun was being buried by distant, darkening thunderheads, we anchored just offshore and prepared a meager evening meal of fried fish, rice, and hardtack bread that Jean-Paul made. By the time we had cleaned our few pans and dishes, and washed some of the sweat off ourselves with river water, the air was darkening and night creatures were awakening. Bats of various sizes had begun their sweeping dives and arches across the water, pursuing the myriad water insects. Howler monkeys had begun their ritual chants while night birds screeched and cried. The water around us came alive with grunts and croaks, and splashes of predators and victims. I had hidden our canvas bag as well as possible, stuffing it into a storage cavity in the bow and hiding it with some blankets. After Jean-Paul retreated to his cabin to read for a while (he slept on top of the cabin under a mosquito net), I slid over and opened the lid, just to check. The good news was, the bag was still there and the device still inside. But I had arranged a small piece of monofilament line across the canvas lip that protected the zipper. It would break lose automatically if someone opened the bag. The line was broken.

I moved over to Will and Eddie in the encroaching darkness and whispered, "We've got problems. Our crazy captain got into the canvas bag somehow. He knows about our little device. He may not know what it is, but he damned well knows it's gold and valuable."

"Son of a bitch got away from us when we were collecting wood and zipped back to the boat," hissed Will. "I knew it!"

"Now we're going to have to be paying serious attention, dudes," Eddie added. " 'Cause he's the one with the gun."

I grimaced at the thought of that big Remington. "Could be he was just curious. Maybe we're making more of this than necessary."

"Yeah, and could be those alligators out there are gonna grow wings and fly away," Will growled. "But I wouldn't bet on it. He said we've got another day on this river — that we won't arrive until the day after tomorrow. We're good company for him right now. More people on the boat make the natives wary about bothering us. But I'm guessing, if he's planning anything, it's going to happen tomorrow or tomorrow night."

"I'm thinkin' we should sleep in shifts — one person awake all the time," Eddie added.

We all agreed on that and I said I would take the first shift.

At that moment we heard the door to the cabin open and Jean-Paul stumbled out, lizard on his shoulder and his bottle of tequila in hand, humming a Beatles song. He was headed to the top of the cabin. We quickly rolled apart and feigned sleep, hoping it would be kind enough to find some of us.

In a few minutes everything got quiet and I could hear soft gurgling snores from atop the wheelhouse. As I lay there, looking up at the star-filled heavens, I found my mind wandering toward the two ladies Will and I were courting...especially one. I could see those eyes, and that long...

Will nudged me and whispered, "You're thinking about the girls, aren't you?"

"Yeah. How'd you know?"

"You were rubbing your own leg and making little growly sounds."

"No I wasn't."

Will chuckled. "So, you gonna tell me which one? The lucky winner?"

"And what happens if she's your lucky winner, too?"

"Then we flip for her."

"Go to sleep," I said. "Dream about the one you want. Because as long as we're stuck on this piece of crap boat, it doesn't matter."

The next day was a continued lazy cruise along the river. A small front moved through and dumped a little rain on us, which was a welcome relief, but two hours later all we had left was its residual humidity, the water it deposited sucked up by a merciless sun. Jean-Paul continued to serenade us with any number of Beatles songs, which was apparently all he knew, or cared to know. He was in excellent spirits, either from our upcoming arrival at the town, or his anticipation of killing us and taking what we had, or both. Our problem was, we really weren't sure he intended to do us harm. What if we played our hand and incapacitated him, and it turned out he was just a weird and curious guy who suffered from bad luck? Then we would have lost our only ally — the only person who could help us at Camerone and watch Eddie's plane while we were gone. But if we waited, and he really was a bad guy...

Ospreys danced with frigate birds in lazy circles above us as we neared Camerone, and pelicans and seagulls competed for the bounties of the now brackish river. Even an occasional manatee and porpoise made an appearance. Unfortunately, behind what should have been somewhat comforting knowledge was the ever-present thought that we were coming to the end of this journey, one way or another.

It was late afternoon when Jean-Paul pulled off his old seaman's cap, wiped the sweat from his face, and announced we needed to make one last foray into the jungle for wood. "Come, *mis amigos*, one last journey into the heart of darkness," he cried, pulling the lizard from his shoulder, putting it in the wheelhouse, and grabbing his Remington. "By this time tomorrow we will be drinking rum and dancing with ugly but accommodating women in someplace similar to civilization!"

"He certainly seems genuine enough," I whispered to Eddie and Will. "Maybe things are going to be just fine."

"Yeah, maybe," said Eddie cautiously. "But I wouldn't bet anything important on that. You dig?"

"Like our lives?" I said.

He nodded. "Yeah, dude, exactly."

When we reached shore in the skiff, all three of us were up front, with Jean-Paul manning the outboard in the stern. Will, Eddie, and I got out and pulled the boat up on land. Jean-Paul stood and moved forward, suddenly bringing the gun up in our direction. He paused on the bow.

"Hold up, *mis amigos*." There was a somberness to his voice I didn't like, and his eyes had gone flat. The Frenchman took a breath, exhaled through his teeth and bought up the gun.

"Oh shit," Will mumbled behind me.

But as Jean-Paul looked at us, we heard an odd birdcall in the distant foliage, then another a little farther away. He paused, glancing around, listening, uncertain. His eyes lost their flatness.

"I think we need to get wood quickly," he said. "Let us get this done, and get away from here. Now."

Ten minutes later we were back at the steamer, with the skiff alongside the stern. Jean-Paul had built a platform just above the engine exhaust for ease of entrance and egress. The Frenchman was a big fellow and the gun made it a little awkward for him. Will was standing by the rail on the deck of the steamer. I was behind him. I saw the Frenchman look up at Will and make a decision. He handed my buddy the rifle and proceeded to step out, stretching for the stern rail of the steamer and stepping toward the platform. But as he did, the skiff shifted, lengthening the gap between the big boat and the little one. He missed his footing and tumbled into the water, banging his head on the platform in the process. Will tossed the gun to me.

The Frenchman's head remained under the surface for a second or two, then he came up sputtering and splashing several feet from the steamer. My partner grabbed the long fending pole on the gunnel and held it out to him. Jean-Paul quickly grabbed it and scrambled forward, onto the platform and aboard the boat. He pulled off his ratty cap and shook himself then looked at me, holding the gun, and I realized I had a decision to make. We stared at each other for a moment. Will and Eddie stood off to the side, as still as concrete statues. An osprey shrieked high above us. Our eyes met and the moment stretched into two or three tension-filled seconds. Finally, I sighed and handed him the weapon. I saw our captain exhale quietly and nod. Again he shook his head like a dog, and turned to the others.

"Come, *amigos*, that wood will not unload itself, and this old tub will not run without it!"

We went to work stacking our wood near the firebox. That completed, Jean-Paul returned to his wheelhouse and the three of us gathered at the forecastle. The engine noise drowned out our conversation.

From the shade of the tarpaulin near the bow, Will shifted into a comfortable sitting position, looked at me and gritted, "Several things just happened in the last hour, and I'm not sure I understand them all, but I think it's possible that he was going to kill us on the shore back there, until he heard those strange calls." He huffed out a confused and slightly angry sigh. "But I'm really not certain of that."

"Let me give you two sticky-assed pot brownies a newsflash," Eddie growled. "I guaranfreakingtee you we were about to be dipped in milk and eaten!" He nodded toward the wheelhouse. "Old Beatles-singin' Bogie over there got spooked about something today and needed us to help with the wood, or we'd be alligator bait now. We need to be layin' some plans, dudes, and time is runnin' out. It's down to tonight or tomorrow morning."

"He's right," Will added, pulling on his mustache nervously. "That thing with you with the gun today. I had no clue what you were going to do. Hell, I don't have any idea what I would have done. But here we are, basically right back where we were. No change in status."

"Not exactly," I said, still staring at the wheelhouse. I waited until our captain lost interest in us then surreptitiously opened my hand by my side, showing Will and Eddie the ammunition that had been in the Remington.

"Holy shit, you took his bullets!" Will exclaimed.

Eddie grinned. "Wicked, dude! Righteous move!"

I nodded at Will. "Yeah. While Bogie was splashing around and you were poking him with the pole, I ejected the five rounds into my hand. Chances are he's not going to have any idea the gun is empty, which gives us an edge if there is a problem. I feel like we need to be thinking about the skiff out there. By nightfall we'll only be a couple hours or so out of Camerone, and that fifteen horsepower engine will move that little boat faster than this old tub. There's a full gas can in the skiff and another by the wheelhouse. We need to get out of here, maybe early tomorrow morning."

"After today, I think we have to go on the assumption that there is going to be a problem," Will said. He turned to Eddie. "Did you bring any of that '*El Tigre*' stuff with you — the Bacardi 151/hashish combo we used on Stinger?"

Our buddy nodded sheepishly. "Yeah, Eddie bring a little. Maybe a third of a bottle."

My partner chewed on his lip for a moment, thinking. "Okay, here's what I suggest..."

The day gradually wound down and we anchored offshore in a small cove surrounded by a thinning jungle, the outstretched limbs of an old rubber tree nearly touching our boat. The sun melted into our river like liquid gold, and its mistress, the moon, edged over the horizon like a silver pendant, so crisp, clear, and extraordinarily large that its valleys and contours were plainly visible.

During dinner under the tarp at the forecastle, Jean-Paul pulled himself from the funk he'd wallowed in most of the afternoon. We figured he was partly embarrassed for his "slip-up," and had been chastising himself for it. He'd been hitting the tequila harder than usual, and had become talkative, which suited us just fine. The more we could learn, the better.

"Tomorrow morning we reach Camerone," he said through a mouthful of beans. "It is nothing more than a mote in God's eye — a small village, a few bars, a tiny fish processing plant, and a couple of bordellos that double as boarding houses. Also an airstrip with a couple of warehouses, run by the *contrabandistas* — smugglers — and controlled by a prick named Ricardo Santello." He shook his head slowly, as if in memory. "*Sacré bleu!* As nasty as God made men, *amigos*. Hopefully, he will be gone, on some errand of evil somewhere."

Will casually glanced at me while taking a bite of rice. I stood up.

"Excuse me, gentlemen, nature calls," I said. "Probably all those beans."

As I headed for the stern, Jean-Paul took another swig of his half-empty bottle, holding it toward me in salute, then returned to his meal.

A few moments later, from the railing at the back of the boat, I screamed, "Snake! Python! Help! Help!"

That brought everyone up from the table. Jean-Paul grabbed his rifle from the cabin on his way to the stern. But Eddie was a little slow in standing. As our captain rounded the corner of the wheelhouse, Eddie took out his little complimentary flight bottle and dumped about half of what he had into Jean-Paul's tequila, not so much as to radically change the color or the taste of its contents. He gave the tequila a quick shake and set it down, then ambled off.

Our captain was, of course, too late. The snake (which never existed to begin with) was gone, and I was explaining to my partner and the Frenchman that it had fallen from a branch onto me, but after a brief struggle it had slipped over the side. We returned to our meal, and Jean-Paul had several more healthy pulls on the tequila bottle. By the time we finished dinner, shadows were growing at the jungle's edge and river mists had begun curling like soft, gray snakes across the water. In addition, Jean-Paul had begun to slur his words slightly, and his motor actions had become far more deliberate.

We sat for a while longer, enjoying the slight evening breeze, our captain continuing to work on his peyote and hashish tequila. He had begun to whisper endearments to his lizard and giggle at the replies only he heard, and complain at how loud the mosquitoes were. Finally, the Frenchman stood up, weaving noticeably.

"It has been a long day, again, *amigos*. I think I will read for a while, then sleep." He twisted his neck back and forth lazily, picked up his bottle and wobbled toward the cabin, but he stopped and turned around. Offering a curious smile, he rumbled, "Tomorrow we will go our own ways, *amigos,* in one fashion or another." Emitting a juicy burp, he continued. "I would just like to tell you that I have enjoyed your company." Then he got a strange look on his face. "Truth is such a difficult thing to find, eh? Buddha once said, 'Three things cannot be long hidden: the sun, the moon, and the truth.'" He waved his bottle at us, almost sadly, and stumbled away, Eddie's formula starting to show in his staggered gait.

We heard him fall onto the couch in the cabin and belch

complacently. There was the gurgle of another long hit of tequila. A moment later I heard the bottle hit the floor and roll gently into the wall as the boat shifted at anchor. In minutes he was snoring.

I looked at my companions. "What in the hell do you suppose that was about?"

"Damned if I know," Will said. "But the good news is, it looks like he's out for the count. He'll be lucky if he wakes up by tomorrow evening."

"Too bad we don't have an orangutan for him," I muttered with a grin.

As the moonlight crept across the deck and bathed us, we agreed to be up just before sunrise. We'd load the boat and disappear quietly.

I slept fitfully again, with dreams of talking iguanas and crashing airplanes, and rivers that never ended. At five a.m. Will shook me awake.

"C'mon, Sleeping Beauty, time to flee the castle," he whispered tensely.

I rolled out of my blanket to find the sun just cresting the horizon, gilding a long smear of gray cirrus that lay against the distant jungle like a mottled ribbon. We took the extra twelve-gallon gas can from the steamer. That, along with the six-gallons on the skiff would get us to Camerone easily. We grabbed the important navigational and communications electronics taken off the Goose, and a package of food and water we had been able to accumulate. Lastly, but certainly not least, I picked up the canvas bag with the golden device. We hopped aboard the skiff from the transom platform and were just getting organized, Will preparing to pull the starting cord on the outboard, when we heard a voice from above us.

"*Sacré bleu*! I cannot tell you how disappointed I am — my new acquaintances sneaking off into the mists, without saying *bon voyage* to their old friend, Jean-Paul — the man who saved them from the wiles of the jungle. And in my skiff, too!"

I noticed he was carrying his Remington, and that he had shifted the muzzle in our direction. The Frenchman, no shoes, wearing nothing but his wretched, weathered pants, was weaving a little, as if the morning breeze was too much for him. His hair and beard were disheveled, his eyes were puffy slits, and his words slurred, but he was still standing in front of us with a gun.

Eddie hissed angrily behind me, "Honkey son of a bitch must have the constitution of a rhinoceros!"

"Jean-Paul, listen, we just — "

He waved me off. "If you must leave, you must leave, but I think maybe that you should offer a parting gift for the boat you have taken the liberty of 'borrowing.'" He smiled, but there was nothing nice about it. "I think I would like the shiny gold thing you have in your bag." His face lost its humor, and his eyes went flat, as they had the day before, by the jungle. The rifle came up menacingly. "And I would like it now."

I decided to play my ace, betting that, in his condition he'd never checked if the rifle was loaded. "We're leaving, Jean-Paul," I said from the bow. "We'll be back in a week for our plane and we'll leave your skiff in Camerone. And you're not getting 'our shiny thing,' that's for damned sure."

The Frenchman shook his head. "Why is it always like this?" he said, gazing up at the heavens. Then he looked down at us and pulled the trigger of the big Remington. The report nearly took me off my seat, and a piece of the railing next to my hand evaporated, leaving a two-inch hole. That, of course, accomplished two things. There was no longer a question about the gun being loaded, and it provided a universal adjustment in attitude.

Will was already digging in the canvas bag, muttering, "Oh yeah, we'll just take his bullets and he'll never know," pulling out the device and handing it up to me.

Jean-Paul gazed up at the sky again. "Now I must shoot these, too, just like the others. What a shame. Why is it that everyone I come to care for ends up dying? What a terrible curse, no?"

I opened my mouth to argue the point. "You're the one who kills — "

Eddie tapped me on the arm. "Save it, dude. Never argue with a crazy person. They'll drag you down to their level and drown you with confident inaccuracies."

I turned my attention back to our mad captain. "Jean-Paul, you don't have to kill us, just let us — "

Another round from the Remington silenced me, the bullet whizzing past my ear, hitting the water next to the boat. We were out of options. Will handed me the golden scepter, which hummed softly as the sun touched it. Jean-Paul stepped down onto the stern platform and knelt on one knee, reaching out across the water to the bow of the little skiff. I was just starting to hand our device across when, not three feet below us, the surface of the water exploded in a maelstrom of boiling spray. Up from the depths burst the head of a huge alligator, shooting upward between the two boats like a malevolent rocket, jaws open, rows of yellow scimitar teeth flashing in the sunlight. Those teeth clamped down on the Frenchman's forearm, jerking him upright with the alligator's momentum, nearly half of that twelve-foot leviathan clearing the surface before it twisted in the air and splashed back down into the brown, swirling water, drenching us with spray and terror, and taking Jean-Paul with it. In the process, the jaws severed our docking line, and we drifted a few feet from the steamer, frozen by the incredible spectacle we had just witnessed, mesmerized by the bloody whirls on the surface, the Frenchman's shrieks still in our ears.

"Whoashit!" Will whispered. "Holy freaking mother of God!"

Eddie broke the shock of the moment. "Get that damned engine started, before he comes back for dessert!"

Will didn't have to be told twice. He ripped at the starter cord, the engine caught, and we quickly pulled away from the steamer. We paused a safe distance away and studied the water for a few moments, still in shock, but there was no sign of our captain or the alligator.

Crazy Eddie exhaled hard and shook his head. "Eddie seen a lot of shit in his life, but that…that…"

Will finally pointed us down river, adding, "I ain't getting out of this freaking boat until it's sitting on dry land," and we headed away in shaken silence.

Possession is nine-tenths of the law, and it's nine-tenths of the problem.

— John Lennon

CHAPTER FIFTEEN

Three hours later the river began to widen as the water blended with the ocean. Flocks of seagulls swarmed over schools of baitfish, giant loggerhead turtles broke the surface for a gulp of air, and schools of porpoises swirled and soared with the current in the green waters. After another hour of puttering along, we sighted Camerone. The town was set into a small bay at the mouth of the river, providing good, deepwater access and protection for larger boats, like shrimpers. There were two sets of docks nearby — one was an old, rickety arrangement of wood pilings and aging lumber slats, the other was fairly new. Some of the pilings on the new one were poured concrete and the wood slats were heavy and in good condition. It was there that the better shrimp boats were moored, along with a number of lobster boats. Some of the lobster boats were way too shiny and well maintained to be fishing boats, and the exhaust systems indicated high-powered engines. We settled for the older docks to avoid drawing any attention.

As we were tying up our skiff, an old man began working his way toward us from a small, adjacent shack. He was probably in his sixties — sparse gray hair, dark eyes that offered little emotion, and leathered skin from years in the tropical sun. He was dressed in white cotton *pantalones* and a loose-fitting beige shirt. The old fellow ambled over and stopped before us. "*Buenos dias, señores.*"

I returned the greeting in Spanish and stood up.

"My name is Eduardo," he offered. "I am the caretaker here. Where you come from?"

I pointed up river. "That way."

He nodded somberly. "Hmmm. Where you going?"

Will pointed out to sea. "That way."

He nodded again. "Hmmm." He looked at our skiff, then back to me, and a little humor touched the corners of his eyes. "You may need an extra gas can, *señor.*"

"Can we leave our skiff here overnight?"

He shrugged with that typical Central American nonchalance. "*Si, señor*, you can leave it here. But if you want it to be here tomorrow morning…"

"Okay, how much? For it to be here tomorrow morning."

His mouth scrunched up, as if he'd just sucked a bitter lemon, and he gave the question some thought. "Maybe thirty, American?"

"How about ten?"

"Twenty?"

"Fifteen."

Eduardo paused. "Hmmm... Okay. Fifteen. In advance, *señor.*"

As Eduardo walked away, very content with the transaction (and knowing that he would have gladly done it for five), we stored our electronics in the center bench hatch and locked it. I grabbed the canvas bag with our clothing and the gold device, and we headed into town.

The area was much as Jean-Paul had described it. A dusty, palm-lined road snaked out from the docks and took us by a fish and lobster processing plant, then wound into town. The airfield was on the same end as the docks, for convenience. A six-foot, chain-link fence surrounded the strip and there were four aircraft tethered in the sun like hooded hawks waiting for their turn at the sky again. A weathered-looking Beech Baron, a DC-3, and a single engine Cessna 182 sat across from an older twin-engine Beechcraft 18, which appeared from a distance to have been well maintained. As we walked along the dusty road, we studied the aircraft and the two metal warehouses near them.

"Maybe we could talk someone into flying us home," Will said, staring at the metal birds.

Eddied wiped the sweat from his forehead with the back of his hand. "And when they ask us how we got here, what do we tell 'em, dude? That we left a seventy-five thousand-dollar aircraft back on the river? And what exactly do we pay them with? Credit cards? No way, José."

I spit a mouthful of phlegm and dust onto the road. "Gotta admit, I agree with Eddie. I'm thinking ol' Jean-Paul was right. We're gonna have to borrow one of those babies." I looked over at Eddie. "You have a preference?"

My one-eyed buddy studied them for a moment or two. "If Eddie had a choice, he'd take the Beech 18. Enough range and size to get us back comfortably, and I like two engines if we're going to run this in one straight shot, up the coast to the Yucatan, then around the end of Cuba and into The Keys."

I felt that edgy twirl in the pit of my stomach at the thought. But at the same time it made me smile with nervous excitement. "Okay, man. Sounds like the one. What we need to do now is find someone to give us a little information on this place and those birds."

We caught a ride on a rickety produce truck, and a few minutes later we were entering downtown Camerone. Basically, bulldozers had pushed back the jungle enough for a handful of wooden houses to be built on each side of a dusty street. Outside the town, shacks made of tin siding and junk lumber were scattered about for the workers at the processing plant, small garden plots and laundry lines next to each one. I could see a bar at each end of town, and the main boarding house/bar/bordello was in the center.

I felt as if I'd drifted back in time. It was like the Old West. The walkways in front of the businesses were made of wooden planks. There was a ratty-looking general store, a public bathhouse, something similar to a restaurant, a barber shop/blacksmith, an undertaker, and a gun shop of sorts, which was located just on the edge of town, a couple hundred yards from the other buildings. Peering in the windows of the gun shop, it appeared more like a Wal-Mart for armaments — everything from machine guns to rocket-propelled grenades. A couple of big men with Russian AK47s across their laps sat by the counter, one stood outside. Jean-Paul had mentioned it was owned by Ricardo Santello. I suddenly realized that Camerone was a serious layover for smugglers from at least three or four countries — not just for drugs, but weapons as well, supplying the warring factions of Nicaragua, Colombia, and Panama.

We ended up in the large bar/bordello, which is always a good place for information. It was late afternoon and sunlight drifted through the grimy windows in sullen trellises. The place looked just like a Western saloon — a long, curved bar against the rear wall backed with a large, gritty mirror with bottles on shelves around it. The floor was a dusty hardwood, stained with booze, blood, and God knows what else, and the gaudy red drapes at the windows had faded to a deadened coral. A handful of garish ceiling fans gyrated with lazy indifference, flailing at the cigarette smoke that hung below them like long drifts of stratus clouds. At the few tables in front of the bar, a handful of locals and smugglers played cards and drank. There were Miami Cubans in guayabera shirts, Colombian rebels in quasi-military attire, Nicaraguan freedom fighters of one sort or another, one or two South Florida smugglers a little out of their element, and a couple of guys who appeared to be CIA Contras trying desperately to fit in.

Will glanced around apprehensively and took a whiff of the place, grimacing. "Smells like somebody pissed in a sweaty boot then poured tequila in it," he muttered to no one in particular.

A band, of sorts, gathered in the corner, composed of an ancient, eerie-sounding harpsichord that looked like it might have belonged to Bela Lugosi, played by a dude who appeared old enough to have known Bela Lugosi, a black guitarist with an afro who hammered an old Stratocaster, a skinny Latin guy blasting away on a trumpet, and a heavy *Miskito* woman singing and swaying laconically while snapping a set of castanets, all of them doing a freaky rendition of The Stones' "Wild Horses." The whole thing had sort of a ghoulish, "early rock/mariachi band on peyote" feel to it. If you closed your eyes, you could just about see Count Dracula's castle burning while being attacked by Jimi Hendrix and a band of angry Mexican villagers.

We took seats at the bar. I ended up next to a burly Latin with a stained shirt, jeans, shaved head, lots of tattoos, and a gold ring in his ear. He shot his tequila and glanced at me with an appraising, somewhat disdainful look. I nodded. He poured himself another shot from the bottle next to him and spoke without looking at me. "You sure you in the right place, *gringo*? This is a long way from Kansas City."

I knew intrinsically this was a watershed moment. He was determining whether I was a fish or bait, and this was not a place to be bait. "Don't I know it, brother," I replied. "If my partner and I hadn't been forced to shoot our way out of that last bank, I wouldn't be here at all. Just a stopover."

That got his attention. He glanced down at the canvas bag at my feet, which I was probably guarding a little too tightly. "What's in the bag, *amigo*?"

I took a shot of tequila. "My partner's remains. He took a round in the stomach and bled out on the way here."

His eyebrows rose and he looked at me. "You had him cremated, eh?"

I glanced over at the band nonchalantly and spoke without looking at him. "Nah, haven't had time for that yet. I just cut him up and stuffed him in the bag. Thought I'd have one last drink with him, for old times sake. But he is starting to smell a little."

That backed the boy up nicely. He took a sip of his drink and nodded, trying to be cool with that. I relaxed. At least at this juncture, I was a fish.

After getting a bottle of tequila and some glasses, I grabbed a deck of cards off the bar and suggested we move to a table near the back. I had always liked playing cards — it calmed me. I wouldn't have called myself a card shark, but I was fairly good. Will took our valuable canvas bag and we settled on a circular table that was just a little larger than the others. We received a few appraising looks from the patrons as we sat down. Will glanced at me and shrugged. Next to us there was a guy sitting at a table by himself. He looked like he could be an American, maybe down on his luck. He was wearing an old pair of khaki pants, a *Guess Who* T-shirt, and a Cessna ball cap, and he had a couple days' growth of beard, was drinking cheap local beer, and playing solitaire. After we poured ourselves drinks, I looked over at the guy and on impulse, took the bottle with a couple of glasses, and walked over to him. He looked up, no particular emotion on his face one way or another.

"I'm guessing you're an American, and a pilot," I said.

He stared at me for a moment. "Canadian, originally, and yeah, I fly, but I'm going to save you some time. I'm not interested in flying you or whatever it is you have, anywhere."

"Actually I don't have anything that needs to be flown anywhere," I said with an unassuming smile. "Just passing through. By tomorrow evening the wind will have forgotten me." I extended my hand. "Kansas, Kansas Stamps."

"Jack Becker," he said, reaching up and offering a disinterested handshake.

"I have a couple of questions, and seeing as how you fly airplanes, maybe you could answer them for me." I sat down uninvited and pushed a glass over to him, filling it, then filling mine. He looked at me cautiously, but didn't refuse.

My new friend picked up the glass and clinked mine, then shot the tequila. "Okay, you bought yourself a question or two, maybe."

I nodded respectfully. "We came in by boat this time, but I'm thinkin' we might come back in an airplane. What do you know about the airstrip here? Have you used it before?"

He offered a thin smile, but there was a bitter twist to the corners of his mouth and a distant look of anguish in his eyes. "Yeah, I've used it before. Lost my partner and my airplane on the end of that strip. Bastards overloaded us with pot and weapons and we buried the plane in the jungle on takeoff."

Wincing, I muttered, "Damn, man! I'm sorry to hear that." I filled his glass again and this time he gratefully shot it, as if trying to cache the thoughts he'd just issued. "Who owns the strip? Who do I get permission from to use it?"

"Santello," he gritted, as if the word itself riled him. "He's the prick who insisted on overloading us. Stick around here and you'll get to meet him. This is his bar. He drives a brand new El Dorado Cadillac. Had it brought over on a shrimper from Miami. You can't miss him."

I paused respectfully, then continued. "Is there security there, like day and night?"

He chuckled rancorously. "Yeah, a couple of drunken guards. You'll pay dearly for it, but don't expect them to do anything but drink and sleep off their hangovers."

"Who owns the Beech 18 that's out there?"

"Santello and one of his overlords, a guy named Choka, but all his runs are sanctioned by Santello. "

Jack pushed his glass toward me and I filled it. He took it in a gulp again. "At least the son of a bitch keeps the plane in good condition. Word is he has a run coming up fairly soon — flying out a couple big cats and a load of pot. Saw them fueling the plane late this afternoon, which means they'll probably go tomorrow, after the cats come in."

"Big cats?" I said incredulously.

He nodded, the alcohol beginning to ease the caution in his eyes. "Yeah, ocelots, jaguars, endangered stuff. They make damned near as much money from them as they do drugs."

"Well, *amigo*, probably more information than I need," I said, getting to my feet as if I was a little concerned with learning things that could get me in trouble. "Appreciate you filling me in." I slid the bottle over. "You keep it. Take care of yourself."

My new acquaintance looked up at me. "Let me give you a bit of advice. I don't know what you're up to, but I recommend you get the hell out of this place as soon as you can. That's what I recommend."

I tapped the tabletop with the flat of my hand. "My thoughts exactly."

Returning to our table, I explained what I had just learned.

"Santello. That's the same guy Jean-Paul mentioned, with more than just a little discomfort," Will said, smoothing his mustache uneasily.

"Yeah," I agreed, absentmindedly shuffling the cards I had carried over from the bar. "I haven't even met him and I don't like him." I looked over at Eddie. "I'm thinking I'd like to harsh that boy's mellow. He's the one who owns the Beech out at the airport."

Crazy Eddie's one eye gleamed in anticipation. "Right on, brotha! We'll cop that jive turkey's wings and bum his bong righteously!"

We were enjoying a quiet laugh when the noise level in the bar fell distinctly. Three men had just walked in. Two of them were large and brutish-looking, obviously muscle — bandanas, worn denim pants, leather vests, and jungle combat boots. But it was the guy in the center who caught everyone's attention. He was tall and a little on the heavy side, with shoulder-length ebony hair and smoky gray eyes with large black pupils — dangerous eyes, devoid of emotion. He was dressed nicely for this neck of the woods — new jeans, an olive green Levi's shirt, and cowboy boots with silver-tipped toes. There were two other aspects that made him distinctive; his two upper front teeth were gold, and his two incisors on the lower jaw were also gold. It was a strange, arresting thing that made you have to look twice. Even more striking was the incredible cat strolling beside him on a leash. It was a young ocelot, probably about thirty-five pounds, marbled brown and black markings on the head and sides, creamy white stomach, and emerald green eyes. It was guarded and somewhat uncertain, but not particularly frightened.

The fellow with the Cessna ball cap hissed vehemently, "Ricardo Santello."

The big Nicaraguan moved with the same fluidity as his cat, but he was far more self-assured. Flanked by his bodyguards, he glided directly toward us, cat at his side, stopping a few feet in front of our table. He looked down, gray eyes smoldering, somewhere between indignant and amused. "I'm sure you are strangers here, so I will afford you a courtesy in your ignorance. You are sitting at my table."

You know, sometimes you meet someone to whom you simply take an instant dislike. I'd run into this kind of guy too many times in my life. It was always the same — they found pleasure in domination. They weren't happy unless someone near them was stuttering and terrified. I knew I should just let it go. I was a smart ass, not a badass. Damn, I knew it was the smart thing to do. But I couldn't. I just couldn't. Out of the side of my mouth I whispered to Will, "You remember Cat Island and Drako?"

Will nodded almost imperceptibly. "Yeah. But I'm not happy about this."

I set the deck of cards on the tabletop, looked up at Santello, and shrugged innocently. "Sorry, buddy. Didn't see your name on the table anywhere. Maybe you could have a couple of nametags made, you know, one for you and one for the table. Then this kind of embarrassing thing wouldn't have to happen."

Santello visibly stiffened, his eyes darkening like chimney smoke. "I don't need no stinking name cards."

"Shades of *Blazing Saddles*," Will whispered.

I struggled to keep from smiling.

"You will give me my table now," Santello said evenly, struggling to keep his cool. He wasn't used to this type of response.

"I'll tell you what," I said, pulling my chair away and leaning back in it slightly. "It was an honest mistake. How could we know? And you've got to admit we were here first. How about we cut cards for it?"

The tall smuggler suddenly looked a lot like Jean-Paul's old boiler with a full head of steam. His complexion had clearly darkened a couple of shades, and his hands clenched slightly, but when I offered to cut cards, his expression garnered a slyness. He was a person who liked to beat people completely — mentally and physically. He liked the game, and I was counting on that.

"And if I cut cards with you, *señor*, what do I get if I win?"

"You can have your boys beat the crap out of us, right here in front of everyone and make your point."

Santello shrugged. "I can do that anyway, anytime I want."

"Yeah, but that really wouldn't prove anything, would it? It would just say you're not as much of a gambler as you claim you are."

That struck our boy in just the right place. He stood there for a moment, then handed the cat's leash to one of his men. Will instinctively stood and offered his seat, a diversion already simmering in that devious head of his. As Santello sat down, Eddie got up and stood back also, leaving just the Nicaraguan and me. The whole bar had been listening to the conversation, and slowly, like lemmings on Xanax, they all began easing over to us, forming a distant, respectful half-circle.

In the process, my buddy had strategically eased himself into the spectators and chosen his spot on the far corner of the circle. Next to him was a smallish Cuban with a black "Fidel" beard and a really bad toupee — scraggly fake hair, wet with sweat, covering what was obviously a very bald head.

Santello looked at me and smiled, but his eyes clearly said, *I'm going to cut your balls off when this is done.* He reached out and shuffled the deck, then took the top third and slowly showed his card — a jack of spades. He pursed his lips and nodded in satisfaction. "Okay, *gringo*, it is your turn."

I glanced at Will surreptitiously, then reached over and took my cut of the deck, but before I could flip it over, Will suddenly turned to the Cuban next to him and screamed in Spanish, "Son of a bitch!" then decked him with a massive right to the jaw. The Cuban's head snapped back, and his fake hairpiece went soaring across the room like a flying spider. My partner pointed and yelled, "Tarantula! A Mongolian Red-eye!"

The word "tarantula" has a remarkable effect on people who live near the jungle. The crowd jumped back as if someone had just dropped a grenade. Before anyone could get a good look at anything, Will dashed over and began stomping furiously on the toupee. He ripped a beer bottle off a table and smashed it on "the spider" screaming epithets about "freaking hairy-legged, poisonous bastards!" Then, before there was really a collective grasp of the situation, he grabbed the thoroughly decimated hairpiece and ran to the double doors, hurling it out into the street.

There was a gaping silence as he came back in wearing a sheepish, apologetic countenance. "Sorry, man. I just hate spiders."

The floorshow over, everyone immediately returned their attention to the main act. Of course, Santello had only been distracted for a second or two. He was watching me like a hawk while my partner pummeled the hairpiece and threw it out the saloon doors.

Suddenly, the room hushed to morgue-level, and all eyes were on me. I crossed myself, took a deep breath, and turned over my portion of the deck. There lay the queen of hearts.

Santello hissed out a breath from between his golden teeth and uttered a vehement series of statements about my character and my mother that would have burned the ears off of a sailor. Finally, he inhaled and composed himself, staring at me with those hate-filled, smoky-black eyes. "Either you are a daring son a bitch, or you cheated. In either case, *amigo*, it's a matter of pushing your luck too far." He paused, raising his hand and wagging an index finger at me. "I don' like you, *amigo*. For son' reason I don' like you at all." Then he lowered his hand slowly and spoke in a venom-laced whisper. "And in Camerone, that is not a good thing."

I nodded, remaining serious. "I'll keep that in mind."

Ricardo Santello rose, his dignity and composure returning. He snatched the ocelot's leash from his bodyguard, and with a final glare at me, he turned and walked out.

The guy next to us, with the Cessna baseball cap, muttered, "You know you're dead, right? I mean just as dead as yesterday's turtle soup." He shook his head in amazement and a profound degree of satisfaction. "But damn, man. It may have been worth it. They'll talk about this moment for years! Hell, I'll talk about this moment for years!"

As we headed over to the bordello/boarding house, Eddie glanced at me. "Okay, how'd you do it, dude? I know you better than to think you'd risk it all on luck."

"Normally, you'd be right," I chuckled nervously. "When Santello came in, I knew intrinsically who he was. So, remembering a trick Will and I had used on Cat Island a while back, I tucked the *king* of hearts into my sleeve." (I was wearing a long-sleeved khaki jungle shirt.) "I had planned to palm it under my portion of the deck when Will got everyone's attention, but it caught in the cuff of my sleeve." I pulled the card out.

Eddie turned pale. "You telling me, dude, that our honkey asses was actually on the line for that card cut?"

I shrugged. "What else could I do?"

"Ooohhh, that seriously bums my groove," our pilot moaned. "And they call Eddie crazy."

Will just smiled and quoted from The Eagles' "Desperado": "You know the queen of hearts is always your best bet."

"By the way," I said to Will. "Very entertaining distraction on your part."

He grinned. "Actually, I was just going to hit the Cuban and yell that he was groping me, but when the wig went flying across the room, it looked so much like a spider I just changed my tack." He smiled. "Couldn't resist the Mongolian Red-eye thing."

Eddie pulled in between us on the boarded walkway, draping his hands over our shoulders. "If you two are done patting yourselves on the backs, we need to plan on splitting this scene *muy rapido*. I mean like rats off the sinking ship, like the last wisp of Superman's cape. That Santello dude is baby-eating, crazy mad. He's gonna go get drunk, and that whole scene is going to eat at him like acid on a Kewpie doll. Then he's going to come for us. You dig?" He got a malicious grin and looked at me. "Will and me, they're probably just gonna shoot — but you...I'm thinkin' probably staked out on an ant pile somewhere and covered in honey."

I winced. "Maybe you could just keep your vivid imagination to yourself."

We were nearing the end of town, maybe two blocks from the gun shop, by an empty lot. I glanced at the sun, which was just starting to touch the mountains in the distance, casting long shadows across the street. It would be dark in an hour. "Nonetheless, I agree with you, man. We gotta get out of here, but I think we're going to need one more distraction to buy us some time while we get that airplane warmed up and ready to go."

We noticed Santello's bright red Caddy was parked at the bordello/bar in the center of town. "Probably working off some of the mellow-harshing you gave him," Eddie said with a grin.

Will gazed down the road toward the airport, then looked up and down the street, chewing on his lip for a moment. He turned to us. "Okay, how about we do this…"

A few minutes later, my buddy walked over to an old man sitting on a walkway by the closest building — rumpled shirt, white *pantalones*, a cotton rope for a belt and a beat up, wide-brimmed straw hat covering his dark, deeply lined face. Will knelt next to him and spoke in Spanish, "If you would be interested, I would give you ten dollars, American, for your hat and your belt."

The old man stared at my friend for a moment, then stood up, took off the belt and the hat, and handed them to him without a single word.

Will gave the man his money, took the two items, and gave me the belt. "I'll be back in five minutes," he said to Eddie and me, putting on the hat. Then he headed down the street.

My partner, who had the distinction of being able to hotwire a car in less than a minute, picked out an old pickup truck parked in the shadows a block from the bar where we had met Santello. While he was working his magic, he could hear the ghoulish rock/mariachi band inside, butchering one of Jimmy Buffett's songs, "Son of a Son of a Sailor." He grimaced and muttered under his breath, "Good God! If Jimmy heard that, the rest of his hair would fall out!"

When Will had the pickup started, he pulled it out and casually drove back to us by the empty lot. At that point we asked the old man, from whom Will had bought the belt and hat, if he would like to make another ten dollars. The fellow agreed that he would. I gave him the money and told him that in ten minutes he was to go into the bar and tell Ricardo Santello that the *gringo* with whom he had played cards today wanted him to come out and look up the street at his Cadillac and his gun shop. The man's better days were past, but there was a roguish gleam in those old eyes. He had heard what happened with Santello that day in the saloon, and it pleased him immensely. He intrinsically understood something was about to happen, and smiled conspiratorially. He was old and had little to lose, and he loved great stories. The fellow ambled off with a limping gait, holding his pants up with his hand.

Will ambled back down the fairly deserted street and slipped into Santello's Cadillac. (No one was guarding it, because no one in their right mind would even touch it.) He hotwired it and drove it down to the end of town, parking in front of the gun shop (which was closed, but had a guard out front). The fellow, a big *Miskito* — ponytail of long black hair, ritual scars on his cheeks, and dark, cautious eyes — walked over. "Hey man, what you do with señor Santello's car?"

My partner pulled down the brim of his hat and shrugged indifferently. "What do I know? He just tell me, 'Pedro, drive my car down to the gun shop. I be that way in fifteen minutes.' It's all I know, man."

The guard tilted his head. "How come I don' know you?"

Will shrugged again, hands out, palms up. "I just come in from Miami, to help him with his big cats. That's why." Will brought his hand up, gesturing. "Oh, he also say for you to go have a drink. He is meeting someone here — it's a private thing."

The fellow stared at Will for a moment, uncertain. "He wants me to leave?"

"That's what he tell me."

The guard became a little wary with that, shifting his rifle slightly. "He wants me to leave? Why would he want that?"

Will sighed, exasperated. "How would I know this, man? You don't like it, go tell him you don't like it. When they finally pull his boot out of your ass, it won't matter whether you understand or not, 'cause you will no longer have a job!"

The guy exhaled hard. "Okay, okay. What do I care?" He turned and headed across the street toward the saloons.

Once Will was certain the fellow had found a bar, he pulled the Cadillac right up to the front of the gun shop, got out and opened the gas cap, took the belt made of cotton and stuffed a good portion of it into the tank, letting it soak with gas, but leaving about two feet dangling outside. About then, Eddie and I pulled up in the old pickup. My partner dramatically pushed up his hat and pulled out a match, like Clint Eastwood in a Spaghetti Western. (I could almost hear the music from *The Good, the Bad, and the Ugly*.) He struck it on the shiny fender, and touched the bottom of the cotton belt with the flame.

Will got into the pickup, and with our precious canvas bag

between us, Eddie hit the gas, taking us through the center of town toward the airport.

Just as we were driving out of Camerone, the old man was speaking to Santello in the bar. They both stepped outside. Ricardo Santello stared up the street toward the gun shop and his red Caddy. The old man chose that time to drift away unnoticed. The Nicaraguan frowned. "What is my car doing — "

The Caddy suddenly went up in an orange fireball, hood flying off like a Frisbee and doors blowing open. The flames leapt over to his gun shop, with all that ammunition.

When we reached the airport gate, the guard — tall, full beard, green Fidel cap, AK47 — bent down and peered at us through the window.

"We're here to preflight Choka's plane," I said in my official voice.

"Where's Jorge?"

"He got some bad *quesillo*, man. Me and my friend, and our mechanic (nodding at Eddie) are taking his flight."

The guard scowled. "How come I don' know you, man?"

"Because Choka just brought us in from Miami to fly for him."

The guy shook his head slowly. "I don't know, man. I don't know you — "

I spat in the dirt angrily. "Then why don't you go get Choka or Santello? Go interrupt them at their dinner and tell them you don't like them not letting you know what they do. After they have cut your tongue out and nailed it to your forehead, you come back and nod to me it's okay, 'cause you not gonna be able to speak no more. Huh, man? You want to do that? Huh?" I paused and let that sink in. "Me and my friends, we wait for you, no problem."

Finally, the guy exhaled angrily. "Nobody tells me shit around here! For all I know you could be some stinkin' *Americanos* trying to steal a plane."

I laughed as heartily as I could, given the hammering of my heart. "Yeah, sure! That's it." I looked at Will and Eddie, who quickly forced out a chuckle or two. "You got us."

"We gonna go steal Choka's plane now, and fly it to Key West," cried Will from the far window. "And by tomorrow afternoon we be drinking tequilas in a quiet little bar on the beach. We even have one for you — the guard who let us steal the plane!"

"Okay, okay, enough!" the man said, heatedly, waving us through. "No more bullshit about stealing planes. It makes me nervous."

We started to pull through the gate when suddenly the fellow straightened up and yelled, "Hey, stop. Stop!"

"Oh, Jesus," I whispered, not knowing whether to take my foot off the pedal or jam it down and make a run for it. The guard was coming over at a good pace and had his gun up. Before I could make up my mind, he was at the window.

"Hey, hey, what was all those explosions about in town?" he said, pointing back at the rising smoke in the distance.

I exhaled the breath I'd been holding. "I got no idea, man," I smiled impishly. "Maybe someone blew up Santello's Cadillac."

"That's not funny, man," the guy scolded, his brows furrowing. "Somebody do that, they be bad crazy."

It was a very nice airplane — older, but in excellent shape, obviously refurbished with care. The two big Pratt & Whitney 985-Rs looked almost new, stainless blades gleaming brightly from the lights on the fence. We piled out of the pickup and opened the hatch, scrambling inside. The seating was configured like Eddie's Goose — pilot and copilot's seats in the cockpit, and one more set of seats behind the cockpit partition. But beyond that, there was a bit of a surprise: inside the cabin were three pallets of marijuana bales. The pallets had locking wheels, so they could be rolled out the extra-wide sliding hatch with little more than a good push. And that wasn't all. In front of the bales was a four-foot by four-foot cage with two beautiful ocelots inside. They sat curled in the corner, hissing with discontent, their huge green eyes watching our every move — some very unhappy cats.

"From plane stealers to a freaking traveling circus," moaned Will. "I just can't wait to see what's going to be next."

I took a glance outside the hatch. Lights were coming down the road from town, and I could pretty much guess who that was. "Time to get out of here!" I yelled. "We've got company. Eddie, you set yourself up in the cockpit and get a preflight going. Will and I will get rid of the cats."

Crazy Eddie never even bothered with a reply. He was in his element. Hell, he was grinning. He loved this kind of thing — putting it all on the line with a set of good wings underneath him.

My partner and I had just gotten the cat container out from behind the pallets of pot, our backs to the hatch, when we heard someone singing in a raspy whisper. *"We're Sergeant Pepper's Lonely Hearts Club Band, we hope you will enjoy the show. We're*

Sergeant Pepper's Lonely Hearts Club Band. Sit back and let the evening go..."

I looked at Will, whose eyes were the size of goose eggs. "Oh, man, it can't be. It...just...can't...be..."

"Aahhh, but it is, *mes amis,"* said a gravely voice from the hatch. "My good friends, taking their golden toy and leaving me to be eaten by an alligator. I am so disappointed, again."

As we turned around, there stood the Frenchman, Jean-Paul — horribly gaunt-looking with dark, hollow eyes, bedraggled beard, thin hair plastered on his head, and clothes muddy and torn. But there were two other significant factors — the pistol he held in his right hand and the blackened stump where his left hand used to be.

"How?" I stuttered. "How? It's not possible."

"Aaahh, but it is," he gritted with a malicious smile. "And I'll tell ya the quick version, because you don't have enough time for the long one." He paused, eyebrows bouncing. "On the other hand, so to speak, I bet you wish you did." Smiling at his own joke, he continued, "To make it short and sweet, the demon alligator grabbed me wrist and drug us under the boat, but when he bit me hand off, he lost Jean-Paul and I hid under the hull, holding my wrist with my good hand to keep from bleeding away. After a minute or so I worked my way back along the hull to the stern, and crawled back onboard. The first thing I did was stick my wrist in the hull-patching tar bucket on the boiler." He paused again, face alight with the moment and the memory. "I can tell you, *amigos,* that hurt worse than the bite, but the hot tar sealed my wound and stopped the bleeding immediately. Then I drank half a bottle of tequila and passed out for a few hours."

The Frenchman took a ragged breath and glared at us with eyes like those of a dragon from beneath his lair, hungry and confident. "But when I awoke I found I was missing *mis amigos* — packed up and left me to the nasties in the river, you had." He grinned with gallows humor. "So, I ate myself a meal, drank some more tequila, and headed for Camerone." He waved his gun in a careless arch. "Well, I get to this quiet little village and find someone has made a mess of it. *'Sacré bleu,'* Jean-Paul says to himself. *'Who would have done this?'*" His eyebrows rose in question. "And he thinks, aahhh, maybe his old friends. And where would they be? Probably looking for an airplane. So here I am, and just in time, it seems."

I sat back on a pot bale in disbelief, the ocelot cage next to me. "Look, Jean-Paul, we thought you were dead," I said, pleading, hands out. "The alligator wasn't our — "

A shot from his pistol interrupted me, slamming into the bale next to us. The cats at my feet yowled and hissed in fear and anger.

"Save the story for someone who cares," growled the Frenchman. "Just give me the golden wand, now!"

Another shot emphasized his words. Again the cats hissed and slammed themselves against the cage door with fury.

Pointing toward the cockpit, I said, "Eddie's got the bag up there. Eddie, bring the bag!" But while I was talking and our nemesis' attention was focused toward the front of the plane, I quickly slipped the rod from the latch of the cat cage, then slammed the roof with the flat of my hand. Both ocelots hit the wire door with the momentum of small freight trains. The door flew open and those twin felines aimed all their pent-up fury at the only creature they could see. Jean-Paul screamed and got off a shot, but it went wide and only served to further infuriate the animals. The ocelots hit our old captain in the chest like linemen on a quarterback and they all tumbled out the hatch in a bundle of fur, claws, and curses. Jean-Paul lost his pistol when he thudded onto the ground, and by the time he had worked his way loose from the wrathful cats, he looked like he'd just lost a fight with a Veg-A-Matic. The last we saw of our old nemesis was a shadow racing into the darkness, screeching curses in English and French about Americans and cats — followed closely by the twin ocelots.

Will joined me at the hatch as we watched Jean-Paul and his new acquaintances disappear into the night. "That boy doesn't have the best of luck, does he?" he muttered. "Sometimes, if you're not careful, you actually get what you deserve."

I smiled. "C'mon, Ringo, it's been a hard day's night. Let's get the hell out of here."

The good news was it looked like we were done with the crazy, Beatles-spouting Frenchman. The bad news was the headlights from at least two vehicles were coming down the road from town. In minutes they'd be on us.

Eddie was instantly back to startup procedure, checking his fuel pumps, setting mixture controls and throttles, then cranking over the big radials. The port engine fired and caught with a burst of rich white smoke from the exhaust. As soon as he had that one purring, he cranked the starboard and it, too, responded perfectly, heavy props whirling in perfect synchronicity, the plane coming alive under us. I closed the hatch as Eddie swung our silver bird around and taxied over to the threshold of the dirt strip. Then I quickly stumbled up front and into the copilot's seat while Will buckled into one of the seats behind us.

A Jeep and a light troop carrier with the canvas top down came rushing through the gate, heading toward the other end of the runway. Inside the truck were half a dozen men with rifles. In front of them, Santello rode in the Jeep with three of his men.

Eddie aimed us down the strip and slammed the throttles to the firewall. The airplane surged forward and the tail came up as we bolted down the runway, but it was a big plane with at least an extra half-ton of pot on board. The two vehicles were on the field and had turned onto the runway. They were charging head-on at the plane, their headlights almost blinding us.

"I don't think we can make it," Eddie muttered. "This bitch ain't coming off the ground, dude."

The truck and the Jeep showed no signs of giving way. Santello was a madman at this point. He would die rather than let us get away. The ground outside the window was racing by in a blur, but the vehicles were almost on us, firing away. I could hear bullets ricocheting off the wings and popping holes in the fuselage. Suddenly, I realized Eddie was right. We weren't going to make it. I was so out of my mind with terror, I had forgotten about the trick an old pilot friend had taught me — how to make a plane "jump" on takeoff. He used it to "hop" haystacks in an old single engine Cessna using the technique. I'd only tried it once before in my life — when Will and I found ourselves in a similar situation years ago on Cay Sal Island in the Bahamas. Basically, you took the plane up to top speed on the ground and snapped twenty degrees of flaps just before you ran into the obstacle in front of you, jerking back on the controls, and the plane literally bounced over it — in theory. But this was a huge, overloaded, twin-engine aircraft.

"Dead one way or the other," I muttered stoically. I turned to Eddie and shouted. "Give me the controls! I got a plan!"

He glanced over at me. "You got a freakin' plan now? Now?"

"Let me have 'em!" I shouted again. A couple of machine gun rounds clipped the metal framing on the windshield and we both shrieked.

"Okay, dude!" he yelled. "But if you kill me, I'm gonna kick your ass when we get to hell!" He was hesitant and he kept his fingertips at the edge of his yoke as I took the copilot controls.

We already had ten degrees of flaps dropped. Santello's vehicles were so close to our nose I could clearly see the tall Nicaraguan standing in the Jeep, holding the windshield with one hand and firing his weapon from his hip with the other, lips peeled back in rage, his golden teeth shining brightly in the lights of the plane. Bullets were ripping through the aircraft with muted snapping sounds and Will was shouting something from the back about never, ever flying with me ever again.

I slapped down the flaps lever so violently I bent the handle, and sucked the controls back into my abdomen hard enough to fracture a rib. I screamed. Eddie screamed. Will was already screaming. Just when I was certain we were dead, waiting for the impact of metal on metal, the old silver bird lumbered into a slight bounce — not a true hop, just a lift of a few feet — so few that Santello had to duck the landing gear.

I heard Eddie whoop with joy and disbelief, but it was a short-lived victory. With the flaps full down, we had managed the hop over the Jeep and the truck, but it had decreased the plane's overall momentum. We weren't climbing yet. Eddie quickly snapped the flaps back to twenty degrees, raised the gear, and took the controls. The old girl responded by starting to climb, but we weren't fifteen feet off the ground and we were nearly out of runway. A few hundred yards in front of us, the surrounding jungle was rising up like a giant dark green monolith, and buried in the winding trunks and vines dead ahead was the wreckage of Jack Becker's airplane (the guy with the Cessna Cap, from the bar). The jungle grew taller right at the edge of the airport clearing because it received more sunlight, and it created a natural "wall" about a dozen feet higher than the tangled labyrinth behind it. It was this wall, about ten feet thick, into which we were hurtling.

"God!" I whispered desperately as Eddie fought to gain altitude.

"No way, José," Crazy Eddie muttered with fatal complacency. "We ain't gonna make it. Tighten your belts, *amigos,*" he added almost sadly. "We're going in." He exhaled hard. "Been nice knowing you, dudes."

But at that moment, as we swept toward that dark green maw of destruction, the jungle wall in front of us exploded into a brilliant, fiery corona, blowing away the tops of the trees in our path and scattering the wreckage of Becker's aircraft. Eddie instinctively sucked in the yoke and bought us a few more feet as we all cried out and flew straight into that flaming inferno.

To this day I don't know how we made it. I'm certain I heard branches scraping the underside of the Beech as we soared through that blazing hole in the green wall. But seconds later we were through the smoke and flames, and climbing out above the jungle, a rising moon casting a silver sheen over the canopy of treetops below us.

Eddie drew a breath and banked away, coming around in a circle and heading out toward the coast.

What we couldn't have known then, what we couldn't have seen, was Jack Becker slowly bringing down the rocket-propelled grenade launcher from his shoulder a hundred yards from the spot where he had lost his partner and his plane. It was his powerful projectile that had ripped a hole through the tops of the jungle and freed us. He smiled sadly, but in his eyes there was a bright, triumphant gleam. "We don't all make it," he said quietly to himself. "But sometimes, some of us do. Now we're almost even, Santello."

The last thing I saw as Eddie brought our plane around and turned us out to sea was the Jeep and the military truck stopped on the airstrip below, Santello's people pouring out, guns aimed at a lone individual in their headlights with his hands in the air — well, at least one hand in the air. There were muzzle flashes in the darkness below. Then we were gone.

The old man sat on the wooden walkway outside Santello's bar. He had no hat and no belt, but he had a bottle of tequila and fifteen dollars American left in his pocket. He watched the big Beech 18 soar across the darkening sky, heading out to sea. He smiled. *Madre de Dios,* what a good story he had to tell.

As a dreamer of dreams and a travelin' man
I have chalked up many a mile
Read dozens of books about heroes and crooks
And I learned much from both of their styles.
                                              — Jimmy Buffett

CHAPTER SIXTEEN

Using the aeronautical charts already aboard the plane, Eddie quickly had us headed north for Cancun. Two and a half hours later we clipped the tip of the Yucatan Peninsula and made the eastward turn for South Florida and Key West, staying well clear of the coast of Cuba. We hit some weather on the last stretch and it pushed us a little farther north than planned, bringing us in over the Marquesas Keys. All of us were dead tired, and mentally weary from the stress of being chased by damned near everyone in Nicaragua, and I guess that's why we forgot about the pot in the cargo hold of the plane. It wasn't until we were coming up on the Marquesas, that Will woke up, stretched, and looked behind him.

"Whoashit!" I heard him yell. "Holy freaking bejeezus! We still got a thousand pounds of pot in the back of this bloody aircraft!"

Eddie slapped the dash in frustration. "Ooohh, man, this is radically bogus. We're already on Key West radar and we don't have a flight plan. You two need to get that reefer out the doors, now! You dig? Before the Feds send somebody up to visit with us!"

While Eddie was mumbling about his mellow being harshed to shreds again, I unbuckled and went back into the cabin with Will. Together we opened the specially designed sliding hatch, wind ripping at us like a hurricane as we held on to guy lines that had been installed in the ceiling to make this kind of thing easier. None of the bales on the pallets were tied down. The whole process was designed for a very low-level water run — normally everything would barely have time to move off the pallets before it hit the sea and was picked up by boats. But in our case, as soon as the pallets were one hundred feet out of the hatch, bales began spreading out across the sky, falling like manna from Heaven. In addition, we had no idea that one pallet contained several ten-pound packets of cocaine.

Even with all the clever forethought by Santello, dumping pot out of an aircraft in flight was still a tricky situation. One wrong move and we'd be making a flight of our own. Nonetheless, with all our excitement that afternoon, we didn't exactly have a monopoly on interesting events in the Marquesas…

Tommy Bob Johnson had been a born-again Christian. He believed in faith, the grace of God, and everlasting life, but, strangely enough, he was a pot smuggler by profession — just pot, nothing else. Some folks argued that his profession conflicted with his faith. He would just smile and say, "Nobody's perfect. That's where Jesus comes in." But the truth was, he was sort of a Robin Hood — making midnight runs in shrimpers and airplanes and continuously spreading the wealth back home. He had anonymously donated one hundred thousand dollars to Florida Keys Hospital, bought a thousand new novels and left them on the doorsteps of the Key West Library, had given fifty thousand dollars to the local VFW, and provided God knows how much money to local businesses, friends, and family. Tommy Bob had pretty much become a legend in his own time, and when the engines on his plane quit and he rode that final load into the sea somewhere off the Caicos, most everyone believed that, regardless of what he had in the back, Jesus was riding copilot with him on the way to the Pearly Gates.

There was a remarkable memorial service for Tommy. Three hundred people came from four different countries. They all gathered together in boats and rode out to the Marquesas (which was one of Tommy's favorite drop spots), forming a large circle off one of the smaller islands. It was a beautiful, clear day — an azure sky slashed by high, feathery streaks of cirrus clouds, and a silky breeze from the southeast. The ceremony was officiated by a local reverend who was known to imbibe a little himself. He, his crew, and his sailboat were anchored in the center of the circle with a huge PA system. It was an absolutely beautiful ceremony and at the end, when each person tossed a hibiscus flower into the sea, there wasn't a dry eye anywhere. The preacher — shoulder-length blond hair, dressed in a tropical shirt and white cotton bell-bottoms — threw his hands up dramatically, face raised to the sky, and shouted. "Lord, we commend our friend into Your arms, but before we leave today, we ask for a sign, a small gesture, that Tommy Bob is with You. Let the wind rise slightly — ruffle the water with Your Almighty understanding. Give us a token of Your compassion and forgiveness."

The preacher paused. High above the congregation the drone of a lone aircraft was heard.

"Just a small sign, Jesus," cried the reverend, hands still extended, trying for the dramatic — a fitting ending for a good man like Tommy Bob. There was a pause. Gradually, it grew uncomfortable. The minister, arms still outstretched, finally started to lower them when suddenly there was a shout. Someone pointed upwards. Another person yelled, looking up, and several others gestured toward the sky. A moment later, the waters around the little flotilla began to explode with crashing marijuana bales. The preacher still had his hands slightly extended, when, not ten feet in front of him, a ten-pound package of cocaine hit the deck and exploded like a white bomb. The poor fellow, shocked to numbness and covered from head to toe with glistening cocaine powder, blinked a couple of times and gazed around at his boat, then slowly ran a finger over his cheek and put the tip in his mouth. He blinked again. "Son of a gun," he whispered incredulously. "Now that's a sign."

Needless to say, that was pretty much the end of the service, because almost everybody was pulling a bale or two into their boat and making a dash for the coast. In what can only be accounted as another miracle, everyone made it in. Even today, hardly a Saturday night goes by in Key West without somebody relating the story of the "Tommy Bob Johnson Marijuana Miracle." Glasses are raised and the traditional toast is offered, "To Tommy Bob, and Jesus!"

We were immensely pleased to find we didn't have a DEA reception upon landing at Key West International. Somehow, the folks monitoring Fat Albert that day must have been taking a smoke break. Customs was fairly simple. I knew most of the people at the airport and we went through the routine fairly smoothly — except for the golden scepter. When we started to get out of the plane, we realized it was still in the canvas bag.

"What about the scepter?" Will whispered.

"Too late now," I said as the customs guy marched across the tarmac toward us. "We'll just have to play it by ear."

The agent looked through the airplane, then took us to the disembarking station. Once we got past the standard questions regarding fruits, vegetables, and animals, and why we had been to Bolivia, the customs agent opened our canvas bag. Will glanced at me, eyes on the verge of panic.

The fellow pulled out the scepter. "What's this?"

I shrugged innocently. "Couldn't resist buying it. It's the latest tourist thing. Supposed to be a replica of the anti-gravity device the Incans used to build their great stone cities. I know it's a stupid shit thing. I mean really, how impossible is that? But I thought the workmanship was good. What the hell, everybody should bring back a souvenir, right?"

The guy looked at it and let the drug dog sitting at the end of the counter get a whiff of it. "If it doesn't interest him, it doesn't interest us," he said indifferently as he stuffed it back in the bag.

As we walked out into the Key West sunshine and hailed a cab, Eddie took a deep breath and muttered, "Groovy, man, just groovy." He looked over at me with a touch of admiration in his eyes. "You got style, honky, and 'nads to match." He put his arms over both our shoulders. "Eddie done lots of interesting gigs, but this one is near the top of the list — very psychedelic, dudes, very psychedelic."

Leo and Lucinda were most unhappy upon discovering they had been taken — or rather, their golden device had been taken. They returned to the motel and paid a concierge to tell them the names of the people who had stayed in room 201. It took another fifty dollars, but Leo also got their home addresses.

Neither of them cared for the thought of going back to South Florida so soon, but they really didn't like the idea of losing that unique little device. They discussed it while sitting in the lobby of the motel. Leo explained that he wanted to waste those "stinkin', scum su...su...suckers" just for fun, now. Lucinda smiled, her turquoise eyes showing a touch of fire, and she signed that she would be content with watching Bobo "kiss" them. She gave Leo a little peck on the cheek, then stood and reached out a long, slender arm to her Cuban lover. Hand in hand they walked out of the motel — the feisty, diminutive Latin and his taciturn Brazilian bombshell. The couple caught a cab and headed back to the airport.

Those of you who have taken extraordinary chances a time or two, and succeeded, know how it feels for the first few days afterwards. Your appetite is sharper, your vision clearer, and all your emotions are as keen as a blade. It's as if you're King Kong — unstoppable, blessed by kismet, one part religiously thankful and another part arrogantly cavalier. And we were all of that. However, as we came down, there were things to be done and revelations to be discovered.

Carina had left a note on our door saying she was returning to the Bahamas for a week to see her mother in Nassau and pick up a few things from her mother's house that would complete her move. She had left the day before we returned.

There was some disturbing news on other fronts, as well. Vanny's father, old Jake, had died while we were gone. As soon as we found out, we were on our way to Vanny's place to console her, and sadly, to our discredit, to compete in our consolation. She did ask if we were successful on our quest, and was pleased that we were, but her grief dampened further interest. In addition, we discovered that the girls had met each other. Vanny put out feelers on Big Pine, checking with friends of hers, and found Carina. They had met and exchanged notes, which could never be considered a good thing for us.

However, we had little time to worry about all of this. Eddie's plane was sitting on a Nicaraguan river region inhabited by wild natives and crazy smugglers. After we had caught our breath and stored our magical gift from an ancient civilization in a safety deposit box, we loaded up my Cessna 182 with some supplies, tools, a carburetor rebuilding kit, a hand pump with a hose, and three twenty-five-gallon drums of fuel, then picked up Eddie and headed back to Central America.

To avoid being over grossed, we departed with about two-thirds our fuel capacity, skipping across to Cancun to fuel again, then down into Honduras, refueling once more at La Ceiba and taking on as much fuel as possible while still being able to get off the ground. We were slightly over grossed at that point, but the old girl still lifted just before the end of the runway. From there we just chased the coast around into Nicaragua, watching for the distinct inlet on which Camerone sat. Three hours later we found it and headed up river, keeping well away from the town.

It was late afternoon when we located Eddie's Goose, still tied up in the little bay on the river. Everyone breathed a sigh of relief as I set the plane down and taxied over to it cautiously. This time we had brought weapons — an AR16, a riot shotgun, and a couple of semi-automatic pistols. Will and Eddie stepped out warily while I covered them with the AR, then each knelt on a pontoon and paddled us over to the Goose, where we tied up. There was no sign of anyone. It appeared Jean-Paul's little friend had deserted the ship. We were pleased to find the plane just as we had left it, and after an uncomfortable night fighting mosquitoes and worrying about natives, we began repairs at the crack of dawn.

Eddie was a good mechanic, and with the right tools and parts, he soon had the defective carburetor rebuilt on the starboard engine. While he was working on that, Will and I emptied the Goose's fuel into a ten-gallon jerry can and dumped it at the edge of the jungle over and over again. Then we pumped in seventy-five gallons of fresh fuel — enough to get Eddie to an airstrip on the coast. It was miserable, hot, sweaty work, but it paid off. After a couple of anxious moments of priming and cranking, the repaired engine finally fired with a healthy burst of white smoke from the exhaust. The port engine fired without a problem. We celebrated with a six-pack of Budweiser and by mid-afternoon both planes were lifting off the water and headed home. Actually, we were both headed for the closest airstrip (other than Camerone), because the 182 was running on fumes. As we soared up into a blue sky laced with feathery white cirrus clouds, I couldn't help but smile. We had done it again. I was reminded of the quote by the writer, Ray Bradbury: *"Living at risk is jumping off the cliff and building your wings on the way down."* We had certainly built our share of wings this time around.

Upon returning home, the next few days were taken up in a somewhat secretive process of learning about the device from Puma Punku. We drove down to Cudjoe Key and took an old road back to the gulf side of the island, where there was a series of marl pits from which they had drawn fill for the highway. A number of large coral boulders still lay scattered around — good practice pieces. We learned the range (up to about one hundred yards before the power faded), the strength of the scepter (practically unlimited), and we discovered it had a "collar" in the center that could be turned to focus the beam, making it tighter so as to move a single object among many. We also tested it on humans, which was a little scary. One day Will just aimed the beam at me from fifty feet away and lifted me into the air like a feather. He took me up to ten feet, then twenty.

"Okay, okay!" I yelled. "That's enough."

Then he swung me from one side to the other, like a pendulum.

"Just remember, sucka, you have to sleep some time," I yelled. "Don't be surprised if you wake up in the osprey's nest on top of the telephone pole outside the house!"

That thought sobered him and he brought me down, turning off the beam with the trigger. But the point had been made. It worked on anything, and responded instantaneously.

Eddie joined us on the tests and we had finally begun to discuss what we might do with the scepter — perhaps a secret meeting with an electronics corporation, or even a government representative, but we had made no hard decisions. The three of us agreed that whatever we ended up with financially, we would split equally, but Will and I did give Eddie five thousand dollars to pay for the use of his plane during the caper.

It was moving into October. The days were growing shorter and their oppressive heat had begun to edge off — that time of the year when the seas lay down beautifully, offshore weed lines rolled back past the outer reefs, and the waters lost their opaque, blue-green color from summer algae blooms, becoming gin-clear. The air no longer held that heavy listlessness, and fat, gray and white cumulus clouds gathered in flocks on afternoon horizons, sheet lightning flashing through their fluffy interiors in startling, effervescent bursts. Will and I dove a couple of afternoons, catching lobster or shooting a grouper for dinner. In the interim, we had taken Vanny to dinner several times, and visited her at home, but the girl's spirit was rightfully dulled by Jake's passing, and neither of us pushed her in any direction. We gave the lady time to set her own course and deal with the loss of her father, but there were times when I hugged her that I had to fight myself not to kiss those remarkably soft lips, to run my hands through that flaxen blond hair, and I knew Will felt the same.

We had received phone calls from Carina, as well. She said she would be back in a few days, that she missed us, and that she would call to let us know when to pick her up in Marathon. She, too, raised those same emotions and needs within us, and increased our confusion. Yet, with the exception of the difficulties with our ladies, life was really very good. We had done the near impossible again. We had a magic scepter and gold coins in the bank, along with lots of dollars from our sale of the golden cross to our buddy Nick Crow. It all seemed too good to be true. I should have been reminded of one of Will's favorite expressions: "No matter how diligent you are, you can only direct so much of your future. Just about the time you're strolling down the street of life, hands in your pockets, a small smile twisting the edges of your mouth, somebody pushes a piano out of a sixth-story window."

It had been a while since Will and I had done a night in Key West, and through it all we hadn't officially celebrated our recent good fortune. It was Saturday afternoon with nothing going on, so we headed into town for a couple of drinks.

Key West was only a couple of weeks away from Fantasy Fest, its annual Halloween celebration of debauchery, decadence, and delight — a glorious rite of sensuality and the senses. It was a liquored, costumed, often chemically-enhanced assemblage where all thought of decorum or morality was lost to moonlight and rum. There were advertisements up for the coming events, announcing the various hotel parties at places such as The Pier House and The Casa Marina, and of course, the annual float parade, wherein everybody who was anybody exerted effort and ingenuity to build a float and crew it with lusty folks attired in modest exotic costumes or simply feathers and spray paint.

We parked my Jeep on Caroline Street, next to The Bull and Whistle, and walked down to The Green Parrot, off Whitehead. We figured we'd start downstream, move on to Duval, and work our way back up. By the time we were fairly snockered, we'd be back at the vehicle.

Aaahhh, Key West, the apex of perpetual Caribbean frolic — palm trees leaning lazily over sidewalks that glisten with steam from afternoon showers, perfumes of hibiscus and jasmine coalescing with the scent of warm bodies, and cacophonies of music from Alice Cooper to Bob Marley drifting through the moist, tropical air, bathing people from every walk of life and nearly every ethnic, political, and sexual persuasion imaginable. There were wasted wanderers baring their souls, or their breasts (or both), sailors out on leave, smugglers out on bail, hippies and Rastamans just plain out of it, and folks from Iowa caught in the Mallory Square "sunset" madness, trying to figure how in the heck they could get back to the cruise ship before the devil found them.

It was still early and The Green Parrot was only moderately packed. The light buzz of voices blended with an old James Taylor tune about Carolina, and there was enough of a breeze coming through the open doors to make it comfortable. We worked our way through the crowd and found a table near the back by the pool tables. After a drink or two and a conversation with a couple of dizzy coeds from the University of Miami, we shot a few games of pool with a burly biker, and a gay guy who seemed a bit taken with Will. We decided to move on.

The drinks had loosened us just enough to give everything a pleasant glow, so without hesitation we found Captain Tony's and started in again. We were enjoying ourselves, relating our recent experiences and laughing about some of them, not really hunting. We both felt we might have found the girl we were looking for, although neither of us had given voice to a name.

"C'mon," Will said, leaning both elbows on the table and gazing at me in a conspiratorial fashion, an eyebrow cocked. "Which one is it? Which one have you got this 'leaning' toward?"

I inhaled and held the breath for a moment, savoring the

comfortable expansion in my chest and head as it mixed with the rum and Coke. I exhaled slowly and offered a wry smile. "Why don't you tell me which one you've settled on?"

"Okay, okay, I'll tell you," my buddy muttered, a sense of surrender in his voice. "This is how I see it..."

He stopped in midsentence, staring behind me at the doors of the bar. Instinctively, I swung around. There was Rick Penchant, smuggler/bandit/idiot extraordinaire, dressed in white slacks, green tennis shirt, and Topsiders. His blond hair had grown back and all the monkey bite wounds on his neck and face had healed, with some minor scarring; but that jutting chin, those dark, arrogant eyes, and that egotistical, "I'm just so impressed with myself" half-smile hadn't changed at all. Apparently, he had learned nothing from the *El Crucifijo de Santa María Magdalena* debacle with us. Just looking at him made me want to give him another lesson. However, the fact that he was an asshole didn't negate the fact that he was a dangerous asshole, and the last thing we needed was a confrontation with him.

Penchant would have been equally surprised to see us. When he left for his treasure/exploration expedition in Colombia and Panama six weeks ago, he had turned loose Stinger, figuring that would be the end of Will and me. Trouble was, he hadn't heard from any of us for practically two months. Stinger never reported back (because he was busy traveling with an orangutan to South America, then healing up enough to chase us to Bolivia), and Penchant's heavies couldn't find us at the time, either. Unfortunately, the same waitress/hooker who learned of our trip from a drunken Eddie, and told Stinger about our plans to find a golden prize in Bolivia, also provided Penchant with "occasional entertainment." She had recently repeated the same story to him, and his interest in us had once again been piqued.

"We need to get out of here," I whispered urgently.

Will nodded. "Damned right, Tonto."

We watched Penchant find a seat up front, a buxom blond in a practically transparent sleeveless white shift on his arm. Once they were settled, the waitress went over and began taking their order. That was our cue. We all but crawled between the tables to the side door and slipped away. Unfortunately, just as we were disappearing like the last wisp of Superman's cape, Penchant glanced up. His eyes went wide with recognition and he cursed under his breath. He started to rise, but realized the futility of it — we were already moving away at a clip. Our nemesis sighed angrily, but was pulled away from his frustration by the attentions of his sexy escort.

Two blocks away, down on Duval, we stopped our casual jog.

"Well, that's sure a buzzkill," Will muttered angrily, catching his breath. "I'd hoped he was still in Panama."

I wiped the perspiration from my forehead with the palms of my hands. "Well, we can rule that out. I'm betting dollars to donuts he'd like to have a talk with us about the gold cross that I'm certain he suspects we stole back. I think maybe we should call it a day. I'd hate to get caught half drunk by him and his boys."

"Roger on that," Will said. "Time to 'split this scene,' as Eddie would say."

Five minutes later we were settling into our seats in the Jeep on Whitehead Street. I rolled down the window and was reaching for my keys when, off to my left just into my peripheral vision, I saw someone crossing the street with a lurching gait — one arm tucked into the left side in a neurologically crippled fashion, hand hanging down loosely, and dragging the left leg slightly with each step. The whole thing reminded me of Igor, Doctor Frankenstein's helper. Before I could do anything, the fellow staggered to a stop a few feet from my window. I couldn't believe my eyes. My jaw dropped as fear and shock grabbed my entrails with tiny, clawed fingers. Stinger! (Albeit a somewhat damaged Stinger). With shabby clothes, slightly glazed eyes, matted hair, a little drool dribbling from the side of his mouth, and a crippled arm, he was the epitome of a very angry Igor. But that wasn't the worst of it. In his good hand he carried a large revolver, and he was bringing it up.

"Aaaahhh!" I yelled in terror.

Will suddenly realized that the guy wasn't a homeless person. "Stinger!" he shrieked. "Holy shit!"

Our badly battered antagonist smiled — at least it looked like a smile, considering his glazed left eye still stared down at the ground and the left side of his face (the same side on which the ear was missing) sagged a little now, as if someone had deflated it slightly, hence the drool. His hair was patchier than before and there were hollow, dark shadows under his eyes, but his one good eye gleamed with the fervor of pure vengeance. He straightened himself, chin jutting out, and brought up the gun. "Thought ya finished me off, laddies, didn't ya? Well, ya didn't! The poison from that bloody bug put me in a coma for a week, crippled me arm and left me with a gimp leg, but I'm here, sure as Mother Mary eats fish on Friday! Surely that I am, lads, to make certain you get to hell before me!"

So intent on putting us out of his misery, Stinger failed to notice the VW bus full of Jamaicans that had just turned the corner on two wheels at Duval, barreling down Whitehead with reefer smoke and reggae music rolling out of the windows, the driver completely lost to any sense of reality, coming in on Stinger's blind side. Our old buddy cocked his pistol. "Say hello to the devil for me, buggers!" he cried, as he backed up a few feet into the street so he could get both Will and me in his sights.

"Wait!" I cried, pointing at the oncoming bus. (I don't know why. I should have just kept my mouth shut.) But Stinger didn't budge, didn't even glance in the direction of the oncoming vehicle. His good eye was a fiery pool of wrath and revenge, every fiber of his being focused on us.

"Ooohhh, you're not foolin' ol' Stinger again. No, lads. No, you're not!" he growled, shaking the muzzle of the gun at us. "I don't give a tiny rat's ass if Jesus and the devil have teamed up and sent all the chariots in hell for me. I'm gonna — "

The bus swatted our Irishman like the hand of God. He looked like a hood ornament, splayed out on the front of the VW, arms spread wide, eyes bulging, still holding the big pistol, just like Yosemite Sam after a run-in with a train.

The vehicle finally came to a stop down the street, after dragging Stinger under it for the last few feet. A crowd quickly formed around it, and by the ghastly expressions on the faces of the bystanders we had to assume the worst. We both exhaled the breath we'd been holding.

Will looked over at me, eyes simultaneously displaying shock and relief. "Ugghh! Ugly way to go. The son of a bitch was like a freaking persistent cat, but I think he just used up the rest of his lives." He frowned, scrunching up his mouth with bitter pity. "You almost got to feel a little sorry for the guy."

"Yeah, I suppose," I said with a grimace. "But it was either him or us. Hell, it's not like I didn't warn him." I shook my head with amazement, and maybe a tad of respect. "He proved to be a resilient and determined antagonist, but I have to agree — that's the end of our problems with the crazy Irishman." We could hear the ambulance in the distance. "Time to go, Ringo. Let God and the devil work it out." I started the Jeep and we drove away.

One thorn of experience is worth a whole wilderness of warning.

— **James Russell Lowell**

CHAPTER SEVENTEEN

The following day we visited Vanny, and she seemed to be doing better. Her blond hair was combed out, catching the sunlight as it rolled off her shoulders, and she was dressed in a yellow tank top and a pair of cut-off jeans, which displayed clearly the better part of her charms. Her old cleverness and sarcasm were returning, as well — a healthy sign of recovery. We had an early lunch together in Marathon at the Seven Mile Grill. A handful of beers and a few of those famous fish sandwiches did wonders for us all. In the process, I explained to her that we were having issues with a guy in Key West who wasn't too happy with us, and we were going to have to abandon our house again for a while. (It was fairly certain that Penchant would come looking for us again.) She was concerned and offered to have us stay with her, but neither Will nor I thought that was a good idea. We had already called a place we knew of in Key Colony Beach and rented a small apartment.

When we dropped Vanny off and she put her arms around my neck in a farewell embrace, that fragrance of orange blossoms and bougainvillea engulfed me like a tidal wave. I could barely resist crushing her to me and kissing those incredible lips. When I watched her hug my friend with equal passion, bat's wings of confusion and jealousy flittered in my stomach.

On the way home, Will mentioned contentedly, "She's something else, isn't she?" He added happily, "I think that girl really likes me."

"I hope not," I said, more sullenly than I intended. I was reminded then of a quote I had heard years ago. I had no idea who had written it, but it was starting to seem appropriate. *"Love is a lot like contracting rabies. Sometime after you've been bitten you know you're getting crazy, but there's nothing you can do about it."*

That afternoon, while we were packing up a few items to take with us to our new "safe house" in Marathon, the phone rang. Will picked it up and answered cheerily, but a moment later his face became hard and wary. He motioned for me to pick up the phone in the kitchen. The voice that I heard chilled me. It was Drako, the sociopath from Cat Island — the one with whom I had cut cards for Carina. His voice was brimming with malevolence, and the confidence of someone who, this time, held all the cards.

"You want your woman back, you do what I tell you. Otherwise I feed her to da sharks."

Instantly every muscle in my body felt electrified and my stomach knotted with dread. "Where is Carina?" I blurted out. "What have you done with her?"

"Don' get your britches all bunched up, white boy," Drako growled, but there was a teasing satisfaction to his tone. He knew he was in control. "She go to visit her mother in Nassau, but she call her sister in Cat while dere, and her sister, she tell too many people. Women, dey got no sense of 'shut yo mouth' 'less you teach dem. I send a couple of my people and dey go get her."

Will, generally the easygoing one between us, came back with such a wrath and viciousness in his voice that it startled me. "You hurt her, you son of a bitch, and there'll be no place on this freakin' earth for you to hide. You understand me? Do you understand me?"

I suddenly realized with a complete clarity which girl my partner had a "leaning" toward.

Drako chuckled maliciously. "You in no position to be makin' threats, conch boy. You do exactly what I say and maybe you see her again, in one piece."

I heard Will draw a breath to respond and I interrupted. "Okay, Drako, what's the deal? What do you want?"

"Smart boy," the Bahamian replied with sweet venom. "Maybe tings go okay for you. I want da gold you find on my island. Don't bother to lie to me. I seen dem gold coins Fabio bring with him. I want what you find. My island. My gold."

I started to say something, but he stopped me.

"I make it simple, I don' know how much you find, but you bring me five hundred gold coins, and you get Carina, all nice and healthy. You call me at The Reggae Cove when you arrive, tomorrow, you hear, conch boy?"

I exhaled slowly. There was no way around this, and more threats weren't going to help. "Yeah, I hear you. We'll keep our word. You keep yours."

We were up before dawn, gathering our gear. The only chance we had was to put Drako at a disadvantage somehow during the exchange. We needed to ensure Carina's safety first, then find a way to take him down. I took a moment to call Vanny, to let her know something had come up and we were forced to fly back to Cat Island. I didn't give her any details. She didn't need the extra stress.

"Somehow we have to make this exchange happen in a territory in which we are comfortable, and we need some leverage," I said as we sat on the porch drinking coffee, waiting for the sun to clear the horizon.

Will stared out at the lightening water, chewing on his lip in thought. "Yeah, I agree. Leverage, exactly. I've been thinking about it. I got a plan. We'll need Fabio's help." He looked up at me and smiled mirthlessly. "That son of a bitch is going to rue the day he screwed with the bunko brothers."

As we ran down Pine Channel, feeling the rhythmic slapping of the floats on the surface, The Guess Who hammering us with "American Woman," and the new sun gilding everything in sight, I felt ready for this, good to go. I was frightened for Carina, but there were few times in my life I could remember feeling more consumed with purpose and passion. We were going to save our girl.

Leo and Lucinda arrived in Miami in time for lunch. They had come into Tampa from South America, in order to keep a low profile, then rented a car and headed south. When the couple reached Miami they dropped off the rental, picked up a newspaper and found an older model Ford Mustang convertible for sale. Leo met with the owner, showed a fake I.D., paid him cash (an extra hundred to keep the license plate until he could register it), then picked up Lucinda and off they went. Top down, both of them were enjoying the ride into The Keys until they moved onto the narrow, two-lane stretch of road on U.S. 1 in Key Largo. They found themselves behind a band tour bus that just wasn't in a hurry. The big lettering on the sides and back of the bus read, "Jimmy Buffett and the Coral Reefers." There was an occasional waft of a rich, sweet-smelling substance drifting back at Leo and Lucinda, along with song after song of life in the islands coming from the open windows of the bus. Most people would have been pleased with all this, but Leo, who only listened to Cuban music, was in a hurry and didn't like to be anywhere that he couldn't see a tall building, was purely annoyed.

"Buncha wacked out yahoos singing about sailboats and palm trees," grumbled the little Cuban. "Who is dis yahoo, Jinny Buffett?"

The trip over to Cat was relatively uneventful, and the weather kind. We crossed the Florida Straits, sailed through the Great Bahamas Banks and over Andros Island, then passed the Exuma Cays and Exuma Sound, and finally glided into Cat. As we neared the island, I eased down to two hundred feet and put the amphibian in a small bay at the northern end, just past Lott Settlement. I dropped off Will with the box of gold coins and the golden scepter — we didn't want to have to clear customs with those items. Prior to departure we had called Fabio, our little Bahamian buddy. He met us at the bay with a rental car. He and Will, along with our more precious items, headed on to the airport at New Bight while I flew over to it. We tied up an hour later outside the terminal building.

Fabio came walking over with Will. He was still the same skinny little fellow with mischievous hazel eyes, big teeth, and long, reddish-brown Rastaman ringlets that curled to his shoulders. But he was dressed much nicer than before — Nike tennis shoes, parachute pants, a bright blue T-shirt and a couple of gold chains dangling from his neck.

"Good to see you again, Fabio," I said as we shook hands. "Wish it was under different circumstances."

"Ya mon, ya mon," he said, his head bouncing up and down. "Me too. Dat stinkin' goat fornicator, Drako — "

"Yeah, I know. Now we've got to figure this thing out, somehow beat him at his own game." I looked out at the island as it suffered in the afternoon heat, almost no breeze, palm trees drooping, and hardly a cloud in the sky. "Well, there's no point in putting things off. Let's find a phone and call the bastard."

Unfortunately, our nemesis wasn't having anything to do with plans about meeting yet, which threw us off our game.

"I don' give a rat's ass what you want," he said. "You do what I say if you want to see dis woman again. You go get a room at Kookie Palms, where you stay before, and I will call you tonight."

"Wait, listen! We need to see Cari — "

The phone went dead.

Will was standing next to me. He heard, and his face was tight with dread.

I put my hand on his shoulder. "We don't have a choice, man. We'll have to form a plan as we go."

Within the hour we had dropped off Fabio at his new apartment and settled into Kookie Palms. Malaki, the owner, was pleased to see us. It was early fall and there were hardly any tourists. As there were no phones in the rooms, we explained to him that we were expecting an important call — one we could not afford to miss. He assured us he would stand by throughout the day. He offered to prepare us an early supper in his small café next to the guest rooms, and we accepted, not wanting to get too far away from our belongings. I had duct-taped the scepter underneath the bathroom sink cabinet, very difficult to notice and hard to find, but that wouldn't work for the thirty-pound box of gold coins, so we simply hid it under the bed and covered it with a blanket. Hell, we weren't going to be more than a stone's throw from it at any time.

We sat in the shade of the covered deck for the next hour or two, drinking beer. At five p.m. Malaki announced that dinner was ready. We hadn't eaten since early morning, the tension and the worry leaving us with little appetite. Our host fluttered around us nervously, making sure our glasses and our plates were full, and the food — broiled snapper and local vegetables — was pleasing, but he seemed almost relieved when we finally left. When I opened the door to our apartment and we walked in, I heard Will grunt behind me, but before I could turn I felt a burst of pain at the base of my skull and the lights went out.

When I came around, I found myself bound hand and foot in the trunk of a car, being jostled miserably as it worked its way down a rough road. I turned my head and it exploded in fireworks, throbbing like a tequila binge hangover. Wincing, I moved my hands and feet around, finding Will next to me. "Hey, buddy, you all right? You awake?"

He moaned, and shifted his position slightly. "Oh, God!" he muttered. "I should have listened to my mother and become a pharmacist."

"Well, it's not like you haven't had some experience with pharmaceuticals."

"Yeah," he groaned. "I keep pushing them out of airplanes. No money in that unless you know the people picking them up."

We had just gathered our senses about us when the vehicle slowed, then stopped. I could hear two men talking up front — something about this being the place, the Orange Creek Blue Hole.

"Oh shit!" Will whispered. The Orange Creek Blue Hole was well known on Cat. It was a truly bottomless marl grotto that had strong, undersea currents flowing from its subterraneous caverns, linking them to the sea. I had a pretty good idea what they intended for us.

The trunk opened and we were unceremoniously pulled out, then dragged over to a tree about twenty yards from the blue hole. The moon was full and satiny white, nearly as bright as day. There were two of them — a couple of Drako's boys. Without much conversation they dropped me to the ground, my back against the tree, and tossed Will down next to me, then they went over to the edge of the blue hole for a moment, probably checking out the best place to toss us in.

At that moment, the weirdest thing happened, and I will remember it for the rest of my life. I glanced over at the edge of the jungle and I saw something. At first I thought it was the moonlight playing tricks, but it wasn't. Sitting on a log not thirty feet from me was a strange, squat-looking, gnome-like creature, sort of like a frog — skinny arms and legs, round body, not more than a few feet in height, but I swear to you, as I live and breathe, the face was strangely human. The eyes were almond shaped and luminescent, the nose was flattish with flared nostrils, and the mouth was wide, with thin lips. It sat there, staring at me with a curious indifference. The head tilted, then the mouth opened slightly. I turned to my buddy and nudged him with my foot.

"Will!" I hissed. "Will! Look! Look at this!"

When I had his attention we both glanced over, but the creature was gone.

A shiver ran down my back and I was reminded of the legendary *nyankoo*, the three-foot-tall gremlin with a human face and mystical powers that villagers across the island have talked about in hushed tones for generations. Cat Island's Bigfoot, or maybe Littlefoot.

"What is it?" Will asked. "What's going on?"

I glanced back at the log. "Nothing. Nothing I guess."

We were offered no time for debate. The two big Bahamians had returned, their faces grim.

"One at a time," the taller one said, frizzy hair, ugly cold eyes, dressed like his partner, in shorts and a Bahamian Islands T-shirt. "We get 'em over to da water, and cut da ropes on dere feet like Drako said." He grinned maliciously. "With dere hands tied, dem conch boys make it maybe five minutes before dey run out of energy. Den dey drown slowly. Dat Drako, he a cruel bastard."

"Will!" I yelled, kicking at them, trying to reach my friend. I got a kick to the face for my efforts.

Will, too, was crying out unintelligibly, kicking and fighting them as they dragged him toward the water.

They got about three-quarters of the way to the blue hole when one of them realized he had left his knife in the car. While they dumped Will and one went back, I suddenly sensed something behind me. I could hear leaves cracking and the stealthy, slow movement of something small and strange-smelling — bitter-tart like the mangroves, and musky. I heard a husky twitter-like sound right behind me, and I froze. The smell became stronger and the hair on my arms stood straight up as my terror mounted. All I could think about was that frightening little gnome-like creature with the human face. The twitter came again, right behind me, just over my shoulder, and my skin went clammy. Suddenly, I felt tiny, clawed fingers touching the ropes at my wrists, pulling at the knots in a methodical, determined fashion. I could feel its warm breath on my neck, but I couldn't bring myself to turn around. I was petrified, but praying whatever it was would free me. In the distance the two men had returned with their knife and were dragging my partner to the water's edge. He yelled out in fear and anger as they cut the bonds on his feet, picked him up, and prepared to toss him into the dark, clear water.

The creature behind me still hadn't succeeded when suddenly it chittered harshly, skittering away into the jungle. I sat there, breathing heavily, moonlight filtering through the foliage, when once again I heard something approach and pause at my back. Whatever it was knelt close to me. I felt a small hand grasp my shoulder tightly.

"You two got a natural way of finding bad chit, mon," Fabio whispered. You know dat? Good damn ting I be comin' over to your place and see dem dumpin' you in dat damn trunk."

I almost cried with relief. They had just thrown Will into the water. They were laughing, watching him struggle.

"Dat boy not gonna last two minutes," one joked. "He already bobbin up and down like a coconut in a bad sea."

"C'mon, Luka," said the other. "Let's go get dey other coconut. I hear a bottle of rum callin' me."

The two men were approaching. Fabio had succeeded in untying my hands, but not my feet. "Be ready, mon," he said as he quickly slid back into the darkness.

My adrenalin was so spiked that when the first one knelt in front of me to untie my feet, I reached out with both hands, grabbed a couple handfuls of his frizzy hair and jerked him into me, head-butting him in the nose. He fell back screaming in pain, blood gushing from his nostrils. Before his partner could react, Little Fabio stepped out of the jungle from behind him with a baseball bat and whacked the boy out of the park. Just for good measure he smacked the other guy, as well. They'd be lucky if they woke up in a week.

My Bahamian buddy stood in front of me. "You know, Fabio got better tings to do than always be chasin' around, beatin' people senseless for you. Maybe you two need a easier hobby dan dis damn adventure chit."

I couldn't help but grin as I ripped at the bonds on my ankles, but Will was still out in the center of the blue hole. I hit the ground running, and when we reached the marl bank, my worst fears were realized — there was no sign of Will. Quickly scanning the surface, I saw a swirl, maybe twenty feet from shore. I kicked off my tennis shoes and smacked the water in a flying dive, but when I reached the spot, there wasn't anything to be seen. Spinning around and treading water, I yelled his name. Nothing. I jackknifed down and did a long circle underwater. Still nothing. I was about to come up for air, when another eight or ten feet below me there was a wisp of my partner's shirt. My heart hammered with fear and hope simultaneously — I would never have seen it had the moon not been full. Clamping my mouth shut, I kicked down furiously, knowing that I was running out of air.

Will was floating listlessly, his clothing billowing out in a ghostly fashion, eyes closed. Still slashing downward in a wild, determined frenzy, I was growing dizzy, and the ringing in my ears was becoming a cacophony. Reaching my friend, I grabbed his arm and started for the surface, but the extra weight was too great a burden on my oxygen-starved body. Sparks were flashing in the corners of my eyes, gray shadows like "floaters" drifted across my irises, and my chest felt like someone was standing on it. I remember realizing in the back of my mind that I was fading out, dying, in some Godforsaken grotto in the middle of nowhere, but I couldn't let my friend go. I just couldn't. I bit my tongue and felt the gush of blood in my mouth, trying to force my body to hold on to life, kicking feebly toward the moon-splayed surface. As everything began to fade to dark gray and I reached the point of succumbing to the fatal instinct to breathe, I squeezed Will's arm in sad apology and finally...inhaled. But as I did, I broke the surface. Gasping desperately, coughing up water, and floundering, I still might not have made it had Fabio not jumped in and dragged Will and me to the shore.

After drawing in a few life-giving breaths I crawled over to my partner, pushed him onto his back and gave him a handful of CPR chest presses. His eyes were still closed, he didn't respond, and his face held a bluish tint. Moving Will onto his side, I slammed him in the back with the flat of my hand once, then again. Still nothing. "Don't you dare die, you son of a bitch!" I hissed out breathlessly, grabbing him by his shirt, pulling him up to me and shaking him, as much in anger as fear. I rolled him over and pounded him once more, hearing myself groan in desperation when there was still no response. I was gasping in terror, blinded with tears, sitting on my haunches on the hard, moonlit coral, holding my friend in helpless despair, when suddenly he coughed out a mouthful of water in a trembling rush, and gagged. I cried out in relief, quickly lifting him up to a sitting position, supporting him with my arms, and continued to slap his back to clear his breathing passages.

As I was holding Will, watching his color return and realizing that I wasn't going to lose him, I was reminded once again of how deep and abiding my affection was for this tall, rangy fellow with his large nose, sandy blond hair, and sarcastic nature. I realized that sheer, genuine affection could stand alone as its own entity, surviving solely on friendship, respect, and honesty. In its purest, most valuable form, it was devoid of sexuality, passion, or any other confounding or distracting physical elements. What we shared was authentic and unadulterated. We were true friends.

I was still holding him, patting him on his back when he coughed again and weakly pushed me back, muttering in a slurred fashion, "Quit squeezing me, you bloody gorilla! I can barely breathe as it is."

I laughed with genuine pleasure. "Sorry, buddy. Don't know what I was thinking."

By the time we got back to Kookie Palms, the moon had reached its apex and was creeping down the other side of the sky, mingling with the stars on the horizon. Malaki was nowhere to be found. We suspected he'd been in on our distraction and abduction, but there was a part of me that said the tall, gentle fellow was probably an unwilling accomplice, most likely threatened with bodily harm or damage to his establishment.

Our room had been torn apart and the coins were gone. However, they never thought to look up under the bathroom sink cabinet (behind the sink itself). No one does, which is why I used that spot. So, we still had the golden scepter. I was past the point of anger, lost now to a cold determination, but my partner was buried in a dark rage. They had taken Carina and our gold, but I knew intrinsically that with him, it was Carina that mattered.

He took the scepter and pressed the trigger in the shaft. The instrument hummed to life. He turned the collar, tuning the beam to a narrow shaft of energy, nodded with grim satisfaction, then turned it off. "C'mon," he said, never even looking at Fabio or me, and walked out the door.

Fifteen minutes later we were pulling up at The Reggae Cove. I had the baseball bat between my legs and Fabio had the can of mace Malaki kept behind the cash register, and a four-foot piece of heavy plumbing pipe.

Will turned to us from the driver's seat before we got out. "Now this is what I want you two to do…"

One of Drako's people was sitting on the porch. He got up and came over, full of confident bravado. He had a gun tucked in his belt. "You be more stupid conch boys than I thought. Drako's gonna —"

I smacked him on the head with the baseball bat and we walked over his body, hardly missing a step. At the door, Will and I nodded to Fabio, then we went in.

 The bar hadn't changed. Fans still struggled with the cloud of ganja smoke that hung just below the ceiling. There was the same smell of mildew and stale beer blending with reefer, the mirror behind the bar still had a bullet hole in it, and reggae music provided the perennial authenticity. There were maybe a half-dozen people at the tables, drinking and playing dominoes. Drako was sitting in the back, dressed in white cotton slacks, a jungle green tank top, and leather sandals, cleaning his nails with a ten-inch stiletto — same slicked-back hair and hard, black eyes, the overhead florescent lights and his sleeveless shirt accentuating the taut muscles in his arms. When we walked in, a look of surprise flashed across his face, but he quickly buried it. Placing the knife on the table, he pushed back his chair and frowned.

"You supposed to be dead. How you do dat?"

Will clicked on the scepter and it hummed, almost anxiously. "We cut a deal with the devil. We promised to send you instead."

"What that shiny thing you got, mon?" the Bahamian asked.

"A little something I dug up for the occasion. Where's Carina?"

Drako shrugged, indifferent. "She here, where she belong." He got that malevolent smile. "But I bring her out for you, so she can see you one last time." He nodded to one of his men and the fellow went into the back. A moment later he came out dragging Carina by the arm, pushing her down into a chair near his boss. It was plain that she had suffered — her white blouse was torn, lipstick smeared, and shame and fear filled those golden eyes, but a terrible, prideful anger burned in them, as well. She gasped when she saw us, a glimmer of hope rising in her countenance, and I had to physically still myself from running to her. I had never felt such a pure, animalist desire to hurt as I did at that moment. I saw Will's hands clench and his face fill with emotion, then go hard as he stared at Drako.

Drako never even got up. He just nodded to the huge black fellow next to him. The man's body rippled with muscles, six-foot-five if he was an inch, with a head like a bowling ball. The guy got an almost happy smile as he lumbered at Will. My partner never hesitated. He pressed the trigger on the device, and the wavering beam shot out at a heavy wooden table on the other side of the room. With a second click Will locked the beam on the table and ripped it into the air, hurling it across the room with such speed that the round projectile blurred. It hit the guy like a bus and buried him in the side of the wall across from Drako, splinters of wood flying through the air like shrapnel. Another man rose up and charged with a machete in hand. Will locked him with the beam and bounced him up and down from ceiling to floor five or six times, then cast him off like a ragdoll. A guy off to my right rose up quickly and made a dash at us. He may have been going for the door. It didn't matter. I caught him in the knees with the baseball bat and I heard bones snap like saplings. Before he hit the ground I backhanded him across the head. There was a collective gasp, then silence. We moved to the center of the room in unison. I stepped off to the side, Will still facing our antagonist and a couple of his terrified friends.

Drako sat up, concerned now, somewhat amazed, but not cowering. I noticed for the first time the semi-automatic pistol in his waistband. He stared at Will, weighing the situation, intuitively realizing that his real antagonist was my partner. "You have some heavy juju, conch boy, but can you dodge bullets?" he asked, his confidence seeming to be returning for some reason. For a flash of a second I saw his eyes shift behind us. Instantly, I knew we were in trouble. As I turned, the bartender was coming out from around the bar with a sawed-off pump shotgun. He jacked a shell into the chamber, but as he did, Fabio stepped out from the kitchen door behind him and tapped him on the shoulder with his lead pipe. As the fellow turned around, our little buddy hit him with a spray of mace, then swung the lead pipe in a whirring arch. It caught the bartender squarely in the jaw, so hard that the big man's teeth bounced off the mirror behind the bar.

I've got to give Drako credit. For all that he'd just seen, he wasn't beaten. He'd decided to make it a contest, mano a mano. He stood up slowly and came around the table, facing Will. He shifted the pistol in his belt, then let his hand drop to his side. I swear to God it was just like the Old West again. I could almost hear the Spaghetti Western music. All Will needed was a cigar and a serape. Everyone left in the room just slid away, including me. There was nothing I could do against the pistol our opponent carried. It had come down to a single moment that would decide this affair.

Will spread his feet for balance, and the two men stared at each other. Bob Marley was crooning about shooting a sheriff again, and there was a steady, monotonous drip of liquor off the edge of the bar where a rum bottle had broken in the melee. The moment stretched out into impossible tension, then Drako went for his gun.

I suddenly realized Will was at a disadvantage because he had to bring the beam to target and lock it with a second touch. His antagonist had only to draw and shoot. Just as my friend locked the beam, Drako fired, and I saw Will flinch backwards from the impact. Still, he threw Drako up against the ceiling before the scepter fell from his hand, a red splotch forming at his shoulder. But there hadn't been enough force in Will's stroke, and the Bahamian was staggering to his feet, gun still in hand. He was badly shaken and his left arm hung loosely at his side, but he realized in an instant that he was going to win this.

As Drako shook his head, trying to clear it, I charged him with the baseball bat. I didn't know what else to do. If I could get to him before he got the gun up… But about halfway into my blitz it was apparent I wasn't going to make it. Drako was bringing his weapon to bear with a hellishly triumphant smile. I screamed — I'm not sure if it was fear or defiance — and threw the bat, my momentum still carrying me at him. It missed easily, twirling over his head as he ducked, and bounced off the wall. I remember I could still hear Bob Marley as the barrel leveled at me. Strangely, my last thought was of Vanny.

Suddenly, Drako's eyes went wide with shock and surprise, and he stood there, frozen like a statue, the gun still aimed at me. I stumbled to a halt as my adversary's black eyes slowly lost their focus and the barrel of the gun gradually lowered, as if it had become too heavy to support. Drako dropped to his knees, and behind him I could see Carina, face contorted with horror and vengeance. The tall Bahamian issued a gurgling sigh and collapsed face-first onto the dusty linoleum floor. From his back protruded the stiletto with which he had been cleaning his fingernails, buried to the hilt.

Carina rushed into my arms, crushing me to her. She was crying and kissing me passionately. In the next instant we separated and were at Will's side. He had taken a round high on his shoulder — not life-threatening, but his arm wasn't much use to him at the moment. He drew Carina to him with his left hand and they held each other with the same passion. Fabio was quickly at our side, guarding us, but there was hardly anyone left to protect us from. The one or two people still intact were cowering against the wall in the back.

"I tink dis be a good time to be somewhere else," Fabio said.

I nodded. "You get Will and Carina into the car. One thing left to do."

As my friends shuffled out the door, I walked to the back and picked up Drako's pistol. There was a guy hiding under a table. I fired a round in front of his feet. "What did Drako do with my coins?"

When he hesitated, I put one more round in the wall next to his head. "In da back room! In da room!" the guy cried in terror. "He got a safe behind da picture!"

I walked back and found the picture. It was a cheap safe. Two rounds in the locking mechanism and the door flopped open. There was our box.

Half an hour later we were at the airport, wanting to be on our way out of Dodge. It was closed after dark, and the gate was locked, but Fabio knew the night watchman. We had no idea how this whole thing was going to go down with the local law enforcement, and I wanted to be gone before it got to that point. Will was hurting, but the bullet had passed cleanly through the upper ball of his shoulder and there was no other damage. Carina had stopped the bleeding with a few items we purchased at a local store on the way to the airport. Will was loving the attention. I'm not sure that he wouldn't have shot himself just for the pleasure of her ministrations. Fabio agreed to return the rental car, and once again, I pulled him off to the side after getting Will and Carina into the airplane. I opened the lid to the box and the gold coins glittered coldly in the moonlight. "Fill your pockets, buddy," I said. "You've damned well earned it again."

Fabio got that big-toothed grin. "You boys a lot of trouble, but you got a fine sense of appreciation." He dipped his hands into the box a couple of times, shoving the coins into the pockets of his baggy shorts. Then he looked up with a warm smile. "You call Fabio next time you in town, huh?"

He started to turn away when I stopped him. "Fabio, just a question; what do you know about this *nyankoo*? You know, the little gnome creature that's supposed to be on your island."

He looked at me strangely for a moment. "You tink maybe you see *nyankoo*?" He paused. "Maybe out at Orange Creek Blue Hole?"

I shrugged in answer, not knowing exactly what to say, but surprised that he knew the location.

He looked over at the moon above my shoulder for a moment, then returned to me and smiled, but it was an odd, knowing smile. "Just a old wives tale, probably... from some old wife." And he was gone.

Five minutes later, so were we.

Adventure without risk is Disneyland.

— Doug Coupland

CHAPTER EIGHTEEN

We were passing over Andros Island and coming up on the Florida Straits. I was starting a gradual descent toward sea level for the final run in. With thousands of dollars in antique gold coins and an ancient device aboard, we didn't want to deal with customs, so we had to dance with the devil again. Will was finally asleep, curled up on the bench seat behind me. It had been a tough night for him, almost drowning and being shot. Carina, who had been sitting with my partner, pulled a blanket over him and moved forward to sit in the copilot's seat.

"He is fine," she said. "Resting well."

We sat in silence for a few moments, then she spoke quietly, without looking at me. "Thank you."

No response was necessary. I just nodded.

"You and Will," she whispered, her voice filled with emotion. "With the exception of my father, I have not known such people like you." She reached out and ran those long, perfect fingers through my hair, sliding them sensuously to the back of my neck, letting them linger there before running her hand slowly down my shoulder and arm, reluctantly letting it slip away. She was looking at me now, and the reflection in her eyes offered a good deal more than gratitude. Carina leaned over and kissed my ear and my neck sensuously, then she drew my head around with her hand and found my lips. The passion in that kiss was profound, yet I suddenly found myself strangely disturbed by it, uncomfortable, as if I was betraying my friend — as if, perhaps, we were betraying more than my friend, and I thought of Vanny. I returned the kiss, but pulled away when the plane lost a point or two of pitch.

We talked quietly for a while, but as we got closer to the coast I was forced to give more attention to my flying, and to watching for DEA aircraft that might be watching for me. Nonetheless, we made it in safely, once again. (I was beginning to understand why so many of my friends were getting rich overnight.) I took a chance and landed in our own Pine Channel, hoping Penchant and his gang had already checked out our place and figured we'd left town. After tying off the aircraft, we stumbled up the stairs and into the house. Carina gave Will a couple of painkillers from my medicine cabinet and put him to bed. I had her sleep in my room and I took the couch. Twenty minutes later we were all asleep.

The morning sunlight crept through the living room windows and softly awakened me. A wan sun had cleared the horizon, but was easing into a stratum of marbled, dark gray thunderheads. Above that, wispy, pink-tinged stratus clouds struggled in an opaque sky. I smelled coffee and that brought me around. As I got up and pulled on my T-shirt, I saw Carina in the kitchen. She brought me a cup of coffee, a warm smile, and a kiss on the cheek.

"Aaahh, I see one of my heroes is awake."

I raised the coffee cup and nodded in appreciation. "How's your other hero doing?"

She took a sip of her coffee. "Good enough, all things considered. But we need to get him to a doctor this morning and have the wound looked at."

Will stumbled out his room, holding his arm just above the elbow. "Let me tell you, this hero crap purely sucks. I need coffee and another Percocet."

By midmorning we had Will at a local clinic, where a doctor looked at my partner's arm and asked questions we chose not to answer. It wasn't his first rodeo. He quit asking questions, cleaned the wound, and stitched it up. Will received a shot for pain, which he appreciated on a number of levels. Afterwards, we had a late breakfast at The Big Pine Coffee Shop, then took Carina back to her apartment on the island. She needed some time to herself, to rest and recuperate. At parting, our lady gave us both passionate hugs and thanked us profusely again.

On the way back to the house, Will was looking out the window when he spoke quietly. "Okay, I guess it's time, so I'm just gonna say it. Carina. She's the one I want. I don't know how that's going to set with you, but that's the way it is."

I was suddenly flooded with relief. "Yeah, I know, and I'm okay with that. In fact, I'm good with it."

Will swung around, pleasure and relief filling his face. "Really? You're sure, man?"

"Oh, yeah. I'm sure."

My partner slapped the dash in exuberance, then winced from the pain. "Hot damn! That's some good news!"

"Yeah, I figure it is," I said hopefully. "But the bad news is, we have some other serious issues to deal with. I'm fairly sure Penchant is trying to find us as we speak. We're going to have to get out of the house again and back to the apartment we rented in Key Colony, until we can figure out how to solve this problem. Speaking of Marathon, we need to drive up and see Vanny, let her know we're okay."

Will was smoothing down his mustache with his forefinger and thumb — that thing he did when he was concerned. "Yeah, the Penchant thing. I'm not sure how to solve that, unless maybe we could find a Mongolian Red-eye..."

I grinned. "I'm not ruling that out."

Forty-five minutes later we were pulling up at Vanny's place. She was out of the door before we had reached the stairs. "I've been worried crazy about you two!" she cried, coming off the deck, her blond hair tied in a ponytail and those reef-blue eyes sparkling with relief. I got the first hug, because I was ahead of Will, but when she saw the bandage on Will's arm she was all over him with concern, hugging him gently and wanting to know what had happened. My stomach did a little flip-flop at all the attention he was getting, but it was okay. He was the one with the bullet wound.

We sat and talked for a while in her living room, we explaining our latest quest and Vanny appearing appropriately impressed. There was no need to be secretive. She and Carina had already met and shared far more than I was comfortable with, and it appeared that they liked each other. She seemed to have turned the corner on her grief and was, by and large, the old Vanny that I knew (and...loved?).

Over the next hour we explained the problem we had with Penchant, and that we would be staying in Marathon for a while, which apparently suited her fine. But I warned that we had to be careful about our contacts, in case Penchant's boys were following us. Finally, reluctantly, we had to leave. Again, that wonderful scent of orange blossoms engulfed me as I took her in my arms and our lips brushed lightly in the process, sending little electric sparks throughout my body, lighting some places more than others. Yet once more I saw that she offered Will the same favors, maybe a little more...but then, he was the one with the wound. I was thinking I might have to shoot myself, just a little bit.

Fabio called that afternoon, while we were grabbing a few things from the house for the apartment in Marathon. He had good news, saying the police were ruling Drako's killing a drug-related gang thing, and they weren't expending much energy trying to solve it. Drako wasn't well liked anywhere, and the general impression was "good riddance." No one apparently saw what happened to Drako —

they were too busy hiding under tables and chairs, and the couple of witnesses who claimed they saw a white guy with a magic wand move people through the air were automatically disqualified as being way too high to be credible.

Will and I returned to our furnished apartment in Key Colony Beach Monday morning to try to lay plans for getting us out of this mess with Penchant. Somewhere along the line we were going to have to give Penchant something more serious to worry about than us. But there was still our nagging issue of lovers and friends.

"We've got to get this thing resolved between us and the girls," Will said with a sigh as we sat in the living room of our new place, Elton John crooning about "Bennie and the Jets" from the transistor radio in the kitchen.

I was staring out through the patio doors at the small patch of beach in back of the apartments. The wind had come up and lazy whitecaps were forming a couple hundred yards out into the water. I swept back my hair with the fingers of both hands in a nervous gesture. "Yeah, you're right, and I think I've got an idea."

Will cocked his head. "Okay, I'm listening."

"First, we call them, both of them, and find out if they feel the same way about coming to a decision on just one of us — or if they really even want one of us. If they agree, we all write a letter to the one we want, so it comes in the mail. That way, if it doesn't work out as planned for everyone, there's no awkward group of people standing around in a room, not knowing what to say."

"Yeah, that's good, that's sensible," Will said, nodding in agreement. "Hell, man, in a worst-case scenario both the girls might want just one of us." He grinned. "And that would be really tough on you — embarrassing."

That afternoon we called the girls, and surprisingly enough there was no resistance to the idea. We all agreed to put letters in the mail immediately, so we would have the results the following day. We gave them both the address of our new apartment and hung up with sugarplums dancing in our heads, then we went out for an early supper.

Unfortunately, it was crushingly crowded everywhere, and the traffic on U.S. 1 was terrible. It was Fantasy Fest week, with the big parade on Saturday night, and every boozehound, biker, and Jimmy Buffett fan in Florida and the Eastern Seaboard was headed for Key West. Truth was, we were no different. With his music and poignant lyrics, that boy from Pascagoula had made himself the very embodiment of the Florida Keys. Will and I were not the kind of people who had heroes — we'd lived it and done it — but we did carry respect for certain people, and Buffett was one of them. For us, his songs had made the good times better and the bad times bearable.

Will turned to me at the noisy restaurant and smiled, surprisingly congenial given the circumstances. "Well, look on the bright side. If all goes well, by the weekend we'll be taking our girls to Fantasy Fest!"

I had to admit, that did put a glow on everything.

The mailman was a young guy — tall, long in his step, and enthusiastic about his job. He showed up right when our landlord said he would, with two letters. I've been in a lot of hairy situations in my life, but I can rarely recall being as nervous as I was when he handed us those letters. I beat Will by a fraction of a second and snatched them out of the mailman's hands. I separated them and scanned the addresses on each — one for Will, one for me. That prompted a mutual sigh of relief — no one was going to be left out in the rain. But there was no return name and address at the top of either. We had to open them to find out.

We inadvertently stepped away from each other and ripped open the letters. Somewhere in the background I remember hearing seagulls calling, and children laughing at the swimming pool out front. Within the first two sentences my chest constricted and I couldn't get a breath. My hands were shaking and I suddenly felt the twin sensations of panic and pity assault me. Anguish hammered down the walls of my hope while sympathy poured out, for Carina, who wrote without reservation of her growing love for me. Carina — not Vanny.

I had only to look at Will's face to see that it mirrored my emotions. "Vanny, not Carina," he whispered, stunned, shell-shocked, trying to suck in a breath. "I mean, I like Vanny, but...I thought for sure..."

Somehow, through this miasma of enchantment, fascination, and liaison, we had missed the signals, read it all wrong. Probably because we simply wanted to see it the way we wanted to see it. In the end, the girls we had chosen had chosen someone else. A radio was playing in the apartment's office. I could just barely make out the soft, rasping of a tune by Bonnie Tyler. *"Once upon a time I was falling in love. Now I'm only falling apart. There's nothing I can do. A total eclipse of the heart..."*

Will looked at me, eyes filled with irony and sorrow. He offered a bitter smile. "How's that for a dream bummer?"

Bonnie was right. It was a total eclipse of the heart.

In this bizarre situation, out of four people, there were no winners to congratulate. We had all lost, and no one was up to phone calls of any sort. Will and I sat around the rest of the afternoon, licking our emotional wounds. Finally, we went out, grabbed a pizza and a six-pack of beer, and came home.

For the next couple of days we seemed to stumble around in a fog of disbelief. Life had slipped out of gear — the engine was running but nothing was moving. One evening we were sitting on the little patio behind our apartment, desolately munching another pizza, watching a reddish-golden moon ooze out of the sea and rise up into a river of ghostly stratus clouds hovering just off the horizon, illuminating their edges with soft fire. Any other time it would have been worthy of wondrous exclamation, but we were all out of wonder, running half a tank low on happy and glad.

I was hunched in torpid silence, staring out at the ocean and sipping on my beer, when Will pulled himself upright in his chair, wincing a little from his wound and leaned forward squinting out at the darkening sea. "What's that? Looks like someone's bringing a boat in."

Sure enough, out of the evening haze across the ocean came an old, gaudily painted commercial fishing boat with a large forward cabin, its inboard engine chugging along throatily, the boat easing its way into the shallows of the beach in front of us. A big black man emerged from the wheelhouse, moved forward and tossed out an anchor, then let the offshore wind catch the craft and set the hook. Without further ado he stood up and waved, then slid off the side into the waist-deep water and waded toward us. Rufus!

Our strange, mystical buddy strode out of the sea like Neptune and marched up the beach, stopping before us at our patio, dripping water on the concrete deck. "Hello, hello, my olden friends, Willmen and Nevada!" He pulled up a chair without invitation and sat down.

We looked at each other, then over to our just off-center Jamaican friend. It was the same old Rufus — T-shirt and shorts, dreadlocks, battered sandals, and that big, toothy smile. "Kansas and Will," I corrected for probably the fiftieth time in our association.

Rufus leaned forward in his chair. "I see you are in firm health. Dat is a good sign for expendable pinballs."

Will huffed. "No thanks to you, I might add."

I glanced around, then back to our guest. "I'm guessing this is not a coincidence. But I'm telling you right now we're not going on any more of your 'interesting journeys'. This last one nearly got us killed a half-dozen times. We've been chased, shot at, attacked by alligators and crazy natives, and in the end I'm not sure the 'special gift' we got was worth all our efforts. On top of it all, while dealing with this, we lost the ladies of our lives in some confusing foul-up of hearts."

Rufus held up his hand. "Actually, olden friends, dat is why I am here, basking in the glow of your presences and bringing greetings from the Grand Messenger for the wisdom of ganja. I may possess a solution to da problem with da blood-pumping organisms in your chests which are presently causing you much difficulty in your heads and lower sexual regions."

Will turned to me. "Okay, I'm lost. Can you decipher that?"

I shrugged. "I think he's saying he can fix our love lives."

"Let me tell you story about the clever mango," Rufus said, softly interrupting. "We all lose at game of life occasionally. But if persistence not work, sometimes you must become da clever mango."

Will sighed, a little less taken with the idea of parables solving his problems. "Rufus, I don't think clever mangos are gonna —"

"Where you got to be, mon?" Rufus said more sternly. "Where have you got to be dat is so important you cannot hear small story dat would fix your pumping organism?"

Will sat back and Rufus continued. "Da mango, he hang in da tree, waiting for some pretty bird mouth to eat him. But sometimes he gets passed by. So what does da clever mango do? He falls to da ground and becomes all sticky-full of juice — juice oozing out, sweet, enticing, attracting all dem pretty bird mouths. You must become sticky, tasty — irresistible. Den da bird who does not want you in da tree cannot resist you on da ground. Da pretty-mouthed birds come down and pluck your seed with pleasure." He looked at both of us. "Is dat not what you want? To have your seed plucked with pleasure by da pretty bird of your choice?"

It was absolutely freaking amazing. He knew! He knew about the loss of Carina and Vanny. I glanced at Will. "How could he know?"

My partner just shook his head. "Beats the hell out of me."

Unperturbed, Rufus reached into his pocket, taking out a small vial of dark blue liquid. "Ancient potion," he whispered. "Very ancient. Was first used when there was snow on da banks of da Nile." He held it up. "You have your women visit you — one-half in one drink, one-half in da other. Dem pretty birds must drink. Dey will sleep soon after, probably eight hours." He held up a finger. "Very important! Da first person dey see — da very first person — dey will love! You understand? If dey see da mailman first, dey fall in love!"

I scooted back my chair, a look of incredulousness on my face. "You gotta be kidding us, Rufus. A love potion? Is that what you're telling me this is? Like 'number nine'?"

Rufus stared at me, those big chocolate eyes unchanging. "Dey don't be no number on it, mon. But, ya mon, dis be 'one size fits all' serious love medicine." He held up his finger again. "Now, dis potion gonna wear off in about six months, but if you love dem and your time together is good, dey will come to love you, too, as it wears off."

"When you think about it, this is a little weird," I said, somewhat uneasy. "We're sort of taking their free will here, if this works."

"Yeah, that may be true," said Will. "But the truth is, no one has what they wanted now. If we do this and it works, everyone is happy."

Rufus nodded, got up, and handed the bottle to Will. "I must go now. Catch tide." He smiled. "Remember, you are captains of da boats dat are your lives — you are not passengers. When you arrive at strange destinations, don't blame any one else for misreadin' da charts." Our old friend gazed at us for a second. "You want your pretty birds, you do what Rufus say. Become clever mangoes. Dis small gift I give you today — for your troubles." With that, he turned and headed back across the beach toward his patiently bobbing boat, leaving us with our mouths open and our heads full of questions.

We sat there in silence for a moment, then Will held up the vial and looked at me, that crooked smile splitting his face. "What have we got to lose?"

The following morning I called Carina, and Will called Vanny, asking them if they would consider coming over to our apartment on Key Colony that evening — telling them that maybe there might be a solution to this confused *ménage*. Both were hesitant — no one wanted more salt in their wounds — but they agreed.

Vanny arrived first, dressed in a light pink tank top that accented her full, perky breasts, and a pair of blue jeans that looked as if they might have been painted on. It was a "look what you're not going to get anymore" thing, and it worked. But her sparkling blue eyes that usually flashed with such fire were tinted with a defiant pain. Carina arrived five minutes later, while the three of us were making uncomfortable small talk. She had chosen a short, white tube dress that clung to her like a needy lover, and a pair of sandals with three-inch cork heels. She flowed into the room with that innate natural elegance, but when she saw us, there was hesitancy in those golden eyes that diminished the confidence she was trying so hard to maintain.

Will and I were no different in our desire for image. Both of us had donned our best blue jeans and deck shoes. I chose a white, tight-fitting polo shirt, and Will, his favorite tropical shirt.

Saying that it was awkward would be an understatement. After an exchange of brief, uneasy hugs, we ushered the ladies to the living room and sat them on our rattan sofa. The sun was just easing onto a pale blue horizon, casting streamers of scarlet and tangerine through the windows, which added to the ambience but did nothing for our situation. There was absolutely no point in wasting time wading through hollow small talk with uncomfortable silences. There were no winners here. No one wanted to catch up on old times. I immediately offered to make drinks and they graciously, if not indifferently, accepted. Vanny, to the point as always, was interested in hearing what this "solution" was that we had to offer, and I assured her it was next on the agenda, after we'd had a chance to relax for a moment or two. I went to the kitchen where I added ice to the blender filled with margarita mix and whipped up a couple love cocktails laced with Rufus' special potion (and two more regular ones for Will and me). The drinks were served and we somehow managed a little small talk for about fifteen minutes. But it wasn't long before our ladies' eyes began to flutter. They eased back into their seats, and within minutes both of them were asleep.

Exhaling softly, I rose from the couch. "I gotta tell you, I'm still feeling a little weird about this."

Will cocked his head at me. "Weird enough to live without Vanny for the rest of your life?"

I carried Vanny to my room, placing her on the bed and covering her with a sheet, gently caressing her cheek and offering a wistful entreaty that she find her love for me again when she awakened. I kissed her softly on the forehead and left. Will carried Carina into his room, and I was certain offered the same supplication with equal fervor. When all was said and done, it was after 10:00 p.m., and my buddy and I had experienced a tough few days prior to all this. So, with sugarplums dancing in our heads, we each took a couch in the living room and were soon asleep.

I awoke to the early morning sun drifting through the windows, turning our living room to soft saffron. I could hear seagulls crying to each other on the beach. Will was snoring peacefully from across the room. Taking a deep breath and exhaling slowly, I relaxed for a moment. It felt so good to be safe. Then I suddenly remembered the night before. Glancing at my watch I recoiled. "Holy moly! Will, it's 9:00 a.m.!" I screeched, jumping off the couch and scrambling over to my buddy while pulling on a T-shirt. "Wake up! Wake up, Cinderella! We're late for the freaking ball!"

Will's eyes popped open and he bolted upright. "What time is it?" he muttered groggily, shaking the sleep away and combing back his long hair with his fingers.

"It's late time," I growled impatiently, pulling him to his feet. "We gotta get into those rooms with our prospective ladies and have them see us, now!"

As my partner slipped on his T-shirt, I walked to my room and opened the door. The bed was empty. I checked the bathroom. No Vanny. Nothing. At that moment I heard Will call to me. There was something in his voice that made that spot in my gut writhe like a snake.

My friend stood in the doorway to his room, staring into it with incredulous dismay. I stumbled over and gaped. Carina and Vanny were curled up together in each other's arms, sleeping blissfully, the most perfect, peaceful, contented smiles on their faces. The bedcovers were in passionate disarray and the girls were naked, covered only by the corner of one mauve sheet.

"Ooohhh, sweet Jesus!" whispered Will. "Vanny must have stumbled in looking for me or the bathroom, and found Carina. Lord! We've lost our ladies to our ladies — again!"

I fervently hoped Will was wrong, but upon waking the two, there was sadly no question that Rufus' potion worked. We had decided to screw with Mother Nature for our own gain, and it had backfired.

Over the next couple of days our mellows were severely harshed as a whirlwind romance ensued between Carina and Vanny. In record time our ladies cemented their relationship and Carina ended up moving in with Vanny. For my partner and me, it was like having heart surgery without anesthesia. The only good news was, we discovered that the girls still held the highest esteem for us, but remarkably enough, it seemed neither carried much of a preference for Will or me — though it seemed at times when Vanny hugged me in greeting there was something in her eyes, a twinge of longing or sparkle, a subdued memory that couldn't quite find its way to the surface. But in the end it made little difference, because she would turn to Carina, caress her, and they would giggle self-consciously at their obvious affection, and my heart would constrict in memory and pain. That could have been, should have been, me...

My buddy and I were back on our apartment patio on Friday evening, sitting in the shade, tired of all the empty-hearted hiding out and missing our house on Big Pine, when Will straightened in his chair and looked at me. "You know what I think we ought to do? I think we ought to go to Fantasy Fest tomorrow night and drink and chase ass until dawn." He offered a beleaguered smile. "In the immortal words of Crosby, Stills and Nash, 'If you can't be with the one you love, love the one you're with.'"

Sitting there, staring at the setting sun, I knew it was a knee-jerk reaction, but that didn't make it a bad idea. "Can't say that I disagree. For the last few months we've been hunted, shot at, tricked, and led in the wrong direction like a couple of blind bird dogs. Maybe it's time for some straight-up, old fashioned debauchery."

Will smiled. "We'll take the scepter, really screw with some heads, huh?"

"I don't know. You think that's a good idea?"

"Hell yeah. Let's have an evening that will bury our sorrows for months to come. Let's make some memories that our grandchildren will be certain are lies!"

I couldn't help but grin at the thought. "We could go as space people — wear the bottom half of our old wetsuits, a couple of tank tops and swim caps, and get all that painted silver! Do some serious freaking out." I paused for a moment. "Actually, it's a great idea. We can hide in the herd!"

Leo and Lucinda knew the two guys they were after had finally returned. They had been sitting in their Mustang in the parking lot of a small curios/shell shop on the other side of U.S. 1, watching the house since noon. The airplane was back, and one of the cars (the Jeep) was gone. Even with their diligence over the last few days, they had missed them somehow. Leo had rented an apartment on Little Torch Key, so it was there they returned for the evening. They would begin their vigil again in the morning.

As it was, there were a number of other people with their own issues that week.

Key West's Umbrella Man, formally Arlington Newberry, was a

bleak-eyed, weary sixty-four years old. He had once been a wealthy stockbroker in Key West, with a trophy wife and lots of people he called friends. They enjoyed his lavish parties, cruises on the yacht, and nights on the town. He enjoyed their unadulterated fawning. But he liked his booze and drugs a little too much, and one night, a couple of joints, a bevy of margaritas, and a serious fall down the staircase left him with about half his mind. He never recovered. Within six months Arlington's wife and his "friends" had relieved him of his money, his home, and his yacht, leaving him out on the street. As time passed, his only possessions became a shopping cart, an umbrella (which he applied at all times, rain or shine), and a Chihuahua named Albatross, that he had found in a parking lot. It was a dozen years ago that he lost his life as a stockbroker, but he barely remembered it now. Arlington lived on handouts and what he could find to sell from the dumpsters he pillaged, sleeping in the park, or whatever shelter he could find. None of his friends from years ago would have recognized him — the shabby clothes, a grimy baseball cap from which protruded graying, stringy hair, and those once clever, bright blue eyes now vapid pools that vacillated between listlessness and invented conspiracy. As people who suffer from his sort of malady often do, he had taken to talking to himself, requiring opinions from Albatross on most decisions.

Arlington sat on the corner of Simonton and Petronia streets, just a block from Duval, umbrella above his head, knowing this would be an exceptional week for him. Once a year when everyone dressed up in strange costumes, they got drunk and lost things. (Sometimes Arlington "helped" them lose those possessions if they were careless about where they placed them.) He knew the dumpsters would be overflowing with good stuff, and his usual list of beneficiaries would have a meal or two for him. He licked his lips in anticipation and ran a hand over Albatross' head. "We's gonna get nice things now. Nice things. Yes, yes." He rubbed the palms of his grubby hands together in anticipation. "Lots of nice drinks nobody misses, and nice tips on tables when nobody's looking, and we's can buy juicy hamburgers with pickles and ketchups. Yes, pickles and ketchups." His bushy, gray eyebrows danced like Groucho Marx's. "Hmmm, we like 'em a lot!" Shaking a finger in admonishment at Albatross, he added, "But we must be clever. Yes, yes. Remember our old motto — know when to buy and when to sell, and when to steal." Those watery blue eyes caught a gleam of delight. "Sure, we's a dirty little man, but we's still clever. Clever rascals. Yes, we's are. Don't you think, Alby?"

FBI Agent James Rodriguez sat in his Ford Grenada in the Searstown Plaza, nursing a cup of robust Cuban coffee and smoking one of the five cigarettes he allowed himself each day. He had been assigned to follow up a report that a couple of the *Banda Pirata Cubano* (Cuban Pirate Gang), originally out of Miami, had been spotted in Orlando about a week ago. The FBI, along with local authorities, had arrested most of the gang that had stolen a large number of pleasure yachts over the last year or so, but a few members had eluded them. One of his contacts in Miami said he'd heard that two of them, a Cuban man and a Brazilian woman, had "passed through, going south," so on a hunch the agent was checking out Key West. Dressed in a pair of gray slacks, a cream-white, short-sleeved shirt, and a pair of dark loafers (his jacket thrown over the seat next to him), Rodriguez was a tall, almost gaunt, thirty-five-year-old Cuban-American with military short, dark hair and bright brown eyes. He liked his job — getting paid to play "cops and robbers" — and he was enjoying being back down in The Keys again, but Rodriguez admitted to himself it was a damned bad time to try to find anybody in this lunatic town. Nonetheless, here he was, sending out descriptions to his "street people" and hoping to get some feedback.

Late afternoon of the following day Will and I returned to our house on Big Pine Key, where we started gathering up the items we needed for our costumes. We weren't exactly in a good mood, given the circumstances, but we were doing what we could to make the best of it. The truth was, we were starting to look forward to a night of feckless forgetfulness in Key West. To get us moving in the right direction, I mixed up a pitcher of rum punch. Glasses in hand, we toasted to another adventure and went to work. I dug out a couple of our old, extra light wetsuit bottoms and found a pair of sleeveless tank tops, then I went to the drug store on Big Pine and purchased two large bathing caps. Will found a can of silver spray paint in the storage shed and commenced to making our costumes all glittery. Once everything had dried, we tried it all on, adding two pairs of dark, wrap-around sunglasses to the package. The rum punch had started to catch us, and when we got a good look at each other we started laughing so hard I had to take a break and mix more punch.

Leo and Lucinda watched what were apparently a couple of

absolute idiots spray paint their clothes, then stumble around the porch laughing at each other so hard that their drinks spewed out of their noses and they had to sit on the steps to catch their breath.

"Dis not gwenna be berry hard, I don' tink," Leo said, shaking his head. "Why don' we go cl…clobber dem now an' take da wand ting."

We decided we were ready to go. We took off the swim caps and tossed them in the car — for the sake of comfort and to avoid looking too conspicuously stupid on the way to Key West. I went into my room to grab some money. As I reached into my drawer, I noticed the "magic gumball" Rufus had given us before we left for South America, and I remembered his words — "Throw at floor or wall. Once it crack open, poof! Everybody go blind around you for five minutes, but do not open eyes for ten seconds after throwing ball, or you too be blind as dead mud duck!" Somehow, through all our adventures there, I had never quite found the right moment for its use. Truth was, I'd almost forgotten about it. On impulse I grabbed it. Turning to leave, I took a glance into the mirror above my dresser — a quick appraisal of myself before a night of unfettered frivolity. My sun-bleached brown hair was lying on my shoulders now — probably time for a trim. The hazel-green eyes that stared back at me still carried a wicked flippancy, but they were tempered by experiences that had added a touch of prudence. The tank top reminded me that I still had a hard physique, probably one of my stronger assets when it came to the unabashed pursuit of barstool princesses. I shrugged and muttered, "It is what it is, and it'll have to do," while stuffing the blind ball into my wetsuit pocket. By the time I got downstairs, Will had grabbed the scepter and was waiting by his car. We hopped into the Camaro and took off.

It was a couple of hours before sunset, one of those days where calm waters and a flawless sky mesh at the horizon in exactly the same color, and you can't tell where one stops and the other starts — scattered clouds literally floating into the sea. A light front had just come through and the air was cool and crisp. We couldn't have asked for a more perfect situation.

Leo and Lucinda were less happy with the situation as the Camaro suddenly pulled out of the driveway and turned West on U.S. 1.

Lucinda signed hurriedly. Leo nodded. "Yeah, yeah, I know.

We'll ju...just follow. Ees okay. Dey got da wa...wand with dem."
He started the car and pulled out of the shell shop parking lot.

The traffic bottlenecked on Stock Island coming into Key West, then eased a bit on Roosevelt Boulevard, but got terrible again as we hit Truman Avenue. We took a left on Varela Street ,then made a right onto Catherine Street, cutting through the suburbs, down toward Duval.

Leo was having fits. A fender bender just before Truman had tied them up for a couple of minutes, offering only a quick glance at the Camaro as it turned onto Varela. They followed as quickly as they could, but lost their prey. Now they would have to prowl downtown for the car.

"Unabefreakin'alievable!" grumbled Leo. "Five freakin' million tu...*touristas* comin' to one place to drink tequila and listen to son' blond-haired yahoo named Jinny Buffett. Who da shit is dis guy?"

We found a parking place on Rose Lane off Duval, put on our bathing caps and wrap-around sunglasses, then shuffled our way through the gathering mass of tourists and locals to The Bull and Whistle, ready to do some serious "forgetting" for a while. It was still early and the place was crowded, but not overflowing. The parade was a few hours away. The bar carried that perennial tincture of alcohol, cigarettes, hormones, and expectation. There was a mixture of local beach people, indifferent islanders, a handful of bikers, and a lot of *touristas* trying their best to find the nirvana Jimmy Buffett was always telling them about. The better part of them were in costumes of some sort, and everyone really liked our silver spacesuits and the wand Will was carrying.

We settled into a couple of seats at the bar and ordered two margaritas. There was a couple to Will's left and an empty chair next to me. Beyond the chair was a heavy biker attired in chains, tattoos, and leather — cold green eyes, a pirate's gold loop in one ear, a full beard, and black hair down past his shoulders. His woman sat next to him — thin but not unpleasant-looking, with long red hair and anxious brown eyes, dressed in a red bikini top and a yellow sarong around her waist. The biker yelled abrasively at the bartender, calling him by his first name every time he wanted something, providing the distinct impression he was a local. The barkeep responded quickly, but without much pleasure, a plastic smile pasted on his face. I knew instinctively the big guy was one of those people who attaches themselves to a bar like a ghoul to a graveyard — something no one wants, but short of an exorcism there's no way to get rid of them.

Every bar has one or two. The biker and his girl were doing shots of tequila, but apparently she had reached her limit.

"C'mon, baby, one more for ol' Wolf," he growled as he tried to force another drink to her mouth while she asked him to stop. In the process, she pushed his hand away and spilled the drink on him. His personality changed in a heartbeat, his face went hard, the veins in his temples standing out as if hard rubber worms had just crawled under the skin. He grabbed her hand. "Dammit, bitch, you stop drinking when I tell you to!"

Neither Will nor I were white knights by any stretch of the imagination, but the guy caught both of us wrong. This was the kind of man who had gone through life bullying anyone and anything that got in his way. There was no fixing him with kindness, understanding, or Jesus. People like this fellow learned lessons only one way.

Will had knocked down several shots of rum from our bottle on the way in to Key West and he was pretty well through his margarita. My boy was feeling his oats, and I wasn't far behind him. He pushed back his stool, winked at me, and stood up. "Earthling!" he shouted clearly in a heavy, mysterious voice.

Wolf paused in the process of bringing up another shot of tequila. He turned and tilted his head. "You talkin' to me?"

Will nodded firmly. "Yes, it is you I talk to. Your woman says she has had enough spirits, so I advise you to leave her be."

"Who in the hell do you think you are?" he growled, somewhere between anger and incredulousness, letting the girl's arm drop and giving my partner his full attention. The people in our immediate vicinity had picked up on the drama and were starting to observe, conversations fading.

Will straightened up. "I am Zodar, from the planet Tamalon, where men treat their women with respect."

Realizing where this was going, I sighed and stood up, my courage buoyed by the distinct advantage that Will held in his hand. "I too am from Tamalon, and I find your disrespect of the female species abhorrent, asshole."

The guy's eyes narrowed and he pushed himself off the barstool, a malevolent smile splitting his hairy jowls, but it quickly faded to viciousness. "Listen carefully, you two goddamned homosectional gay boys. Keep your freakin' noses out of this, or I'll beat the shit out of both of you after I make her drink her tequila, you hear me?"

Will and I had long since come to the conclusion that we didn't care who someone loved. The gay thing wasn't our cup of tea, but the gay bashing thing just didn't sit well with us. I turned to Will and brought my hands up, making a series of arcane gestures and signs. My buddy nodded and confirmed with a few of his own. I turned back to the biker.

"My friend says he would like to bet you fifty earth dollars that he can stop you from being an unmitigated asshole, maybe even cure you of this disease once and for all — just him against you."

I took out a fifty-dollar bill and slapped it on the countertop, and Will brought up the scepter, holding it in front of him with the business end down.

The biker looked at us for a moment, then burst out laughing. "Let me see if I've got this right," he said, smiling, hands out, palms up, looking around at the audience, which was growing. He was enjoying this — an ass-kicking always brightened his day, especially with a lot of attention. "You're gonna pay me fifty bucks to kick your shiny boyfriend's ass while he holds his dime store ray gun, huh? You two idiots are a lot drunker than you look." He took out fifty dollars and put it over mine, then poured another shot of tequila and sat it in front of his woman. "For you, bitch, just as soon as I take care of this." Then he turned to Will, while I stepped back.

Everyone adjacent to us did the same, moving discreetly away. No one wanted any of the spaceman's blood on them or in their drinks. A nervous, anticipatory hush fell over the bar, like Romans at the coliseum before they released the lions. Someone coughed in the back of the room.

Will brought the scepter to his side and hit the trigger. The beam hummed down at the floor just like Luke Skywalker's light saber. Wolf offered one final, ugly grin, then lumbered confidently at my partner, tucking his head, moving into a crouch, huge tattooed arms raised with clenched fists, beady green eyes glittering with malicious pleasure. The yellow-naped parrot in the cage behind the bar (who had witnessed more than one of these occasions) undid his door and clawed his way to the top of the cage. He flapped his wings excitedly and screeched, then yelled, "Kick his ass! Kick his ass! Aaawwk! Muck him up good!"

But within the flick of an eye my friend raised the scepter and locked the beam on his antagonist, sweeping the astonished, suddenly quite concerned biker to the ceiling, holding him there just long enough for the fellow to get some perspective on his predicament, then stuck his head in one of the whirring, commercial grade ceiling fans to loosen him up.

While the biker was yelling, the parrot was dancing on the top of his cage, flapping his wings and shrieking, "Bite his freaking ear off! Aaawwk! Kick him in the nuts! Aaawwk!"

Will pulled Wolf out from the fan and flung him against the far wall, hard enough to jiggle the boy's eyeballs. I was sure I heard something crack when he hit and collapsed to the floor.

My buddy turned to me with a smile. "I'm getting pretty good at this!"

"Yes! Yes indeed you are, Zodar!" I said with a smile of my own. "I can see why all the women on our planet love you."

The biker was moaning, struggling to his feet.

"Excuse me," Will said politely. "My work on this planet is not yet done." He turned and beamed the beaten and befuddled biker once more, ripping him from his feet and sticking him in the ceiling fan again, adding a few more cuts and bruises to his collection. Then he pulled him over to where we were, perhaps ten feet above us, and held him there. "Tell me, Mr. Wolf, have you learned anything negative yet about the propensities of being an unmitigated asshole?"

Wolf gagged a little and spit out a tooth, but before he could do much more, my partner sighed dramatically. "I'll take that for a 'no.'" Will twirled the shrieking biker through the air and slung him down the entire length of the bar top like a hockey puck, right into the wall a few feet from the bar. With the exception of the squawking parrot, who was really enjoying himself, the room went silent. Most everyone was hiding under their tables or gaping with stunned amazement (and a good deal of appreciation for the space guy). Wolf was crumpled up against the wall, bleeding in a half-dozen places and very possibly suffering from a concussion and a fractured arm.

As my buddy strode toward him, raising the scepter, Wolf cringed like a beaten dog. "No! No!" he screamed in a near pubescent voice. "No! God, stop!"

Will snatched him up again and held him in the air. "It is a common agreement here that you are..." Will looked up at the ceiling in dramatic deliberation, finger to his lips, as if trying to find the right word. Then he brought his eyes back to our biker. "A butt-faced asshole, as we would say on Tamalon. But I would like to confirm that you know this. Tell me. Tell me, Mr. Wolf, that you are a butt-faced asshole, and that you are never returning to this bar."

The parrot screamed, "Butt-faced asshole! Butt-faced asshole! Muck him up! Muck him up good!"

I could see people giggling now.

Wolf hesitated for a second and Will started him toward the ceiling fan again. "No!" he screamed. "I'm a butt-faced asshole! God! I'm a butt-faced asshole!"

My partner raised him into the fan just enough to clip the top of his head again. When Wolf quit slobbering and begging, Will added, "And you're not coming back here, ever. Correct?"

A slight move toward the fan had him blubbering, "Never! Never coming back. I promise! I promise!"

The parrot was just beside himself, bouncing around on the top of his cage and flapping. "Butt-faced asshole! Never coming back! Aaawwk! Knock his dick in the dirt! Aaawwk!"

The people were relaxing now — laughing at the parrot and whispering with incredulousness to each other.

Even Will was having a hard time keeping a straight face. Finally, he carried the thoroughly vanquished bully to the door of the saloon. He looked at him hard. "Remember, we are watching you now. You are on the list."

Wolf had no idea what that meant, but he whimpered at the thought. Then my buddy and his scepter tossed him a good twenty feet into Caroline Street. Wolf's girlfriend garnered a slight smile, and ordered a rum and Coke. When Will returned, we got a two-minute standing ovation. Needless to say, the people of Tamalon didn't pay for a single drink that night, and the parrot had learned a new phrase regarding butt-faced assholes, which he used with enthusiasm throughout the evening.

As we were bringing peace and justice to Planet Earth and enjoying our newfound popularity, Leo and Lucinda had been combing the streets around Duval for our car. They finally found it, and by the purest of luck found a parking space a block away. They got out and Lucinda glanced around at all the costumed revelers. She signed adamantly at Leo regarding the need for costumes — that they would stand out like a ballerina in the barrio without them.

Leo was resistant. "I don' need no son' a bitchin' costume!"

But she looked at him, those large, dark eyes gleaming sensuously, and signed, "C'mon, baby," batting her long eyelashes. "Maybe we use them later on tonight, for our own private Fantasy Fest."

Half an hour later she and Leo were leaving one of the costume shops on Duval. Lucinda had gone with a titillating combination of feathers and spray paint, worked artistically over a very tiny bikini.

Leo was a little devil, literally, complete with horns and a curving, spiked tail. It was perfect, but Leo still wasn't happy. "Unabefreakin'alievable! A red yahoo devil!" But the promises from Lucinda calmed him — or rather, moved him — to acceptance.

However, neither of them was aware of another coincidence that had taken place only moments before — one that Leo would have found far less pleasing. When they were parking their car, FBI Agent James Rodriguez had been having dinner at a small café on the other side of the street. He was raising another forkful of *arroz con pollo* to his mouth when he saw the distinctive couple exiting their Mustang and discussing costumes.

"*Madre de Dios!*" he whispered, the fork suspended in air, his face displaying stunned disbelief. There they were! The people he'd been trying to catch for over six months! Right in front of him!

His first impulse was to go over and take them right now, but he knew that wasn't good protocol. He got up, dropped some money on the table and walked quickly to his vehicle at the front of the restaurant. Grabbing his car phone, he called his office in Miami. The orders he received were simple. "Do not attempt apprehension without support. Other agents are en route, from north of Marathon. Continue to observe and follow, as they may lead to additional suspects."

We finally bade our new earthling friends adieu, moving out of The Bull and Whistle onto Duval, and into the wild gaiety that was Fantasy Fest. An ancient golden moon had risen into the heavens, hovering over us in benevolent understanding. It had seen it all before, from Stonehenge and Alexandria, to the streets of Rome and the palaces of Europe. From Peking to Haight Ashbury, some things never changed. The crowd was thickening, a thrumming hive coming alive with anticipation of the parade, thousands of people up and down Duval raptured in a rummed-up, spaced-out, mild hysteria of spontaneity, shuffling along the street in a glorious tequila/herd mentality. Glittering, painted bodies swirled in the moonlight, feathers and leather and imagination running rampant as liquor splashed into willing lips and over eager faces, restraint and self-consciousness washing away in riotous rivers of rum. The floats were just coming into view, each providing a theme from the exotic and bizarre to the clever and crazy, all accompanied by wildly attired or barely attired partiers and a cacophony of music, lifting spectators and participants higher and higher into an undulating chimera of sensations, sounds, and scents that were no less than a fest of fantasy.

The mobile displays of cleverness began to roll by and the excitement in the crowd raised another notch as candy and beads were tossed out to the spectators. Coming up on our left was a float whose theme was outer space, complete with a funky rocket ship and several wildly attired space people. When they saw Will and me at the curb, they waved, encouraging us to come aboard. Both of us were nearing three sheets to the wind and we'd acquired a couple of ladies from the bar, but the invitation was simply too much to pass up. Abandoning our newfound attractions, my buddy and I broke away from the press, grasped the side of the float, and scrambled aboard. In the process of crawling onboard, I tripped over a little fellow in a devil suit and sent him sprawling. I apologized and he started to cuss at me in Cuban, but a tall, feathered lady in the crowd grabbed him and the sea of people separated us.

There was one other individual who observed with interest as the two aliens boarded the float. He had been watching them since they arrived on Duval, eyes shimmering with a combination of elation and wrath. He moved away, struggling through the crowd — places to be, things to do, grand entrances to be made.

At first, as our display moved along, we just waved and threw candy. But somewhere along the line, Will turned on the scepter and started fooling with the crowd — lifting people up and depositing them on balconies, or on the float rolling along in front of us, or if they were really hot-looking, setting them down with us. There are still folks today who tell of people flying through the air in the 1982 Fantasy Fest, but the reports were never really taken seriously because, let's face it, how do you gather any credibility when all the witnesses were flat-assed hammered? However, the scepter was starting to run out of power. We had learned in our time studying it that the device would hold a charge for about five hours before it wound down. The wand would still hum, and the globe and crystal at each end would still glow, but it would no longer lift objects. It could be rejuvenated slightly by turning it off for a while, but the best thing was to recharge it with sunlight.

Even without the use of our wand, my buddy and I were enjoying ourselves immensely. We were on the front of the float, waving, throwing candy, and drinking excessively. The moon was directly above us, absolutely incandescent in its brilliance — so bright the night seemed lit like midday. A shapely spaceperson had just refilled my drink, when above the din of the crowd I heard an airplane, and a moment later I saw a large, high-winged, single engine Cessna come across the face of the moon, silhouetted like the proverbial witch on a broomstick. The plane was nearly above Duval Street, at about two thousand feet, when the cargo door slid open and someone jumped out. Immediately a white parachute blossomed — one of the new parafoil designs that were far more controllable. Once the fellow had it all in hand, he turned it toward the parade. Many of those in the crowd had noticed as well and were pointing, assuming it was some sort of promotion for Fantasy Fest. I studied the man controlling the parachute. He appeared to have bandages over much of his body. Damn, he looked familiar, even at a distance. There was no question he certainly seemed to be heading toward the float parade. Will was watching as well, with an odd expression on his face.

As the fellow soared down, not so much gliding with pleasure, but dropping like a hawk, the glistening moon bathed him and I finally got a better view. Aside from the near rigor mortis set of the jaws and teeth, I realized that his face was really banged up, and one arm seemed to be tucked over the guy wires in a semi-useless fashion. But it was those eyes, those crazy gray eyes…

My jaw dropped, and before I could get the words out, Will cried, "Holy freaking crap! Stinger! I think that's Stinger!"

That wasn't the worst of it. I noticed that, bound against his chest with duct tape, was what appeared to be a row of reddish dynamite sticks, the fuse dangling down the front of his vest. Now that he had locked on his target, Stinger was screaming a barely audible volley of curses, a small butane torch in his good hand streaming out a searing blue flame. I found myself scooting back, bumping into Will, immersed in the impossibility and terror of the moment. The people around us were pointing and exclaiming excitedly.

I suddenly realized with a lurid clarity that the crazy Irishman intended to kill us in some sort of banzai-kamikaze attack. He had just lit the fuse, and it was sparkling its way up toward the dynamite. The crowd, lost to blind revelry, had no idea what was happening. They didn't care if it was Jesus or the devil parachuting in, as long as he brought beer. I could hear our old antagonist screaming profanities, shouting about how "ol' Stinger was going to get the last bloody laugh!"

Just when it looked like he was probably right, I noticed a flock of late-roosting pelicans coursing downward across the sky, headed for the salt marsh at the edge of the airport — big birds, probably a dozen of them. Stinger's glide path was taking him right toward the V.

He came down, quartering from above on the pelicans — it was the last thing the birds were expecting. It was the last thing Stinger was expecting. He jigged when he should have jagged and his chute caught the last three or four birds in the V. Suddenly, what had been a graceful, albeit vengefully gliding device, became a twirling mesh of out-of-control nylon sheeting and guy wires, unmercifully tangled with absolutely freaked out, squawking, flapping pelicans. With an enraged gray and white bird straddling his neck, trying to swallow his head like a luckless mullet, Stinger was slapping frantically at the pelican and the last of the burning fuse, shrieking epithets about godless winged demons and freaking horrible timing. As the collapsing parachute swirled in a slow, failing arc above Duval our mad bomber managed to get out a couple more scathing expletives before that Wile E. Coyote look filled his eyes and the fuse found the dynamite.

I've got to tell you, it was as if someone tied a cherry bomb to a parakeet. In a fiery flash of thunder and smoke our old antagonist simply became part of the universe — just bits of bandages, tufts of nylon, and fluffs of pelican feathers floating through the air and settling quietly around the suddenly stilled crowd. There was a lingering odor in the air, somewhere between grilled chicken and napalm. Suddenly, someone started clapping, another person joined in, and a moment later people were cheering up and down the street. The freaking tourists thought it was all part of the Fantasy Fest show!

Will gazed up at the star-ridden sky, where Stinger had just been so vengefully soaring, then turned to me and shook his head. "I think that was the last life for our tenacious cat. He finally be on his way to meet the Grand Messenger of Ganja."

I couldn't resist a small smile of relief. "Sometimes, if you're not careful, you actually get what you deserve."

With the entertainment over, the revelers of Duval quickly returned to reveling. A beautiful space girl filled our glasses with something highly alcoholic, and we reverted back to the task of drinking ourselves senseless and throwing candy to the crowd.

The float behind us was a pirate thing, done like the deck of a ship with sashes, cutlasses, and muskets for the guys, and string bikinis for the "prisoners." There was a lot of rum drinking and capturing of booties going on. The crowd was really getting into it. We were about halfway through the parade when I noticed the head corsair on the float suddenly eyeing Will and me strangely; head cocked, eyes narrowed. He was a big guy, dressed in tight black pants and a long-sleeved white pirate shirt open to the waist, but with the scarf around his head, the eye patch and the wide-brimmed hat, it had been difficult to tell much about him. Yet his movements did seem familiar. All of a sudden his demeanor changed and he marched over to one of his buddies, chatting seriously, suddenly ignoring their surroundings. The big pirate took off his hat to wipe his forehead, and my stomach knotted. I could see small scars along his neck...where a crazed monkey had bitten him. Penchant! In an instant I was at my sotted partner's side, dragging him back from the attentions of the crowd. Behind us, Penchant was marshaling his crew for a boarding. If we'd had the scepter at full power, we could have easily held them off, but as it was, we were forced to more conventional tactics — basically retreat and run for our lives. But the timing was bad. We'd been drinking all afternoon and I was having trouble walking straight, let alone conveying the seriousness of our situation to my sloshed companion, who was well ahead of me in the race to inebriety. It helped when he finally got a look at Penchant and his boys coming over the back of our float, cutlasses drawn.

"Holy crap!" he gasped, sobering some, grabbing me and desperately looking for an escape.

The weight from all the people on one side of the float was causing it to tilt sideways. There was a bottom rail on one of the upstairs balconies coming up. If we could jump at just the right moment, we might be able to grab it and climb to safety — maybe run across a couple of roofs to the alley behind.

Rick Penchant was struggling with his balance on the cockeyed platform, but he was grimly moving forward, a vicious, confident smile slicing his face, his men close behind. The porch rail was coming up; the crowd was surging around us as our off-course float careened in toward the sidewalk. The people were loving it, cheering the pirates. Screw those spacemen in the cheap outfits. One or two were even trying to grab our feet to slow us down. The music was blaring, the surrounding horde was clearly nearing a point of frenzy.

I looked at Will and intrinsically he understood. Just as Penchant reached out for us, the crowd swept in and we leapt, arms extended. Both of us performed a highly unsuccessful imitation of Superman taking off, missed the porch rail by a good foot, and hit the concrete sidewalk like lead bars. The last thing I remembered was my forehead hammering the pavement. Somewhere in a red, reverberating fog, it seemed I heard Penchant saying, "Take them and their toy to the safe house. I'll be there as soon as I can." Then rough hands grabbed me and I faded out.

If grace belongs to God, there are those who say that luck belongs to the Devil, and that he looks after his own.
                                                    — **Sarah Dunant**

CHAPTER NINETEEN

Vanny's arms were around my neck and she was telling me how sorry she was. She had made a mistake; I was the one her heart wanted. My lady was kissing me, licking my ear and neck sensuously, and I was moaning how good it felt. Her tongue was curling behind my ear and I was thinking I didn't remember it being that long…

I awoke, bound hand and foot on a rug, face to face with a cocker spaniel, who was now licking my eyes and nose. Will was equally trussed and lying next to me, just coming around. I had a lump on my forehead the size of a tennis ball. My partner was groaning about being slugged. As soon as my eyes focused, I shook my head and shooed away the dog, then took in our surroundings — a bedroom with one bed, a nightstand with a lamp providing our light, shades pulled on the window. The door to the room was open about six inches, and with a quick, snake-like wiggle I was able to position myself to see out into a large living room/dining room with a kitchen off to the left. Two of Penchant's "pirates" were playing cards at the living room table — still in costume, big guys with dark hair and tight, scowling mouths. They looked like they could almost have been twins. Our scepter was sitting on the kitchen counter. The hyper spaniel bounced around the table a few times before they ran it off.

"We need to get out of these ropes," I whispered. "I can guarantee you whatever those boys have planned, we're not gonna like it."

"No time like the present," Will said as he wriggled over next to me, back to back, and began trying to work the knots at my wrists.

I could feel the ropes loosening some when there was a knock at the door. One of the card players grumbled about nobody touching his cards and got up. I edged my way around so I could see what was happening.

The fellow walked over and opened the door. There stood a diminutive red devil accompanied by a tall, rather exotic-looking woman attired in spray paint and feathers. The little devil spoke, holding up a piece of paper with the picture of a Cadillac convertible on it.

"Chu guys are son' lu…lucky sons a bitches. We only got one mo…more application left, and it's churs."

The big guy looked at him skeptically. "What the hell are you talkin' about? We don't got time for this." He was moving his hand toward closing the door, but the little guy stepped forward.

"Before chu close dat door, man, let me tell you di...dis. Only take a minute. Every Fantasy Fest all da hotels in Key West chip in and buy a br...brand new Cadillac for one lucky winner. Dey pay us to pass out free tickets for it. All chu gotta do is fill out a ticket and chu can win a fr...free Caddy."

The other guy had come over, listening, but they started to hesitate. "Nah, nah, don't think we're interested —"

The devil pulled his companion to the forefront. "My assistant will entertain you with a three feather dance while you sign yo...your ticket and look at a picture of de Cadillac." He smiled lasciviously. "And she only got two feathers."

His lady shimmied and moved a plume down her body sensuously, her large, dark eyes glimmering with mischief. A minute later the two guys were at the table enjoying the entertainment and looking at the picture of a Cadillac Leo had snatched off a "for sale" poster board, while he dug into his pockets for the tickets. Actually, they were far more interested in the sensuous dance the assistant was providing. So much so that neither of them noticed as the devil slid behind them, pulled a heavy leather and lead blackjack from his waistband, and clubbed them both on the sides of their heads.

At first, as I was watching this whole thing unfold, I couldn't figure out why those two looked familiar, but when the devil started talking, Will, who had wriggled up next to me, went rigid.

"That's them! The couple from Bolivia! The people who stole the scepter!"

I blanched. "Get that knot untied, man!"

As frantic and dedicated as Will was, he didn't have enough time. Partially because the freaking cocker spaniel kept getting in the way. Leo checked the guys he'd blackjacked. They were out for the count. Then he and his "feathered assistant" began a leisurely search of the place. It didn't take long for them to find the scepter, and us. I don't know which they were most happy about. They stood above us like a couple of cheetahs over a fresh kill.

"Well, well, lookie what we got he...here," snarled Leo. "We been followin' chu assaholes for a while! All da way fron' Bo...Bo...livia."

The tall woman didn't speak, but her eyes were equally vehement. She signed at Leo and he nodded.

"Chur, why not? Go get Bobo. Just what dese assaholes deserve!"

His lady's eyes brightened with vengeance, and she disappeared. Leo shooed the spaniel out of the room and closed the door.

Will looked at me. "You don't think...not the.... Oh, man, they wouldn't do that to us, would they?"

Leo leaned over and smiled rancorously as Lucinda came back in, carrying Bobo's round wicker basket. "Oohh, yes we would, assaholes!"

Lucinda set the basket down between us as we lay on our backs, tied like sacrificial lambs, our heads anxiously turned toward it, and cracked the lid about halfway while lifting a reed whistle that she wore on a string around her neck. She blew on the whistle with one long breath — an eerie, high-pitched wail almost out of the range of human hearing. For a moment nothing happened; all I could hear was our breathing. Suddenly, there was a nearly imperceptible shuffle in the basket. Long, hairy legs extended themselves, stretching from sleep, black, beady eyes coming alive in the dim light. A moment later I saw the first legs appear out of the darkness and slowly grasp the rim of the basket, moving out with the meticulous tenacity of an octopus emerging from its lair. Soon the head was over the edge, then the almost wooly-looking, brown body. I heard Will whimper...or was it me?

Lucinda signed and Leo nodded, entranced. "Now it gotta make a choice..."

Will was the best friend I'd ever had, but at that moment I found myself shamelessly hoping that Bobo liked mustaches. My dear friend was already blowing at the spider, trying to turn it toward me.

"No offense," he whispered between breaths. "But I'm allergic to spider bites."

Unfortunately, it worked. Bobo turned in my direction. It hardly mattered. We both knew there would be no winner in this game.

In seconds the huge, hairy creature had crawled out of the basket and onto the silver material of my shirt. I was frozen with terror. Lucinda signed and Leo interpreted. "If you move, it will st...strike instantly. Maybe you be lucky and it will not bite. Maybe..." But he bore an ugly, knowing smile when he said it.

The spider was inching across my ribcage and onto my breastbone, high-jointed legs moving in a slow, synchronized rhythm as it crept toward my exposed neck and face. I heard myself moaning mindlessly, in revulsion and fear, locked onto those soulless black eyes as if I were a mouse facing a boa. Within moments the spider was on my neck, then moving up the side of my cheek, clawed appendages gripping my flesh like tiny needles, firmly embracing me, its silky belly dragging across my skin, cold eyes glistening with malevolence. I wanted to throw myself into a convulsive roll and bounce away like an epileptic snake, but I could hear the words reverberating in my ears, "If you move, it will strike instantly!" The sweat of terror glistened on my skin and it delighted the senses of the creature, evoking its instinct to kill.

Suddenly the phone on the nightstand rang — once...twice... three times...four times...

Leo couldn't stand it. He snatched it off the cradle. "Yeah?" he said, noncommittally.

It was Penchant. "I'm on my way. I'll be there in less than five minutes. You better not have hurt those two, because I want to kill them personally when I get there. Got it?"

"Yeah," Leo grunted, and hung up.

The creature was spread out on my face, its huge, hairy mandibles clicking like castanets in front of my unprotected eyes. Suddenly, it rose up on its haunches, displaying that glossy, black underbelly as it prepared to strike.

"Wa...wait!" Leo called out. "Don' let Bobo kill him! Dere's sonbody else coming o...over dat's gwenna kill 'em! Much better for us. We don' got no involvement dis way. C'mon! Get Bobo and we gwenna get outta here."

The spider raised its head, curved fangs now clearly exposed, and leapt. I finally screamed, just as the woman deftly grabbed the arachnid from behind with two fingers and dropped it back into the basket. She signed angrily at Leo.

"Yeah, I know, I know. Me too. But dis is better," he said as he scooped the scepter off the bed, then knelt next to us and patted me on the cheek. "Don' get to feelin' too good about dis, asssahole. You still a dead sonabitchee." Then the devil turned to his mistress and took her hand. "C'mon baby, we find another dinner for Bobo. Right now I take you ba...back to da motel bar and we drink margaritas and stare at dat ceiling full of stars 'til we too drunk to walk."

Agent James Rodriguez had followed his quarry to a house off Margaret Street. He watched the little guy in the red devil suit and the tall, hot-looking woman dressed in feathers and spray paint knock on the door and engage in conversation with a couple of men. They were permitted inside. A few minutes later the woman came out to retrieve a basket from their car, then went back inside. Five minutes later the couple emerged, the lady having added some sort of decorative wand to her costume. They got into their car and drove away. As he followed, the call came in from headquarters in Miami. His backup had arrived in Key West and he was being patched into them.

"I'm headed north on Margaret Street — no, wait!" he said. "They just turned west on Truman. Looks like they're headed somewhere local. You two take Roosevelt Boulevard to where it meets Truman Avenue and wait at the tennis courts at Bay View Park. As soon as they get where they're going, I'll call and we'll make the bust together."

Arlington Newberry, aka Umbrella Man, was having an exceptional evening. So many people so drunk — lots of stuff that was simply going unattended. He gleefully pushed along his shopping cart, umbrella over his left shoulder, attired in a colorful tropical shirt he had discovered on a nearby bench and lit by a wonderful buzz from the many partially consumed cocktails he had found along the street. His mange-plagued Chihuahua, Albatross, was riding in the carriage, chewing contentedly on the remains of a steak bone. Arlington had also "found" a couple very nice cameras and three pairs of expensive sunglasses that evening, which he would take to the pawnshop tomorrow. He giggled at the thought.

"We's don't need no silly costumes," he said slyly to Albatross, with a slight alcohol-induced slur. "We's gonna sell cameras tomorrow and get monies to buy hamburgers with ketchups and pickles!" His eyebrows bounced with anticipation and a smile split his wide lips, displaying graying teeth that hadn't graced a toothbrush in years. "Yes. Yes! 'Licious hamburgers!" Then his face became more serious. He pulled off his old ball cap, pushed away a few strands of stringy brown hair from his watery blue eyes and shook a finger at Albatross. "But nows, but nows we's needs to be lookin' in dumpsters. Lots of plenty good things in dumpsters after tonight!"

During the evening he had worked down Duval to Truman and turned east. A couple of weeks ago he had found an old, abandoned shed behind a vacant house off William and Olivia Streets, near the Key West Cemetery, which had become his temporary abode. Everything in life was temporary for Arlington and Albatross.

As soon as the front door closed, Will and I were frantically squirming into one another like mating snakes, furiously tearing at each other's bonds. We both heard Penchant tell Leo on the phone that he was going to kill us when he got to the house. Inside of a minute I had a hand free. Moments later we had our hands and feet untied, but we had run out of time. I had just managed to stand, when the front door opened and in stepped Penchant the pirate, still in costume. Leo had left the bedroom door ajar and I could plainly see him, and he us. There was no escape. The spaniel bounced over to Penchant and he kicked it away, muttering something about girlfriends and their freaking idiot dogs. He pulled a chrome revolver from his pocket and smiled.

Will and I backed up against the far wall as he came into the bedroom, but as we did, my hand brushed the Velcro pocket in my silver painted wetsuit — where I had tucked the magic "blind ball" Rufus had given me. Gradually, without a lot of attention, I eased it out.

"Ooohhh, I been waiting a long time for this," Penchant snarled as he brought the gun up level with our midsections. "I thought Stinger would take care of you, but somehow he got sidetracked."

"You got that one right," I whispered.

Penchant's head tilted and his eyes narrowed suspiciously. "What do you know about Stinger? The waitress/hooker we both know said he followed you into South America."

"I'll tell you the honest truth," I said. "All we know about Stinger is bits and pieces." That got a sideways glance from Will. "Our impression is he's had some problems keeping himself together lately."

Our antagonist cocked his head, curious, but decided to pass. He waved his gun dismissively. "Doesn't matter. What matters is, we're all here together and it's payback time." He straightened up. "Now, there's one other issue. Where's that golden space gun of yours? I'm pretty well certain I saw you use that to lift a couple people into the air tonight. Seems like a toy I'd like to have."

I grunted. "Man, that ship has sailed. You're about twenty minutes too late. A Latino couple broke in, popped your boys on the head, and took it."

Penchant stared at me, digesting that, and finally realizing that it was probably true, given the situation. The spaniel came bounding in again, dancing around our buddy's feet with truly misplaced affection. Penchant kicked at him. While he was distracted, I got a firm grip on the gumball. I remembered Rufus saying it should be thrown against something — it had to crack open for its magic to work, blinding everyone in the room for five minutes. I whispered to Will out the side of my mouth. "Hey buddy, you remember the blind ball I told you about?"

Will nodded almost imperceptibly. "Yeah, close your eyes beforehand."

"Uh-huh," I muttered, as I brought my hand up and side-armed the ball toward the wall next to Penchant, the gleam of victory lighting my eyes.

However, the damned spaniel was next to Penchant when I threw the ball. The freaking dog leapt up and caught it. I couldn't believe it! Will and I were flinching crazily, blinking like neurotic owls, hands over our eyes, trying to keep from going blind if the thing exploded, but still wanting to know what was happening.

Penchant watched me throw the gumball, and saw the dog catch it. Now he was on high alert. "What the hell are you doing?" He pointed the gun at the dog jumping around on the bed, throwing the gumball into the air and catching it while we were cringing and blinking. "What's that? What's wrong with you two?"

"Just really nervous," I replied, jerking again as the dog tossed the ball in the air and caught it. "Never been shot before."

Our nemesis shook his head, somewhat bewildered by the whole thing, but he got over it. "Well, I'm gonna put your mind at rest regarding the experience." He aimed the gun at my chest and I quit blinking. But at that moment the dog decided to bite the gumball. There was an immediate explosion, which I'm certain loosened several of Fido's teeth. The animal issued a terrified yowl as his mouth blew open, and a bomb burst of miniscule, saffron-like particles filled the room instantaneously, like a golden fog. The good news was Penchant was instantly blinded. But so were Will and I. So was Fido.

Penchant grunted, "What the hell!" Then wailed, "Jesus! I'm blind. I can't see!" But when he heard us shuffling around in front of him, the concern for his present plight was overwhelmed by his desire to shoot us as many times as possible. If Will hadn't anticipated him and dragged me down, the movie would have ended there.

As we hit the floor, bullets slapped the plaster above us. We quickly scrambled along the wall on our hands and knees toward the large window I remembered on the far side of the room, burbling little terrified shrieks as bullets dug holes in the plaster around our heads. Our antagonist was hurling curses into the darkness that would have shriveled the devil's schlong. The dog was going nuts — running headlong into things, yelping and howling, then doing it again. Fortunately, he created a great distraction. Penchant got so pissed he started shooting at the dog. Suddenly, I heard the distinct clicking sound of a hammer on empty cartridges. As I felt for the windowsill in the darkness, it got quiet.

"What the hell did you do to me?" Penchant muttered in an angry whine. Then his anger got the better of him. "I'm gonna kill you sons of bitches with my bare hands. I'm gonna dig your eyes out with my fingers!"

I heard him stumbling over things in a fury on the opposite side of the room and I knew we were running out of time in a number of ways. We had used up at least two of the five "blind minutes." I didn't want to be around when everything started to wear off. Penchant was an asshole, but he was a large, well-muscled asshole. I found the window latch and got my fingers under it. Our buddy had just charged into the other wall and knocked something off of it that sounded like it was made of glass from the shattering sounds. He screamed in rage. I pushed back the shades, jerked up the window and punched out the screen with my fist, then reached out in the darkness behind me and grabbed Will. "C'mon, Ringo, time to go."

The dog seemed to have recovered from the exploding gumball, but was still bouncing off the walls and barking like a crazy thing. Penchant got a handle on our direction and charged the darkness again, tripping over the dog and battering the wall right next to Will.

I scrambled out the window and collapsed onto a hedge of some sort. Will landed on top of me a second later. Suddenly, I realized I was starting to see gray outlines on the periphery of my vision. The magic gumball was wearing off. We could hear Penchant cursing like a madman, still offering remarkably imaginative descriptions of what he was going to do to us.

"The boy does have an extensive vocabulary," Will muttered caustically to no one in particular.

We were crawling slowly toward the curb when the bedroom window exploded behind us and our raging nemesis came flying out, tumbling onto the lawn. Struggling to his hands and knees, he shook himself like a dog and listened. Will's head hit the bumper of a car in the street and he yelled out in pain. That was all Penchant needed. He charged at us on all fours like a wounded gorilla. My partner and I quickly felt our way to the doors of the vehicle, threw them open and climbed in, slamming them behind us, seeking protection as much as anything, but praying for a key in the ignition. In the driver's seat, I fumbled at the dash and my prayers were answered. The engine fired but didn't start. The bellowing gorilla was at the car. Frantically, I ground the ignition again and pumped the pedal, effectively flooding the carburetor. Penchant had staggered to his feet and was feeling his way around for a door. Will leapt over the seat with the deftness of a frightened squirrel and hammered down all the door locks, but that didn't slow our antagonist much. He screamed and punched one of those meaty, ham-like fists through the back window, just behind my head, and started grasping around for the door-lock knob. I'm sure I screamed, furiously grinding the starter. But at that point my prayers were answered, again, and the engine started.

I realized that I could see shapes now, probably enough to navigate. But it hardly mattered. We were getting out of there. I slapped the car into drive, mashed the gas pedal, and we lurched onto the road, still dragging our berserk, treasure-hunting buddy as he grasped the outside door handle with one hand and tried to rip my head off with the other through the broken-out window. Will slid over and bit him on the forearm. We were already up to twenty miles an hour. That and the bite were too much for Penchant, and with a final, desperate howl he fell away, tumbling into a ball for about fifteen feet before splaying out on the pavement.

We cruised slowly up Margaret Street for a couple of minutes, waiting until our vision returned, then picked up speed and snapped around a handful of corners to be certain no one was following us. Finally, we stopped under a banyan tree off Watson Street. I exhaled a heavy sigh of relief. "Well, at least we're still alive."

"Yeah, but so is Penchant," Will muttered dejectedly. "On top of that, we lost the scepter to those two Latino maniacs, and there's no way in hell to find them. They're probably halfway to Miami by now."

"Maybe not," I said, looking out at the backed-up Fantasy Fest traffic crawling along on Truman Avenue, considering that statement. "I heard the little guy say something about going back to the motel bar, drinking margaritas and staring at a ceiling full of stars until they were drunk." I turned to Will. "Think about it — a ceiling over the bar with stars on it."

My friend's eyes brightened and we both said it at the same time. "The tiki bar at the Sea and Sky Motel at Windsor and Truman!"

Will clapped his hands ecstatically. "Damn, man, you're right!

That's it! That's the bar!"

Agent Rodriguez had followed the strange couple when they left the house on Margaret Street, staying well back to avoid being made. In less than ten minutes his suspects had pulled into the Sea and Sky Motel off of Truman. They got out and headed toward the tiki bar.

Leo was ecstatic. They had hit the big time. The crazy wand thing was going to go to the highest bidder, and they would be rich. No more having to steal boats or rob people. It was the good life for them. Lucinda casually put the scepter under her arm as they walked.

"Hey," Leo said. "Don' chu wanna hide dat?"

She looked at him and signed. "Why? It's crazy fest here. We fit right in with it. Besides, I want it with us."

The diminutive devil smiled, picked up his red tail with one hand, took his lady's with the other, and they ambled over to the motel. Time to celebrate. They found themselves seats at the little tiki bar outside the motel and ordered margaritas, just tickled with themselves.

Rodriguez parked near Leo's car, then watched the two settle into seats at the bar. He lit a cigarette, took a deep, satisfying drag, then called his team, who were still waiting by the tennis courts at Bayview Park. "Okay, gentlemen. I have our targets and we are ready to move. I'm at the Sea and Sky Motel on Truman Avenue. Get your asses over here, now."

As with so many internal agencies in the U.S., Rodriguez and his team were jealous of success, and refused to share it if they didn't have to. Agent Rodriguez had considered calling the Key West police for backup, but decided against it. This was going to be his night to shine, and no one else's.

It took us a few minutes to find a convenience store with apparel. We needed to get out of the space outfits, as everyone we *didn't* want to find us had seen those. Will and I purchased fruit-juicy shirts, a couple pairs of shorts, and two wide-brimmed, touristy straw hats, then headed toward the Sea and Sky. Parking well away from the motel, we strolled up casually, trying to keep to the shadows. Fantasy Fest was still in full swing and the tiki bar was doing well. As we passed it, Will glanced over and stopped, then he pointed.

"There they are," he said with a quiet incredulousness. "There they are!" He leaned forward and squinted through the colorful ground lights on the walkways. "And there's the damned scepter, tucked against the bar at their feet. Damn, man, that's a brazen couple of thieves."

I looked at my partner. "We're going to need a distraction."

Will chewed on his bottom lip for a moment, staring at them as he thought, then nodded and turned to me. "Okay, I'm gonna need some women's makeup, a tube top, a pack of 'strike-anywhere' matches, a disposable razor, and two shots of Bacardi 151 rum." He leaned into me. "Now, this is what I'm gonna do, and this is what you're gonna do..."

We went over to the motel gift shop, which was still open because it was Fantasy Fest. Will purchased eye shadow, flaming pink rouge, bright, ugly-red lipstick, and one of those elastic bands for tying up women's hair. In addition, he found the bottom half of a puke-yellow sarong he liked, and a purple tube top. Then he excused himself to the men's room. When he came out five minutes later, I involuntarily gasped. My partner had slipped the tube top over his naked, skinny chest and wrapped the sarong around his waist, disguising his shorts. He had shaved off his mustache, rouged his face, lipsticked himself unmercifully, and applied the black and red eye shadows almost tastefully until he looked like a strange, blond Egyptian. He had taken the fuzzy elastic band and tied off his long hair on the top of his head, rather than at the back. To all this he added a serious alternate lifestyle swish to his hips and sway to his walk. I wouldn't have called him fetching by any stretch of the imagination, but arresting he was. In the meantime, I had gone to the bar and purchased his shots of 151. I handed him the plastic glass. "Hot damned, man, you gotta be the ugliest 'homosectional' on the face of the planet!"

Will beamed. "Showtime!" he said, that old, mischievous grin of his breaking through the thick red lipstick.

While Will was grooming himself for the show, Agent Rodriguez's backup arrived, pulling in next to him at the motel parking lot. They took a few minutes to settle on a plan, then moved out.

I walked around the bar and into the shadows diagonally behind where Leo and his woman sat. Will moved around to the opposite side of the bar, picked his target, and the show began.

There was a middle-aged tourist couple sitting at the round tiki bar, sharing drinks and talking intimately, both of them attired in shorts and colorful T-shirts. Will swished onto the deck, then sashayed up directly behind them, sat his rum on the bar, grabbed the unsuspecting fellow by his shoulders, swung him around, and planted a huge kiss right on the guy's lips. Then he pushed the astounded fellow back and said in a demanding, somewhat wounded tone, "Now, can you tell me that means nothing to you? After all this time, baby? With you and me? Absolutely nothing?"

The guy just sat there, stunned, his lipstick-smeared mouth hanging open, wide eyes staring at Will as if he were some sort of apparition from *The Rocky Horror Picture Show* (and he could well have been).

My buddy didn't give him a moment to recover. "You promised me you were going to leave your wife!" he screeched, and walloped the guy with an open-handed left, hard enough to knock his eyeballs sideways.

His drinking partner looked at him. "Wife? Wife?"

Conversation in the bar had come to a full, dead stop. There wasn't a soul under that thatched roof who wasn't locked into the drama. The woman with the guy was backing up in her barstool, wondering who in the hell this dude really was, not at all wanting a piece of the crazed gay bitch with hairy arms and an Adam's apple.

At this point I was moving in on our targets, creeping out of the shadows and coming up behind them. It didn't matter. I could have been riding an elephant and they wouldn't have noticed.

Will threw up his hands in theatrical dismay. "How could you do this to me? I threw away my career as a porn star for you! I let you do that 'special thang' to me!" He gazed around at his audience as if everyone understood, eyes wide with indignity. "That special thang!"

The guy finally marshaled enough of his senses to respond. "I... I... Are you sure you've got the right — "

Will cried, "If I can't have your baby, no one will!" He snatched up his high-octane rum and pitched it onto the man's crotch, and with a flick of a wrist produced a match, struck it on the back of a chair, and tossed it into the fellow's lap. There was an immediate "poof" and an instant blue flame engulfed the delicate area. That was it for the lady friend. With a shriek she was scrambling out of her chair and on her way back to Michigan. The guy issued a high-pitched wail and literally backed up onto the bar top, knocking over customers' drinks and liquor bottles, and for a few moments pandemonium reigned. Bartenders furiously shot the mistaken lover's crotch with water from their bar guns as if they were hoping to quench some of the steamy affair they had just witnessed, while tourists sat agog at the spectacle, taking in every moment so they could be sure to tell the story with riveting accuracy when they got back home. *Holy cow! This Key West was some kind of place!* The locals were enjoying it, but for them it was just another night on the island. While the bartenders fought the flames of passion, and the fellow screamed terror-filled, moving descriptions of how his dick was burning off (although it really wasn't), my partner simply turned and sashayed away from the chaos. He did pause one last time at the edge of the bar, swinging around dramatically, pointing, and screaming. "I'm never doing that 'special thang' with you ever again!"

Leo and his lady were totally engrossed. They never even noticed as I began to ease up behind them. But at that moment Leo straightened abruptly. He saw the men in slacks and long-sleeved shirts coming in from the parking lot, moving with purpose. Quickly looking around, he spotted a third, closing from the patio side — gray slacks, short-sleeved cream shirt — where all the foliage might have provided a getaway. After all his years in the business of crime, he had developed a finely tuned radar for law enforcement. He grabbed Lucinda's arm and nodded toward the approaching agents. She instantly understood.

"We got to split up," he whispered tensely. "I meet ch...chu at da regular place, in Miami. Okay?"

His lady nodded and began to rise, first reaching under the bar and grabbing the scepter.

I cursed in the darkness, at first because I thought they were leaving, but the tenseness in their faces made me glance around, and I saw the approaching agents. With a harsh expletive I looked over toward Will, just outside the lights of the bar. He, too, had picked up on what was happening. I backed away to a palm tree on the periphery and waited as he circled over to me.

Leo and Lucinda slid off their barstools casually, but as their feet hit the ground they were on the run. Lucinda headed back toward the motel, a completely unexpected move. She dashed into the lobby and down one of the corridors. Agent Rodriguez went after her. Leo, moving surprisingly fast in his devil costume, cut diagonally across the parking lot and headed for his car. The other two agents set out after him, truly surprised, because they had parked their car right next to his. In his haste, one of the detectives tripped on a decorative sidewalk light and went sprawling onto the concrete, knocking the breath out of him. The other found himself cut off by a tour bus that had just pulled in. The little Cuban made it to his car unscathed but gasping for air, heart hammering in his chest. He unlocked the passenger's door, reached into his glove compartment and pulled out a small, semi-automatic pistol. He bolted over to the FBI vehicles and shot out the front tires of each. Glancing at the approaching detective, he grinned and hopped into his car. A moment later he was screeching out of the parking lot, watching the agent in his rear view mirror as the guy hopped up and down in frustration, screaming what Leo was certain were obscenities.

He would have been just fine. He would have made it away clean, but that five-foot-one Cuban ego got him. Leo stopped his car in the driveway, just before Truman, got out and turned to the impotent Federal officer in the distance. "Hey!" he yelled. "What chu tink of dis, you weasely-assed dip shit?" He put his hands behind his head and thrust out his hips, laughing and humping air at the fellow in the ultimate Latin gesture of disrespect. He still would have been okay, but when the little Cuban got back into his car and headed out, he had to roll down the window and shoot his antagonist a bird, just as he turned onto Truman. "Screw you!" he yelled, waving his middle finger in the air and sticking his head out the window. "Chu neber gwenna ge...get Leo Lickker, you floppy-shlonged mutha —"

This, of course, took his eyes from the road, because he had to see the look on the agent's face, and in the process he ran smack-dab into the front of an oncoming Winnebago, piloted by a zoned-out couple from Ohio. Sometimes you've just got to leave well enough alone.

Umbrella Man watched the accident from behind his shopping basket. It scared him a little, watching the police and the ambulance arrive, but he did end up with two nice, shiny hubcaps. It had been a long night, from North Duval all the way to Truman, then east a few blocks, but it had been worth it. Such prizes he had found. He was only a block or two from his present abode and he was looking forward to curling up on his old mattress with Albatross.

Lucinda made a mad dash into the motel and raced along the inside corridor. With those long, lithe legs she was about halfway down the hall by the time Agent Rodriguez came bolting through the front doors and spotted her. As she ran, Lucinda frantically watched for an escape. She found it in an exit to a laundry room, which led to the parking lot on the north side of the complex. She went out the door and made a left, taking her toward the end of the building where the garbage for the motel was collected and stored. The tall Brazilian had just reached the end of the building when she saw an FBI agent clear the same door she'd just exited. She threw herself against the wall, panting with exertion and fear. *Think! Use your mind. Don't try to outrun him. Outthink him!* The woman realized she had to hide the golden wand. If she could cache it somewhere fairly safe, they could come back for it. If they were caught with the device, it was gone forever. Glancing around frantically, Lucinda noticed there were three dumpsters next to the side of the building surrounded by a thick hedge of bougainvillea. She ran over and stuffed the ancient device underneath the bottom of the hedge, then hurried across to the low, four-foot chain-link fence that enclosed the back of the complex, separating it from the dense foliage of the compound. Taking one of the large feathers that adorned her body, she carefully attached it to the top of the wire fence. Then the Brazilian temptress raced to the back doors of the motel and entered, moving up the hallway, making a right at the next turn then a left at the following hallway. She had a plan.

Rodriguez was in good physical shape. Even though he smoked a few cigarettes during the day, he was one of those "a mile every morning" guys. After spotting the woman, he made the trash area in less than a minute. He glanced around quickly, gun out, moving forward cautiously. He'd already been made a fool once tonight. It wasn't going to happen again. As he edged around the dumpsters, Rodriguez glanced at the fence and saw the feather. He cursed vehemently in Cuban for a moment, then grabbed his walkie-talkie and called his partner. The other agent answered instantly. "Where are you? Did you get her?"

"No, the *puta* got away over the back fence. We need to secure the east and north sides of this block. Get Key West PD on that right away. What about the other one?"

"We got him. He's in the back of my car. He's a little banged up. There was an accident. But he'll be okay until we can wrap this up."

Rodriguez exhaled with a touch of satisfaction. At least it hadn't been a total screw-up. "You maintain surveillance at the motel. I'm going after the woman."

Will and I watched the whole drama from the motel tiki bar, my friend having disappeared into the men's room for a few moments, removing all the makeup and putting on his normal clothes. After an hour it was fairly obvious that the woman had gotten away. The crazy Cuban was still being held in the back of the FBI sedan, handcuffed to the door with an agent watching him. A half hour later, the Feds decided to wrap it up and settle for one out of two.

Rodriguez was nearing apoplexy. He had royally screwed this situation. The whole thing should have been an easy bust. He should have had both of them and been halfway back to Miami by now. Finally, after the tires had been changed on their vehicles, he sent the other two agents on to the mainland with the Cuban. Reluctantly, he started his car, lit a cigarette and huffed out the first drag in anger and frustration, then drove away. He got as far as the light at White and Truman streets, waiting for it to turn, drumming his fingers on the steering wheel, when suddenly he stopped dead. In the next instant he spun his car around in the intersection and was fighting his way through the traffic back toward the motel.

He flashed his badge at the surprised night manager. "I want to see the room the two suspects paid for, now!" *Son of a bitch!* It had never even occurred to him to check the room.

The detective quietly slotted the key, then threw the door open. Lucinda was sitting on the bed, smoking a cigarette and packing her things.

Once again we watched from the bar as another of our nemeses was escorted to an FBI sedan in handcuffs and taken away. Will held up his glass and I clinked it with mine in a toast.

"Here's to local law enforcement," I said with a smile.

Will nodded, a good deal of relief flooding his eyes. "Yeah. Not all that talented, but persistent." Then his face sobered. "Okay. They got the bad guys, but I didn't see anybody with a golden scepter, and I've been paying attention."

I took a sip of my margarita, staring at the motel. "She hid it. Somewhere during or after the chase, she hid it. The question is, where? I think we need to have a look at her room."

We told the night manager that we were reporters for *The Citizen* and offered him forty bucks to let us have a private look. He shrugged, took the money, and gave us the key. Fifteen minutes later we'd been through everything. No scepter. There was, however, that wicker basket with the huge hairy spider inside sitting on the bureau next to the television. Just seeing it gave me the heebie-jeebies. As a final thought we got down on our hands and knees and were feeling around under the box springs of the bed when we heard the door open. I figured it was the manager.

"Just about done," I said. "I think we're finished."

"Ooohh, you have no idea how finished you are," growled a familiar voice.

I looked at Will. "Holy freaking moly! It can't be!"

"But it is," said Penchant, holding what I was certain was a reloaded pistol. He closed the door and strode slowly, confidently into the room. He waved the gun at the bed next to us. "Have a seat, boys. We need to have a talk."

There was no point in arguing. We sat on the bed, backs against the headrest.

He continued. "When I got my sight back, I started looking for you two. The police scanner in my car was all abuzz about a happening at the Sea and Sky Motel, and you know, something just told me I better check that out. Sure enough, who do I see at the bar but my old friends, once again up to no good, I was sure. So I parked my car away from all the activity and found a place to watch you, and here we are again." He held up a finger and his eyes narrowed. "Only this time, I'm going to kill you before you have a chance to do any of your song and dance routines."

Our treasure-hunting antagonist leaned against the bureau, only a foot or so from the wicker basket and I inadvertently glanced at it. Penchant caught me. Looking down at the basket, then back at me, he raised his eyebrows in question. "Something in there of importance? Something I should know about?"

I shook my head. "Nope. Nothing."

He got that ugly smile. "Well, maybe I ought to just check for myself." He gazed at us and tilted his head. "Jewels, maybe? Precious stones like the ones on that space gun of yours?"

"Nope. Not even close."

Penchant was easing off the lid as he spoke, keeping his eyes and his gun on us. As the lid slid off sideways, Bobo the spider quickly crawled out and onto the sleeve of our buddy's pirate shirt. In seconds it had scrambled up his arm and onto his shoulder. Penchant felt that, but by the time he glanced down, Bobo had reached his back, just below his collar. I could almost see those hairy mandibles clicking with delight. Penchant felt around in the basket, finding nothing. He turned it over. Still nothing. Angry now, figuring he'd been played again, he issued a foul expletive about our parents and barnyard animals, and brought up the gun. "All right. No more screwing around. You guys didn't go to all this trouble for nothing. Where's the space gun?"

"We don't know," Will said. "If we knew, we wouldn't be

looking for it, would we?"

"Wrong answer," snarled Penchant, staring at my partner. "I count to three and I kill you first." Then he looked at me. "Then I count to three again, and kill you."

"We don't freaking have —"

"One," said Penchant.

"Don't do this — "

"Two." The spider had reached the collar on his shirt.

"We can find it if you give us time — "

Penchant's face went hard. "Three," he said, but as he raised the gun and fired, Bobo leapt and nailed him with those long, curved fangs. Penchant screamed with surprise and pain and the shot meant for Will's head took out a piece of the wall an inch from his ear.

"Damn! What the hell?" he yelled, instinctively reaching up and coming away with a monster spider in his hand. He screamed again and flung Bobo against the curtains of the sliding glass doors. But his hand also came away with blood on it.

"Jesus!" I screamed. "That's a Mongolian Red-eyed Tarantula!"

"A freaking what?" cried Penchant, holding his neck, eyes wide with alarm.

"God, no!" yelled Will with equal fervor. "Only one in three survive the bite of a Red-eye!"

"Get your head between your knees so the blood doesn't rush to your heart!" we yelled in unison. "It's your only chance! Get your head between your knees!"

Fifteen minutes later we were walking Penchant over to the Greyhound bus station across from the Sea and Sky Motel — his arms over our shoulders and ours over his. One of the strings that held our old buddy's ankles to ours had come loose and his right foot was dragging a little. Will's new hat was on his head, my sunglasses were fixed over his glazed eyes, and a half-smoked cigarette Will had found in the hallway ashtray at the motel was stuck between his stiffening lips.

"I was thinking New Jersey," said Will in a contemplative fashion. "It's a more expensive ticket but it'll be a while before they find it no longer matters where he is."

"Sounds good to me." We stopped for a moment, waiting to cross the street. I exhaled and turned to my partner. "Do you think we should be writing this stuff down? It would make a great story."

Will thought about it for a second or two, watching a Greyhound bus pull into the station. Finally, he shook his head. "Nah...nobody would believe it."

Most people live their lives like a candle, burning just enough to keep back the darkness. Eventually flickering and sputtering, they quietly fade away. But some, a few, live like a flare — flaming brightly with white-hot passion, illuminating the world around them, never particularly afraid of being extinguished. It's always your choice to be a candle or a flare.

— **Capt. Ross Murdock**

CHAPTER TWENTY

While we were buying Key West's infamous treasure hunter a ticket for his final bus ride, Bobo the spider discovered that the sliding door to the courtyard gardens was open. He wiggled his way out into the lush, tropical surroundings and glanced around contentedly. As fate would have it, not an hour later he encountered, of all things, another Brazilian Wandering Spider, just hanging out on a banana palm — a female stowaway from a South American sailboat that had docked in the harbor a month before. It was love at first sight.

As the two hairy arachnids were getting to know each other, Umbrella Man was making one quick pass through the garbage bins at the back of the Sea and Sky. It was generally his last stop at the end of the day. Humming dementedly to himself, he picked through the dumpsters, discovering a small treasure or two, but it was late and he was tired. However, as he turned to go, he caught a glimpse of something under the surrounding bougainvillea hedge.

My, my, whats could that be? he wondered to himself. *We's needs to see it. We's needs to touch it.* He got down on his hands and knees and crawled under the hedge, reaching out, grasping the shiny, golden shaft, and pulling it out. When the glow of the security lights touched it, he gasped with wonder and delight. "Oohh my, my! Pretty, pretty stones!" That sly smile split his grubby face. "Oooh, we's are a dirty little man, a dirty little man, but we's are clever — clever like a rat," he whispered, his eyebrows bouncing up and down with glee. "We's likes us when we's clever, yes we does! Shiny, shiny stones, pretty metal!"

Arlington held up the device and watched the light reflect off of it. "We's needs a rock, or a hammer. Yes, a hammer," he muttered confidently as he wiped some saliva from the side of his mouth with the back of his hand. He drooled a little when he got excited. "Something heavy to knocks them jewels off the ends, so we's can sell 'em. Yes, so we's can sell 'em, and have a juicy hamburger with pickles and ketchups. Yes. With pickles and ketchups!" He was already rummaging through his basket for an instrument of destruction.

We slept until noon the next day, then went to Island Jim's for a late breakfast. The Key West Citizen had front-page coverage on the capture of "two fugitives wanted in connection with boat hijackings in the Caribbean." In the local news section there was a remarkably good photo of militant gay Will accosting the tourist whose crotch was on fire. The caption read "Fiery Affair Quenched at Local Bar."

While we were enjoying a chuckle or two and sipping mimosas, Arlington Newberry and his faithful companion, Albatross, were showing a Key West pawnshop owner some really unique crystal-like stones they had hammered off of a golden device — a device which might well have belonged to a star-traveling civilization that stopped here and there and built remarkable, uniquely functioning monuments representing their capability, to remind and encourage indigenous, evolving civilizations of the spark that existed within all of them. These travelers may well have constructed magnificent edifices so that generation after generation could cast their eyes upon them and know, unequivocally, that the power of spirit kindles greatness in all things and that the universe is an unending panorama of possibility — that their future and vision, however narrow at the moment, could grow into a wondrous garden of intellect, technology, and service to their fellow travelers on the path of man.

Coincidentally enough, the guy who owned the pawnshop was a retired government technician who had once worked in a top-secret electronics facility. He still had friends. Within forty-eight hours there were personnel in government Jeeps and dark sedans scouring every inch of every back alley in Key West, looking for one of those remarkable golden scepters that hadn't been brutally broken into several pieces. Umbrella Man was a sly bargainer. He didn't give away his information or his find easily. When all was said and done, he had a lifelong free pass to McDonald's in Key West for as many juicy hamburgers as he could eat, with ketchups and pickles included.

When Leo and Lucinda were interrogated by the Feds, they told of the scepter, using it as a bargaining chip. Given the information gleaned from the pawnshop owner and Umbrella Man, their firsthand information of the operation of the device was considered very valuable. They were permitted to make bond. Within three days of being released, they had obtained false identifications and passports, had booked a flight for South America, and were sitting in the appropriate concourse at the Miami Airport.

"Flight number 454, now boarding for Rio De Janeiro," said the gate attendant into the microphone.

Lucinda rose from her seat with fluid grace and took Leo's hand, helping him up. The cast on his arm, from the accident with the Winnebago, was cumbersome and annoying, but the doctor said he would heal just fine. Rio De Janeiro was a good place for a new start — lots of stupid rich people and nice boats. She kissed him on the forehead, then, hand in hand the tall Brazilian temptress and the feisty, diminutive Cuban walked down the boarding ramp and into the aircraft, proving that crime doesn't always pay, but it's never boring.

The only mar in the whole affair was that they were forced to wait before taking their seats while a fellow with long blond hair, wearing a white sports coat and blue jeans, showed up late and was allowed to board first class ahead of them. There were stickers on the guitar case he carried that read, "Havana Daydreaming," "Margaritaville," and "Come Monday."

"It...it's dat stinkin' Caribbean cowboy again!" Leo huffed, stamping his feet in an angry little dance, reaching back for the leather blackjack in his pocket. "Jinny Buffett! Jinny Buffett! Everywhere I go! Is he twins? Who da hell is dis guy? I'ne gwenna bop him!"

While gradually recovering from the bizarre loss of our ladies, we ran into Rufus at Coco's Cantina on Summerland Key a few days later. It appeared to be a coincidence, but we both knew better. Rufus was already aware there had been a screw-up somehow — probably heard it from the Grand Messenger on the mystical coconut telegraph.

"You little pinballs seem to like complications more dan most," he said, shaking his head and offering a wry smile. "Now listen, little mangoes. Like I tell you before. Dis potion gonna wear off in about six months. Best thing you can do is spend much time around da pretty bird you want, so she grow to appreciate you while she under da influence of da potion." He sighed. "Den maybe we try again with special potion, if we have to." He looked at us with a gaze somewhere between fondness and frustration. "Try to stay out of trouble for a while. Swim with da tide, little fishes. Rufus got other things he got to do, okay mons?" He started to walk away, then stopped and turned back to us. "Oh, by da way, da golden device you found — dere be something similar, hidden in another place not too far away." He smiled knowingly. "If you be interested, it come to you." Then he was gone.

Will looked at me, eyes registering an amalgam of intrigue and uneasiness. "Something similar?"

I shrugged. "Well, we've got six months for the potion to wear off on our girls. We're going to need something to do."

Acknowledgements

I owe a debt of gratitude to a number of people for the success of this novel. For their proofing talents and valuable suggestions, which made this a far better book, thanks so much to Robert Simpson, Mark Medford, and of course, my lady Bonnie Lee, whose first editing contributions are simply invaluable.

I also wish to offer a special thanks to my editor, Cris Wanzer, for her unflagging efforts to make this book all it could be, and to Kathy Russ for her exceptional "final eyes" edit and insight on this.

About the Author

Michael Reisig has been writing professionally for almost two decades. He is a former newspaper editor and publisher, an award-winning columnist, and a best-selling novelist.

Reisig was born in Enid, Oklahoma. The first son of a military family, he was raised in Europe and California before moving to Florida. He attended high school and college in the Tampa Bay area. After college, he relocated to the Florida Keys, establishing a commercial diving business in which he served as the company pilot, traveling extensively throughout the southern hemisphere, diving, treasure hunting, and adventuring.

From there he turned to journalism, putting many of his experiences into the pages of his novels and columns, then going on to manage, then own, newspapers.

He presently resides in the Ouachita Mountains of Arkansas where he fishes and hunts and writes his novels, and occasionally escapes to the Caribbean for further adventures.

Other Novels by Michael Reisig

The Road to Key West

The Road to Key West is an adventurous/humorous sojourn that cavorts its way through the 1970s Caribbean, from Key West and the Bahamas, to Cuba and Central America.

In August of 1971, Kansas Stamps and Will Bell set out to become nothing more than commercial divers in the Florida Keys, but adventure, or misadventure, seems to dog them at every turn. They encounter a parade of bizarre characters, from part-time pirates and heartless larcenists, to voodoo *bokors,* a wacky Jamaican soothsayer, and a handful of drug smugglers. Adding even more flavor to this Caribbean brew is a complicated romance, a lost Spanish treasure, and a pre-antediluvian artifact created by a distant congregation who truly understood the term "pyramid power."

Along the Road to Key West

WHAT IF YOU DISCOVERED A DEVICE THAT MADE PEOPLE TELL THE TRUTH?

Fast-paced humor-adventure with wacky pilots, quirky con men, mad villains, bold women, and a gadget to die for...

Florida Keys adventurers Kansas Stamps and Will Bell find their lives turned upside down when they discover a truth device hidden in the temple of an ancient civilization. Enthralled by the virtue (and entertainment value) of personally dispensing truth and justice with this unique tool, they take it all a step too far and discover that everyone wants what they have — from the government to the Vatican.

Along the way, from Key West, into the Caribbean, across to Washington D.C., and back to America's heartland, Kansas and Will gather a wild collage of friends and enemies, from a whacked-out, one-eyed pilot and an alluring computer specialist, to a zany sociopath with a zest for flimflam, a sadistic problem-solver for a prominent religious sect, and the director of presidential security.

The New Madrid Run

The New Madrid Run is a tale of desperate survival on an altered planet. In the aftermath of a global cataclysm caused by a shift in the earth's poles, a handful of survivors face the terrible elements of a changed world as they navigate a battered sailboat from the ruins of Florida into the hills of Arkansas via a huge rift in the continent (the New Madrid fault).

Brothers of the Sword/Children of Time (prequel to *The New Madrid Run*)

Two complete novels spanning three hundred years—bound together by a lost Spanish treasure and the eternal journey of spirit and soul. A captivating tale of the past and the present—of romance, rescue, and revenge.

The Hawks of Kamalon

Great Britain, Summer, 1944

Drawn thousands of light years across the galaxy ten men and eight aircraft are greeted by a roaring crowd in a field before the provincial capitol on the continent of Azra; a land in desperate need of champions.

The Old Man's Letters

Meet Jake Strider, a cantankerous country sage with a caustic wit and a ribald sense of humor. *The Old Man's Letters* chronicles some of Strider's most notable correspondence to his son over almost two decades. It's a hilarious, remarkably perceptive panorama of rural life, from bizarre tales of crazy friends to poignant political and social points of view. This is a guaranteed "laugh out loud" read.

Made in the USA
Lexington, KY
10 January 2019